TEEN
THO
07/14/25

Thompson, L. T.

Devils like us

Devils Like Us

Devils Like Us

L. T. THOMPSON

BLOOMSBURY
NEW YORK LONDON OXFORD NEW DELHI SYDNEY

BLOOMSBURY YA
Bloomsbury Publishing Inc., part of Bloomsbury Publishing Plc
1359 Broadway, New York, NY 10018
50 Bedford Square, London, WC1B 3DP, UK
Bloomsbury Publishing Ireland Limited, 29 Earlsfort Terrace, Dublin 2, D02 AY28, Ireland

BLOOMSBURY and the Diana logo are trademarks of
Bloomsbury Publishing Plc

First published in the United States of America in June 2025
by Bloomsbury YA

Copyright © 2025 by L. T. Thompson

All rights reserved. No part of this publication may be: i) reproduced or transmitted in any form, electronic or mechanical, including photocopying, recording, or by means of any information storage or retrieval system without prior permission in writing from the publishers; or ii) used or reproduced in any way for the training, development, or operation of artificial intelligence (AI) technologies, including generative AI technologies. The rights holders expressly reserve this publication from the text and data mining exception as per Article 4(3) of the Digital Single Market Directive (EU) 2019/790.

Bloomsbury books may be purchased for business or promotional use.
For information on bulk purchases please contact Macmillan Corporate and
Premium Sales Department at specialmarkets@macmillan.com

Library of Congress Cataloging-in-Publication Data available upon request
ISBN 978-1-5476-1519-3 (hardcover) • ISBN 978-1-5476-1520-9 6 (e-book)

Book design by Jeanette Levy
Typeset by Westchester Publishing Services
Printed and bound in the U.S.A.
by Berryville Graphics Inc., Berryville, Virginia
2 4 6 8 10 9 7 5 3 1

To find out more about our authors and books visit www.bloomsbury.com
and sign up for our newsletters.
For product safety–related questions contact productsafety@bloomsbury.com.

For Cara

Devils Like Us

I
CAS

When she was ten years old, Cas Sterling saw her best friend's father die.

She watched the man bleed out on a forest floor, his chest heaving, his fingers twitching by his sides. It took an excruciatingly long time for his life to leave his body—minutes, although it felt like years. Cas woke up screaming.

It was just a dream. It had to be a dream.

That was before Cas had made up the rules—and so when her nanny, Miss Eloise, came running, Cas spilled the whole story. Through stuttering breaths, she told Miss Eloise about Mr. DeWindt. She told her nanny about the knife and the blood and his eyes cut from his own head. Miss Eloise brought Cas hot chocolate and rubbed her back until she could stop crying.

"This is what happens when you steal those wretched gothic novels from Mrs. Smothers," Miss Eloise said, shaking her head. "They put such ghastly images into your mind."

But Cas hadn't read any of the cook's novels in months, and she knew that this scene hadn't come from the pages of a book. This had come from somewhere else.

Cas was shaky and feverish for days, and her head ached constantly. Her mother sent her to bed and called Doctor Gregory.

When Remy DeWindt came by to meet Cas for their usual adventures, Miss Eloise allowed her up to Cas's sickbed, where Remy and Cas read books of riddles and played games for the whole afternoon. Remy won five chess matches in a row, as was typical whenever Cas reluctantly agreed to play against her. Once Miss Eloise had left them alone, they brought out the playing cards and switched over to twenty-one, where Cas could better hold her own.

And all the while, Cas debated how much to tell. It had only been a dream, after all. But it was about Remy's father.

Was it just a dream? Cas had a terrible feeling.

"Any word from your dad?" Cas asked tentatively as Remy dealt the next round: a three and an eight for Cas, the king of spades for the house.

"Still nothing," Remy said, placing the second house card face down on the bedspread between them. "Mother keeps saying he'll be home soon, but . . ." She shook her head. "I think she expected him to be back by now. Even she seems more worried by the day."

Close to two weeks before, Remy's father had left town in the middle of the night. Supposedly he'd been called away on business—at least that's what Remy's mother claimed. But the rumors had already started to fly. Mr. DeWindt had always been an oddity in Windover—too forthright for polite society, too willing to voice the sorts of opinions that offended traditional sensibilities. He'd stopped going to church a few years back with no explanation. Cas was deeply envious of this.

Mr. DeWindt had built his own pyre of dislike among the town's old guard, and now his sudden unexplained absence had set that pyre ablaze. Mrs. Sanderson at the general store was telling everyone who would listen that Mr. DeWindt was a devil worshipper and had run away to join a cult. The Sterlings' housekeeper believed he'd fled town to escape a mountain of gambling debts, and Cas had overheard her own mother speculating that he likely had some other woman and had abandoned his family to run off with her out west.

Cas was sure the rumors were nonsense. But even Remy had her misgivings. She'd already confided in Cas about the long nights her father had spent locked in his study, and his nervousness lately around strangers coming to the house, and the argument she'd seen between him and the local pastor on the very night her father had disappeared.

Cas studied her cards for longer than she really needed to before deciding to hit. Remy dealt her another: the two of spades. Cas flicked the corners of the cards against each other, weighing the options.

"Are *you* worried?" Cas pressed.

"Of course I am," Remy said. "It's not like him to be away for so long."

Remy was Cas's best friend in the world. They'd grown up just a few houses apart—they'd learned to do chores together, and then they'd neglected their chores together, and they'd exhausted their mothers and antagonized Cas's nanny and snuck off together to run wild through the woods outside of town. Cas had never kept a secret from Remy.

Cas hit again, and Remy dealt her a queen. Remy added up the cards and smirked. "Bust," she said. "You're terrible at this game, too."

"I have to tell you something," Cas said.

She told. It was a mistake.

Cas created the rules for herself after that. *Because* of that. When the dreams started happening during the day, too, she held fast to the rules. When she confirmed that they weren't dreams at all, that they revealed events that would soon come true, she buried that knowledge deep in her soul and plastered over it with a cocksure attitude and a smile.

She's been following the rules for nearly half her life now, and she never lets herself forget them. She never slips.

The most important rule has always been this:

Don't tell anyone what you saw.

Cas wakes late on a morning in March with a railroad spike pushing through the front of her skull, and she knows right away that another vision is coming.

Her head is pounding. Her brain feels pinched. Their maid Penelope has pulled the drapes wide—the *nerve* of her—and when Cas manages to squint her eyelids open, the light streaming through the bedroom window makes her groan.

"Morning, miss," Penelope says from across the room, where she's laying out clothes on the chair by Cas's dressing table. She's chipper, as always. Cas ignores her, as always. "Sorry to wake you. Only your mother sent me—Mr. Ashworth has come by for a visit. He's waiting for you downstairs."

"Oh, damn it all," Cas says.

Penelope flinches.

"Not you, Pen," Cas says quickly, squeezing the bridge of her nose as if she might pinch off the knifepoint that's stabbing into her brain. "Sorry. Just . . . *damn*. He's back in town already?"

"It seems so. Do you not want to see him? I thought you and Mr. Ashworth were friends."

"We are. It's fine."

It's not fine. Henry Ashworth is the last thing she needs today. Cas presses the heels of her hands to her eyes, hard enough to make spots dance against the insides of her lids.

Damn these headaches.

Damn these visions.

She's gone through this routine enough times to know what's coming. The headache will build for hours or sometimes days. Eventually it will crest, and Cas will black out. And then, after she's come to, she'll be stuck in bed for the next week, shaky and sick, while her mother hovers and scolds Cas for being ill and refuses to let Cas even take a piss by herself.

And, of course, in the brief moment of her unconsciousness, Cas will have watched someone else die.

"Which one today, do you think?" Penelope asks, and Cas drops her hands to see Penelope holding up two cotton day dresses in different colors. "The pink brings out the color in your cheeks. But I'm sure your mother would love to see you wear the green—why, just yesterday she was saying how you hadn't so much as tried it on since the dressmaker sent it over, and it really is a lovely thing. Just look at this embroidery . . ."

She keeps talking, though she doesn't seem to require any response from Cas, thank god. Cas lets herself stop listening. It's not that she doesn't want to see Henry, exactly. Penelope is right: she and Henry *are* friends. They have been since they were ten years old. Cas had been reeling from Remy DeWindt's recent decision to cut Cas out of her life, and Henry was still reeling from the death of his sister the year before, and it turned out that both of them enjoyed hiding under the serving table at their parents' evening parties and stealing macaroons off the tray. Cas had known Henry forever; she'd always thought him boring. But his sister's death had unlocked a wildness in him, like he could suddenly see the ridiculousness of their world. Like he felt stifled by the high society of Windover in all the ways it had always stifled Cas, too.

They're too old to hide under tables at parties now, and they've had to shift to pointed eye contact across the room and occasionally making faces at each other when Cas's mother says something outrageous. At the Pendleton family's annual Christmas party a few months back, Henry hadn't wanted to do even that much. It's as if he's been slowly sanding off his most interesting edges, reshaping his public self into the perfect model of well-mannered New England youth. Cas can still provoke the real Henry into showing himself sometimes—but only sometimes, and only ever in private. More and more, she can't figure out where she and Henry stand.

She especially doesn't know where they stand since the Pendletons' Christmas party, when Henry had pulled Cas into the entrance hall and told her he's in love with her.

"Are you all right, miss?" Penelope asks, and suddenly she's standing right in front of Cas, peering down into her face. "You look a little pale."

Cas swats her away. "Just a headache."

"Should I bring you up a glass of water?"

"No—I'll be fine."

"Or send for Doctor Gregory?"

"*No.*" As much as Cas would prefer to hide away in her room today, she'd also prefer to put off the doctor and her mother's suffocating attention for as long as possible. Henry had gone back to Harvard the morning after the Christmas party; they haven't spoken since. But Cas is going to have to face this sooner or later.

The problem is that she never actually *said* anything in response to Henry's confession; she'd smiled, and she'd laughed nervously a few times, and then the Hirsch sisters had saved her when they'd come barreling into the hall to announce the dancing. But Henry hadn't seemed upset as he and Cas went to join the quadrille. Maybe he'd taken Cas's smiling to mean she felt the same way. Is he going to expect a clearer answer today? Is Cas going to have to tell him she's in love with him as well? It would be a lie, but a kind one.

Cas eyes the two dresses draped over Penelope's arms. Honestly, they're practically the same. They always are. "You choose," she says. "Please. I don't care which."

Penelope debates for several more minutes before she holds up the pink one and says, "Let's see if this helps with your pallor." She spends an eternity pinning up Cas's hair and pinching her cheeks to put some color in them, while Cas grits her teeth and considers jumping out of the second-story window. Cas doesn't really mind Penelope, usually. The maid has a constant need to be moving at all times, which Cas can relate to well enough. But Penelope always seems to point her energy in a direction: tidying up the room, poking at the fire, relaying the gossip she's picked up from the other maids in town.

Cas just gets restless.

Henry is already settled in the parlor by the time Cas makes it downstairs. According to Cas's mother, the Sterlings' parlor is decorated in an homage to the old rococo style. Really it looks like the room has devoured someone's flower garden and then retched it up again. Everything is covered in a floral print: floral rug, floral curtains, floral upholstery on the sofa.

Henry in his dark jacket stands out as the only non-flower in the room. He's sitting stiffly on the sofa, though he springs to his feet when he spots Cas in the doorway.

"Miss Sterling," he says, as if he and Cas haven't known each other since they were toddlers. Cas wrinkles her nose at him. Henry glances around, confirming they're alone, then amends, "Cassandra. Cas. It's good to see you."

"And you." Cas drops into the armchair across from him and props her boots up on the floral-cushioned piano stool. "Is your term finished, then?"

"Not yet, but we have a few days off from classes. I caught the train home last night. I was hoping you and I could . . . talk."

He puts a certain emphasis on the word *talk*. Cas doesn't like it. "Is that a new waistcoat?" she asks, deflecting.

"Is it?" Henry looks down at the waistcoat in question, which has a shawl collar and a subtle paisley pattern. "I suppose. The salesman told me it was the current fashion. Listen . . ."

He leans in, and this is the moment, isn't it? He's going to press for an answer that's several months overdue, and Cas will have to either lie to his face or break his heart.

But Henry glances at the open door to the front hall, where Penelope is now dusting the bannisters. He straightens, clearing his throat.

"How would you feel about going for a ride?" he asks in the stiff, proper voice he's taken to using in public. "It's a little chilly, but the sun is out. We could take the carriage to Long Beach."

Cas's head pounds at the thought. A ride to Long Beach is nearly an hour round trip, which means nearly an hour on a winding country road with no way to flee this conversation.

"I'm not feeling well, actually," Cas says. "It's probably better if we—"

"She'd love to go," says a voice from the parlor doorway, and her mother whirls into the room wearing a broad smile and a dress as floral as the wallpaper.

Her eyes catch Cas's boots on the piano stool. Her smile drops.

"Feet," she snaps. "Down."

Cas puts her feet down.

"It's wonderful to have you back in Windover, Mr. Ashworth," Mrs. Sterling resumes, beaming again at Henry like he's Jesus Christ himself. "Cassandra would love to ride to the shore with you. I'm sure you two could use some time to catch up."

"That's just what I was hoping for," Henry says.

"Excellent. Would you like to take our carriage, or have you brought yours? Either way, I can have our driver act as your chaperone. Should I have Mrs. Smothers pack you a picnic?"

"I have a headache," Cas cuts in.

"You have no such thing," her mother says. "Some fresh sea air will do you good."

Henry's eyes dart between Cas and her mother. "I came in my carriage," he says after a moment. "And a picnic would be wonderful, thank you. That is, if it's all right with you, Miss Sterling?"

Somehow they're back to *Miss Sterling* again. "As if I could possibly stop this boulder now that it's rolling downhill," Cas says. She means for it to come out as a joke. It doesn't. Her headache is cutting her already short temper even shorter.

"Cassandra," her mother hisses at her.

Henry pretends not to have noticed. "I'll go have Thomas bring the carriage around."

Cas waits for the front door to close behind him before she wheels on her mother. "I really do have a headache."

"You're fine," Mrs. Sterling tells her. "You are going with him, and you're going to enjoy it."

This is all part of her plan to have Cas and Henry married someday. Both of their mothers have had it plotted out for ages. The Ashworths' house, on the far side of town, isn't nearly grand enough for a family of their standing, and the Sterlings' house, grand though it is, lacks an heir. This is Cas's fault for being born an only child and for not being born a boy, apparently. Property laws are a load of bull.

Henry will marry into the Sterling family, and then he'll inherit the Sterling family home, and all the worries of both their mothers will be solved. Henry's confession at the Christmas party only makes this arrangement more convenient. Cas's mother doesn't know about that development yet. Oh god; she's going to be insufferable about it.

As much as Cas *wants* to hate this tidy railroad track of a life lined up ahead of her ... she doesn't hate it, really. She can't. Not when a life with Henry is better than any other life Cas could hope for. Henry is kind, and he's familiar, and he's in love with her, apparently. He knows Cas is no housewife; he claims he won't expect her to be. They'll both have to perform in public, of course, but once they're safe at home, they can do as they please. Henry and Cas had talked through these logistics long before any romantic feelings were involved. Cas can only hope the logistics still hold.

There are worse futures, she knows. She ought to be grateful.

Still, sometimes the idea of doing this for the rest of her life—of donning her fine dresses and entertaining company and using the proper fork at dinner, all so she can collapse in her room at night and breathe for a few hours before she has to do it all over again—makes Cas want to walk into the sea.

"Look at me," Mrs. Sterling says now.

She waits until Cas has stood and met her eyes. It takes effort. It's been years since her mother raised a hand against her, but Cas can still feel her own muscles tense, waiting.

"You are to smile at him," Mrs. Sterling says. "You are to be attentive. You are to use proper manners and to hold your tongue." She drops her voice low. She's a snake in the grass getting ready to spring. "Do *not* botch this, the way you've botched everything else in your ungrateful life."

Which is how Cas finds herself strolling along the shoreline at Long Beach later that morning, trying to ignore the pounding of her head and the churning of her stomach as she and Henry walk.

Long Beach is a peninsula less than half a mile across, covered with tall seagrasses and patches of sand. The ocean spreads out on either side. The walking path isn't crowded this early in the season—mostly couples out for a promenade, though Cas refuses to count herself and Henry among that number. She spots Abigail Payne arm in arm with some gentleman from the next town over—a Mr. Growden? Mr. Grove? Cas can't remember. Abigail smiles and waves at her. Cas mirrors her before balling her hands into fists and shoving them into her coat pockets.

"I know I ought to continue straight into law school in the fall," Henry is saying, "but with the elections coming up, I've been thinking of taking time off. Getting some real hands-on experience with a campaign. It's infuriating to be stuck in a classroom instead of actually doing something useful in the world."

He waits, and Cas realizes she hasn't said a single word for several minutes. Henry must have noticed, too. Cas blinks her eyes in the sun and tries to focus.

"That makes sense," she says.

Henry nods, seemingly satisfied. "There's a senate candidate in Boston who'd be a dream to work with. You'd like him. His whole platform is about equality, about building a government that works for *all* people."

It's a relief to hear him still talk like this. Sometimes Cas worries that Henry's private-school education will squash the morality straight out of him. But he's still the same Henry he always was, whose political ambitions come from a genuine desire to help people. He used to go off on all sorts of idealistic monologues about it, back when he and Cas would sneak out to get drunk on terrible wine they were too young to know was terrible.

"It would mean I'd be away from Windover for a while longer," Henry continues, "but . . . well, so would law school. And I could still come home to visit. I know you're not much of a letter writer, but . . ." He gives Cas a sidelong glance. "I've missed you."

They've meandered far enough down the beach that no one else is in earshot. Cas rubs her throbbing forehead. Henry stops walking.

"About the Christmas party," he says.

Oh god, not now. "What about it?"

"I wanted to apologize."

Cas was bracing for the worst, but this isn't at all what she expected. "Apologize?"

"I know you don't feel the same way about me," Henry says, the words coming out in a rush. "I never expected that you did. Only it seemed right to tell you how I felt, because ... well, we've always been honest with each other, haven't we?"

Cas feels a little dizzy—from the relief, or the headache, or both. "I suppose?"

"Anyway, I shouldn't have sprung it on you like that, and I wanted to make sure you knew that it doesn't change anything between us. That is, it doesn't change anything for me. I'm not ... you know ... *expecting* anything other than the life we'd already planned."

He looks like he means it, and good god, it would be so much easier if Cas *were* in love with him. But it turns out Henry knows she isn't, and he's not even upset about it. He doesn't even mind that their inevitable marriage won't be a love match, but instead a mutually convenient business arrangement between friends.

Cas needs to get her head on straight. "Yes, that's ... good," she says. "That's ... that's ... that's really good. We're good, then."

Henry's mouth quirks. "We're good," he says.

It should be a massive relief. It *is* a massive relief. So why does Cas feel worse now than she did before?

We've always been honest with each other, haven't we?

Cas isn't sure she's honest with anyone these days, but she's probably more honest with Henry than she is with anyone else. That ought to count for something, right?

"So," Cas says in a desperate bid to change the subject, "you're going to hold off on law school, then?"

Henry accepts the bid smoothly as they resume their promenade. "Law school will still be there later. Oh, I saw your father on campus last month—did he tell you? I think he's friends with the head of the library there."

Cas's mind is drifting again. The sun has turned too bright, too warm—Cas shouldn't have worn a coat. It's stifling. A wisp of sea breeze blows cool on her face, and Cas savors it. Ahead of them, a woman watches her three small children playing in a sandy patch. Two of them are methodically piling the sand into a large mound, while the third methodically knocks it down.

Cas's old nanny, Miss Eloise, used to bring her here when she was younger. Cas would run up and down the shore for hours. She'd kick off her shoes and hike up her skirts and wade barefoot through the freezing shallows. She'd gaze out at the empty ocean and imagine drifting away on it, the only person in the world.

For those glorious afternoons, Cas hadn't had to try to be Miss Cassandra Sterling—halfway watching herself from the outside, through the eyes of her mother or the people in town. Wondering just how much of herself she'd have to carve off to live up to her family's name. For a brief time, Cas could just exist as Cas.

Miss Eloise had left when Cas was ten, not long after she'd had that first vision.

There's something uncanny about that child, Miss Eloise had murmured to Mrs. Sterling on the morning she'd packed her bags. She probably hadn't thought Cas could hear her.

Cas and Henry are still walking, but a silvery, flickering haze has started to crowd in Cas's periphery. She closes her eyes, and the insides of her eyelids are all silver sparks. She opens them, and the whole world is silver sparks.

Not now, she pleads. But she knows what it means. It's coming, it's coming.

"I need to stop for a moment," Cas interrupts. Her own voice sounds much more distant than it did just moments ago.

Henry stops alongside her. "Are you all right?"

"Just feeling a little faint." That's not the half of it, though. The pain in her head is cresting now—she might be swept away on it at any moment.

"You should sit down and rest," Henry says.

"I will. You can go on ahead."

"I'll do no such thing." Henry is squinting at her now. "You need to rest. You look terrible."

"Thanks for that."

"I mean to say—"

"Go to hell, Henry," Cas says, and takes off walking again.

Henry follows, tragically unfazed. Cas has told Henry to go to hell too many times for the sentiment to hold any bite.

Cas steps off the path, scanning for anything she can duck behind for a little privacy. The beach is clear and open. Cas shouldn't have come here. She should have kicked up a fuss and refused outright. Her mother would have been furious, but at least then Cas wouldn't be swooning on this very public beach, about to have a very public fit. The visions don't usually come on this quickly. She'd figured she'd have more time.

Obviously she'd figured wrong.

From somewhere behind, Henry takes her arm. The fabric burns against her skin. "Don't touch me!" she gasps.

He lets go. Cas unbuttons her coat and lets it drop in the grass. The fresh air on her arms helps, but it's not enough. Her view has almost been overtaken by the flickering haze now. She can't see a damn thing.

"Cas, wait," Henry is saying.

"Don't—"

But the pain in her head spikes so sharply that she stumbles, and Henry catches her, one hand clamping onto her elbow, the other around her waist. She can't get away. She can't get away. The world is all swirling sparks . . .

And then she's in the vision.

She doesn't feel her body falling as she goes under; she never does. She simply flickers from existing in Long Beach at one moment to existing in another place entirely. It's nighttime now. A gravel street. Windover, the south side of town. Over the peaked roofs of the run-down boardinghouses there, the moon shines in a clear sky.

A girl is running down the road. Her loose red hair streams behind her, glinting like flames in the moonlight. Her chest huffs for breath in time with the bounce of her boots. But she's silent as she runs. The visions are always silent. Not just quiet, but a total absence of noise; not like Cas's ears have been muffled with pillows, but like she's stopped having ears at all. The girl's face is pale and sharp, with wide-set eyes that shine glassily with fear as she glances backward over her shoulder.

The girl's face is familiar. Cas's heart sinks. It's always worse when she recognizes them. In only a second she's placed her—a figure Cas has seen around town many times, hovering behind Remy DeWindt at the dressmaker's shop or crossing the common arm in arm with her. It's Fionnuala Robinson, a maid in town and Remy DeWindt's closest friend. The girl who had swooped into Remy's life only a year or two after Cas had left it, who now fills the space there that Cas used to hold before she had to make the rules. Before Remy had cut her off.

Far behind Fionnuala, maybe fifty yards down the road, something is moving—a dark figure Cas can't quite make out from the shadows of the buildings around it. Somehow, though, Cas senses it's drawing closer. Whatever it is, it's giving chase.

That's when Cas hears something. The visions are silent, always, and yet there's a sound: a whimper from the air beside her.

She turns.

Cas has been so fixated on the girl and the shadowy figure in the distance that she hasn't noticed the figure right next to her. Looking at him, her eyes won't quite focus, like they know he doesn't belong in this scene. Like they know he's an intruder.

It's Henry.

Henry, with his eyes wide and terrified in a way Cas has never seen, even in those worst days after his sister had died. Henry, with beads of sweat trickling down his high forehead.

Henry, watching the whole thing.

II

FINN

As a child, Fionnuala Robinson had begged her mother to bring her to confession. The priest back in County Mayo, Ireland, heard confessions every Saturday afternoon at the old stone church in Knockadine, and even before Finn was old enough for the sacrament, she trailed along whenever her mother went. Finn would study the faces of the parishioners as they entered the confessional to present their sins, and then she'd study them again as they left. She always thought she could sense a sort of relief about them on the tail end, a straightening of their shoulders. It was as if they'd lugged a huge bag of rocks into the booth with them and then abandoned it, leaving the rocks behind.

She started taking the sacrament herself when she was eight or nine, and she finally understood. She finally felt that lifting weight of forgiveness. It was the promise of the thing—the assurance that God had cleared you of every sin you'd committed up to that point. The absolute knowledge that if you were to die in that moment, you'd be spared from hell.

Even back then, Finn had nightmares about hell.

Finn doesn't know how long it's been now since she last went to confession. Perhaps once or twice just after she and her brother had left Ireland for Massachusetts, but certainly not in the years since. Yet she still can't set foot in a house of God without thinking about those Saturday afternoons in the Knockadine church. It's like she's haunted by that younger version of herself, who still felt a scrap of hope for the salvation of her own mortal soul.

The church Remy DeWindt has dragged Finn to this morning is a far cry from that drafty stone parish of Finn's youth. Instead of slanting walls and a thatched roof that leaks, this small country church has tidy clapboards, tidy shingles, and an interior so newly whitewashed that it seems to glow. The parish is Congregationalist, or perhaps Presbyterian now—Remy had tried to explain it on the long walk over, but Finn is fuzzy on the differences between the various threads of Protestantism. In any case, there are no statues of Mary here, no elaborate stained-glass depictions of saints. And there isn't a confessional booth in sight.

"We appreciate your help on this," Remy says as the grim-faced caretaker unlocks the office door. "I'm sure you're juggling a lot right now, but it will mean the world to my mother to have some of her brother's books."

"I'll be glad to be rid of them, honestly," the caretaker says. She's clearly in a hurry—when Remy had presented their story, the woman had agreed without even looking at the letter Remy and Finn spent the last two days forging. "Your uncle's left us with quite a mess to sort through. God rest his soul," she adds quickly.

Remy's laugh is a perfect balance of sympathetic and polite. "He never could throw anything away. It always frustrated my mother to no end."

Even knowing that Remy's mother has no relation to this parish's late pastor, Finn almost believes her. The caretaker gets the door open at last, then steps back to reveal a small office, every surface inside it piled with papers and books.

"Is all of this his?" Remy asks.

"As I said. You're welcome to whatever you'd like. Is there anything else I can help with, or . . . ?"

She clearly hopes there isn't. Remy doesn't answer, though. She's already distracted, examining the bookshelves with that hungry keenness she gets, a hound closing in on its mark.

"We'll manage from here, thank you," Finn tells the caretaker. She thinks she's done a decent job of muffling her accent until she catches the look on Remy's face—perhaps not so decent, then. But if the caretaker has any questions about why one of the girls going through the dead pastor's office is so obviously and unavoidably Irish, she doesn't ask them. Remy thanks her once more, smiling sweetly, and as the woman leaves them to it, Remy flicks the latch closed behind her.

"Right," Remy says, dropping the false smile in an instant. Finn has watched this transition for years, yet she still marvels at how easily Remy shifts from the perfect, polite, respectable young lady back into this focused researcher, who only Finn ever gets to see. "We don't have a lot of time. I'll start with the papers if you take the books."

Finn sets to work along the lowest of the bookshelves, skimming the titles printed on each spine. On their walk to the church this morning, when Finn had asked what, exactly, they were hoping to find here, Remy had said, "Just the usual—anything strange. Anything that seems out of place."

What she'd really meant, of course, was *anything occult*. Finn has been privy to Remy's investigation for long enough to know what to flag: Anything that might reveal an interest in prophetic omens, or divination, or unseen planes of the world. Any sign that this pastor was researching mysticism or magic. It all seems so far removed from this clean, white-walled church; it's hard to imagine that the pastor here had been part of the same strange net that had ensnared Remy's father.

But Remy insists this man had ties to the Order, just like all the others. His name was on her father's list of members. She'd been scheming up ways to dig into his affairs for over a year before the news came last week that he'd passed. And death has a way of letting a person's secrets drift to the surface.

"Look at this," Remy says, holding up a ledger of some kind. "*Eden Theological Seminary.* He was sending monthly donations there in support of a local scholarship student—but the money cuts off last year."

"Graduated?" Finn guesses. "Or dropped out? Or . . ."

"Or another disappearance. I'll have to do some digging. If it's the last, Pastor Cole was recruiting awfully close to home."

She tucks the ledger into her bag and continues on to the next bundle of papers. She's mesmerizing when she's like this—so focused, so clearly in her element. There's something about the way she goes perfectly still as she's reading, the way her dark curls fall around her face. Her mouth pinches at the corners, dimpling the round, warm pinks of her cheeks. Finn imagines touching a fingertip into the centers of those dimples.

And then promptly shakes herself. Fool, she thinks. She returns to the bookshelf. At least Remy is too immersed in a dead man's papers to notice Finn's reddened face, betraying her as always.

Finn tugs at her collar, trying to adjust the scapular where it's scratching beneath her dress. She'd inherited the scapular from her mother—a necklace of sorts connecting two small squares of wool, each embroidered with golden thread. The piece that hangs down Finn's front bears an image of the Virgin Mary in profile, a halo perfectly encircling her head. The piece down the back has words.

"It's a promise from Our Lady," Finn's mother had told her when she'd given it to Finn so many years ago. "See? *Whosoever dies wearing this garment shall not suffer the eternal fire.*"

The promise had offered more comfort back then than it does these days. Finn doesn't know why she even wears the scapular anymore. She's certain enough of her own damnation; a few words embroidered on a piece of wool aren't going to save her.

Finn reaches for the next book—a perfectly innocuous collection of Calvinist essays. But as she shifts it there's a *thump*. Something at the back of the shelf has jostled out of place.

Finn moves the surrounding books, widening the gap. She peers through.

There, pushed all the way behind the rest of the row of books, is a slim leather tome. The title is embossed in faded gold on the cover: *Grimoirium Verum*.

Finn skitters back a step.

"What is it? What's wrong?" Remy asks.

But Finn is frozen. Remy scrambles to her feet and squints between the books to see. She pulls in a sharp breath through her nostrils.

"That's a grimoire. I'm sure of it." There's victory in her voice—she's caught the rabbit at last. "What's a Protestant pastor doing with a spellbook hidden in his bookshelf?"

She reaches for it, and Finn can't stop herself. She grabs Remy's arm. "Don't."

"What, touch it?" Remy shakes her sleeve loose and pulls the grimoire out. "It's not as if I'm going to burst into flames. See? It's fine."

"Be careful."

Remy starts to flip the book open, then pauses, as if only now realizing the actuality of Finn's fear. She presses the cover closed again, her face softening.

"Sorry," Remy says. "I know you believe in all of..." She flaps the grimoire at her. "I can wait till later to look at it more closely. Only I think my father had this same book in his collection. And you have to admit that *this* raises suspicions, doesn't it? It's proof that my father was right—Cole wasn't just supporting the seminary's public front. He was tied up with the Order, too. We should check the other shelves, see if he tried to hide anything else back there."

As they search behind the other rows of books, Finn wills her pulse to return to normal. The echo of Remy's words hangs in her ears: *I know you believe in all of...* As if Finn has any other choice. *Belief* feels like too flimsy a sentiment, anyway—like saying one believes in dirt or pickled beets. There's no *belief* needed for something you've seen, something you've held in your own hands.

Remy, meanwhile, has spent the better part of a decade digging through the library of occult books her father left behind—yet her interest is purely academic. It's all in pursuit of her investigation; she's made it quite clear that she doesn't believe a word of it. She and Finn have had the argument too many times now for either of them to offer anything new.

They spend over an hour combing the office before Remy finally admits they need to head home. Both of them have mountains of work waiting for them back in Windover. Finn's employer, a cantankerous woman named Mrs. Darner, had instructed her to scrub the parlor floor, the entryway, and all of the house's silver cutlery—all of which Finn did yesterday, but not to Mrs. Darner's ridiculous standard. Finn will do it again, but she resents it. Remy, meanwhile, has her own family's house to maintain, on top of the dozens of other odd jobs she picks up around town to coax the DeWindts' lean budget into balancing. She's always dashing off to help with the neighbor's new baby, or to mend trousers, or to tutor someone's child in French.

Perhaps, Finn thinks, as she watches Remy shove a few more pages from the pastor's desk into her bag, the two of them are overdue for another of their nights in the woods. It's been several weeks since they last went, and besides, Remy never says no to the suggestion, though she never suggests it herself. They can slip out to Dungeon Rock for an evening, to drink and talk and look at the stars. To shrug off their respective responsibilities, if only for a few hours.

When they make their way outside, the bells of the church have started to chime. It must be eleven. Remy swears.

"Later than I'd hoped," she says, already heading down the church's drive. "We'll have to make it a quick walk back to town. I'm supposed to have the Russell children for a piano lesson at noon."

Finn has to trot to keep up with her. "Some of us can only walk so quickly," she mutters. "Not all of us have your ungodly long legs."

Remy laughs. It's loud and deeply unflattering, a world away from the gentle chuckle she usually pulls out in public. Finn much prefers this one. "I don't think my legs are ungodly long. Maybe yours are just ungodly short. Nearer to the ground, nearer to hell, and all that."

Finn knows she doesn't mean anything by it, but she can't help glancing at Remy's bag, where that damned grimoire is now tucked away. It feels dangerous, explosive, like carrying around a loaded cannon.

Remy has tracked her gaze. "You're thinking about the book again, aren't you?"

"No," Finn lies.

"I'm not going to *do* anything with it. I promise. It's just for research."

"I know."

And Finn does. Remy may be a skeptic, but she isn't a fool. Whatever spells or summoning rituals are described within that book's pages, Remy would never be reckless enough to attempt them. Besides, she's far better at planning and scheming than at ever putting those schemes into action. Even after all these years of her investigation, Finn has no idea what Remy intends to *do* with all the strange secrets she's uncovered.

Sometimes she thinks Remy doesn't know herself.

There's a clatter of cart wheels on the road ahead of them, and then a rig and a pair of horses round the next bend through the trees. A trio of women ride behind the driver, who has a clerical collar and a slick of wheat-blond hair under his hat.

"Oh no," Remy breathes. "Is that—? Tell me I'm wrong, please. Is that Pastor Dekker?"

"It's Dekker," Finn says, and Remy blanches.

"What's he doing here? Did he somehow know *we* would be here?"

"How could he have known?" Finn asks.

"I don't know. He's a snake. He seems to know everything about everyone in town."

"Would you like us to dive into the trees to hide?"

But Pastor Dekker has already spotted them. He pulls the horses to a stop in the middle of the road, hand raised in greeting.

"Ah, Miss DeWindt!" he calls out. "What a pleasant surprise."

He doesn't acknowledge Finn; most people don't. Instinctively, Finn has fallen into place a few feet behind Remy, just as she used to when she was still working as the DeWindts' maid. It's been ages since Remy's family could afford a household staff, though Remy kept the staff on far longer than she ought in her efforts to maintain appearances. She kept Finn on even longer than the rest; in the end, it was Finn who forced the split and left for old Mrs. Darner's, where she's worked for the last six years. But old habits die hard.

Remy's polite smile is firmly back in place now. "Quite."

"What brings you so far from Windover?" Dekker asks.

"We're not terribly far," Remy says, though they are. "We're just out for a walk. It's a fine morning, isn't it?"

"It is indeed. Well, *we're* on our way to visit dear Mrs. Holcombe at the church up ahead—the caretaker, you know. You heard about Pastor Cole?"

"Oh yes," Remy says. "Such a loss."

"We're bringing Mrs. Holcombe some pastries and flowers," one of the rig's passengers chimes in. She's one of the Hirsch girls, though Finn can't remember which one. She glances at the other two riders: a slightly older woman named Lizzie Pendleton, and . . . Imogen Walters.

Jesus, Mary, and Joseph. Of all the luck.

"How is your family these days?" Dekker is asking, thankfully ignorant of the way Imogen Walters is gnawing coyly on her bottom lip and trying to catch Finn's eye. "I don't believe I've seen your mother for services in some time. Should I be concerned?"

There's an undercurrent to his words: clearly *Remy* should be concerned for her family's reputation if word starts getting around. "She . . . comes when she's well enough," Remy says.

"Of course. I do offer home visitations, you know, if she ever feels inclined."

Remy's smile is nearly wide enough to hide the way she's gritting her teeth. "I'll be sure to let her know."

Imogen Walters chooses this moment to blurt out, "Good morning, Miss Robinson." Finn has been silently praying that Imogen would take the hint and compose herself—but *this* is the opposite of composed. With a flutter in her voice and a very obvious flush to her cheeks, she stammers out, "It's . . . it's lovely to see you."

Finn offers her a lukewarm curtsy. "Mrs. Walters," she murmurs. To Remy, she says, "We should be getting back, shouldn't we?"

"Right," Remy says. "Right. Lovely to see you, Pastor. We'll just be on our way."

She maintains her smile as Dekker bids them farewell and jolts the horses forward. When the rig has disappeared down the drive, Remy buries her face in her hands.

"I can't believe this," she says as she and Finn start toward Windover again. "Nothing feels like a coincidence with him.

And now he wants to visit my mother at home...I'm going to have to drag her to church on Sunday, aren't I? I swear he's determined to keep us all under his thumb—as if he hasn't done enough already."

The *done enough* is because Dekker was almost certainly involved with Remy's father's disappearance. Finn hadn't known Mr. DeWindt well; he'd hired Finn and her brother only a few months before he vanished. In her memories of him, he's kind and warm. Or perhaps that's simply the way Remy talks about him.

"Dekker does seem unusually invested in your family," Finn admits.

"I think he's unusually invested in every single person in Windover. You're the lucky exception, I suppose."

"You could become a Catholic," Finn suggests, then snorts. "Or a heathen."

"Can you imagine the rumors *that* would launch?" Remy says. "Lord, what a mess. Do you think he's planning to look through Cole's things as well? He might even be looking for the grimoire."

"Nothing to be done about it now, is there? Unless you'd like to run back and offer it to him."

Remy does not, of course, run back and offer it to him. "What was that between you and Imogen Jenkins, anyway?" she asks instead. "Or Walters now, I suppose. It's so strange that she's married."

Finn tries to keep her face neutral, though her cheeks are warming. "Hmm?"

"The blushing, the *good morning*. I didn't know you two even knew each other."

"In a manner of speaking."

"Oh lord." Remy stops in the middle of the road. "Tell me you didn't."

"Didn't what?"

Finn meets Remy's gaze and holds it steadily until Remy's cheeks go pink, too—which is good. It's better, somehow, to turn it into this strange challenge, to dare Remy to say it aloud. Especially since Finn knows she never will.

Remy looks away first.

"Imogen's husband is older than us," Finn says once they're walking again. "And he's often away in Boston. Imogen likes to have . . . companionship, sometimes, when he's gone."

"Oh lord," Remy says again. "Stop."

"You're the one who asked."

"I take the question back."

It's an open secret between them—not even a secret at this point, really, not since last year when Remy had walked in on Finn and Mary Lassiter sweaty and tangled in a tent at the Lynn Cattle Show. It had been a humiliating experience all around, made worse because, even as Finn's hands had been sliding under Mary's blouse, her mind had been drifting to dimpled cheeks, and long, dark curls, and the sound Remy might make if she were ever kissed like this . . .

Finn's mind is a traitor. Mary deserves better. Afterward, Finn and Remy spoke about it only once, on one of their nights in the woods, when Remy was drunk on cheap port and Finn was too far in her own altitudes to do the decent thing and fling herself off the rock.

"It's not as if I don't get the *appeal*," Remy had said. "It's not as if I haven't thought about girls, or kissing a girl, or . . . I mean, doesn't everyone? It's just that the rest of us aren't so brazen as to *act* on our... There are rules, you know. There's common decency. And Christ, Finn—*Mary Lassiter?*"

In the months since, Finn has wondered what would have happened if they'd had that conversation sober. She's wondered what Remy might have said if Finn had gently informed her that, though Finn has only her own background for comparison, she's not so sure that imagining kissing girls is the universal experience that Remy believes it to be.

It doesn't matter. Even if Remy *were* interested in girls in that way—even if somehow, by some miracle, she was interested in Finn—Remy would never ever do anything about it, and Finn isn't about to push the issue. Despite the drifting of her unruly mind, she's long given up on that particular fool's paradise. It's fine. It's completely fine. Finn is fine with it. She knows herself well enough to know what she wants, and *she's* perfectly capable of action. Plenty of other fish in the sea.

Even though it's been years since Finn has gone to confession, she still practices one part of the sacrament regularly: the examination of conscience. She keeps a constant list of her own sins running in her mind, adding to it with each new wrong. The list is endless at this point. Once her fate became inevitable, she more or less stopped trying.

But she keeps the list anyway. It's strangely satisfying, like picking a scab. When Mrs. Darner makes her wash all the china three more times after it's already clean, Finn adds to the list: *Fantasized about murdering employer.* When she answers her brother's question of how she's doing with "Fine, I'm doing fine," she adds: *Lied to Kieran.* When she slips in through the back door of the Walters' house on cool spring evenings when Mr. Walters is out of town, she adds: *Fornication, and also sodomy.*

She knows she's an abomination. Probably she's even more abominable for dragging sweet Imogen down with her. Finn never stays the night; she flees back to her own empty bed so she can lie there alone in the dark, hating herself. But shame is an old friend. It never keeps her away for long.

Now, as she and Remy set off on the long walk back to Windover, Finn adds a broad item to her list of sins for generally impure thoughts. She usually has to around Remy. Under Finn's dress, the wool of her scapular shifts a little, just over her heart.

III

CAS

In the years since that first terrible vision of Remy's father, Cas has seen many deaths. She's seen a woman burned alive in a house fire. She's seen a man snap his neck by tumbling from a horse, and a child, even younger than Cas had been at the time, fall to his death from the cliffs near Nahant. She's seen three different men die from gunshot wounds and two die while working at the railyard in Salem.

But Cas has never before seen a death like the one that's coming for Fionnuala Robinson.

Fionnuala keeps running down the darkened Windover street. But something is detaching itself from the shadows behind her—or maybe the shadows themselves are detaching. The figure is nebulous as smoke. It isn't human-shaped, exactly, but it isn't fully *in*human either—it walks on two legs, more or less, even as it dissolves and re-forms, even as it moves at an impossible pace and radiates a cold that sinks deep into Cas's bones.

Fionnuala seems to know it's there. She seems to know it's gaining on her. She keeps glancing over her shoulder, marking the monster's progress as it closes the gap between them. A kind of dual panic is building in Cas's chest: panic for the girl, for her death at the hands of this ghastly thing, and then a completely separate panic for herself. And for Henry. And for whatever is going to happen outside the vision, back on the beach, when she and Henry both wake and Henry has seen what he's seen.

Fionnuala has nearly reached the edge of town now. She races onto the little stone bridge that crosses Cedar Brook. Ahead of her, the world widens—no more buildings. Just open farmland and woods beyond.

But the terrible figure is upon her.

A curl of smoke reaches out from its depths. A tentacle. An arm. A shadowy hand with its palm extended. When the hand plunges into Fionnuala's back, through her chest, her mouth opens in a silent scream. Then the hand crumples into a fist. Her body goes slack.

In an instant, Fionnuala's life flickers out. A candle snuffed.

Then Cas is on Long Beach again, flat on her back, gasping. After the silence of the vision, sound hits her like a wall: The roaring waves. The rustling seagrass.

And somewhere, a voice that isn't hers is screaming.

"Henry," she says.

The word catches in her throat. She tries to sit up, and the world spins. Thoughts are coming in fragments: Henry. Fionnuala Robinson. That shadowy figure on the bridge. Fionnuala Robinson is going to die. There's a monster coming for her, something ice-cold and evil, something Cas can't unknow the existence of.

And Henry knows it, too. Henry didn't just see Cas fainting. Henry . . . *saw*. All of it.

"Henry!" She gets it out louder this time. Shakes his shoulder. He's on the ground beside her, fumbling in the sand, his face covered in sweat. The touch jerks him out of his yelling. His eyes dart around wildly, as if still searching for that shadowy hand.

"What the hell," he chokes out. "Where is it? Where did it go?"

"You're all right," Cas says, partly to Henry, partly to herself. "You'll be all right in a minute."

The others on the beach have taken notice; the children who'd been playing in the sand are now staring openmouthed as their mother tries to pull them away. Abigail Payne and her companion have already started toward Cas and Henry, their brows pinched with worry. As Cas struggles to her feet, as she drags Henry upright, too, she runs through the list of rules she made back when this was all new: Play it off as a normal fainting spell. Don't let on that anything strange has happened. Don't tell anyone what you saw.

"Come on," Cas says, pushing Henry back toward the path. They only need to make it to the carriage. Once they're away from prying eyes and ears, Cas can figure out how to fix this.

But Henry doesn't move. "That thing," he says. "What was it?"

"Nothing. It wasn't anything."

"You saw it, too, didn't you?"

"No, I— We can talk about it in the carriage—"

"What was it?" Henry demands.

But it's too late. Abigail Payne and Mr. Growden, or Mr. Grove, have reached them.

"Are you both all right?" Abigail asks. Her face is a perfect picture of concern, though she's probably thrilled about the gossip she's about to gather. "That looked like quite a commotion."

"Fine," Cas says. She paints on a smile like the one her mother uses when Cas says something crass in front of company. "We're just fine. I only swooned. Mr. Ashworth must have tried to catch me, but . . . well, either I got him by surprise, or he needs to spend a bit more time lifting weights." She forces a laugh, the kind of fluttery little giggle she's heard girls like Abigail Payne use. "Still, he's such a gentleman for trying, isn't he?"

"Chivalry isn't dead after all, eh, Ashworth?" Mr. Growden, or Mr. Grove, says. (Growve, Cas compromises.) He taps his fist to Henry's shoulder in that affable way the men around town always seem to. It's absurd that even in this moment, as her entire life is crumbling apart, Cas feels a stab of jealousy. Something about the easiness of it, the masculine self-assurance.

Even if Cas knocked someone's shoulder like that, it wouldn't be the same.

"At least the thought counts for something," Growve goes on. "You'll have to join us in Saugus for dumbbells some morning."

Henry doesn't answer. He's still staring at Cas as if the others don't exist.

"That thing," Henry says again. "That . . . *demon*. Is that what it was? A demon?"

Abigail Payne's eyes widen, her mouth forming a perfect O. Growve has staggered backward a step. Cas tries for another giggle, though the panic turns it nervous and high.

"You must have fainted for a moment, too," she tells Henry. "You had some sort of dream—"

"It wasn't a dream," he cuts in. "It was real. It *felt* real."

"It's just the heat getting to you." Even as she says it, gooseflesh breaks out on Cas's arms. Now that the vision has passed, the early spring chill is settling back in.

"You saw it, too. You must have. It was right—"

Henry spins in a wild circle, searching. But there is no monster here—only a beach full of onlookers, and Growden and Abigail Payne still frozen in shock. "It was right there in town! A demon!"

"We should get home. You're not well," Cas tries. She reaches for Henry's sweat-slicked hand, but he jerks it away.

"You saw it, too!" Henry says again.

He's the most heated Cas has seen him in years—probably since they were thirteen and ranting about the unfairness of the universe. The desperation is written so clearly on his face. He needs confirmation. He needs Cas to believe him.

Cas recognizes it—because she felt that desperation once, too.

But she made the rules for a reason. She remembers Miss Eloise packing her suitcase. She remembers Remy DeWindt glaring at her over their game of twenty-one.

Don't tell anyone what you saw.

Cas hates herself for it, but she says it anyway: "I didn't see anything."

For a long moment, Henry stares at her. Then his shoulders slump. "But . . . you said . . ."

"I have no idea what you're talking about."

It's the final nail in the coffin. It's enough. Henry deflates. His hand is limp in Cas's grip as he lets her lead him away. He doesn't know how she's betrayed him. He doesn't know this is all her fault.

Cas pulls him up the path, past Growve, who looks like he wants to say something but can't find the words, past Abigail, who watches with one delicate hand pressed over her mouth. That hand will drop away as soon as Cas and Henry are gone. Abigail Payne is going to tell the whole town.

And even though she's awake now, even though Cas knows it's not here, not now, not happening to her, she can almost feel the same cold she felt in the vision when the demon, or whatever it was, closed in on Fionnuala Robinson. She can almost feel the dark, shadowy hand plunging into her own chest. Clenching around her heart.

IV

REMY

Nearly three weeks after Remy's father left home without explanation—one week after Cas Sterling told Remy a horrible story that prompted Remy to end their friendship forever—a package arrived at the Windover post office. It was addressed to Remy's mother, but Mrs. DeWindt hadn't left her room in days, and so it was Remy who fetched the package and Remy who opened it. The package contained a small leather-bound journal and a note written in her father's hand:

My love,

I didn't choose to leave you; this is the first thing you should know. Please tell Remy, Prue, and little Gracie that I didn't choose to leave them, either.

I was taken, unwillingly, by members of a group that would recruit me to their cause. I've been walking this group's halls, learning their secrets, digging for information—but they'll realize soon how much I know. They'll also realize that I believe their cause to be a morally abhorrent load of rot. I plan to run, though not to you; I won't endanger you or our daughters. So long as this order still exists, so long as its members hold influence, I'll be hunted. I cannot come home. I'm sorry.

I send the enclosed journal to you for safekeeping. <u>Do not read it.</u> Lock it inside the compartment beneath the window seat in my study. If I don't return home to you, burn it. Tell no one. Neither this note nor this journal ever existed.

I love you.
—C

Remy read the journal, obviously. Her father had always encouraged her inquisitive mind, and so she chose to disregard his underlined instruction, which was probably only meant for Remy's mother, anyway. Most of the journal was blank, but her father had filled in the first sixteen pages of it with lists and half-explained notes—everything he'd learned about the group that had taken him away. The group was a secret society based at a Christian Congregational seminary school in Maine. The founder seemed to have a fascination with all things supernatural.

But whatever Charles DeWindt had learned about the group's intentions, he didn't write it down. His notes were both incredibly thorough and incredibly inadequate. One list was labeled *Members* and contained two dozen names—including that of Windover's local pastor, Joseph Dekker. Another list was labeled *Disappearances (Victims?)*. This list had only six names, though Remy has been able to add ten more to it as she's conducted her own research in the years since. Another page of the journal contained no words at all—only a charcoal sketch of a strange, sigil-like symbol, a ring of markings encircling a sort of hourglass shape.

When Remy had unlocked the window seat in her father's study, she'd discovered a collection of nearly fifty other books. Their subjects varied, but all of them pertained to the occult. It appeared her father had been researching this order for years before its members had found him. Remy has now read all of those books, too.

In her mind, the note her father had sent eight years ago had laid out her task quite simply: If her father can't come home because of these men hunting him, then Remy will help take them down. Once their order is dissolved, her father can safely return to Windover. Everything can go back to the way it's meant to be.

It's the *how* that she can't figure out. Remy is still working on that part.

Two days after their visit to the dead Pastor Cole's office, Remy still hasn't had a chance to look through the grimoire Finn found. She's barely had a chance to sleep. The past forty-eight hours have been filled with housework, and paid work, and a last-minute childcare job that Remy accepted from a neighbor, because her youngest sister, Grace, needs a new pair of boots and there hasn't been extra money for months.

This is the struggle—the impossible balance Remy has to maintain. She needs time for her research if she's to have any hope of bringing her father home. But *without* her father at home, there are a thousand other tasks to cover, a thousand bills to pay and never enough money to pay them with. Her mother had become a ghost after Remy's father left; for eighteen months, she barely got out of bed. She's seemed more present of late, but she still isn't her old self. It's up to Remy to take care of her and to raise Prue and Grace as well.

And that's not even accounting for their family's reputation. Remy has spent years trying to stitch back together the tatters left by Mr. DeWindt's unexplainable absence. If she can just make herself useful to enough people in town, if she can just smile and say the right things and prove herself to be a polite young lady, maybe the whispers about her disgrace of a father will finally die, and everyone will move on.

At least today, as Remy and Finn make their way to Mrs. Sanderson's general store, the gossip is about someone else.

"Did you hear about Henry Ashworth?"

This is the question on everyone's lips as the two of them elbow their way into the shop. The general store is packed full today; Mrs. Sanderson reigns from behind the counter, too busy talking to bother with fulfilling orders. Remy grinds her teeth. Mrs. Sanderson likes to keep both of her hands on the crank of the Windover rumor mill; she's responsible for spreading most of the wilder stories about Remy's father, including a few even before he'd disappeared. Unfortunately, the Sandersons own the only general store for miles, and so Remy must fake a smile and politely bear it.

At least Finn has come with her, as she usually does. It's not that Remy ever *asks* Finn to accompany her here; it's just that anytime Remy mentions needing to do her family's shopping,

Finn always seems to have something to pick up for old Mrs. Darner, too.

"The whole thing sounds harrowing, absolutely harrowing," Mrs. Sanderson is saying as Remy tries to work out who's in line and who's here only for the scandal. "Miss Payne was practically trembling when she told me."

"Our Miss Cassandra was badly shaken by it, too," Mrs. Smothers, the longtime cook for the Sterling family, says. "Still sick in bed today. She was right there when it happened, you know."

"Oh, I heard," someone else chimes in. "The poor dear."

Remy doesn't think anyone who's ever met Cas Sterling could reasonably call her a *poor dear*, but she doesn't say this. She has better things to focus on than whatever trouble the well-to-do Henry Ashworth has gotten himself into. At her side, Finn looks as if she's glowering, though Remy knows better; this is simply Finn's neutral expression. Her thin mouth and sharp brows just fall into a glower if she isn't deliberately molding them into something else.

Remy nudges her way toward the front counter. After this, she can go home and get started with supper. Maybe she can squeeze out a few hours afterward to dig into the *Grimoirium Verum* at last—assuming she's not dead tired. And assuming she can afford the extra candles for light. She checks the price list on the wall and does a quick calculation.

No candles today, then.

"What did happen, exactly?" old Mrs. Hirsch is asking. "Davey told me what *he'd* heard, but it was shocking."

"The truth *is* shocking, I'm sorry to say." Mrs. Sanderson doesn't sound sorry in the least. "Apparently Mr. Ashworth and Miss Sterling were out for a walk when poor Miss Sterling swooned—and instead of catching her, Ashworth just snapped. Started shouting like a madman about *demons*, of all things."

Remy feels suddenly self-conscious. No one is staring at you, she tells herself, though she's certain that everyone is. Demonology hadn't been her father's primary focus, but it comes up in several of the books he'd collected. It's strange to hear the word *demons* spoken aloud in the general store—as if the secret parts of Remy's life are seeping out into the open. Finn has reached nervously for the collar of her dress, rubbing the strands of her scapular.

"Good riddance," someone is saying. "Demons? He ought to be locked up."

"Are they sending him to Worcester? Or the new asylum in Boston?" Mrs. Hirsch asks.

"No, no; his parents are trying to cover, of course," Mrs. Sanderson says. "I'm told they're pulling him out of Harvard and shipping him off to some other school."

"A *school*?"

"A seminary. Some fancy place in Maine."

Remy has nearly reached the counter, but at this, she stops so abruptly that Finn bumps into her from behind. This piece of her father's story isn't common knowledge—and yet she's certain that everyone *knows*, somehow. Could Henry Ashworth really be on his way to Eden? Maybe it's a different seminary. Maybe there are dozens of seminaries in Maine.

No one is staring at you, Remy recites in her mind. No one is whispering. They're not paying you any attention at all.

"Why a seminary?" someone has asked. A snort. "Are they hoping to drive the demons out of him?"

"Perhaps we should come back later," Finn murmurs.

"I'm fine," Remy tells her. "It's fine. Let's just get what we need."

And it *is* fine, until Mrs. Sanderson says, "Well, the pastor helped them set it all up, didn't he? And we have to trust that Pastor Dekker knows best."

Remy is knocked from her own body.

Physically, she's still standing there in the general store. But her mind has flown far outside herself. The parallels here have surpassed coincidence. There are not dozens of seminaries in Maine, and there's only one with a connection to Pastor Dekker. Had Dekker sat in the Ashworths' parlor, patting Mrs. Ashworth's hand as he'd made his bid? Remy recalls the day she'd walked in on him talking to her own mother, offering her charity. *Just until you're back on your feet*, Dekker had said. *Just until your husband returns. I'm part of a certain group, you see, and we'd be happy to look after a family like yours.*

That was months after Mr. DeWindt had disappeared, months after the journal had arrived with Dekker's name written on the list of members in Remy's father's hand. Her mother was so listless in those days that she might have accepted the pastor's offer without question—but Remy convinced her not to. Remy swore she could support the family herself in the meantime. They needed money, yes, and in the coming years as the savings ran out, they'd need money even more badly. But not from *him*.

Something brushes against Remy's elbow—a hand. Finn's hand. For just a moment, Finn touches Remy's sleeve, pulling her back to herself. Grounding her.

"But I always said this would happen, didn't I?" Mrs. Sanderson is telling the group. "Ashworth just got unlucky. It only takes one bad egg to leave its stink on a town for years. One ... *strange* influence. Oh, Miss DeWindt—I almost didn't see you there." Her eyes have narrowed slightly. "Speaking of the devil ... any word from your father lately?"

The reason Remy can never quite convince herself that people aren't staring or whispering about her is that, sometimes, they *are*.

Beside her, Finn has stiffened. On the counter in front of them are several large storage baskets of dried beans. Finn looks at Remy, who's frozen, heart pounding, and then at Mrs. Sanderson, who's smirking slightly.

Finn hooks her elbow inside the rim of the nearest basket and tugs.

With a rushing sound, dried beans cascade onto the floor and explode out in every direction. Beans skitter under the shelves and beneath people's boot heels. Someone yelps; someone else nearly slips and has to grab on to a display rack, which sways ominously. Finn, meanwhile, has already locked a hand around Remy's elbow and started dragging her back toward the shop's door.

"Oh, clumsy me," Finn says in the loudest and most theatrical voice Remy has ever heard from her. "What a clod I am! I'm so sorry for the mess—I'd offer to help you tidy up, but I fear I'd only make it worse. Sorry again. Deepest apologies."

She shoves both herself and Remy through the door and out onto the street.

"Walk," Finn says. "Now. Before someone comes after us."

Remy walks.

They're a full block away from the general store before Remy's pulse begins to slow. Two blocks away before she settles back into her own body, the adrenaline releasing its grip on her. Three blocks away before the shame finally hits. Mrs. Sanderson's snide comments are nothing new; Remy should be able to keep her composure better than this by now. Finn shouldn't have to swoop to her rescue, to cause a ridiculous scene just so Remy can save face.

Remy wishes she weren't so goddamn grateful for it.

When they've reached the DeWindts' front gate, Remy finds her words at last: "You shouldn't have done that."

"It was an accident," Finn says immediately.

"Mrs. Sanderson looked furious."

"Good. Mrs. Sanderson is an arse."

"She's going to make you pay for that whole bushel, you know."

"Or I could flee town." Finn must see something on Remy's face, though, because after a moment, she sighs. "I'll go back this evening and purchase the lot of them. Beans will wash; I'll tell Mrs. Darner I bought them on special. I can pick up your order while I'm there, if you'd like. I'll bring it by here in the morning."

Remy should decline. She should thank Finn for the offer but assure her that she needn't bother; Remy can manage returning to the general store perfectly fine on her own.

She doesn't decline. She's not sure she *can* manage it. The idea of facing Mrs. Sanderson again so soon is making her stomach twist.

Remy spends five seconds considering, then five seconds hating herself, before she nods and says, "I'll pay you back."

"I know you will."

It's always been like this; Finn has been coming to her rescue ever since the beginning, when Finn—still employed as the DeWindt family's youngest maid—had entered the study one evening to find Remy poring through one of her father's occult books. Remy had startled and dropped the book. She'd been certain this girl would go telling the whole town that the rumors were true—that Mr. DeWindt had been a devil worshipper, and now his eldest daughter was, too.

But Finn hadn't said a word as she'd picked up the tome from the rug. She'd smoothed the pages flat, and then she'd handed the book back to Remy. As it turned out, Finn had known about Mr. DeWindt's secret library for months. She'd been volunteering to clean the study herself so that the family's housekeeper, a devout Christian woman with notoriously loose lips, wouldn't dig up the hidden key and find her way into the window seat.

Remy still recalls Finn's hint of a smile as she'd offered the book back to her. Remy had been alone in her research for that first year or so—but she hasn't been alone since.

"A seminary in Maine," Remy says now, as if saying it aloud will manifest an explanation. "It has to be Eden, right? Especially with Pastor Dekker involved. But do you think Ashworth actually knows anything?"

Remy is itching to write all this down in her father's journal—*her* journal now, considering she's filled far more pages of it than those first sixteen that he'd sent. The pieces are all here, surely; she just needs to rearrange them into the shape of an answer.

Finn hasn't spoken. She isn't looking *at* Remy but past her—at the huge colonial-style house at the end of the road. The Sterlings' manor. Remy's gaze moves automatically to the far upstairs window, a habit that eight years of estrangement hasn't managed to break.

Cas Sterling is peering out at them from her bedroom window.

When they were children, Cas's pointed chin and snub nose had given her a mischievous, elfin look. She's grown into the features, though. Her heavy brows seem to speak whole sentences on their own. Now, as she realizes Remy and Finn have spotted her, those brows lower as if to say, *Oh. You.*

Remy whirls away. Of course it's Cas Sterling, taunting Remy with the life she used to have—the life she still *could* have if only her father were still here. Remy takes a long breath, and then she gathers up everything in her mind—Mrs. Sanderson's words, the seminary in Maine, Pastor Dekker, Henry Ashworth, her own swirling mess of emotions—and tucks it neatly away. She imagines herself stashing it all inside the window seat in her father's study. She imagines slamming the bench shut and locking it.

Still, she can *feel* it there, poking at the back of her mind as she and Finn say their goodbyes and part ways. When Remy glances back up at the Sterlings' window, Cas's face is gone.

V

CAS

For several days after the trip to Long Beach, Cas is kept to bed. She's going to tear out her own hair from boredom. Doctor Gregory visits each morning, taking Cas's temperature and letting her blood and ignoring her insistence that she's perfectly fine, or at least will be in a few days. Doctor Gregory doesn't seem to believe her. He says that so long as she's feverish, she needs rest and constant supervision, which means her mother hardly leaves her bedside.

It's bad enough that Cas feels like she's been trampled by a dozen horses and then briefly set on fire, as she always does after a vision. Her mother just makes everything worse. She's endlessly attentive—and yet her attention isn't really about Cas. It never is. She wrings her hands and worries aloud about what people in town are saying right now. More than once, she brings up the dinner party that she and Cas would both be attending if Cas hadn't had the audacity to fall ill.

"You can still go to your party," Cas tells her.

"And how would that look—me dining and socializing while my daughter lies on her deathbed?"

Cas rolls her eyes. "I'm not dying."

"Well, it would look even worse if you *did* die. And you haven't even married! You do know that if you die without marrying, there's no one to inherit this house when your father passes. Oh, why must you strain my nerves this way?"

Her mother hasn't admitted to her own role in forcing Cas to go out with Henry that day. And she never will. Every time Cas tries to ask about Henry, her mother shushes her like she's a child.

"The doctor has said you should avoid any stress. You're just to focus on getting well."

Which means that whatever's happening with Henry, Cas has reason to be stressed.

On the third evening of this, Cas takes matters into her own hands. If she has to spend another night listening to her mother fret about the inheritance, Cas is going to set the house ablaze just to be done with it all. She asks her mother to bring up a fresh cup of tea, and then throws on a coat over her nightgown and tiptoes down the stairs after her. She makes for the back door.

There's one harrowing moment when she has to slip past the open doorway of her father's study—but he's busy admiring one of his fancy old books, and he doesn't look up as Cas darts down the hall. Even if he'd seen, would he have bothered to stop her? Unlikely. In Cas's experience, unless she's disgracing the Sterling family name or endangering his precious library, her father doesn't bother much with her at all. He'd wanted a son, and instead he'd gotten Cas, much to both of their disappointment.

He probably doesn't even know she's been ill.

The chilly evening air outside feels glorious on her cheeks. Cas skirts around the edge of the house and then sets off up the road. Windover is a small town, just a few long, sparse streets all radiating out from a central common. The Sterling manor is on the town's western edge, nestled against the Lynn Woods. The

Ashworths live on the far east side. Cas takes a more circuitous route than usual in an attempt to avoid people, but the streets are quiet. She doesn't see a soul.

Outside the Ashworths' house, Cas debates throwing rocks at Henry's window to get his attention, just like the good old days, when they used to sneak out. But the panes over his bedroom are dark now, no candlelight within. Cas knocks on the front door.

"Cassandra," Henry's mother says when she answers. She blinks at Cas for a moment, then glances over Cas's shoulder, scanning the street behind her. The back of Cas's neck prickles. "Darling. You'd better come inside."

Mrs. Ashworth settles Cas in the parlor with a cup of lukewarm tea before she drops the news that Henry is gone.

The way Mrs. Ashworth tells it, Henry—by pure coincidence and certainly not because of a recent damning incident on Long Beach, which she doesn't even mention—has decided to drop out of Harvard mid-semester and instead enroll in seminary school. He's already left town. He's on a private charter sailing north to some island off the coast of Maine. As she talks, her husband, Henry's father, sits in his armchair without a word, smoking his pipe and occasionally tugging on the curtains as if making sure they're fully drawn.

"It's supposed to be a wonderful program," Mrs. Ashworth tells Cas. "One of the best in the country."

"A seminary school," Cas echoes, as if saying it again might make it make sense.

"It's sudden, I know, but there was an open seat, and he couldn't pass up the opportunity. You know how long Henry has wanted to become a minister."

"Has he?" Cas feels like she's hearing about a complete stranger. For years Henry has told her about his plans to run for congress. He has never ever spoken of a plan to go into the clergy.

"I'm sure he mentioned it," Mrs. Ashworth says. "From time to time. Maybe he talked about it more when he was younger, before Cecilia..."

Her voice wavers slightly on the name, though, and her smile cracks. This is just like after Cecilia's death, then: Mr. and Mrs. Ashworth carrying on with their lives, trying to convince the world they were fine, even as their daughter lay in the ground. Cas spent years hearing Henry complain about this, and yet only now can she start to understand his frustration—this particular pinch of grieving when it feels like no one else is.

But this *isn't* like after Cecilia's death, either. Mrs. Ashworth's tone is strangely urgent, as if she's desperate for Cas to stop raising doubts about this story and simply believe it. Mr. Ashworth flicks back one corner of the curtain to peer through the window yet again.

"I'm sure you miss him," Mrs. Ashworth is saying. "But it'll only be for a few years. Once Henry has finished his training, Pastor Dekker has said he'd be happy to—"

Cas nearly drops her teacup. "Pastor Dekker?"

"Well, of course. Didn't I mention...?"

She glances at her husband, though, suddenly uncertain. Mr. Ashworth clears his throat.

"Dekker's the one who found us the opening at Eden," he fills in. "It's the seminary where the pastor did his studies, too."

Cas sets down her cup with a clatter. Now she *knows* something is wrong. Because eight years ago, Pastor Dekker was the last person to speak to Mr. DeWindt before he vanished.

Remy had seen it all from her bedroom window and told Cas about it the next morning. Her father and Pastor Dekker had been arguing in the back garden. The pastor looked angry. Her father looked frightened. When Remy woke, her father was gone.

Not long after that, Cas's first vision showed the gruesome details of what happened to him.

Now Mr. Ashworth lets out a long puff of smoke from his pipe. Mrs. Ashworth sets her teacup back onto its saucer and takes Cas's hands.

"The pastor came to visit us when he heard about . . ." She shakes her head. "He thought it might be best for Henry to take some time . . . away."

She squeezes Cas's hands. Cas can barely feel the touch.

"It was either that or the mental hospital," Mr. Ashworth says, yanking the curtains shut again. "At least this way he'll have a career out of it."

Cas is spiraling. She knows she's spiraling. She doesn't know how to stop.

She spirals as she finishes her tea and they fall into talking about the weather. She spirals as she tells Henry's parents goodnight and escapes back into the clear, cold evening. She spirals as she walks, aimless, mindless, absolutely no idea where she's going.

It's not as if she has any real reason to worry, does she? The parallels are tenuous at best. But there *are* parallels: Remy's father, gone. Henry, gone. Both of them hurried away without even time to say goodbye.

And the pastor somehow tied to both.

Why had Pastor Dekker even gotten involved? And why had he left the Ashworths so shaken? Cas isn't surprised that Henry's parents went along with Dekker's plan, despite their obvious misgivings. They'd needed a viable cover to send Henry away until the gossip dies down, and Harvard is too close, too connected. This seminary in Maine is as good an escape as any.

But why had Henry agreed to go? Why would he willingly throw away his political career, all the plans he'd been telling her about just days ago, to enroll at Dekker's old school?

Cas tries not to think about that very first vision, but her mind pulls up the images all the same: A pair of severed eyes. A blood-soaked knife in the dirt. Mr. DeWindt's body twitching as the life left it.

Maybe Henry *hadn't* agreed to it.

Maybe he hadn't gone so willingly after all.

Cas doesn't know exactly how she pulled Henry into the vision with her. It had been an accident, clearly. Everything about the visions feels like an accident. And yet Cas had lied about it to Henry's face afterward—which had been very, very deliberate. She hadn't had any other choice, had she? She was following her own rules. Abigail Payne was going to tell everyone either way, and what difference would it have made if Cas had vouched for Henry on the beach? Would it have changed the story Abigail told? Or would it have just gotten Cas shipped away somewhere, too?

Maybe Cas *should* be shipped away somewhere. It was her fault that Henry had seen what he'd seen. And when he'd needed her, Cas had abandoned him to his fate, alone. She might as well have called him mad herself.

Cas doesn't mean to end up in the center of town—she means to stick to the side streets and keep avoiding people, but her feet have their own idea. The lamps surrounding Windover Common are all alight. Mrs. Sanderson is locking up for the night, and the last of the general store's usual crowd are dispersing toward their homes. Cas ducks her chin into the collar of her coat and pretends she's a ghost. She's out and about in her dressing gown, hair a sweaty mess, and surely by now everyone knows about Henry. Just because Cas is spiraling doesn't mean anyone else gets to see her do it.

But as she hurries across the street, she catches a flash of red hair. For a second, Cas is right back in the vision, watching the girl running toward the bridge just a few blocks south of here.

Now, though, Fionnuala Robinson isn't fleeing from a monster. She's walking across the common with two large sacks from the general store cradled in her arms. Her freckled face is pale in the lamplight, and her eyes are such a dark brown, they're almost black. She looks . . . young. Too young. She's only Cas's age, probably, and whatever resentment Cas holds over the way Finn Robinson took her old place at Remy's side—Cas can't blame Finn for that.

Cas has been so focused on the situation with Henry that she almost forgot a girl is going to die.

Cas has never really understood the visions. She's never really tried to. They're just an unfortunate thing she's learned to live with, because she doesn't have a choice, because she doesn't know what else to do. She can't warn the victims—no one would believe her. Remy DeWindt had proved that well enough. And she can't prevent the deaths once she's seen them.

She used to try, but it never stuck. Once, when she'd had a vision of old Mr. Saunders being thrown from his horse, Cas had snuck into the Saunders' stables and set the horse in question free in the woods. Mr. Saunders was furious. He spent a week accusing everyone in town of being a horse thief, until the night when he had too much liquor, accused the wrong man, got into a drunken fight over it, and died anyway from a knife to the chest.

The visions don't always come true, exactly. But the deaths in them always come to pass—one way or another.

And yet Finn's death was unlike any Cas has ever seen. The shadowy figure on the bridge, the fist through her heart . . .

"Miss Robinson!" Cas calls before she can talk herself out of it. "Fionnuala!"

Finn spins toward Cas's voice and almost drops the sacks in her arms. She watches Cas approach with a glower settled on her face. "Can I help you?"

"Yes," Cas says. "I mean, no. I . . ."

Cas already regrets this. What had she been planning to say? *Just some friendly advice—you should try to avoid being chased by large, shadowy monsters for the moment. Trust me.* It's absurd. She knows it's absurd.

She scrapes wildly for something more normal to talk about and lands on Finn's sack of goods. "Doing your evening shopping?"

"Just picking up an order for Mrs. Darner," Finn says in her even lilt. "Some of us work for a living."

She says it so flatly that it takes Cas a moment to even recognize it as a jab. "Oh," Cas says. "Right."

"And you? Out for an evening walk?"

Finn is taking in Cas's disheveled hair, her flushed cheeks, her dressing gown under her wool coat—her spare one, because she never did retrieve her usual coat from where she dropped it in the grass on Long Beach. Because of course she *has* a spare winter coat. Maybe Cas is imagining it, but she thinks Finn's face softens a little. She's not quite frowning anymore, though she's not *not* frowning.

Cas remembers the scream on her face in the vision the moment when the shadowy figure touched her.

"I have to tell you something," Cas blurts out at the exact moment that Finn says, "I'm sorry about your friend."

"My—Sorry, what?" Cas says. Oh. Henry, she thinks. "Oh. Henry," she says. "Right. Um, thank you."

Finn studies her. Cas doesn't think she's ever heard the girl say more than two words before. On the far corner of the common, a few rowdies stumble out of the pub, arms thrown over each other's shoulders. As always, a stab of longing pushes through Cas's stomach at the sight. Their easy camaraderie, their unabashed laughter, the angular frames of their bodies. Christ, she wishes she were a man.

"Do you know where he went?" Finn asks finally.

"Yeah," Cas says, mouth dry. "Yes. I just found out. He's at some seminary in Maine. I think it's called Eden."

For a bare second, Finn's eyes go wide—and then her face switches back to its impassive glower, so quickly and deliberately that it's clear she's trying to hide the reaction. Because that *was* a reaction. When Cas had said *Eden* . . .

Cas is still working on a follow-up question when Finn asks, "What were you going to say?"

"Sorry?" Cas says.

"You said you had something to tell me."

"Oh. Yes. It's . . ."

This was a mistake. Cas made the rules for a reason. Is she really going to ruin the end of this girl's life by telling her what's coming for her? And this is Remy DeWindt's best friend—what if she runs back and tells Remy about this dire prediction Cas has made? Cas imagines the two of them laughing at her over it. She wants to punch a wall.

"I don't know," Cas says. "Nothing."

Finn's eyes narrow slightly. She clearly doesn't believe Cas, which is fair. Cas wouldn't believe Cas, either. The rowdies across the square have disappeared down one of the side streets. The stragglers from the general store are gone. Cas and Finn are alone.

Then Finn says, "Do you know Dungeon Rock?"

Whatever Cas had expected from her—a scoff, an eye-roll, a demand for honesty—it wasn't this. Cas stares. Of course she knows Dungeon Rock. She and Remy used to play there, scrabbling up and down the boulders while Cas's nanny yelled at them to be careful. It's deep in the Lynn Woods, and it has a legend surrounding it about buried pirate gold. She and Remy could never resist.

But Cas hasn't been back to Dungeon Rock since their fight years ago. And if Finn knows about the rock, Cas is guessing Remy has.

"Yes," Cas says, trying very hard to keep her face completely free of jealousy or bitterness. She doesn't think she succeeds. Finn's gaze is still picking her apart. "I know it."

Finn hoists her two sacks from the general store over one shoulder. "Meet us there this time tomorrow night."

"Us?"

"Remy and me. She'll want to talk to you. Or she won't, but I'll make her anyway. I suspect the two of you have a lot to discuss. This time tomorrow, all right?"

Finn says it all so quickly, and maybe Cas is less recovered from her vision than she'd thought. Her mind is reeling. She doesn't really know what she's agreeing to.

It doesn't really matter, though, because of course she's going to agree to it. "All right," Cas says.

"And . . ." Finn gives her one last appraising look. "Don't do anything rash before then, all right?"

"What's that supposed to mean?"

But Finn is already walking away. For one horrible moment, Cas thinks she's going to turn south, just like she had in the vision—but she veers in the opposite direction, back toward the old Darner house a few streets over. Finn stalks away under the flickering streetlamps, silent as a cat.

VI

REMY

It's impossible for Remy to walk through the Lynn Woods without thinking about Cas Sterling. Back before Remy's father left, before she and Cas stopped speaking, the two of them used to run wild here. They would beg Cas's nanny to take them on a hike, promising to behave themselves—but as soon as they hit the trees, they would race off and leave poor Miss Eloise far behind. They'd peel off their boots and their stockings and run barefoot through the mud, tripping over the gnarled roots that crossed the path. They'd scramble up the sides of Dungeon Rock and survey their world from its peak, wild and invincible and free.

Remy doesn't let herself feel that kind of freedom anymore. Her leisure now is carefully rationed: the trips she takes for her investigation, and the nights spent digging through her father's research, and the occasional evenings when she and Finn can escape to the woods for a night of drinking and talking under the stars.

This is their purpose tonight. When Finn had stopped by the DeWindts' house that morning, she'd handed over Remy's order from the shop, and then she'd asked if Remy might like to visit the rock that evening. And, yes, Remy would like that very much. She'd slipped out after supper, after her mother and sisters had all retired to their rooms, and met Finn at their usual spot at the edge of the woods so they could walk together. Finn carries an old whale-oil lantern to light their path. Remy tries to keep her mind in the present. She tries *not* to think about those years with Cas Sterling—but it's impossible. The trees here cast a spell, conjuring ghosts at every turn.

So when Remy spots the figure waiting for them up ahead, she thinks for one otherworldly moment that *she's* done this, that her own memories have taken material form.

Cas Sterling is sitting at the base of Dungeon Rock.

"Oh," Remy says, freezing mid-step.

"Oh," Finn echoes. Then, "She's on time. I thought she would be late."

Her tone is too unfazed for there to be any doubt: Remy has been set up. "What's *she* doing here?" Remy demands.

Finn brushes a wayward spiderweb from the path and keeps walking. "I invited her."

"And you couldn't have warned me?"

"If I'd warned you, you wouldn't have come."

Ahead of them, Cas is sprawled on a rock with her feet kicked out ahead of her, unaware she's being watched. One of her legs is bouncing up and down in that incessant way Remy recalls even after all this time. This is a mistake. Remy's certain this is a mistake. She ought to turn right back around.

She doesn't turn back. She takes a long breath and follows Finn into the clearing.

Cas leaps to her feet when she sees them. "Hello. Glad you made it. I wasn't sure if you were coming."

"We wouldn't have abandoned you to the wolves," Finn tells her. "You found it all right?"

"I'm here, aren't I?"

But there's an uncertainty about her that disarms Remy a little. She remembers Cas Sterling as many things; *uncertain* isn't one of them. Cas's fingers are drumming against her skirts as she and Remy survey each other. Remy used to find Cas's constant fidgeting funny; now it exhausts her.

"Hello," Cas says again, though this time it sounds like a question. Whatever she's winding up to ask, Remy does not want to answer it.

It's not as if she and Cas haven't spoken in the years since their falling-out; Windover is too small a town for them to avoid bumping into each other on occasion and exchanging the proper hellos. But they haven't *spoken* since that day eight years ago. Not in any real way. In their last true conversation, Cas had described a scene that would haunt Remy for the rest of her life, and then Remy had called Cas *horrible* and *deluded* and declared that their friendship was over.

Without a word, Remy circles around the rock formation and stalks to the usual tree: a giant oak with a rotted hole in its trunk. When she thrusts a hand into the opening, the bottle of brandy is still there, nestled where she and Finn had hidden it weeks ago. She draws it out. A beetle is crawling up the bottle's neck.

Remy flicks the beetle away, pops out the cork, and takes a swig.

Cas is gaping at her. Her gaze drifts to the dark gap in the tree's trunk.

"We used to play here," Cas says. "That's the spot where we used to leave messages for the faerie king."

Remy passes the brandy bottle to Finn with as much nonchalance as she can muster. "Yes," she says. "And?"

"And now it's your liquor stash."

"Once again—and?"

Cas bursts out laughing. All at once, the tension hanging between them breaks. "I only wish I was the one who thought of it."

Finn draws a quick sip of brandy and then hands the bottle off to Cas, who tips it back, chokes, grimaces, and thumps her chest with one fist as if trying to push the liquor down.

"That's . . . interesting," Cas says when she's swallowed.

"Not all of us can afford the finest vintage," Remy snips. She tries to snatch the bottle back, but Cas is already taking another drink and dodges away from her hand.

"I didn't say I didn't want it."

It's a strange sort of dream as the three of them climb up the stony mound and settle on the wide landing at the top. Dungeon Rock always seems out of place in these woods—like God had lost hold of a handful of boulders while sculpting the Massachusetts landscape and simply hadn't bothered to pick them back up again. According to town legend, back in the seventeenth century, a pirate had once sailed up the river to flee from the British navy and had hidden himself in a cave under these rocks. He'd lived in the cave for years, holed up with the boatload of treasure he'd managed to haul with him.

Then an earthquake had collapsed the cave entrance, and both man and gold were sealed in. The cave became a dungeon became a tomb.

When they were eight, Cas and Remy had tried to dig for the treasure here. Remy had spent days scouring through local records, comparing different versions of the pirate story, forming a plan—and then Cas had gotten tired of planning and had simply started in with a shovel. Needless to say, they did not find any treasure.

And now Cas Sterling is here again, passing the bottle with Remy and Finn, all of them pretending that this whole gathering is normal.

"Well?" Cas says, looking not to Remy but to Finn, who has set the lantern in the middle of their triangle. "What's this all about?"

"I'm wondering the same thing," Remy says, though when she turns to Finn as well, Finn only stares back at her, one eyebrow raised.

At last, Finn says, "I think you know."

"I absolutely do not."

"All right," Finn says. "Miss Sterling—"

But Cas grimaces as if she's just been forced to drink something even worse than cheap brandy. "Please. Just Cas."

"Cas, then. Tell Remy the name of the seminary where your friend Mr. Ashworth is headed."

Cas hesitates for only a moment. "Eden," she says. "Do you know it?"

Remy tries to keep her expression steady, though the name has hit her like a gut punch. "Maybe," she says. "It ... could be familiar."

Finn makes an annoyed, guttural sound. "And, Remy, tell Cas about the postmark on the package your father sent you."

"Wait," Cas says. "Your father sent a package?"

It's too late to craft a lie; even if Remy tries, Finn will probably just snitch on her again and tell Cas everything. Remy tips her head back against one of the spindly trees that's managed to grow up among the rocks. "Yes, he sent a package. A journal with some of his notes. It was meant for my mother, technically, but I... intercepted it." She sighs, then admits, "The package was postmarked in Eden."

There's a rattle and a moment of scrambling as Cas nearly drops the brandy bottle. "Well," she says, "you could've led with that."

"I don't see what it matters."

"Are you joking? What were his notes about? In the journal."

"Nothing important."

Finn actually laughs at that, sharp and mocking. "Right," she says. "*Nothing important.* And that's why you've spent all these years obsessed with that place, investigating their seminary and their secret society and—"

"Secret society?" Cas cuts in.

Finn lets that hang as she and Remy enter into another silent standoff. This is the most Remy has heard Finn speak in front of anyone besides herself or Kieran. She's feeling the betrayal on several levels.

"Come on," Cas says. "You can't just say that there's a secret society and then not say more."

Finn takes a long breath. "The Order was founded about five years ago—"

"Ten," Remy corrects automatically.

Finn smirks, victorious, and Remy realizes too late that she's let herself be baited. Finn had made the mistake on purpose; she'd known Remy wouldn't be able to resist clearing up the facts. Remy closes her eyes, pressing her skull back against the tree trunk, hard. She tries to imagine that she's somewhere else, without an audience, thumbing through the familiar pages of her father's journal.

"The society was founded by one of the same men who founded the Eden seminary," she says. "He's still head of the school now: the Reverend John Smith. Which is a name that makes research difficult, of course. His group has members all over New England—plenty of pastors and former seminary students like Dekker, but others, too. Bankers. Political officials. Old-money bigwigs." When Remy opens her eyes, Cas is watching her intently. "They call themselves the Order of Lazarus."

"Lazarus," Cas echoes, like she's trying out the syllables. She frowns. "Why does that sound familiar?"

"Well, the Bible, obviously," Remy says. At Cas's blank look, she adds, "Lazarus is the man Christ raised from the dead."

Cas's frown deepens. "I thought Christ raised *himself* from the dead."

"That too, but he raised Lazarus first. Lazarus was sick, and his sisters asked Jesus to heal him—but by the time Jesus arrived, he had died. So Jesus brought him back to life instead. Don't you go to Sunday services?"

"Of course I go to Sunday services. I just don't pay attention during them."

Finn lets out a snort that she quickly covers with a cough.

"Well, they're dull as all damnation!" Cas says, flicking the bottle's cork at her. "Or they're about my own personal damnation, which is even worse. Pastor Dekker's a worm—even without all this secret-society business, I knew *that* much. He's always consorting with my mother, and making his pointed sermons, and—"

"Pointed sermons?" Remy asks before she can stop herself.

Cas scowls. "Oh, right—of course *you've* never had to sit through him telling the whole congregation about how you, specifically, are disgracing God. Because *you're* perfect. He never uses names, of course, but when he's staring straight at you through his whole tirade about how women are meant to be submissive..."

But Remy hasn't bothered to stifle her ugly laugh.

"What?" Cas snaps.

"Oh, please, spare me."

"*Spare* you?"

"You get to do whatever you want!" Remy bursts out. "And everyone still adores you, because you're richer than God! Meanwhile, I have to behave perfectly every single second of my life, and even then, my whole family's reputation is on the brink."

"Can we focus, please?" Finn cuts in. "Remy, tell her about the donations."

Remy wants to fight this out. She wants to take all her frustration at the double standard she's held to and pack it into a ball and hurl it at Cas Sterling's head. But she doesn't; Finn is right. Finn knows her too well, knows exactly how to ground Remy when she's about to lose herself.

Cas has deflated, too. Remy takes a long breath and buries her anger, just as she always does.

"The Order's main work is officially charity," she says dully. "Its members are funding all the usual causes—missionary programs, scholarships, food for widows and orphans. Pastor Dekker even offered funds to my mother once." Cas looks horrified at this, and Remy adds, "She didn't accept it! I convinced her not to. There were obviously strings attached, and I knew by then that Dekker was up to no good."

"Christ," Cas says. "Pretty audacious of him to even offer. He really is a worm."

"Anyway, the charity gives them a cover, and it fits well with Smith and his seminary. But the numbers don't add up. Even just from the records I've found, there's a lot of money unaccounted for. Obviously the charity work isn't all they're doing."

"Oh god," Cas says. "It's ritual murders, isn't it?"

"No, it's not *ritual murders*," Remy scoffs.

Finn gives a doubtful hum. "Well . . ."

Remy glares at her. "We don't know that they're doing ritual murders. Though there have been a few . . . disappearances."

Panic pitches Cas's voice as she echoes, "Disappearances?"

"Not people like Ashworth," Remy says quickly. "Not the wealthy sons of wealthy families from Massachusetts. These are people who can vanish without being missed. And spread over enough years that the authorities never took notice. I only know about them because of my father's journal—he'd started keeping a list. And then, a few years ago, when I was exchanging letters with a student at the seminary, he confirmed the names from my father and gave me some more recent ones that fit the pattern."

Cas clearly has not found comfort in any of this. She's leaning on her elbows, cradling her forehead like she might be sick. "Oh god. This is bad, isn't it? This is really bad. And now Henry's there, and— Oh god. How long does he have?"

Her hands are snarled in the front of her hair. When they were children, Remy always envied Cas's hair—long and thick and chestnut brown, and always silky smooth, no matter how little effort Cas put into keeping it that way. Even now, with Cas's fingers worrying it into knots, Remy suspects the tangles will come loose easily enough.

"They're not going to make someone like Ashworth disappear," Remy says again.

"Not if we can reach him first." Cas straightens, chin jutting out with some newfound resolve. She turns to Remy. "You know where this place is, right? You've even been writing to a student there. You can easily get us inside."

Remy knows right away where this conversation is heading, and she doesn't like it. "A *former* student. He's graduated now. And it's not that simple. Just because I've done a little research doesn't mean we can show up at the seminary to see your fiancé."

Cas gives a long-suffering sigh. "He's not my fiancé."

"Why are you so fixed on this, then?"

"Because he's my *friend*!" The unspoken end of the statement hangs in the air afterward: *Like you used to be.* "And because it's my fault he got sent there."

"How is it your fault?" Finn asks.

Cas's gaze darts away. "It's not. I don't know."

She seizes the bottle of brandy and tips back another gulp. Her face pinches again as she drags a sleeve across her mouth.

"That really is foul. If only storing it in the faerie king's tree could improve the taste."

She's deflecting, and they all know it. Still, Remy is too relieved that Cas has dropped her previous line of thinking to dare push back. "He was never a very powerful faerie king, as I recall. Most of our requests to him went unanswered. Didn't you once write him a letter asking him to murder Joseph Bryant?"

"Joseph Bryant deserved it," Cas says.

"Well, Joseph Bryant is still alive and kicking, so I suspect the faerie king's powers were limited."

The night around them has turned chilly, but Remy can feel the alcohol warming her from the inside. It's making this conversation bearable, at least. Wearing away the sharp edges like ocean waves working at sea glass.

"It wasn't a letter I left, anyway," Cas says, flopping back on the rock and propping her arms under her head. "It was a hairpin, I think. We had a whole system, remember?"

"Right," Remy says. "I'd forgotten. A ribbon to ask for good weather, a button to ask for help..."

"And a hairpin to ask for murder?" Finn asks.

Cas shrugs as well as one can while fully lying down. "Like an offering. I had to whisper my intention into the tree, too, of course."

"Of course."

"Tell me what happened with Ashworth the other day," Remy says.

There's a very long pause, made all the longer because Remy is entirely unaccustomed to Cas maintaining a silence for more than a few seconds. Remy can't see her face, but her boots are tapping against each other in an anxious sort of way.

"You don't want to hear it," Cas says at last, her tone guarded.

"I'm asking, aren't I?"

"You won't believe me."

"Give me a chance," Remy says, and it takes a single moment, as Cas's tapping boots go very, very still, for Remy to realize her mistake.

When Cas had first brought up the subject over their card game years ago, she'd warned that Remy wasn't going to like it. Remy had promised to keep an open mind, even as she'd felt the dread building inside her. She'd told Cas those exact words: *Give me a chance.*

Cas had. And then Cas had told her about a man in a silk coat cutting out Remy's father's eyes, slashing his throat, leaving him to bleed out on the ground. The image has burned itself into

Remy's unwitting mind. For years, she's wished that Cas hadn't given her the chance when she'd asked for it.

She wonders, for the first time, if Cas has spent these intervening years wishing for just the same.

"My father was doing research about clairvoyant visions," Remy says all at once.

The words seem to come from someone else. She has the disconcerting feeling of watching herself in a mirror image. Still, as Cas sits up, slowly, to stare at her, Remy suspects deep down that she owes Cas this much. Something is happening here, something too big to hold in her hands alone. Even without believing Cas's story from back then—and to be clear, Remy *doesn't* believe Cas's story—but even without believing her, Remy can still offer her this.

"I didn't know about the research until later," Remy says. "But I found his books after he left. He'd gathered a whole library of them. Books about prophecies, and death omens, and methods of divining the future. And . . ." She swallows and makes herself say it. "And people who have visions of things before they happen."

What would her father have made of Cas's story—the dream she'd claimed was more than a dream? Remy doesn't want to look at that question too closely. But it's difficult to deny that there's a thread here, tying these scraps together.

"I've had . . . those," Cas says finally, haltingly. "Visions like that. Of things that haven't happened. Of . . . deaths."

For the barest second, her eyes flick to Finn. Has Cas assumed that *Finn* is the skeptic here? But Finn is listening quietly, her face neutral. Cas pushes on.

"I had one the other day. On the beach. Except that somehow Henry saw it, too. He'd grabbed my arm as I was about to go under, and . . . I don't know. He got pulled in."

Remy swirls the brandy bottle, watching the last of the amber liquid slosh against the glass. Anything she offers here is purely academic, isn't it? She can cite the research without it meaning anything more.

Slowly, she says, "I've read a number of theories about physical touch as a means of spiritual connection. It's why participants at a séance might be asked to clasp hands, or why psychics might claim they can glean information about an object by touching it."

"Right," Cas says, blinking. "At any rate, clearly *I* knew that we'd just been inside a vision, but Henry didn't. He kept yelling about what we'd just seen, which . . . drew some attention, I suppose. And put Pastor Dekker onto him. What does Dekker want with him, anyway?"

Remy can feel them both watching her keenly. "In the note my father sent with his journal, he said the Order was trying to recruit him to their cause."

"What cause is that?" Cas asks.

"I don't know. It's not charity work, though—I can tell you that much. When they realized he wasn't going to join them . . . well, that's when he ran."

"You think they're trying to recruit Ashworth," Finn says.

"Don't you?" Remy says.

The sky above them is peppered with stars now, flecks of white paint splattering a dark fence. Remy rehearses her next words twice through before she says them. She may well not deserve this second chance—but it's been presented to her anyway. She cannot mess this up again.

"I'm not saying I believe you," she tells Cas. "I'm not saying I believe in prophecies, or visions, or any of this. But I think the Order of Lazarus does. I think my father was researching all of this because he knew the *Order* was researching it." She swallows. "And if, hypothetically, a person *was* having visions of deaths before they happened... I think that's something that Pastor Dekker and his Order would be very, very interested in."

"And they think it's Henry," Cas says.

For a moment, all three of them are quiet. Remy has the spiraling sensation that they're retracing a story that's already been written. The thought makes her a little lightheaded.

Then Cas says, "So we're going there, right? We're going to get Henry out of that place. How quickly do you think we can find a ship to Maine?"

It's their treasure hunt at Dungeon Rock all over again—Cas abandoning all of Remy's planning to simply start digging instead. "Hold on," Remy says, "I don't think we should—"

"I'd bet Kieran could find us a ship," Finn says.

"Kieran?" Cas asks.

"My brother. He's a sailor, works on some of the merchant ships out of Salem and Boston. He'll know which captains are heading north."

"Stop and think about this," Remy urges, though they both ignore her.

"Kieran... Robinson?" Cas is saying. "He's your brother? I knew that. I can see it now that you mention it. You have similar faces."

Finn frowns in a way that makes her face look nothing like Kieran's. "Have we?"

"I've just always gotten distracted from, you know, his face. He's got those muscular shoulders, and those *calves* . . ."

"Jesus Christ," Finn says. "Stop talking."

"You think he could get us a ship?"

"No," Remy cuts in. "No, absolutely not. We can't just drop everything and run away to Maine!"

"Why not?" Cas asks.

"Some of us have responsibilities here!"

Finn nudges the toe of her boot into Remy's leg. "Is that the only reason? Because I know you don't want to believe it, but I think your mother and sisters can manage without you for a week or two."

Remy glares at her. "You can't seriously be considering this. Even if we *could* get to Eden, we have no idea what to expect there."

"I've seen your journal," Finn says. "I'd say you have a better idea of what to expect than nearly anyone else."

"It's not the same! And we have no plan, no way to get Ashworth out or—"

"You always were a genius at planning, though," Cas says. "You'll mastermind something."

Remy is simultaneously touched and annoyed. "That's not how it works."

"I don't understand," Cas says. "Why have you been investigating all this time if you're not going to *do* anything with it?"

And Remy finds she doesn't have an answer. Not a good one, anyway. Not one that will make sense to anyone else. She's spent eight years throwing herself into this research, filling her every spare moment with it as she runs herself ragged—but maybe that isn't quite the whole of it. Maybe she's just been *running*. Keeping herself so busy that there's no time left to feel anything else.

For years, she's been living two lives, keeping these two parts of herself in a delicate equilibrium. There's the Remy who's been digging, who would do nearly anything to help her father—and then there's the Remy who keeps that first self of hers in check. Who maintains appearances and behaves just as she's expected. Remy has crafted this second persona with such care, studied the people around her for years, learned the rules of what to say and how to say it. Maybe good manners alone can't repair the DeWindt family name—but they can keep the eyes off her. They can give enough breathing room to let her still investigate in secret.

Going to Eden—taking even a single step down this path Finn and Cas are edging toward—would destroy that equilibrium in a second.

They're both watching her now, waiting for her to agree to leap off this cliff with them. The hope in Finn's dark eyes is terrifying, as if she can see straight to that wildness Remy used to have as a child. The wildness Remy might have again.

"I'll think about it," Remy says at last. Offering even this much sets her hands shaking—but still, Finn's face falls. It isn't enough. It isn't what Finn wanted from her. "Just . . . let me think about it, please."

"Sure," Finn says flatly. "You think about it."

She clearly doesn't believe Remy will, though. She clearly thinks this is a *no*. It shouldn't hurt so much, that disappointment on Finn's face. Remy wishes she could be the version of herself Finn was hoping for—but she can't. She doesn't know how.

Cas takes the bottle from her hand, tips back the last few drops from it, and then says suddenly, "Do you think I could get shoulders like Kieran Robinson's if I started hoisting crates and sail lines all day?"

Finn's expression of disappointment shifts to disgust. "Jesus Christ."

"Have you ever hoisted anything in your entire life?" Remy asks, more grateful for the diversion than she'll ever admit.

"Well, no, but I've never had proper motivation. For shoulders like *that*, though..."

"Jesus *Christ*," Finn says again.

"I'm sure *that* will win you a husband," Remy says. "Maybe you can get all your gowns specially tailored to show off your new muscles."

Cas waves the empty bottle at the sky. "I was never cut out to be a housewife. I'll run off to a deserted island and become a hermit, and then I'll spend all day lifting boxes and grow absolutely massive shoulders and no one can stop me."

As they climb down from the rock, as they hike back to town and go their separate ways, Remy keeps thinking about those years of running through the woods. Does she even have the capacity anymore to feel that unabashed freedom? Probably not. She spends too much time now restraining herself, too much time living for everyone else. That sort of freedom comes only for people who know who they are and what they want.

Remy has no idea anymore.

Remy doesn't expect anyone in the house to be awake as she slips back inside after their meeting in the woods. It's late, though she's not sure *how* late; alcohol always muddles her sense of time. Close to midnight, surely.

But as she tiptoes through the darkened kitchen and skips over the spot where the floorboards creak, something catches her gaze: a flicker of orange from down the hall.

She tries not to sigh. Her mother must have forgotten to snuff one of the candles before she went upstairs. It's hardly the first time; these little bouts of forgetfulness have grown less frequent, but they still happen. Her mother will retreat into herself for weeks or months, quiet and unreachable, drifting through the house like a wayward wraith—and then she'll come back. She's always come back before, anyway.

Remy pads down the hallway toward the light. At least she's awake to catch it this time, to put out the open flame. Sometimes she still marvels that they made it through those first few years after her father left without letting the house burn down.

But the candle in the hallway holder isn't lit. Instead, the light is flickering from the room on the right—her father's study. The door to it is ajar.

Remy frowns. Did she forget to close up properly after she finished her research last night? Did *she* leave a candle burning all this time?

She steps inside the study and freezes.

Her mother is sitting at the heavy oak desk, the family's account book spread open before her. She doesn't move when Remy enters.

"I didn't think you'd still be up," Remy says.

Her mother startles a little. The quivering light from the candle on the desk makes the lines of her face look deeper, somehow.

"Oh," her mother says. "Hello, darling. Did I wake you?"

"I was out with Finn," Remy reminds her.

"Right. Of course." Her mother's lips bend in a distant sort of smile. "And how is Finn?"

Remy tries not to think about the bite of Finn's disappointment. "She's fine," Remy says. "Are you . . . all right?"

"Of course, darling. Just looking over the accounts."

"You don't need to worry about that. I've got it handled."

"I know you do," her mother says. "I can still worry, though."

She closes the ledger. Remy knows what the numbers inside the book show: they're barely scraping by. Remy's piecemeal income covers the family's daily essentials—usually—but they ate through all of her father's reserves in those first few years he was gone, while Remy's mother was in no mental state for financial planning and Remy was clinging desperately to the way things were before. She waited far too long to cut costs the way they should have. Now the savings are gone, and they're overdue on property taxes, and the house is going to need repairs sooner or later. The sensible choice would probably be to sell this place and move the family somewhere smaller.

Remy is absolutely not going to sell this place. Not when her father is still on the run, unable to come home. Not when this house is their last tie to their old lives before he left.

Maybe Remy is *still* clinging desperately to the way things were before. It's not a thought she's willing to entertain just now.

Remy's mother studies her for a long moment. Her mother's eyes are a pale blue gray, a shade that both of Remy's sisters inherited. Remy got her father's eyes, though: wide and dark brown, like black tea left for a long steep.

"Come on," her mother says. "We should both get to bed." She starts to stand, and Remy reaches to pull out the chair, but her mother shakes her off, smiling. "I can manage, Remember."

Her mother is the only person who ever calls Remy by her full name. She's the only person who calls her sister Prudence instead of Prue, too. The old Puritan virtue names came from her side of the family; Remy's father always detested them. Not for the first time, Remy notes the strangeness of having a name that's also a verb: *Remember*.

As if she has any other choice. As if she can ever forget.

So Remy lets her mother manage. Her mother does seem more like herself these days. Maybe Finn is right—maybe her mother and sisters really would be fine without her for a week or two. The idea of it makes Remy strangely uneasy.

"I'll be up in a few minutes," Remy says. Her mother kisses her cheek and leaves the candle with her as she disappears into the hall.

For a long moment, Remy stands in her father's study, thinking. She *should* get to bed—morning will come too soon, and then she'll have too many chores to do and not enough rest for doing them. But she fetches the key to the window seat instead. Her father's collection is the exact opposite of the library in the Sterling manor, where Cas and Remy once got into terrible trouble for daring to flip the pages of a volume on its display stand. Mr. Sterling's books are all rare first editions or original manuscripts; they're meant less for reading than for presenting to guests after supper so the guests can quietly admire their expense.

The bookshelves in the DeWindt study are well stocked, too, but the most interesting holdings are secreted away, the private collection of a man obsessed. These books *have* been read, many times over.

Remy unlocks the window seat and lifts the lid. She draws out both the journal and the most recent addition to the library here: Pastor Cole's copy of the *Grimoirium Verum*.

She brings the two books to the desk and hunches over them in the candlelight. She'll read for just a few minutes—just to settle her racing thoughts. When she opens the journal, she lets herself linger on the earliest pages, the ones with her father's writing. Here is the list of names, with Pastor Dekker identified as a member. Here is the strange hourglass-like sigil he'd sketched in charcoal. For years, Remy has tried to identify this symbol: She's scoured through her father's library twice over. She's sent queries to five different archives, along with the Boston Athenaeum. All her searching has been fruitless; no one has seen a symbol like it.

The rest of the journal is filled with Remy's own notes—observations she picked up from her father's books, and every detail that her student correspondent had revealed, and her own grasping theories about what the Order of Lazarus might be pursuing: They want to ascertain the future. They want to raise the dead. She still doesn't have any real answers. Nearly eight years of research, and this is what she has to show for it.

She flips the journal to a blank page, then turns to the *Grimoirium Verum*. The book's spine naturally falls open to a section in the middle—a conjuring ritual of some sort, though Remy will have to spend more time with the Latin to parse it out. But there's something wedged between the pages that's caused them to part here. A scrap of paper.

Remy takes out the note and unfolds it.

Exodus 12:11. Matthew 10:26.
We're watching DeWindt.
—J. S.

Even as she scrambles for a Bible, Remy's mind is making a list of the marvels contained in this brief missive. First: her father's name. Second: the signature, *J. S.* Unless Remy is very much mistaken, this note came from the Reverend John Smith, the head of the Order himself. Third: her father's name. Fourth: the condition of the paper—still crisp and white. The grimoire itself is old, its pages yellowing, but this note must have been received and stashed inside the book only recently.

Fifth: her father's name.

What does it mean? *We're watching DeWindt.* It's a threat, a warning. It's also a promise. The present tense of the sentence is zinging through Remy's veins: It's the best indication she's had in eight years that her father is still alive. That he's still out on the run somewhere, still hunted by the Order of Lazarus—and maybe hunting the Order in return.

And if the Reverend John Smith is watching him, that means the Reverend John Smith knows where he is.

Her father's old Bible isn't hidden in the window seat; it's on one of the shelves behind his desk, out in the open, surrounded by books of law. Remy's heart is racing as she searches for the two verses cited in Smith's note. The first is from the story of the Passover—the Lord's instruction to eat the meal *dressed for travel, with your sandals on your feet, and your staff in hand.* Is it a code—a command for Pastor Cole to prepare to come to Eden? She forces herself to pause and copy down the verse in her journal.

What would it feel like finally to take action—to dash off to Eden with Finn and Cas? She hadn't realized her mind had been mulling over the logistics, but when she reaches for them, the logistics are there: She'd just need some excuse for her absence. She could invent a job for herself—something out of town. The Higgins family moved to Boston a few years back; she could claim that Mrs. Higgins has asked for her help with the children for a few weeks. There'd be no income, of course, but Remy has earned a little extra this week; if she has her mother cut back on a few things, they can weather it.

Remy can't believe she's even considering this. *We're watching DeWindt.* She can't believe she's never truly considered it before.

She's found the passage in Matthew now:

For there is nothing concealed that will not be disclosed, or hidden that will not be made known.

Remy reads the line three times. A code. It must be. She doesn't know the details of this message, and yet she feels the meaning of it in her trembling hand as she writes it down. She feels it in her racing heart: Something is about to happen.

Something is starting.

VII

FINN

Finn is still awake when Remy appears below her window in the wee morning hours.

The servants' quarters in the Darner house are on the very top floor, tucked away with their own separate entrance and staircase. The design is intended for the family to see and hear their domestic staff as little as possible—offensive on principle, but Finn has to admit that the setup has its perks. Since Mrs. Darner's current domestic staff consists only of Finn, she can entertain guests and nighttime visitors in perfect privacy. Sometimes those guests are Remy, who spreads her books and notes all over the kitchen table while Finn gently forces her to eat something. Sometimes those guests are other girls from town, who spread other things.

When Finn hears the rattling on her windowpane, she assumes the visitor is of this second type. It's past midnight, after all, and she saw Remy barely an hour ago. Perhaps Imogen Walters has come by for a romp. Good. Finn could use a little fun and a little self-loathing.

Finn raises the curtain and peers down into the back garden.

It isn't Imogen Walters.

"Finally," Remy says once Finn has gotten the window open. She's trying to whisper, but she's also trying to be heard by

Finn two stories up, and the whisper is fairly loud. Fortunately, Mrs. Darner sleeps like the dead. "I've probably tossed a pound of gravel by now, but my aim is terrible. Can you come down? I need to talk to you."

Finn's heart starts to hammer for no good reason. It continues hammering as she snatches her dressing gown and hurries down the stairs. Most likely Remy has just stayed up reading and wants to share some new lead she's found. Or she's here to tell Finn off again for arranging that meeting with Cas Sterling. She's definitely not here for a romp. Finn knows that. Her heart is ridiculous.

But there's a strange resolve in Remy's eyes when Finn meets her at the back door.

"So I've thought about it," Remy says straightaway. "And I think we should do it."

"I'm sorry?" Finn says.

"I think we should go to Eden."

Finn stares at her, waiting for the catch. Remy stares back. Her hands are twisting together, fingers knotting and unknotting.

"Really," Finn says finally. Despite her best efforts, her skepticism leaks through.

Remy sighs. "*Yes*, really. Look, you and Cas were right. What's the point of all the research, if not for this? And I was looking in that grimoire—the one we found the other day—and I found this."

She shoves a scrap of paper at Finn.

Finn is keenly aware of Remy's gaze on her as she reads. "*We're watching DeWindt.*"

"They still have him under surveillance," Remy says. "Which means he's still out there, and they know where he is. I looked up these verses, too. Whatever they're planning, I think they're getting close. So we should go. We'll go, and we'll get Henry Ashworth, and we'll find out what we can to help my father."

Something about this doesn't sit right with Finn. When they'd talked back at the rock, when Remy had said she'd think about it, Finn had known she wouldn't. She'd been certain that Remy's mind was already made up. Had Finn misread her so badly? Or was this one mention of Remy's father really enough to change her mind? She knows the hope that Remy still carries after all this time—that her father will return, safe and sound, even after eight years without a word. Finn can't help but be a little more pessimistic.

"Say something, please," Remy says.

And yet this is the result Finn had wanted, isn't it? This is why she'd told Cas Sterling to meet them at the rock. Finn thinks of that oddly intense conversation with Cas on Windover Common. Cas needs this. Remy needs this.

And what does Finn need? She doesn't know.

From far off in the trees, there's a high keening sound like a woman screaming—probably a fox, but Finn can't help but think about her mother's old stories about banshees, those wailing voices that herald death.

"All right," Finn says at last.

The grin on Remy's face sets Finn's heart hammering all over again. "All right?"

"All right." Reluctantly, Finn feels herself smiling, too. "I'll talk to Kieran in the morning. Let's go to Eden."

Less than twelve hours later, Remy appears outside the Darner house once more. This time, she's brought with her an armful of papers, her leather-bound research journal, and Cas Sterling.

"I hear we're breaking into a seminary," Cas says as Finn ushers them into the kitchen.

Remy takes over the table there as usual, though now she covers its surface not with her typical books but with maps, train timetables, and various lists she's already scribbled out for their journey.

"You pulled all this together overnight?" Cas says in wonder, picking up a packing list and then setting the page down in a different spot. Remy moves it back, frowning.

"And into the morning. We don't have time to waste. Finn has already asked Kieran to find us a ship to Maine, and we'll need to be ready for whenever it sails."

"How long of a trip is it, anyway? A day?"

"At least two, and that's if the weather cooperates."

"Ugh." Cas has plucked up Remy's research journal now; she starts to open it, but Remy snatches it from her hand. Cas moves on to the next paper in reach, unoffended. "Why did this secret society have to build their seminary so far away?"

It's likely a rhetorical question, but Remy has never passed up the opportunity to talk about her research, even as she sets the journal carefully out of Cas's reach. "There's something about the specific site, I think—a freshwater spring on the premises that's supposed to have some kind of spiritual cleansing properties. If you believe in that sort of thing. Sit down. You're making me nervous."

Cas sits, though it does little to tamp down the restless energy that's still crackling off her like electricity. It's the same energy Finn had noticed during their encounter on the common—though it seems to have found direction now, like a bolt of lightning.

However familiar a sight Remy and her papers are in the Darner kitchen, Cas Sterling seems decidedly out of place here. She's too brightly colored for the dingy room, a figure transplanted into the wrong painting. Perhaps, Finn thinks, a lifetime of money gives a person some indefinable sort of glow.

Cas shrugs out of her coat and tosses it to the floor, where it lands with a strangely metallic clamor.

"Oh, I forgot," Cas says, and suddenly that indefinable glow of wealth becomes significantly more defined as she digs a bag of coins from the coat's pocket and plops it on the table. "You said we'd need funds for traveling, right? I present to you: funds. Courtesy of my father's secret gambling stash that he doesn't know I know about."

The bag is enormous. It's possible that the coins inside are only shillings. It's also possible they're golden eagles.

"Won't your father notice this is missing?" Remy asks, tipping the bag sideways to peer at its contents. The coins inside are not shillings.

"Maybe, but none of us is supposed to know he has it, so it's not as if he can go around asking. He hides it behind that case in his library where he keeps those damned Jonathan Edwards manuscripts. Now *there's* irony for you."

"Jonathan Edwards," Remy says absently. "Is he the minister who oversaw the witch trials?"

"No, Edwards is the one who preached about the sinners and the angry God tossing everybody into brimstone. So? Will this be enough?"

Even by her barest estimate, Finn suspects the bag holds upwards of two hundred dollars. "Jesus, Mary, and Joseph," she mutters, and puts on the kettle for tea.

They spend the better part of an hour talking through the plan, or rather, Finn and Cas spend it listening as Remy tells them the plan. There are supplies to gather, travel and lodging to arrange, excuses to make as to why they'll each be leaving town. There are logistics to put in order to keep everything running at home while they're away. Remy doesn't mention outright whatever concern she might be feeling about leaving her mother and sisters here alone, but Finn can sense it weighing on her—tightening her shoulders, pressing that crease of worry into place between her dark eyebrows.

"It's probably better if we dress as boys for the journey, right?" Cas says. "We'll draw less attention that way. Finn, do you think your brother could buy some new clothes for us?"

Remy snorts into her tea. "You always did look for any excuse to wear trousers."

"They're comfortable!"

"I'm not disagreeing! And it's a good idea. Besides, I don't want to end up on your hit list like Joseph Bryant."

Cas's voice holds a note of murder as she mutters, "*Joseph Bryant.*"

The two of them have fallen into such a comfortable rhythm already—reminiscing and trading jabs as if they've been friends for years. Which they have, of course. The fact of it peeves Finn more than it ought. Of course she'd *known* about their long-shared history when she'd arranged their reunion last night—but she could do without the constant reminders of it.

"That was Joseph Bryant's crime, you know," Remy is saying, and with a start Finn realizes this is addressed to *her*—Remy is catching Finn up, bringing her into that shared history, too. "A group of us were putting on a drama of 'Sleepy Hollow,' and Cas wanted to play Mr. Crane. Joseph Bryant said she wasn't allowed."

"What a bastard," Finn says.

"Right?" Cas says with such vindication that she nearly upends her stool.

"When your message to the faerie king didn't work, didn't you end up punching him?" Remy asks.

"No, no, of course not!" Cas says. "I *tripped* him."

They have to disperse shortly after that; Finn is shocked Remy could carve out even this small segment of time on such short notice. She's apparently planning to tell her mother about a short-term governess job in Boston that will take her away for two weeks—plenty of time for them to sail to Maine, find Ashworth, and do whatever investigating Remy intends. Finn is going to have to find a replacement to help old Mrs. Darner while she's gone, though she's putting it off as long as she can.

The next afternoon, Kieran sends a note that he's found what they need, and Finn meets him on the old stone bridge just south of town. They perch side by side on the arch of it, dangling their feet over the lazy waters of Cedar Brook as they talk. This has always been their meeting place when Kieran returns from his latest sea voyage. The bridge is worn and fuzzy with moss, and though it's fully mortared, it's always reminded Finn of the drystone walls that crisscross the fields back in County Mayo.

"It's called the *Leonidas*," Kieran tells her. "The captain seems like a nice enough fellow. Sets sail from Boston three days from now. He'll be offloading cargo at a few ports up north, including your Eden. So that'll do, won't it?"

He clearly knows the answer, though; he's grinning already.

"That'll do just fine," Finn says.

His grin, impossibly, widens. He drums the heels of his boots against the side of the bridge in a gentle rhythm. "Are you going to tell me now why you're running off to some town in Maine?"

Finn has been weighing cover stories all afternoon—though her brother is so trusting that she could make up nearly any excuse at all and he'd likely believe her. Still, she hesitates. She's added *lied to Kieran* to her mental tally of sins far, far too often.

"We've just got some business to attend to," she says finally—an omission rather than an outright falsehood. "Nothing too difficult. We'll be there and back again in no time."

"Hmm," Kieran says.

"What d'you mean, *hmm*?"

"I just worry about you, little sis."

There's a gentle look in his eyes that Finn doesn't like. Kieran is four years her senior, but he's always been a boy of soft edges, and Finn has always been the opposite. She scowls.

"Well, you needn't," she says. "I'm more worried about *you*, anyway."

"Me?" He scrubs a hand on the back of his neck, where the skin is still burned pink from his most recent time at sea. "What're you worrying about me for?"

Finn raises an eyebrow at him. They both go quiet. It's the sort of quiet that happens when two people are recalling the worst time in their lives from opposite sides of the memory: the time when one of them had nearly died and the other had watched him nearly die. Finn wonders if she'll ever be able to look at her smiling, shining brother without the image tarnished by that awful winter years ago—Kieran's ghost-pale face, his cheeks hollowed by sickness, his consumptive breaths rattling in his chest like any one of them might be the last.

He's rubbing the back of his neck again now, clearly uncomfortable. "Oh, stop with that. You needn't worry about me, either. I'm fit as a fiddle. In the prime of health."

He makes a show of flexing his arm muscles as if to drive the point home, and Jesus Christ, now Finn is remembering Cas Sterling's preoccupation with her brother's shoulders. As Kieran changes the subject and Finn lets the subject be changed, she tamps down the guilt that's always inside her, lurking.

He's fine now, Finn thinks over and over, like a prayer. He's going to be fine.

It's difficult to convince herself; Kieran has always been too gentle for his own good. Once, when they were children, he found an injured bird by the side of the road and bundled it inside his jacket and brought it home. He stayed awake with it all night so he could feed it every hour. When the bird died, Kieran cried for three days.

Finn would have left the bird where it lay. She told Kieran this when he first picked it up, and again when they got home and discovered that the bird had shat in his jacket. Kieran had smiled and ignored her. He was endlessly kind, while Finn was ornery and selfish and short-tempered. Somehow, her brother had inherited only their parents' virtues, and she'd gotten all of the vices.

In a way, it finally made sense when, a few years later, Finn started noticing girls. She'd always sensed a badness in her—something innate, something that no sacrament of confession could touch. The realization of her unnatural desires only confirmed what she'd known all along.

Finn makes a detour to the DeWindt house on her way home from the bridge. When she tells Remy about the *Leonidas*, she expects Remy to balk—their plan is suddenly very real and approaching very quickly. But Remy only nods once, her jaw tight.

"All right," Remy says. "I'll tell Cas in the morning."

And then she positively throws herself into the planning. The next day, she's right back at the Darner kitchen table, and she spends more than half of their remaining time bent over the papers there. This is how she always seems to do these things: laboring over every detail, leaving no stone unturned, no matter how small or improbable that stone may seem.

Which makes it all the stranger how few follow-up questions she'd had when Cas Sterling had announced that, allegedly, she can see deaths before they happen. The visions Cas had described seem very much in line with Remy's usual topics of research—and yet Remy had seemed almost uninterested. Or perhaps *unsurprised*. Finn has known since the beginning that Remy and Cas had some sort of falling-out years ago, around the time of Remy's father's disappearance. She's always assumed the rift was Cas's choice—that Cas Sterling's perfect, pampered life hadn't prepared her for the DeWindt family's troubles, and she'd dropped Remy like a moldy piece of fruit.

Finn is starting to suspect there's more to it.

They set off for Boston the day before the *Leonidas* is to sail. Finn meets Remy at three o'clock, and they board the afternoon coach from Windover to the rail depot in Lynn. Finn tries to pretend that this is just another research trip, one of the countless outings Remy has dragged her on before. But her twisting stomach doesn't believe the lie.

Remy smiles politely and trades pleasantries with the other coach passengers. Finn clutches her carpetbag against her knees and silently watches as the town that's been her home for the past eight years disappears from view.

This is the last time you'll ever see this place, a voice in her mind keeps whispering. *The last time you'll cross the bridge over Cedar Brook. The last time you'll glimpse these woods.* Remy insists they'll be back soon, of course; her mother is expecting her return within the fortnight. But the voice still nags in Finn's head. No matter what happens, when all of this is over, Finn can't shake the feeling that she won't be returning here.

Cas has made plans to meet them on the train platform, and she arrives only ten minutes behind schedule. Remy must've accounted for the delay, because she's the picture of calm as Cas finally jogs toward them, out of breath and pink cheeked.

"We should hurry. I've just ditched my driver, but George is very dogged and is definitely going to come looking for me when he realizes I'm not in the carriage," Cas says in a rush. She doesn't break stride as she reaches them—just continues on toward the train's open doors and assumes they'll follow, apparently.

And they do follow. "Don't *you* look grand," Remy says as they board. This is because of Cas's outfit: a fashionable gown paired with a floor-length cloak of blue silk and velvet. The cloak alone probably cost more than Finn's yearly wages.

"Oh, don't." Cas sounds genuinely pained. "I told my mother I'd been invited to tea at the Lyman estate. It was the only cover I could think of that she couldn't bully her way into attending. And then she still insisted on picking out my clothes. Your brother got us the goods?"

She's looking at Finn now. Finn pats her carpetbag. "He did."

"Thank god. I can't wait to get out of this."

"What will your mother do when she discovers you're *not*, in fact, having tea at the Lyman estate?" Remy asks as they work their way up the train's aisle.

"Murder me, I expect." Cas drops into an empty section of seats and starts pulling the pins from her elaborately pinned hair. "Stop giving me that look. Why worry about a problem now when it'll still be here waiting for us later?"

Remy continues giving her the look, which is one of horror. "*Because* it will be here waiting!"

Cas shrugs. "So I'll deal with it then."

Remy shakes her head, but she settles onto the bench across from Cas. Finn sits down beside her. When the whistle screams its parting cry, she clenches her hands into fists against her skirts.

The last time you'll see this train station, her mind whispers. *The last time you'll visit Lynn.*

She never did find a replacement for old Mrs. Darner. She never even told her employer she was leaving town. She'll be fired, of course. She ought to care about that fact more than she does. Mostly, Finn feels relief. There will be nothing in Windover for her to come back to, except Kieran, and he'll be back out to sea again in a few weeks. He's barely in Windover these days anyway.

The bench where Finn and Remy sit is facing backward when the train lurches into motion. As the wheels start to grind with a shriek of metal on metal, Finn switches to join Cas on the opposite side. She fixes her gaze out the window, turning her focus frontward.

Not at what they're leaving behind—only at what's coming.

VIII

CAS

Boston is a teeming knot of people, nearly a hundred thousand lives intersecting and separating all at once. As soon as their train crosses the Charles, the smell hits Cas like a wet rag to the face—a combination of soot, seawater, and raw sewage. Just a few decades back, this part of the city was an old mill pond, and then a dumping ground for human waste. Now it's transformed into this grid of streets and shop fronts, but its history hangs in the air. The stink permeates everything.

The train leaves them at the depot on the north side of the city, and they make their way toward the docks on foot. Everywhere Cas looks bares something new and exciting. The crowd in the street spans every walk of life: servants in their work clothes, gentlemen talking business in the doorways of pubs, children running barefoot from house to house. The chaos is blissfully anonymous. No one much cares about three young ladies from the North Shore joining their ranks. Cas's focus keeps getting pulled in eighteen different directions, and more than once she falls behind and has to jog to catch up with Remy and Finn.

It's not that Cas hasn't visited Boston. She's been to a few concerts at the Melodeon, and her mother is always dragging her here for parties, ones that are supposed to be "the event of the season," though they seem to have the same bland food, bland conversation, and bland-faced socialites as every other party Cas has attended.

But Cas has never come to Boston on her own before. She's never been in charge of her own plans and her own lodging and her own life. Her visits have always been carefully orchestrated affairs—whisked from the train station into a closed-curtained carriage and then into a stately house or concert hall, and then whisked back home again.

Cas has never really gotten to *see* Boston until now. She's never gotten to exist as part of the city.

And now, she can't get enough of it.

When they're nearing the harbor, they ask around until they find a passably reputable hotel just off Hanover Street. Its clapboard facade tilts a little to the left, like the building is as tipsy as the patrons of its barroom. Cas dips into her father's unwitting donation to get them private lodging for the night, and she, Remy, and Finn lock themselves into their room upstairs. It's cramped and drafty, though thankfully the sewage smell is mostly covered by the downstairs pub's stink of fried fish and beer. Street noises drift up through the room's grubby window.

"At least it's only for one night," Cas says.

"I don't know what you're imagining a ship's steerage to be like, but I promise you it'll be worse than this," Remy tells her.

Finn has opened her carpetbag and now starts laying out clothes on one of the beds. Her brother has picked a marvelous spread for them: lightweight linen shirts, loose duck trousers, sweaters and peacoats for the colder weather as they make their way north. It's all typical sailors' garb, though too crisp and clean and clearly unused to belong to anyone but a greenhand.

Cas can't bring herself to care. She keeps running her fingers over the piles of rough fabric. For years, Cas has been staring down a life that's entirely for show: marrying Henry, both of them acting out their happy pantomime of domestic bliss. Already, this adventure feels real in a way she'd forgotten anything could.

She shucks off the ridiculous cloak her mother had insisted on, and then the ridiculous puffy-sleeved dress, too. She wads them both into a ball and tosses them into a corner of the room. Something inside her has snapped. Henry had been Cas's one tether to a normal, half-tolerable future—and now Henry is gone, and that future along with him, even if (no, *when*) Cas rescues him from Eden. It took only one morning at Long Beach for her entire world to fall apart—and yet as she stands in the rubble, it's hard to mourn the loss. More and more, this outcome feels inevitable.

She remembers Finn's warning when they'd parted ways on the common last week: *Don't do anything rash.* Maybe Finn had sensed even then how close Cas has always been to simply throwing her whole life away.

Finn is staring at her now. Her eyes dart to the bundle of fabric in the corner and then back to Cas.

"What's wrong?" Cas says.

"You're not going to leave those behind, are you?"

Cas shrugs. "Why not? It's not like I have use for them now."

"That cloak alone must've cost a fortune!" Finn says. "Isn't that silk? You can't just leave it in the corner of a hotel."

"You're welcome to it, if you're so keen on it," Cas tells her.

Finn doesn't reply, but she smooths the cloak back out and folds it carefully, with all the expertise of someone who's made a profession of smoothing and folding other people's fine clothes. Cas feels a prick of shame at that, but she pushes it away. She turns her attention to the new clothes.

Cas finds that if she hikes up her stays and tugs them tightly enough, they can pull her chest almost flat. Remy helps her tie the laces, and then Cas stands in front of the room's smudgy mirror, admiring the straight lines of the body reflected there. It's squeezed and uncomfortable, and also absolutely glorious.

"We should cut our hair," Cas says.

Remy is hopping on one foot as she tries to get her leg through a pair of trousers. Across the room, Finn has gone very still. She eyes Cas in the mirror image.

"Why bother?" Remy says. She pokes her foot through at last and catches her balance on a corner of the bedframe. "Plenty of sailors wear their hair long."

"Plenty wear it short, too," Cas says.

"Just tuck it up into your hat. Or tie it back in a queue. It'll work just as well, and it'll save you the ages it would take to grow it long again."

Cas doesn't mean to say it. The words just get away from her, a warm block of butter slipping through her fingers: "Maybe I'm not going to grow it long again."

Now Remy's eyes find her, too. Cas focuses on her own reflection, tries to ignore the warm flush on her neck and the familiar twinge of guilt, or maybe longing, in her stomach. There she's gone again, disobeying her own rules. She shouldn't have said that out loud. Shouldn't have even thought it. Remy is right: They can play the roles they need for this journey just as well without cutting their hair. It isn't necessary. It isn't practical.

Cas wishes she hadn't started this conversation. Remy already knows too much. She remembers too many of Cas's wild pieces from when they were children, the pieces Cas hadn't yet learned to hide.

Cas isn't supposed to show anyone how much she *wants*.

But now that her mouth has said it aloud, her mind can't stop thinking it. She can't let the idea go.

"Your mother would be furious," Remy tells her.

"That sounds like encouragement to me."

"And what would Ashworth say when you show up to rescue him and have your hair chopped off? What would *everyone* say?"

"You don't have to cut yours," Cas snaps.

With effort, she drags herself away from the flat-chested image in the mirror. She snatches one of the shirts from the bed and pulls it over her head. The fabric isn't soft, exactly, but it's airy and light, and it feels like a second skin in a way her fine gowns never have. When she emerges from the head hole, Remy and Finn are both still staring at her.

"Do we have any shears?" Cas asks.

"No," Remy says, but Finn pulls open her carpetbag and takes a pair of sewing scissors from it without a word.

"Perfect." Cas plucks up the scissors and offers them to Remy. "Here. Help me."

"Absolutely not."

"Finn, then. Cut my hair."

Finn's face slides into the glower she always seems to keep close at hand. "Don't order me about."

Cas drags over a rickety chair and plops down onto it, backward, so she's straddling it—because she's wearing *trousers* now, she can *straddle* things, how marvelous. She folds her hands under her chin and points her best pleading look back at Remy, just like she would have when they were ten years old. "Rem. *Please*. I've never asked you for anything—"

"That's an outright lie," Remy says.

"—and it'll look like garbage if I cut it myself."

"It will look like garbage if *I* do it!" Remy sputters. "Cas, I'm not cutting off your hair!"

"Fine." Cas is suddenly very aware of her own physical form. She's aware of her heart pounding, of her chest compacted beneath her tightened stays, of the blood pumping through this body of hers. Cycling through her legs and arms and trembling fingers and back to her heart. She hoists herself from the chair and stands. Her knees wobble, but only for a moment. "Fine."

"Think this through," Remy pleads.

But Cas is tired of thinking. By the time Remy has gotten the words out, Cas has already pulled a handful of her hair tight, and she hacks the whole lot of it off just below her ears.

Cas gazes down at the severed fistful of her own hair. She breathes in. She breathes out.

"Oh, Cas," Remy says from somewhere far away. She doesn't sound surprised. Sad, maybe, or resigned, convinced that Cas will regret what took only a second to do, just as she's always been convinced Cas will regret her impulses.

But something in Cas has gone very quiet—something she'd never realized before now had been whirring. She's pushed the wish down for so long. Ignored the warm clench of jealousy at the boys in town, the twinge of wanting. Not to be *with* them. To *be* them. Her whole life has been struggling through the water, doing her utmost to stay afloat, and still knowing she's never going to get a good breath of air. Knowing that the best she can hope for is to not drown.

Cas has spent so long focusing on only that, on not drowning. She hasn't let herself really imagine anything beyond it.

Cas opens her hand, and an avalanche of wavy chestnut hair falls around her boots.

"Cas, you *didn't*." Remy is staring down at the loose hair littering the floorboards. "Your mother— Lord, *my* mother— What will everyone—?"

"It's already done," Cas says. She brushes her fingers across the newly cut strands. All ragged, but her head feels exquisitely light. "So it doesn't matter. I don't care what my mother says, anyway."

"You look ridiculous," Finn says.

Cas bristles. "If you want to criticize, you could've helped."

"You need to even it out." Finn's eyes have narrowed appraisingly. "Shape it. Especially with hair as thick as yours. You can't just cut it off in a straight line. It makes your head look like a triangle."

Cas genuinely can't tell if she's trying to help or trying to be rude.

"Lord," Remy says again.

Somewhere on the street outside, voices are arguing in thick Boston accents. Horse hooves and cart wheels rattle on the cobblestones. At this hour in Windover, the road outside the Sterlings' manor would be nearly silent—the whole world deferring to Mr. Sterling's demands for peace while he reads and smokes his evening pipe. Here, there's no deferring. There's only *life*. It sets Cas's pulse a little faster.

Cas holds out the scissors to Finn, handle first.

"Fix it," Cas says. Finn starts for another scowl—*Don't order me about*—and Cas amends, "Please? Can you fix it?"

Finn softens a little. She ruffles her fingers through the jagged ends of Cas's hair.

"Mmm," she says. "I can try."

Finn works quietly. Carefully. Much more gently than Cas would've expected from this gruff, standoffish girl. It's clear she's done this before, and Cas wonders if she's cut her brother's hair, if she's trimmed Kieran Robinson's ruddy curls around his ears just like this. Cas tries to sit still while Finn's fingers move, shaping each section around the curve of Cas's head. The sewing scissors snip, soft as breath, and more hair drifts onto Cas's arms and shoulders and trousers.

"There," Finn says at last. The lilt of her accent sounds gentler now. "That's not half bad."

Cas brushes away the cut hair and crosses to the mirror. The evening sunset from outside the window combines with the candlelight from within to give the image a warm, orange glow. Cas studies the face in the glass.

The familiar pointed jaw, ending in a stubby chin. The familiar snub nose. The too-heavy brows that Cas's mother always has opinions on, the ears that always stick out, just a little, somehow less prominent now with the waves of hair cropped close around them. All of these are features Cas has seen in the mirror every day since forever, and yet . . .

And yet.

When Remy speaks, her voice holds something like wonder. "Cas . . . you look like a boy."

"Not half bad," Finn says again. Behind Cas in the reflection, the corner of Finn's thin mouth has quirked up.

Cas runs a hand through the newly cut hair. The young man in the mirror does the same. The facial features are so familiar but also new, somehow. Everything inside Cas has gone very still.

Because the reflection doesn't show Miss Cassandra Sterling.

It's Cas. Mirrored there for possibly the first time in his life.

"Well," Cas says.

His throat feels thick. He can't stop looking at the mirror. There's a warm feeling in his chest, a tingling, glowing sensation as something inside him begins to thaw. He's aware of Remy and Finn still watching him. He swallows. He tries again.

"Well," he says. "I suppose that's that, then."

IX

REMY

Cas tries, at first, to play it off as a lark—to pretend that this new self of his is just another part of their journey.

It isn't a lark. Remy can tell. She can sense the shift in him, and her mind makes the adjustment with surprising ease. Maybe it isn't a surprise at all. Most of her memories of Cas Sterling—of the *actual* Cas, not the stiff, proper young lady Remy has exchanged awkward nods with for the past few years—involve running through the woods, escaping from their duties, breaking the rules of their designated sex at every chance. In a way, it's been stranger to see Cas wearing dresses and attempting to play the part. In a way, the trousers and the hacked-off hair make much more sense. Something about him has pushed into place, the answer to a riddle that Remy hadn't even realized she'd been trying to solve before now.

Remy, Finn, and Cas take supper in the barroom downstairs and then set off toward the harbor in search of the *Leonidas*. The ship won't set sail until dawn, but Remy needs to see it tonight. She needs to speak with the captain and confirm every detail. A growing dread has been humming through her all afternoon. She's certain that something is about to go terribly wrong.

The haunting glow of the harbor at night only fuels her fear. The docks are crawling with sailors—nearly all of them men, plenty of them drunk or rowdy. Remy had been hesitant about her new clothes, but she's glad for them now. She keeps tugging down the brim of her tarpaulin hat, checking that her hair is still tucked up under it.

But no one pays their group any mind as they follow the curve of Commercial Street along the waterfront. They're just three more boys dodging through the crowds, preparing to take to sea.

"All right," Remy says when they've reached Union Wharf. It's hardly the largest of the dockyards they've passed, but it thrums with activity even at this hour. Workers roll barrels onto the ships berthed at each dock, or into flat-bottomed barges to take the cargo out to the larger vessels anchored in the harbor. A lanky clerk, possibly the dockmaster, frowns at the three of them as he notes something in his ledger. Remy tugs on her hat once more and tries to sound like she knows what she's doing. "According to Kieran, we're looking for a brig."

Finn grunts in affirmation. But Cas is staring blankly.

"It's a type of ship," Remy tells him.

"Well, that narrows it down."

"A midsized vessel, two-masted, square-rigged on both of the—"

"They all just look like ships to me," Cas cuts in. He nods at a tiny schooner tied just ahead of them, its sails neatly furled. "Ship," he says. Then at a three-masted barkentine a little farther out. "Also a ship."

"Just look for the one labeled *Leonidas*, then," Remy says, and they set off along the wharf.

Though Remy won't admit it, she's not very confident in her ship-identifying skills, either. All her nautical knowledge is pulled from books. She's never actually been out on the ocean before. She's spent the last few days planning out every step of their travels, and then planning for possible contingencies, and then planning for even more contingencies in case those earlier contingencies fall through. But this is all new to her, a whole world of unknowns.

Remy can't plan for what she doesn't know.

The bells from the New North Church chime the hour—nine. The names on each of the hulls start to blend together. Remy's arm is aching from carrying her carpetbag; she trades it to her other hand. The ache moves to that arm soon after. It's Finn's fault she has it; Finn had taken one look at the flimsy, half-rusted lock on the door of their hotel room and insisted that they keep their bags with them.

"Complain all you'd like," she'd said, "but I'll not start a journey with our door kicked in and all our things stolen while we're out."

Remy isn't complaining, though. It's inconvenient, yes, but there's a comfort in having her bag tucked safely under her arm, and within it, the familiar weight of her research journal.

There's also a comfort in knowing that this city is putting Finn on edge, too.

Not that Finn shows it much. She walks with a heavy, confident stride that makes her look fierce and untouchable. Remy, meanwhile, feels like she's wearing her own nerves like a brightly colored scarf. Finn falls into step beside her.

"It's going to be fine," Finn says.

Against all reason, this attempt at reassurance only manages to do the opposite. "I know that," Remy says. "Why are you telling me that?"

"You've got that worried look."

Remy frowns. "I don't have a *look*."

"Oh yes you do," Cas says, wedging himself between them as they walk. "It's the look you always used to get when you realized we were about to get in trouble. The . . ." He furrows his brow and scrunches his mouth so tightly that he looks like he's having bowel troubles.

Finn waves him away. "No, it's more like . . ." She glowers into the middle distance, nose wrinkling. Remy regrets the series of events that has brought them all here. She feels distinctly ganged up on.

"I do *not*," she says.

Cas, for his part, has been giddy all evening. He won't stop ruffling his newly shorn hair. When the bartender back at the hotel had asked offhandedly, "You lads enjoying your night about town?" Cas had barely waited for the man to turn away before he'd caught Remy's eye and mouthed, "*Lads* about town!"

"How can you worry on a night like this, anyway?" he asks now. "We're in Boston! That bartender called us *lads*! Everything's going to plan!"

"There's plenty more that can still go wrong," Remy says.

"Well, we've managed steps one and two well enough."

"What were steps one and two?"

Cas skips a few feet ahead of them and twists around, walking backward to show Remy and Finn the tally on his fingers. "Step one was getting to the city. Step two was the costume change.

And we got dinner already, so I'd call that step three handled, as well. Ha!"

He turns frontward again just in time to smack directly into a passing sailor. The sailor whirls, glaring. She's tall and light-skinned and, surprisingly, a woman, though any comfort Remy might take from that fact vanishes at the sight of the enormous rifle strapped to her back—long and gleaming and very deadly-looking.

"Oh, sorry," Cas says, his tone far too casual. Remy's heart has jumped into her throat.

"*Oh, sorry,*" the sailor mocks. "Sure you are, you little ganef. This is a pickpocketing scheme, right? A clumsy one."

The sailor is patting down the pockets of her cropped jacket as if searching for what's missing. It's a men's jacket, and yet the fit of it on her isn't quite masculine. It's something else altogether. Remy struggles to focus.

"We're sorry," she says, trying to drag Cas away. "He's not a pickpocket. Just a clod."

"He's a thief is what he is. I know all your little tricks. I've used most of them. You can't filch from a filcher."

"I didn't filch anything," Cas says.

"We'll see about *that*."

The sailor's hand moves toward her rifle, and Remy's mind leaps to the worst possible outcome: A violent altercation. The three of them dead in a dock fight. No one left to even bring her mother the awful news.

But one of the sailor's crewmates has appeared, a smaller Black woman who takes her companion by the elbow.

"Did they actually take anything?" the newcomer murmurs. Her partner's silence stands as answer. "Then leave it."

The sailor leaves it.

For several seconds afterward, as the angry sailor and her companion stomp off toward the next dock, Remy stands rooted, waiting for her body to realize that it isn't, in fact, about to die. Finn lets out a long breath. Cas, though, only scrubs at his hair and then starts walking again as if nothing has happened.

"Maybe you should be *more* worried," Remy snaps at him as she and Finn jog to catch up.

"Tried it," Cas says. "It didn't agree with me."

"Aren't you worried about your dearly beloved?"

Cas's easy expression sours a little at that, which shouldn't feel like a victory—but it does. "He's not my dearly beloved," Cas says.

"Even so. You're acting like we're out here on some grand adventure instead of on a rescue mission."

"Can't it be both?" Cas reaches for his hair yet again, though the gesture has turned agitated. "Of course I'm worried about Henry. But this *is* an adventure. I can't tell you the last time I got out like this, no maids or chaperones or—"

"This isn't a game!" Remy cuts in. "Some of us have responsibilities back home. I'm not going to give my mother any more reason to worry, not after . . ." She shakes her head. Those early days of waiting for her father, and then not waiting for him anymore, are somehow raw even now. "We're finding Ashworth, and we're helping my father, and that's it."

Cas freezes. At Remy's mention of her father, something terrible flashes across his face—and then, just as quickly, his expression turns to stone. His chin juts out in that stubborn way Remy still recalls from when they were young.

"I'm going to start looking on the other side," Cas says. "We'll find the ship faster if we split up."

He isn't wrong—though it's fairly obvious that this new plan is really an excuse for him to storm off. As Finn watches him stalk away between the warehouses that divide the wharf, her eyes narrow.

"What was *that* about?" Finn asks.

"No idea," Remy lies, and they continue along the row of ships.

Finn lets it rest for only a moment. "That may work on some people, but not on me. I can tell when you're turning cagey."

"I'm not cagey," Remy says.

Finn snorts. At the dock up ahead of them, a pair of familiar figures stands guard at one of the gangplanks: the sailor with the rifle and her companion. Even from here, Remy can make out the sharp lines of the sailor's jacket.

"Hmm," Finn says. "We can skip that next dock. Best not start another fight."

"It wasn't me who started the fight."

"Even so."

Remy hesitates, though. The ship the sailors are stationed beside looks like a brig, or at least something in the brig family. As she and Finn draw nearer, Remy tugs her hat lower and scans the ship for the name—just to be thorough. Just in case it's the *Leonidas*.

But her eyes snag not on the nameplate at the stern but on the figurehead at the ship's bow. It wears a long, hooded cloak, painted all black and carved so expertly that it looks almost like real fabric billowing in the wind instead of something made from wood. A pale, gaunt face peers out from under the hood, its eyes dark holes.

Remy's stomach twists over. Not gaunt—skeletal. The figurehead's face is a skull.

Then she sees the symbol carved into the figurehead's chest.

"Finn," Remy says.

"I've not forgotten, you know," Finn is saying, unaware that Remy has stopped following her. "I know you're hoping to change the subject, but—"

"*Finn*. Look."

Finn stops, then sighs, then returns to Remy's side. Finn looks. Her breath catches.

"Oh," Finn says. "That's . . ."

Yes, it is.

The symbol from Remy's father's journal—the strange hourglass shape that Remy has spent eight years trying, and failing, to identify—is etched into the paint of the skeletal figurehead's cloak, just over where its heart would be.

"We need to find out everything we can about that ship," Remy says.

"Do we?"

Remy turns to stare at her, incredulous. Finn stares back. Finn knows better than anyone else how long Remy has been hunting for this. Now Remy has caught the scent at last—has finally, *finally* found a lead—and Finn thinks there's any choice at all but to follow it?

"I'm not saying it isn't strange," Finn says. "It's very strange. But is this really our priority right now? Or are you just trying to distract yourself from whatever else is going on by diving into research like you always do?"

Remy's protest is automatic: "I don't do that."

"You do it constantly."

"Well, I'm not doing it now. This isn't a distraction. This feels relevant. It feels like . . . Well, in a matter of days, we're going to be in Eden. *At* the seminary. Shouldn't we be arming ourselves with all the information we can get before then?"

Finn's skepticism is written plainly on her face, but she doesn't say anything. Remy thinks. She can feel the scraps of a plan stitching themselves together. She needs a way to access the ship's registration records without risking another brush with those sailors. The tall sailor's accusation is still fresh in her mind.

"Have you seen where the dockmaster went?" Remy asks. "The lanky one. He had a ledger with him. I'm guessing it might have notes on the vessels that are docked here."

One of Finn's eyebrows arches. "And *I'm* guessing that he's not going to give you a peek, if that's what you're thinking."

"I was actually thinking that we might borrow it from him."

Finn's other eyebrow arches now, too. It's a sharp expression for her already sharp face—one that's meant to force a retreat. But Remy has received this look too many times before to be affected.

"We'll give it back," Remy assures her. "I only need it for a few minutes, and then we can leave it somewhere he'll find it again."

"You keep saying *we*, but I don't think you mean *we*," Finn says.

"You can do it, can't you?"

She's seen Finn put this particular skill to use. That is, she hasn't seen it, which is rather the point. Last year, Louisa Springer had made a snide comment about the shabbiness of

Remy's bonnet, just loudly enough to ensure she'd be overheard as Finn and Remy passed her on the street. Finn had brushed up against Louisa as she walked by, then waited until they'd rounded the corner before presenting Remy with her prize: the velvet ribbon from Louisa's own hat. Even in replaying it afterward, Remy couldn't spot the moment when the theft had occurred.

Cas is no pickpocket—but Finn is. Finn can move like a ghost when she wants to.

It's clear she doesn't particularly want to now. But she studies Remy, considering.

At last, she says, "I'll need something to swap it with."

Which is as much of a concession as Remy is going to get. She tries not to grin as she opens her carpetbag. She's brought a few books that might suffice. Her research journal is too important to risk, of course, but she's had a vague plan to catch up on some reading once aboard the *Leonidas*, and she's packed accordingly: an occult text in French that she's been painstakingly translating, and a tattered French-English dictionary, and the *Grimoirium Verum*.

Finn stares at the spread, aghast. "You've been carrying these around this whole time?"

"The dictionary will work, won't it?" Remy says, testing the weight of it in her hand. "It's even about the right color."

"You're absurd, you know," Finn tells her, but she accepts the dictionary. "The dockmaster's to your left—No, don't look. You go ask him for directions, and try not to be dodgy about it. We'll regroup behind those barrels. No, *stop looking*. Jesus, Mary, and Joseph."

Remy has no idea whether she's being dodgy or not as she asks the dockmaster how to find one of the other wharves she remembers from her map-studying. He seems exasperated as he explains the route. Remy sees Finn pass behind him as they talk—and yet she still can't be certain that Finn has pulled it off until a few minutes later, when she and Finn are nestled together out of sight among the barrels as planned. There, Finn presses the small ledger into Remy's hands.

"You're a miracle worker," Remy tells her.

"Hardly," Finn says, though she looks pleased. Remy flips open the book to the most recent entries.

The ledger does indeed contain information about each ship that's berthed here, though the listings are disappointingly brief: the vessel's name and port of origin, its owner, its next destination, and an inventory of its cargo and supplies. Remy skims a finger along the entries until she finds the berth number for the ship with the skeletal figurehead.

The ship is a brigantine, according to its records. The name is in Latin; Remy could probably scrounge up a translation, but it doesn't seem important just now. The cargo on the registration is all perfectly innocuous: flour, tea, spun wool. The ship arrived from Provincetown, Massachusetts, two days ago and will be departing tomorrow morning for Bangor, Maine. The owner is listed as a Mr. Edward Hobbes.

Remy runs through the list in her father's journal of known members of the Order of Lazarus. There's no Edward Hobbes among them. It could be an alias, of course. But it isn't much of a lead.

"What exactly are you hoping to find?" Finn asks, leaning in so she can read the ledger over Remy's shoulder.

Remy isn't certain what she'd been hoping for. But she's certain she hasn't found it.

Still, the thought occurs to her: Bangor, Maine, isn't terribly far from Eden. She examines the Latin of the vessel's name again, trying to recall the meaning. Finn must be studying the same; she reads it aloud, almost to herself, though they're so close together that her breath tickles Remy's ear as she does.

"The *Memento Mori*," Finn whispers. A pause, and then she says, "We should find Cas. I have a bad feeling about all of this."

Cas finds them first. Remy hasn't even chosen a suitable location to leave the dockmaster's ledger before Cas has spotted them and set off running toward them across the wharf, his jaw set. Without a word, without stopping to catch his breath, he grabs both of them by their arms and starts hauling them back toward a narrow space between two of the warehouses.

"What are you doing?" Remy says, ignoring Cas's attempts to shush her. "Get off me."

He releases her sleeve, but he doesn't stop moving until he's shooed both her and Finn into the gap, out of sight of the crowds.

"The good news is I found the *Leonidas*," he says without preamble.

Remy's dread spikes to a piercing pitch. She doesn't want to ask. She asks anyway. "And the bad news?"

"Pastor Dekker is on board."

The gap between the warehouses isn't nearly wide enough for pacing. Cas manages to do it anyway. Three short strides, a turn, then three strides back again, bouncing between the granite walls like a marble in a gutter.

"How?" he says as he turns again, so fiercely that Remy half expects to see a scuff mark on the cobblestones. "How did Dekker find us? Did he follow us?"

"I don't know," Remy says.

"Or did my mother send him after us? God, it's like he manages to be everywhere at once. He's probably listening to us even now."

His pacing is making Remy dizzy; she closes her eyes. "Why would your mother send him after us? Doesn't she think you're in Lynn?"

"Yes, but—I don't know." A scrape of boot against rock as he pivots yet again. "He's always doing my mother's dirty work, isn't he? Anytime she doesn't like something, suddenly Dekker's declaring it a terrible sin and agreeing with her that I'm going to hell."

"Jesus," Finn murmurs.

"We don't even know if he's here for us," Remy says. She leans her forehead against the cool granite wall, eyes still closed, trying to think. "He could be sailing to Eden for some other reason. Maybe he's going to check up on Ashworth."

Judging by Cas's furious footsteps, Remy doesn't think he's much comforted by this.

"Did he see you?" Remy asks.

"No," Cas says. "I don't think so. I bolted as soon as I spotted him. Where were you two, anyway? I couldn't find you."

"We were . . . It doesn't matter."

"It does, though. It really does. Because Dekker's here, and our whole plan's gone to hell, and—"

"It hasn't gone to hell," Remy cuts in. "We just need to make a few adjustments."

When she opens her eyes, Cas has stopped pacing at last, though he's so worked up that it seems he could start again at any moment. Remy takes a long breath.

"I found a note that the Order's leader had sent to another member," she tells him. "It instructed him to be ready to travel. Dekker might have received the same message. But even if he's heading to Eden—that doesn't mean he knows *we* are, too. So it doesn't change our plan."

Cas gapes at her. "I am absolutely not sailing on the *Leonidas* with Dekker."

"No, you're right," Remy says. "That part of the plan *has* changed."

Finn's eyes have narrowed again, and not for the first time, Remy wishes that Finn weren't quite so good at reading her.

"I know what you're thinking," Finn says. She does not sound pleased about what Remy is thinking.

"The log said it's sailing for Bangor tomorrow," Remy says. "That's close to Eden. It's practically next door." An exaggeration—the distance between must be nearly forty miles, *and* Eden is on an island, which could make the travel more complicated. But Remy has been poring over maps for the past three days, and the other two haven't. Neither of them questions her.

"That's not really what this is about, though, is it?" Finn says. "You just want to investigate that symbol."

"Symbol?" Cas says. "What symbol?"

Remy ignores him. "Is it so awful if I do? We'd be sailing in the right direction, at least. Maybe we can get some answers along the way."

"Will one of you *please* tell me what's going on?" Cas says.

Remy digs out her research journal and shows Cas the page. As she fills him in about the symbol, the ship they saw, and the symbol *on* the ship they saw, Finn moves to the end of the alley and peers back out across the wharf. Her shoulders are hunched inside her coat.

"I can't believe you two picked a dockmaster's pockets," Cas says when Remy has finished. "And without me! What if you'd been arrested?"

"Would you rather get arrested *with* us?" Remy asks.

"Well, no, but I'd also rather not have to spring you both from jail by myself. So maybe yes. This mystery symbol," he says, eyes fixed on the journal page. "We're assuming it's connected with your secret order, right?"

"It's not *my* order," Remy snaps.

"Right, I know. I just mean . . . This symbol is tied to the Order of Lazarus. And this symbol is on that ship. You do realize that probably means the ship is *with* the Order of Lazarus?"

"I put together that possibility, yes."

"So your plan is for us to set sail with the very same people who took Henry?"

"Not the very same people," Remy says. "It's not as if it's the same crew. If you don't want to come, though—"

"I'm coming," Cas says. "Obviously I'm coming. I just want to be clear about what we're getting ourselves into."

Remy hadn't expected the relief to hit her so hard. But she also hadn't expected Cas to agree to all this. He's right that the plan is risky. It's dangerous. It could very well get them all killed.

But it could also get Remy closer to finding her father than she's ever been before. She's put off this journey for so long—but now that they've begun, she's not ready to give up on it just yet.

Both she and Cas look to Finn, whose back is still toward them as she watches the skeletal brigantine and the two sailors stationed at its gangplank.

"Fine," Finn says.

Remy had been bracing for an argument, and the lack of one leaves her stumbling to catch her balance. "You'll do it?"

"Yes," Finn says. "Fine. I don't see what other options we have. But there's another problem that I'm not sure you've thought through. We don't know if that ship is taking on passengers. And even if they are, I feel fairly confident that they won't be willing to take *us* on."

"Why wouldn't they?" Cas asks. "I still have the money we were going to pay Captain Barnes."

Finn scowls at him. "Money doesn't solve everything, you know."

"No, but it solves a lot of things."

"Not this." Finn turns back toward the ship, arms folded. "The issue here is that the sailors we'd need to convince think we're pickpockets."

"Oh," Cas says. He joins her at the mouth of the alley and follows her gaze. "*Ohhh*. That's ... unfortunate."

"Maybe we don't need to go through them," Remy says.

Cas raises an eyebrow. "You think we can ask someone else on their crew?"

"Maybe we shouldn't *ask* at all."

Remy silently counts to five in her head as they both put together her meaning. Finn gets there first. "You want to stow away."

X

FINN

It's possible that Finn doesn't know Remy DeWindt at all. Who is this wild imposter who suggests stealing from a dock official, and sailing two hundred miles on a ship with dubious associations, and then wants to *sneak aboard* said ship? Remy follows the rules. She *loves* rules. Hell, she made Finn go back and pay for the beans she'd knocked on Mrs. Sanderson's floor.

But perhaps, in the absence of the social pressures back home, this *is* the real Remy. Perhaps that rule-abiding girl has been the imposter all along. Finn thinks of the dogged way Remy approaches her research, the forged letters and half-truths she's used to get information, the light in her eyes when she makes a new discovery. That same light is shining in her eyes now. For years, only Finn has gotten to see this side of Remy—and now this side of her is stepping out into the wider world.

Finn isn't quite sure how to feel about that.

"We've already got our bags with us," Remy is saying. "We can slip aboard tonight, while it's still dark. The ship is scheduled to leave tomorrow—it'll probably sail out with the morning tide, same as the *Leonidas*. We'll be on our way to Maine all the same, and we just might overhear something useful on the journey."

"Yes," Cas says. "Absolutely, yes. Let's go sneak onto a boat." He squints out at their target. "Ship. Brig. Whatever it is."

"A brigantine, technically," Finn tells him.

"A w*hat*?"

"The lowest sail on the mainmast, it . . ." She shakes her head. "Never mind. Doesn't matter."

She turns her focus again to the two sailors stationed at the brigantine's gangplank. They're standing very close to each other, heads dipped low as they talk, huddling together against the harbor wind. Finn feels the same prickle of recognition she'd felt when they'd first run into these sailors on the dock earlier. She hadn't been able to place it right away, but it's been gnawing at her—the gentleness with which the sailor's companion had taken her by the arm. The way her anger had softened at the touch. Even now, as Finn watches, the woman with the rifle brushes invisible grime from the sleeve of her companion's jacket and then lets her hand linger there a moment too long, fingers trailing down the other woman's arm.

Good lord.

Something warm flickers in Finn's stomach, quickly followed by irritation. She understands the urge—sweet Mary, does she understand it—but would it kill them to be a little more subtle? Or to look a little less pleased with themselves? Finn has wooed, and been wooed by, enough lasses around Windover to recognize a pair of fellow deviants. If her instincts are right about this, Remy's plan to sail on this particular ship is either a brilliant idea or a terrible one.

Probably it's both.

Remy and Cas are bickering again, debating their strategy for getting aboard.

"Do we just cross our fingers and run up the gangplank?" Cas asks.

"Really? That's your plan?" Remy's voice is scathing. "We'll need a diversion, at the very least."

"Right. And once they're distracted, *then* we cross our fingers and run up the gangplank."

But as Finn scans the wharf around them, she finds herself scraping together the pieces. A group of dockworkers has crowded around a makeshift table nearby, playing some sort of card game. A few men on the edge of the throng are smoking pipes. A little farther up the wharf, outside one of the warehouse's doors, a pile of lumber waits to be loaded onto a barge. The wood will be bone-dry; it's been stored far from the water's edge, and there hasn't been rain in weeks.

Finn pushes her carpetbag into Cas's arms, and he's surprised enough that he accepts it.

"Go wait near the gangplank, but don't draw attention to yourselves," Finn tells both him and Remy. "Do you see that hatch in the middle of the deck? It should lead down to the hold. Once the crew's all looking this way, make for the opening. I'll be right behind you."

Remy grabs her by the elbow. "What are you doing?"

"Making a distraction."

"Not alone, you aren't."

"That's the whole point, isn't it?" Finn says. "I'll give you time to get aboard."

"What about you, though?"

"I'll be quick."

Remy still hasn't let go of her arm. "Tell me what you're planning, and I'll do it instead."

"I'm better at sneaking about," Finn tells her, shaking her sleeve loose. "It's the first thing they teach you at maid school. Just be ready."

As she takes off toward the group of card players, she can hear Remy swearing and Cas muttering, "Did she really go to maid school? Is that a real thing?"

Finn begs a spare match off one of the pipe smokers with surprising ease; perhaps he's feeling generous, or perhaps he's trying to focus on the game and simply wants to be rid of her. She cradles the match in her palm and takes her place beside the pile of lumber, crouching in the shadows. Across the wharf, Remy and Cas have left their shelter between the warehouses and are now loitering about a dozen yards away from the sailors at their gangplank. Good—Remy is going along with the plan, even if she isn't happy about it. Finn can deal with that later.

She strikes the match against one of the logs.

That is, she *tries* to strike it. The match doesn't even spark. She tries again. Nothing. Cheap, unreliable piece of rubbish—no wonder the man had offered her one so willingly. His matches are garbage.

Finn considers. She could go ask the man for another. She could borrow a lantern. She could try to light a stick from one of the streetlamps and bring it back here. But tonight has been so full of surprises: the two women leaning so close together on the dock; the gleam in Remy's eyes; Cas's contagious excitement; the thrill of what they're doing, and what they're about to do.

And something deep inside Finn flickers—a fire she hasn't let herself feel in a long time.

She closes her eyes.

It's been years since she last tried to do this. Even more years since she learned *how* to do it. For a moment, as she digs into that deep, yawning place inside her, she thinks she'd been mistaken—that the fire there is gone, sputtered out, left too long without air.

She pushes deeper, though, and she finds it, burning strong as ever. She reaches for it, stinging and hot and alive.

When she opens her eyes, the match is burning steadily in her hand.

From there, it's a simple thing: Toss the match into the pile of lumber. Wait just long enough to make sure it catches. Get the hell out. Finn is halfway across the wharf before she hears the shouts behind her, the cries of alarm as the bystanders realize and try to douse the flames. When she glances back, the whole pile is ablaze. Even with the wood's dryness, it shouldn't have gone up that quickly; perhaps Finn egged it on more than she'd meant to.

Perhaps she ought to feel worse about that fact than she does. She adds *destruction of property* to the list of sins in her mind. She's spent so many years going through the motions, moving through her life in a fog—but in this moment, her head feels shockingly clear.

The silhouettes aboard the brigantine have all gathered at the bow to watch the commotion; the two sailors have abandoned their post. The figurehead's skeletal smile has a hellish gleam in the dancing firelight. When Finn looks to the hatch in the center of the ship's deck, she can just see the top of Remy's tarpaulin hat as it disappears below.

Finn darts across the gangplank and through the hatch herself.

The lower deck is empty, thank goodness. Finn follows the ladder down another level to the cargo hold, which is nearly pitch-black. A few shreds of lantern light slip between the boards from the cabins above.

A hand clamps around her wrist.

But it's only Remy, bent over double to account for the low ceiling and gesturing wordlessly at her. Finn follows her toward the stern, squeezing between the crates and supplies stockpiled here.

"I can't believe you did that," Remy whispers at her through the dark.

"It worked, didn't it?"

"It was incredibly risky. And rash."

"More rash than picking a dockmaster's pockets?"

There's a pause, and then Remy says, "I shouldn't have asked you to do that."

This isn't her usual fretting, Finn realizes; there's an edge of panic to her words. Finn had worried her badly by running off on her own.

"It was fine," Finn tells her. "We're fine."

The hunched shape of Cas emerges ahead of them, waving them over to the back of the hull.

"I think this is a smuggling ship," he whispers. "Look." He's crouched beside what appears to be a solid wall, but when he digs his fingernails into a crack between the wooden planks, a panel dislodges. The darkness through the gap there seems to grow even darker. "Hidden compartment, see? I was trying to figure out why this space felt so much smaller than it had looked from the outside—why the hold wouldn't run the full length of the ship. And it turns out it does."

Finn hadn't even noticed the discrepancy in the hold's size; she doubts a customs agent would catch it, either. She and Remy both stare at him, and they must do it for too long, because Cas scrubs a hand over the back of his neck, suddenly flustered. It's a gesture that reminds Finn of Kieran. She makes a mental note not to underestimate Cas Sterling.

They pile themselves into a secluded corner of the hold, wedged together behind a line of barrels. Finn doesn't much mind the cramped conditions—not when she's pressed against Remy's side from shoulder to ankle, their breathing gradually evening out and coming into alignment as they settle. Remy rests her head on Finn's shoulder. They're all quiet. Eventually, Remy's breathing slows as she falls asleep.

Perhaps Finn is forgiven, then. Her earlier reasoning as to why *she* ought to be the one to cause the distraction—that she's the stealthiest, that she'd have the best luck on her own—is a better excuse than the real one, anyway. The real reason is this: Of the three of them, Finn knows she's the most expendable. The least needed. If she'd got caught, Remy and Cas would still have been able to make their way to Eden without her. They'd be perfectly fine on their own.

And besides, Finn has the least to lose. She always does.

Finn tries to sleep, but she's awake for hours. Over and over, she sees the skeletal figurehead flickering in the firelight.

Over and over, she feels the same skip of her heart that she'd felt when she read the brigantine's name written on the ledger page: the *Memento Mori*. The meaning of it sinks into her bones.

Remember that you must die.

Finn must drift off at some point, because she wakes from a deep, restful slumber to find the brigantine pitching in the open sea. The calm of the harbor feels far behind them. It's likely morning, though the hold is dim as ever. Footsteps stomp on the deck above. Remy is nowhere in sight; Finn tries not to miss the weight of her head on her shoulder.

A pair of eyes appears in the darkness beside Finn's hand, and she jumps. But the eyes are attached to a small black cat.

The cat blinks up at her.

Finn blinks back.

The cat mewls and nuzzles its cheek against her fingers. Finn gives in and scratches the soft fur of its face, rubbing its ears with her thumb. There are patches of white on the cat's stomach and paws, but otherwise its fur is all black, and its glowing green eyes seem to peer out from the center of a pit.

"Where did you come from?" Finn murmurs. She hadn't really meant to say it aloud, but her words bring Remy peering around the barrels. Or maybe it's the cat's purring that Remy hears—it's much louder than Finn would have expected from such a small body.

"You're up," Remy says. "Good. It should be safe for us to move about now—they won't hear us with the racket they're making up on deck. I've found the crew's provisions, I think. Careful with that thing—it might have fleas."

"She doesn't have fleas," Finn says, examining the cat, who's now crawled onto her lap. "Probably."

"Is it a spy?" Cas asks. He's hunched in the opposite corner, clutching a bucket and looking slightly green. "Is it going to report back to the crew that there's stowaways?"

"She's not a spy," Finn says.

"Sure," Cas says. "Fine. But if it *does* turn out to be a spy, I'm blaming you."

Finn gives the cat one last pat, then nudges her off so she can help Remy look through the supplies.

The hold is stuffy and dim, a burrow of crates and barrels all lashed down under nets. Finn and Remy find a cask of fresh water among the crew's stores and crack it open. They've both been blessedly unaffected by the ship's rocking so far; Cas, meanwhile, has already brought up his supper from last night and everything he's tried to eat since. He stays glued to his bucket while his stomach makes its protests known—though the bucket is a sorry solution when there's nowhere in these cramped quarters to empty its contents afterward.

In the stolen shreds of daylight that have made their way below, Finn and Remy return to the false panel and investigate the hidden cargo hold Cas had found during the night. The brigantine, they discover, is smuggling spirits: barrel after barrel of strong whiskey, oaky and sharp enough to burn the mouth. Remy protests as Finn uncorks one of the barrels—"It's not even noon!"—but she accepts a dented cup of the stuff anyway. It's nice, Finn thinks, as she watches Remy relax. She likes getting to see Remy come loose like this. It's such a rare thing; for as long as Finn has known her, Remy has always prioritized her responsibilities to her family, cramming in her own wants and needs only around the very edges.

Recreation suits her, though. They've stumbled onto a rare kind of abandon here: lounging in the hold, sipping on undeclared liquor, laughing and then catching themselves and muffling their voices as best they can. It's all so much like those nights she and Remy have spent in the woods, when Finn forgets about everything else—no worries about Kieran, no list of sins in her mind. The whole world narrows to just the two of them. Those nights with Remy at Dungeon Rock are the closest thing to divinity that Finn has known in a very long time.

They stay in the hidden compartment well into the afternoon. When their empty stomachs start to complain, Remy crawls out and retrieves handfuls of salted fish from the crew's stockpiles. She has to crouch to climb back through the opening. Her sailors' trousers hug around her legs.

These new clothes suit her, too, Finn thinks absently, then realizes she's ogling her friend's backside. She adds another sin to the list, face burning.

"Cas is asleep," Remy says as she settles into place at Finn's side.

"Probably for the best," Finn says.

"Mm. Probably."

"How are you feeling?" Finn asks, taking her share of the food.

"Finding my sea legs well enough." Remy looks at the whiskey barrel beside them and laughs. "With no help from you, I might add."

"You took very little prodding," Finn tells her.

The cat is pacing from Remy to Finn, whining for scraps. Finn tears off a nibble of fish and offers it to her. The cat eats it from her palm.

"So how exactly are you planning to eavesdrop on the crew from here?" Finn asks.

Remy's lips purse. "I'm working on that."

"At least you've brought plenty of reading for the meantime."

"I know you're poking fun, but I stand by it. When else am I going to find this much uninterrupted time for studying?"

"You could try asking for it," Finn says. "For more time."

Remy scoffs. She and Finn have had versions of this conversation before. Finn usually stays out of Remy's family affairs; she knows she can't fully understand. After all, her own family consists of only herself and Kieran. But she's goaded by the whiskey, or by the sight of Remy so carefree for once. She pushes on.

"Your sisters aren't so much younger," Finn says. "They're older than you were when you took over the finances, aren't they? And your mother seems to be improving. Are you so sure that all of these responsibilities have to keep falling on you alone?"

"That's not . . ." Remy shakes her head. The carefree look is gone. Perhaps Finn shouldn't have brought this up after all. "It won't be forever," Remy says. "Only until my father is back. And that's what we're working toward now, right?"

"I suppose." Not for the first time, Finn wonders what Remy is hoping to find in Eden. It's one thing to rescue Henry Ashworth. It's quite another to try to take down the Order of Lazarus. "So we're helping your father and helping Cas at the same time?"

Remy considers this. "I suppose," she echoes.

"What happened between the two of you back then? Between you and Cas."

Finn is half-afraid to pose the question—not because she worries that Remy won't answer, but because she worries Remy *will*. Finn isn't sure how much of this history she truly wants to know. For all these years, she's convinced herself that she knows Remy better than anyone else—but Finn doesn't know everything. Perhaps she never will. There are parts of Remy's life from before that Remy still keeps at a remove.

Remy is gnawing on a piece of fish now, her brow furrowed. "We just grew apart."

"I know there's more to it than that."

For a long moment, the only sound is the waves crashing against the ship around them.

"He . . ." Remy starts, then falters—pausing either on whatever's about to follow or simply on the new pronoun. Finn doesn't understand, exactly, the enthusiasm with which Cas has embraced their new identities, but she's been following his and Remy's leads. "He told me he'd had a dream. Or a . . . premonition, I suppose. About my father."

"Oh." Finn hears Cas's voice from that night at Dungeon Rock: *Visions of things that haven't happened. Of . . . deaths.* She's afraid to ask. She has to ask. "What did he see? In the premonition?"

"It was after my father left, but before the journal arrived. Cas told me . . . Well, he claimed that he'd seen my father dying. Horribly."

Finn closes her eyes. A loose nail is protruding from the planks in the hull behind her; she shifts against it, lets the sharpness jab into her back. "You don't believe him, though," she guesses.

"Of course not. Would you?" Then Remy seems to remember who she's speaking with. "Oh right. You absolutely would."

"Don't do that," Finn says, and Remy sighs.

"Sorry—you're right. I'm sorry. It's not even that I think he was lying, exactly. I believe him that he had a dream about my father. I mean, we were both so worried—it makes sense that his sleeping mind would . . ." She waves a hand in place of a conclusion.

"But you think it was just a dream," Finn says.

"You've seen what Cas is like. He's impulsive. Likes to jump to conclusions. He doesn't think things through." Remy snorts. "And now just imagine him when we were ten."

"Taking your father out of it, though. Setting aside what Cas told you back then. Is the rest of it so impossible? Do you believe him, that he's had other visions of deaths before they happen?"

"I think *he* believes it," Remy says.

"That's not what I asked."

Remy looks at her in the dim light, and Finn looks back, and suddenly the stoic, composed face that Remy wears is completely gone. Underneath, there's only fear—a fear that she's been carrying all this time, that she keeps buried. When she speaks, it's barely a whisper.

"I can't," Remy says.

Finn isn't sure which one she means: that Remy can't believe Cas's visions—or that she can't do what Finn had suggested, can't remove Cas's claims about her father from the larger question like that. Perhaps she means both. Perhaps they're the same thing.

For the first time, Finn understands why Remy has remained a skeptic about all the mystical, magical things she's spent the last eight years studying. If Remy opens that door, even just a crack, she can't control what comes through. Believing anything from her father's books is too close to believing in prophetic visions, which is too close to believing that Cas's visions might be real.

And if Cas's visions are real, that means Remy's father is dead. That he's been dead for years.

Finn remembers those awful days after her own parents' deaths, when it still didn't feel true. Even with all the impossible things Finn *does* believe, she can't fault Remy for her need to ignore. To discredit. Something fierce and protective has roared to life inside Finn's chest, desperate to guard her friend from this thing that might break her.

They've been quiet for too long. "Well, like you said," Finn says finally. "It was probably just a dream he had."

"Right," Remy says.

Something creaks out in the main hold. *Cas*, Finn thinks, her heart sinking—he must have reawakened. He must have come looking for them just in time to overhear the worst possible part of this conversation.

But they wait, and Cas doesn't appear in the compartment's opening. There's another creak. Then the sound of footsteps. Someone is climbing down the ladder.

The cat has perked up in Finn's lap, ears pricked toward the sound. After a moment, she leaps through the opening and darts off into the darkness toward the noise. Finn feels a sudden warmth—Remy has reached over to grip her hand. They stare at each other in the dim light, eyes wide and waiting.

The footsteps are coming closer. Now Finn *hopes* it's Cas—even if he's overheard Remy and Finn talking about him, that's a manageable problem. They'll manage it. Finn really, truly hopes it's Cas.

A face ducks through the opening. It isn't Cas.

"Just as I thought," a tall woman says in a soft British accent. She extends a brown-skinned hand to them, calloused palm up. "Come on, get out of there. Your other friend, too. We're going to the captain."

XI

CAS

Cas *knew* the cat was a spy.

"I suspected we had company," the sailor who's found them is saying as the small black cat winds around her ankles. "This little stinker can't go an hour without getting attention, yet no one had seen her all day. No one besides you lot, I suppose. Come on—upstairs. All three of you."

Cas's half-awake mind is still scrambling to catch up. They've been found out—that's the gist of it. They're on a strange ship that's far out to sea by now, and this captain they're about to meet might very well be part of the Order of Lazarus, and none of them is in any condition for a fight. Cas is still stumbling every time the ship pitches, and Remy and Finn both stink of whiskey for some reason. As the sailor leads them up the ladder and into the main belly of the ship, all three of them follow her without protest.

The ceiling here is a little higher, at least; Cas can stand upright, though it's a near thing. The sailor has to duck her head. She nudges them down a narrow passageway, through a narrow dining area, and into a narrow office of sorts, where a desk fills most of the tiny room. A dark-skinned man in a silk waistcoat is leaning over it, studying a chart.

"Ah, Mita," he says. "I've been thinking that—"

Then he catches sight of Cas, Remy, and Finn clustered in the doorway with her. He frowns. No one has to inform Cas that this man is the captain; he radiates a quiet kind of authority, even caught off his guard, even with his shirtsleeves rolled to his elbows. If Cas is honest, he hadn't expected the captain of the ship to be a Black man—and yet the past twenty-four hours have already laid bare what a small sliver of the world Cas has seen before now. He decides to adjust his expectations accordingly.

"Stowaways," the sailor, Mita, is saying. "I found them down in the hold."

"I see."

With dragging deliberation, the captain rolls down his sleeves, refastens the cuffs, and then retrieves an elegant wool coat from the back of a chair. His dark hair is laced with gray and twisted into long, tight coils that he's tied back with a piece of cord. When he pulls on the coat, it's perfectly tailored.

The silence stretches. Then it stretches some more.

"Well?" Cas says.

The captain raises an eyebrow at him. He still doesn't speak. Patience has never been Cas's strongest suit, and the quiet is crawling over him like an itch he can't scratch. Or maybe it's the intensity of the captain's gaze—he studies them all as if he's flipping through their pages, reading them as easily as he might read any of the books on the shelves behind them. The bookcases must be built into the walls, each shelf fronted with glass-paned doors to keep the contents in place. They're stuffed full, though the glass is too cloudy for Cas to make out the titles.

Cas forces himself to stay quiet for another count of ten before he blurts out, "Are you going to throw us overboard?"

The captain's eyebrow arches a little higher. "Would you like us to throw you overboard?"

This feels like a trick question. "No," Cas says.

"I'll take that into consideration, then. How long have you been aboard my ship?"

The captain has a slow, measured way of speaking, the sort of voice that might politely ask a mountain if it would move aside, please, and might very well have that mountain comply. But none of them answers right away. Finn is standing with her arms crossed, scowling at the captain as if in challenge. Remy's expression is more guarded. At her side, her fingertips are pressing one by one against her thumb, slowly, as if she's counting up a sum.

Cas waits for her to take the lead, to fix this somehow, but she doesn't. She just keeps pressing her fingers together.

"We only boarded last night," Cas says finally. "In Boston."

"I see. And *why* did you sneak aboard my ship in Boston?"

"We're . . ." Cas realizes too late that he has no good response for this, and he pauses for an agonizing moment while his mind forgets every word it's ever learned. "Traveling."

"That," the captain says, "doesn't answer my question."

Remy seems to shake herself. "We're trying to make our way north," she says. "To Maine. But our original travel plans fell through, and we panicked. I had seen that your ship was headed for Bangor, and—"

"And so you thought you could use us for free passage?"

"We can pay you," Cas says quickly. "For the passage."

From behind, Finn kicks his leg. From in front, the captain's eyes narrow a little.

"You do have money, then," the captain says. "And yet rather than use it to buy tickets on an actual passenger ship, you chose to stow away on this one."

"We're so sorry," Remy says. "It was a foolish idea. I can see that now."

The captain studies her. "How old are you all?"

"Eighteen," Remy says. Cas isn't quite—his birthday isn't until next month—but he doesn't correct her. Remy pushes on. "We really are sorry for the trouble. We'll do whatever we can to make it right."

The captain and the sailor, Mita, seem to be having an unspoken conversation. Cas's heart has started to skitter. The stays that are holding his chest flat are too tight, squeezing his lungs. He wriggles a little in place, trying to adjust the bindings.

"It's a strange thing," the captain says. "My crew and I were in Boston looking for someone. Someone I care quite a lot about finding." He pauses for a moment, then says, "My partner. I had thought that our search for him came up with no leads. But instead, we got . . ." He gestures at the three of them.

"We don't know anything about that," Cas says quickly. "We're just . . . traveling. To . . . Maine." Even as he says it, he can hear how suspicious he sounds. Realizing this does not do anything toward making him sound less suspicious.

"To Bangor," the captain says.

"Well, Eden, really," Cas corrects without thinking.

Remy's glare lands on him in an instant—but the damage is already done.

"Eden," the captain echoes. "On Mount Desert Island?"

There's no point denying it. Remy nods.

"That's miles from Bangor," the captain says. "You've certainly planned your route poorly."

There's a new coldness to his tone that Cas didn't expect. It's like dipping a hand into the washbasin on a winter morning and finding the water frozen over. The captain and Mita have resumed their silent conversation. Well, Cas can play that game, too. He finds Remy's gaze and raises his eyebrows at her, trying to send a message of his own: *We can try to fight them, if it comes to that.*

But Remy's eyes widen. *Are you mad?*

"Dozens of vessels sail from Boston every day," the captain is saying. "Hundreds, even. Surely one of them had Eden more directly on its route than our little ship."

"As I said," Remy tells him, "we had made other travel arrangements. They . . . didn't work out."

"Clearly. What business do you have in Eden, anyway?"

"We're visiting a friend there."

Remy delivers this smoothly enough. But the captain's eyes narrow even further.

"Is that so?" He glances at Mita again. "Maybe we *should* toss you overboard. Plenty of ships do when they find stowaways, you know. It saves them on fees and paperwork."

Cas's heart is really running now. "We can cover any fees, too," he blurts out. "If that will help."

Finn kicks Cas's leg again, harder. It wouldn't normally be enough to knock him over, but the deck rolls, and Cas has to grab on to one of the bookcase's doors to keep his balance. He catches Remy's eye again and sends another message: *No, really. I think we can fight them.*

Remy frowns at him. *Absolutely not.*

Cas attempts to nudge his head at their two combatants without letting said combatants see the gesture. *It's three against two.*

And then what? Remy's furrowed brow seems to say. *Even if we beat them, we're still on their ship.*

We'll figure it out. They have to try, anyway. It's better than being tossed into the sea. Remy is unconvinced—Cas knows she's unconvinced.

He does it anyway.

Without warning, Cas flings back the door on the bookcase, seizes the largest book he can find, and hurls it at the captain's head. He doesn't wait to see if it connects. He whirls toward Mita, dodging her hand as she tries to restrain him. Beside him, Remy and Finn have sprung into action, too—thank god. The two of them rush the captain, an artless but enthusiastic monster of eight limbs.

Which leaves Cas to face Mita. He thinks of the handful of fights he's witnessed, the knocks he's seen thrown among the rowdies outside the pub on Windover Common. Cas has never punched anyone before. But he's thought about it plenty of times.

He forms a fist and takes his best swing at Mita's gut.

She catches his fist in midair. Stops the momentum with a single palm. It's like punching a block of wood. In an instant her hand is clamped around his wrist, pinning it neatly to his side. Cas aims a second swing, with his left hand now, but Mita stops it just as easily. Pins his other arm, too. He tries to slam his forehead at her face, thinking he might be able to break her nose, but she slips deftly out of the way and he instead cracks his head into the wall where she'd just been.

Stars explode across his vision. He swears. He staggers—Mita's grip on his arms is probably all that's keeping him upright. His stomach is churning. If he vomits again, he's going to try to aim it at her shoes.

There's a slam of a door from somewhere close by, and then a voice is shouting, "Hey! *Hey!* That's enough!" In an instant, their escape attempt is over.

Two more crew members have burst into the office and restrained Remy and Finn. Even through his jostled senses, Cas recognizes the two sailors from the dock. The angry one with the rifle has shoved Remy face-first against the wall, and her grip seems to tighten as she takes in their group.

"I know you," she says. "You're the thieves from the wharf."

"Thieves?" the captain says. He's leaning on his desk, breathing hard but otherwise unruffled; his head shows no sign of being hit with a flying book. Apparently Cas's aim was off.

"We're not thieves," Remy says.

"They didn't take anything," the other sailor clarifies. "We ran into these boys back in Boston."

She's already released Finn, and now she gestures to her companion. The angry sailor scowls but lets Remy go.

"We're not thieves," Remy says again, shaking out her arms. "And . . ." She hesitates, then pulls off her tarpaulin hat. Her long, dark curls drop around her shoulders. "And we're not really boys, either."

"Well, *they're* not boys," Cas says.

In the second of silence after the words have escaped, Cas waits for the familiar regret of saying something without thinking it through. The regret doesn't come. It wasn't a statement, exactly, but it *was* an implication—and yet it doesn't feel like a lie. He's been reveling in this new self since Boston, this answer to a question he hadn't known he could ask, every moment so warm and right—even as he's known it couldn't last. Because how can it? The future is squeezing in on him, tight as the bindings around his chest, aching and thrilling and terrifying all at once.

Mita has let go of his arms; Cas doesn't know when she released him. He rubs his forehead and ignores Remy and Finn staring at him and reminds himself to breathe. His friends' eyes are still on him, though, picking him apart. *Well*, they're *not boys*. He waits for someone to correct him.

The correction doesn't come, either.

When he finally meets Remy's eyes, there's an understanding there. Cas's chest feels warm—she's backing him on this, then. Cas can do this, *be* this, for a little longer.

The smaller Black woman from the wharf has stepped forward, or as far as can be managed with so many people crammed inside the small office. She sizes up the three of them.

"Got that out of your systems, then?" she says. "Good. Surely we can work this out peacefully. I'm Kit—first mate. This is Striker, our boatswain"—the sailor with the rifle scowls at them—"and Mita, our carpenter. And, of course, Captain Edward Hobbes—captain and owner of the *Memento Mori*."

"It's very good to meet you all," Remy says with perfect poise, as if she's just arrived at a tea party back in Windover. Cas half expects her to curtsy. Once she, Finn, and Cas have introduced themselves, she turns back to the captain. "We really don't know anything about your missing partner. I swear it. I'm sorry that we can't be of more help. We're just trying to get to Maine. I . . ."

A muscle shifts in her jaw. She seems to consider her next words carefully.

"I'm looking for someone as well," she says. "Someone who might be in Eden, or who was there once, anyway. I care quite a lot about finding him, too."

The warm glow in Cas's chest flickers out. *Someone who might be in Eden.* She doesn't mean Henry. Even now, Remy is hoping that she can find her father alive. Cas had thought that they'd reached a kind of understanding when they'd talked back at Dungeon Rock—but Remy still doesn't believe him, does she? It shouldn't sting so badly after all this time.

"We should drop them at the nearest port," the angry sailor, Striker, is telling the captain. "If you're feeling kind. Or drop them here, if you're feeling less kind."

Kit, the first mate, looks appalled. "Striker!"

"What? It's not a bad swim."

"We're not dropping anyone!"

"Captain," Mita cuts in.

Her tone holds something like a petition, and for several seconds the room falls quiet as the captain considers his options.

"They can stay," he says at last.

Striker and Mita both let out huffs of air—Mita's a relieved sigh, Striker's a snort like an angry bull. The captain ignores them both. He turns the full force of that scrutinizing gaze onto Remy, Cas, and Finn.

"You can stay," he says again. "And we'll take you to Eden."

He offers it almost as an afterthought, as if this *isn't* an even better outcome than they could've hoped for. Cas wonders if he's misheard. "Really?"

"You'll pay your way, of course. And we'll be keeping our original route to Bangor first. It won't add much of a delay—a day or so depending on the wind. Once we've delivered our cargo there, we'll continue to Mount Desert Island."

He traces this route on one of the charts on his desk as he speaks. Remy has leaned in close to see. She has to be equally shocked at this turn, though from the outside, Cas would never guess it.

"Thank you," Remy tells the captain when he's finished. "Truly."

Captain Hobbes straightens. "I'm not doing this as a favor. It's business. As it happens, I have cause to go to Eden myself." He glances at his sailors. "Might as well pick up the extra passenger fares for a trip we'd be making either way."

If this explanation is meant to placate Striker, it doesn't work; she's still glaring at the three of them as they discuss payment and Cas hands over the money that had been meant for Captain Barnes. Still, Cas can hardly believe his luck. They're back on their way to Henry, and in the meantime, they'll be sailing with a crew who all believe Cas is a boy. True, that crew might be part of the Order of Lazarus—but the danger of it feels more distant now. The fear and excitement are wrestling inside him, and right now, the excitement is winning.

"Mita will show you to your bunks," the captain says, already turning back to the papers on his desk. "Thank you."

It's a clear dismissal. Cas, Remy, and Finn let themselves be dismissed.

"You'll have to forgive the captain's manner," Mita says as she leads them back from the office and along the lower deck. "He's not always so standoffish. But these last few weeks have been difficult for him."

"Because of his missing partner?" Remy guesses, and Mita nods. "A business partner?"

Mita's mouth quirks. "More like life partner. He and the captain have been together for years—for richer, for poorer, in sickness and in health, till . . ." She breaks off, smile widening as if at some private joke. "It's all very romantic."

"Oh." Remy considers this. Cas waits, ready to clamp a hand over her mouth if she starts to say something awful, but she only offers, "Well. I'm sure the captain is very worried, then."

Mita hums in agreement. "We all are. Here," she says, gesturing them into a low, angled cabin at the very front of the ship. "You three will have the fo'c'sle all to yourselves."

A heavy curtain separates the fo'c'sle from the rest of the crew's quarters, but already Cas can guess why these particular bunks are free despite their relative privacy. The tossing of the waves can be felt everywhere, but it's strongest here at the bow. As they all stow their bags on the narrow bunks built into the walls, Cas's stomach tries to lodge a complaint. He politely tells it to shut up.

Out in the main crew's quarters, Mita is chatting with a few other sailors, who are lounging on more wooden bunks. This sailing crew is nothing like the ones Cas has read about in books; the mix of genders and races alone is far more varied than he's been led to imagine. It's possible the books lied to him.

"I'm sorry about the detour to Bangor," Remy says, her voice low enough that only Cas can hear.

Cas frowns at her. "Sorry?"

"About the delay. Inevitable, but even so. I know you're eager to see Ashworth."

She sounds like she's consoling Cas over a lost pet. "Oh," he says. "It's . . . fine."

It shouldn't be fine, though. Cas's stomach sinks. When the captain had laid out their journey, Cas should have thought of Henry straightaway, because every day longer that it takes to get to Eden is another day of Henry trapped in that place, alone and frightened and in danger. Cas's first emotion should have been concern—not that thrill of excitement at the prospect of staying on board this ship for a little extra time.

Remy was right to chastise him back on the wharf. He's gotten swept up in the adventure of it all, in haircuts and trousers and the zing of rightness in his chest, instead of focusing on Henry. And Cas *is* worried about Henry. Of course he is. Over and over, when he tries to sleep, his mind replays that terrible morning on the beach.

But Cas has never been good at holding in his head things that aren't directly in front of him. And there's so much else in front of him now to focus on—a whole world of revelations he's never even let himself consider before.

When he'd introduced himself as a boy back in the ship's office, none of the crew had questioned him. They hadn't even blinked.

It's too much to process; Cas's nausea is mounting. The ship bounces again, and he clutches at his stomach. One of the boys in a nearby bunk looks up from the book he's reading.

"Still getting your sea legs?" the boy says with a sympathetic wince. He can't be much older than Cas, and he's clean-shaven and wiry, handsome in a quiet sort of way. "It gets easier, I promise. My first time at sea, I spent a whole three days puking my guts out."

An older man in the neighboring bunk pokes his head out with a laugh. "Leo, mate, that's not as comforting as you seem to think it is."

"But I'm not puking my guts out *now*," Leo says. "I haven't puked my guts out in a long while. The vestibular system just needs time to adjust. To find a new equilibrium."

"I think I need fresh air," Cas says, and Leo nods, and Cas hurries up the hatch and onto the main deck so he can puke his guts out over the side of the ship.

The sun is starting to lower over the ocean now. The edges of the clouds glow orange like they've been set aflame. Cas leans on the railing and lets the sea spray hit his cheeks. It helps. It calms his stomach somewhat—though when the nausea has passed, there's nothing to distract him from the restless feeling growing in his chest. Excitement, or guilt, or both. The clouds along the horizon are a dark, violent gray.

It's possible a storm is coming.

After that first vision—after Cas had shared too much of himself and destroyed the only real friendship he'd ever had—it was Henry who had filled the Remy-shaped gap in Cas's life. Henry's sister, Cecilia, had died barely a year before, and suddenly the tiresome boy from Cas's parents' social circles had sprouted a personality. When Cas suggested they play a prank on his mother during one of her tea parties, Henry laughed and agreed immediately. When Cas showed up outside Henry's window with a bottle of stolen wine, Henry snuck out to join him without question.

When Cas drank far too much one night and ended up crying into Henry's shoulder about how his mother was right and Cas was always, always going to be a disappointment, Henry listened and comforted him and assured him that *he*, Henry, did not think Cas was a disappointment.

Cas and Henry have always been alike—both of them the wrong shapes for these roles they're supposed to fit, both of them just trying their best. Even as Henry has given up his rebellious streak, even as he's buried that part of himself in public, it's still there underneath. He and Cas are still a pair. And now the Order of Lazarus has taken Henry, thinking *he's* the one having visions.

God, Cas hopes Henry is all right.

Remy had said that the Order would try to recruit Henry, the same way they'd tried to recruit her father. How long will they keep Henry alive when he refuses—or when the Order realizes they've taken the wrong person? Henry left Windover almost a week ago; he's certainly arrived at the seminary by now. It'll be another three days at least before Cas and the others can reach him. Will they get there in time? Or will the Order have already made him disappear—or done to him what they did to Remy's father?

Still... Mr. DeWindt's murder hadn't been an immediate thing. How many days had passed between DeWindt's disappearance and his death? The circumstances aren't quite the same, and yet there's comfort in the precedent, however loose. Remy's father had been gone at least a week before Cas had that vision of his death. Maybe two weeks. Cas can't remember the date, exactly, and besides, the timings of the visions have never been very precise.

"Leeward side," a voice says from right behind him, and Cas spins to find Finn and Remy joining him at the rail.

"What?" he says.

"You should be on the side that's sheltered from the wind," Finn tells him. "For . . ." She makes an inelegant gesture that evokes the reappearance of a stomach's contents. "Trust me."

"I'm all right now," Cas says.

Remy is gazing out at the horizon as if it's an equation she's trying to solve. Her research journal is tucked in one arm, cradled against her hip like a newborn.

An idea occurs to Cas.

"When was the package postmarked?" he asks suddenly.

Remy blinks at his lack of transition. "Sorry?"

"The one from your father," Cas says. "With his journal. You said it was postmarked in Eden. What date was it sent?"

Remy pauses for so long that Cas thinks she's not going to answer. But then she says, "The seventeenth of June. Why do you ask?"

"And what was the date when he left home?"

An even longer pause this time. Remy's brow has furrowed as she considers him.

"The fifth of June," she says at last.

Twelve days, then. Cas lets himself breathe. The Order had kept Mr. DeWindt alive for a minimum of twelve days. If they follow the same timing for Henry, twelve days will be enough. More than enough. Cas and the others are scheduled to reach Eden on the tenth day since Henry left Windover.

Remy is shaking her head; she must have given up on trying to follow Cas's jumbled thoughts. Instead, she says, "We'll need to be careful these next few days. I don't like how easily the captain agreed to help us."

Cas props his elbows on the railing to look at her. "You'd rather he *didn't* agree?"

"No, of course not, but—what did he mean, that he has his own cause to go to Eden?"

Finn snorts. "I have a guess."

"It certainly sounds like he's on his way to meet with the Order," Remy agrees. "Do you think he's planning to turn us in?"

Cas isn't sure why he feels a need to defend the captain, but he does. "Plenty of people go to Eden without going to the seminary. Maybe he's just making a delivery."

"Sure," Remy says. "A delivery to the seminary."

"You're awfully quick to assume the worst of people."

"And you're awfully quick to trust them," Remy snaps. Cas had thought this was a lighthearted conversation; now he wonders if he'd misjudged the tone. "Why are you asking about the postmark on my father's journal, anyway?"

"No reason," Cas says quickly. Remy is frowning at him. She's not going to let him brush this aside. "I was just . . . thinking about Henry."

Her frown softens. "Oh," she says. She doesn't press him for details. She returns to watching the horizon with that same focused glint in her eye.

Across the deck, Mita is untangling a length of rope, her ink-black hair billowing in the wind. The handsome boy from the crew's quarters, Leo, has come up on deck, too, straightening the brim of his cap to shield his eyes from the sun. Striker calls out to him in a language Cas can't place and throws an arm around his shoulders—it's the first time Cas has seen Striker anything but angry. Leo bats at her good-naturedly. The two of them look like siblings—though Cas can't decide whether he's based that guess on their similar appearances or simply on the comfortable way they have with each other.

This latter piece isn't only Striker and Leo. The whole crew seems to notch together so easily. Cas feels like he's spying through a window into this floating world of theirs, his face pressed to the glass, wishing for ... something.

He knows he needs to keep his guard up. He knows Remy has good reason to be suspicious of these sailors. Still, he finds himself wondering at this strange little ship they've found themselves on, at this strange little crew.

Three days. They'll reach Henry in three days. Cas has to trust that they'll arrive in time; worrying won't get them there any faster. In the meantime, there's no reason why Cas shouldn't enjoy his time at sea—why he shouldn't savor these next three days of being *him*.

Might as well enjoy it while it lasts.

XII
REMY

The storm catches them that night, long before Remy has managed to fall asleep. Sleep has never come easily for her. At least it hasn't for the last eight years. If she slept well before that, she doesn't remember. Her whole life is split into the time before her father left and the time after—and sometimes the time before feels like a dream, a golden era of cheerful family suppers and evenings at the chessboard in her father's study, playing through different strategies over and over until the fire had gone cold. Remy's mother and father had been sickeningly in love; her father was always pressing kisses into his wife's hair or gently tangling their fingers together in passing. Remy used to be embarrassed by these displays. Now, the memory of her parents' easy affection makes her chest ache.

She knows that their lives weren't perfect back then. The money troubles had already started; her father's law practice had never turned the profit that it ought. And her father was boisterous and affectionate and warm, except when he wasn't—when he'd turn quiet and troubled, locking himself in his study for days, muttering alone in the dark. Remy's mother would always say he was ill, though Remy caught the hesitation in her voice as she said it. Once her father had recovered, once he'd returned to his usual self, he never offered any explanation at all.

Tonight, as Remy lies in her bunk on the *Memento Mori*, she tries to quiet her circling mind by focusing on the good memories of that time before. It's a well-worn path she's taught herself to follow, a sort of meditation. Usually, she can use those memories to imagine her father's homecoming, a return to those golden days.

That homecoming is closer than it's ever been before. And yet as Remy tries to walk herself through the imagined scene—her mother's tears, her sisters' excited chatter as their father ducks through the front doorway of their house—it doesn't feel real in the way it usually does. Other pieces keep seeping through. Worries. Misgivings. The note from the Reverend John Smith—the note with her father's name—is tucked between the pages of her journal in her bag, but even that isn't enough to quiet the doubts that the darkness allows to fester.

Remy isn't going to sleep tonight.

She swings her legs out of bed and nearly loses her footing—the ship is pitching badly, much more than it had been that afternoon. Remy's boots have been tossed clear across the cabin, but she manages to find them and pull them on without waking Finn or Cas. She slips past the curtain, past the sleeping sailors in the main crew's quarters, and out into the central area of the ship's lower deck.

Voices are shouting on the main deck above. Remy eyes the ladder, thinking vaguely of climbing up through the hatch to find out what's going on. She has no real plan beyond distraction—maybe Finn was right about her. Maybe Remy *does* throw herself into her research as a way to ignore her worries. She doesn't see what's so wrong with that.

Just as she starts toward the ladder, though, she hears a pair of much quieter voices coming from a door off to the side—the ship's galley. Lantern light flickers through the gap in the doorway, and Remy can just make out the profiles of Striker and Mita talking inside.

". . . still don't see why he agreed to change course," Striker is saying. "Since when do we take on passengers?"

"Well, we have before," Mita tells her. "And he said he was planning to reroute us to Eden anyway, wasn't he?"

"I thought he was bluffing about that."

Mita snorts. "Since when does the captain bluff? Besides, you saw that note from Díaz. That's the closest thing he has to a lead."

Almost without meaning to, Remy has been creeping toward the galley's door until she's poised just outside of it, her ear angled close to hear. It's a vulnerable position, and yet this feels important. It feels like a potential lead of her own.

"Why keep the stowaways, though?" Striker asks. "Is it truly for the money?"

A pause. "I think the captain always has his reasons."

"Just seems like a liability. I don't trust them."

"If it makes you feel better, I don't think the captain does, either."

"Right, so why risk them running around? And we all know he's been a bit . . . off . . . lately, what with—"

Several things happen in very quick succession: From the deck above, a bell begins to clang. From inside the galley, the voices cut short. And then, before Remy can hide, before she can do anything at all, Striker and Mita fling open the door to find Remy braced just outside it—very obviously eavesdropping.

Striker scowls, though her next words are directed not at Remy but at Mita: "What was I just saying?"

Remy scrambles for an excuse. "I didn't mean to—I wasn't—" The bell is still clamoring up on the deck; it's very distracting. She grabs the first idea she can think of. "I felt the waves picking up," she says. "I thought I might see if I could help."

Striker's expression is incredulous as she looks Remy up and down. "You," she says. "Help."

"What does that bell mean?" Remy asks.

"It's a call for all hands," Mita explains, though her face is difficult to read. "They'll need all of us to brace for the storm."

Indeed, the other sailors are emerging from the crew's quarters now, tugging on jackets and boots as they make their way up the ladder. A few of them give Remy questioning looks, but no one stops to ask.

"Right," Remy says, inching back toward the fo'c'sle to make her escape. "I'll just—"

But Striker steps into her path, blocking her. There's something about her that fascinates Remy, even now—the way she plants her feet so surely, the way she squares her shoulders. The way she occupies space. "It's all hands," Striker says simply.

"Striker," Mita murmurs.

"She has hands, doesn't she?"

Mita only shakes her head and starts up the ladder herself. Striker gives a flourishing bow and gestures Remy ahead of her—a clear invitation, or a challenge. She's probably expecting Remy to cower. *Remy* is expecting Remy to cower.

With shaking hands, Remy climbs up through the hatch and onto the main deck.

The rest of the crew is already at work, at least a dozen figures racing fore and aft. Some wrestle with lines, while others dart up into the rigging. Captain Hobbes stands planted in the middle of it all. His long coat billows out behind him. The rain hasn't started in earnest yet, but drops of water spit from the sky and spatter against Remy's cheeks.

Remy tries to make sense of the chaos around her as she follows Striker across the deck. The sailors are in the process of taking in the sails—tying the sheets away so the wind can't catch them, so the pulling storm won't capsize the ship. The captain shouts an order, and a sailor loosens one end of a line while another tightens the opposite side. Another order, and another pair of sailors does the same. One of the square sails high above them curls in on itself.

It's not chaos at all. It's a perfect choreography. Remy wishes she could freeze the scene into a diagram, something she could study in a book. She wants to puzzle out each step of this routine, but it's all moving too quickly for her to follow.

Mita and Striker are standing at the base of the taller of the two masts. A minuscule figure hangs on to the highest crossbeam there, binding up the curled sailcloth. At first, his feet seem to dangle over nothing. Then Remy spies the thin footrope he's balancing on. From the deck, the rope looks nebulous as a spiderweb.

"He'll need more hands for the topsail," Striker is saying—and then she turns to Remy. "You. Greenhand. You're with me."

Remy wonders if she's imagining the catty glint in Striker's eyes. "What, me?" she says.

"Who else would I be looking at? Come on. We're going aloft."

"Striker," Mita warns again, but Striker waves her off.

"She said she wanted to help!"

Another sailor calls Mita's name, and she hurries away. Striker appraises Remy.

"We're going to help Gabe furl the sails," Striker says, voice raised over the wind. "That means pulling them up and tying them into place around their yards—those long beams on the mast that the sails hang from."

"I know what a yard is," Remy says, although she hadn't.

"What's that baffled look for, then?"

Remy tries to scrub the baffled look from her face. "I've just never . . ." She makes a vague gesture to indicate all the things on a ship she's never done before—which is to say, everything. "I don't have any training," she says. "Don't I need training for this?"

Striker shrugs. "It's the sort of thing you learn by doing."

Remy has always hated learning by doing. She prefers learning by *learning*. But Striker is already ushering her toward the web of rigging that stretches from the ship's sides up to the mast. Remy stares up the mast again—and up, and up. She tries to imagine herself climbing this and can't. It feels like make-believe.

In all her planning for their journey to Eden, Remy made no preparation for any scenario in which her feet would have to leave the deck.

She and Striker have reached the base of the rigging now. Striker grabs onto the ladder-like ropes and hauls herself up onto the railing as if she's done this hundreds of times. Because she likely has. Remy's terror must be apparent, and as Striker gazes down at her, her face seems to soften, just a little.

"Here's your training," Striker says. "Always climb up on the windward side. Keep your hands on the shrouds instead of the ratlines. Announce yourself before you lay on the footrope. And keep one arm on the yard the whole time."

It's so many unfamiliar terms that Remy laughs without meaning to. "Oh, is that all?"

Striker smirks. "Or just watch what I do and do the same."

What Striker does is this: she starts climbing up the rigging, hand over hand, foot over foot.

What Remy does is this: Nothing. She stands frozen, deliberating. She should go back belowdecks. She still can. She can take the shame, can handle Striker's inevitable mockery afterward. Better a little mockery than to break her neck by falling from the yard. Better to accept that she's not cut out for these heroics. She never has been.

But all she can think about is the way Finn had looked at her back at Dungeon Rock—hopeful and alight, like she was seeing Remy not as she *is* but as she *could be*. Cas would climb this rigging and go aloft without a second thought. Finn, too. Her friends are bold sometimes in a way that Remy doesn't understand, in a way she's never been able to claim for herself, no matter how badly she may want to.

And she does want to. That's a revelation in itself.

She doesn't feel the rain on her face anymore. She's out of her own body, watching herself stand there, hands clenched, knuckles white.

Take the rigging, she thinks, and she watches her hand uncurl and grab on to the ropes.

Pull yourself up, she thinks, and she watches her body pull itself onto the railing as the ocean churns below her feet.

Climb, she thinks.

She climbs.

It's strange how simple it is once she's started—no different from climbing the ladder into the attic back at home, and yet different in every way. The ropes are sticky with tar, and it clings to her palms. The tempest crushes against her back. She understands suddenly what Striker had meant about climbing up on the windward side: here, the wind pushes her *into* the rigging instead of trying to yank her off it. The ship jolts, and yet she isn't knocked loose. She can feel her heartbeat in each of her clenched palms. She can feel it in her teeth. Slowly, slowly, she makes her way up.

The worst comes just before she reaches the first yard, where the last segment of rigging is stretched at a different angle to attach to the platform. Remy starts up onto it, and the ship tosses again, and then Remy is hanging, clinging to the ropes nearly upside down, more aware of gravity than she's ever been in her entire life. Her stomach swoops. The waves below her are so angry. They could take her in an instant.

But she gets a hand on the edge of the platform, and Striker is there, hauling her up, clapping her on the back as Remy wraps both arms around the mast. The panic still surges inside her, but something else is surging, too. Pride, maybe. She's terrified, but she's *here*, goddammit, she's here inside her own body, carried aloft by her own muscles and bones.

"All right, Greenie," Striker says. "Halfway there."

It takes everything in Remy not to swear. When Striker starts up the next segment of rigging, Remy follows her. She tries to find the rhythm of the climb, to time her breaths with each movement of her hands and feet. The muscles in her arms have started to burn. Blood pumps warm beneath her skin, and rain falls cool on her face.

But she can feel it now. She's settled back into her own body, settled into herself. She can feel *all* of it.

There's no platform at the top of this second set of rigging—only a narrow plank where Striker waits with the other sailor who they'd seen from the deck. He's finished furling the highest sail and come down to join them.

"Meet Immortal Gabe," Striker shouts as introduction.

Remy is clinging to the yard, trying to catch her breath. "Immortal?"

"Haven't died yet, have I?" Immortal Gabe says with a grin. "You're one of the new ones, right? What're you doing way up here?"

"She's helping," Striker tells him. The words seem more sincere now than they had before. As Striker quickly lays out the steps of their task—climbing out along the yard, wrapping up the sail, tying it down—Remy can almost believe that it's manageable. But when she steps out onto the footrope and feels it bend beneath her, she nearly swoons.

"One arm to work, one arm to hold the yard," Striker calls from behind her.

Remy shouldn't look down. She absolutely should not look down.

She looks down, and it's a mistake. The deck below her is both farther and nearer than she imagined—far enough that a fall would very likely kill her, near enough that Remy can still see every plank of it perfectly and can imagine in excruciating detail exactly how her body might break upon it. She can't do this. She's not made for this.

But something in the gray night catches her gaze: a flash of bright, coppery hair.

Finn and Cas have both come abovedeck, too. They must have heard the bell, or noticed that Remy was missing, or both. Cas is helping one of the sailors tie down a line—or attempting to help, anyway—but Finn stands alone at the base of the mainmast, staring up at Remy. Their eyes lock. Slowly, Finn's ever-glowering mouth twists into a smile.

Remy locks her arm around the yard and edges out along the rope. It holds her. It's terrifying, but it holds.

Together, she, Striker, and Immortal Gabe pull up the loose sail. Together, they bundle it against the yard and lash it into place. It's all part of the same orchestrated dance Remy had watched the crew performing from down on the deck, and she feels like she understands something now, or at least is on her way to understanding it. Maybe she could learn to move within this teeming machine, if she were given enough time.

The rain has picked up by the time they finish and start back down the rigging. The ship is pitching a little less violently now, though, with the sails secured, and the world feels steadier. Remy's feet find the deck again at last, and she clutches her knees, trying to breathe, trying to let the stress run its course through her body. When she straightens, she finds Striker grinning at her.

"Not bad, Greenie," Striker says. She considers Remy for a moment, all her earlier hostility gone. "It's Remy, right? Not bad, Remy. I have to admit—that took some guts."

Remy shakes out her burning arms. "You didn't give me much choice."

"There's always a choice," Striker says. Then, "Have you ever fired a rifle?"

Remy stares at her, trying to find the connection between this question and everything that came before. The connection isn't there. She shakes her head.

"I can teach you," Striker says. "If you'd like to learn."

Remy has the sudden sense that she's passed some sort of test, one she hadn't known she was taking. It shouldn't make any difference. She doesn't need to impress these sailors—she only needs information. She, Finn, and Cas will learn whatever they can and then be on their way. They can't trust anyone else aboard this ship. Remy knows that.

So why does she feel herself glowing under Striker's approving gaze? Maybe Remy can use this. Less than an hour ago, this sailor had been glaring at Remy and treating her like a spy. Because Remy *was* spying, but even so.

Now Striker is offering to teach her how to shoot.

"It's a good skill to have," Striker is saying. "Trust me. Much better than whatever that was that you and your friends tried to pull on the captain, anyway."

Remy's cheeks are hot. "That was *not* my idea."

But Striker just laughs, her face tipped back in the rain.

"Captain thinks we'll weather it from here," Kit says, sidling up beside Striker and wrapping an arm around her waist. She pulls her close—*very* close. "The storm should pass in the next hour or two."

"And then you're going to make us undo everything we just did, aren't you?" Striker says. Kit smirks up at her.

"That's the job. If you don't like it, you can find a new boat."

"I suppose I'll stick around a *little* longer," Striker says, smirking right back. Then she leans down, cups a hand to Kit's cheek, and kisses her.

Remy freezes.

She waits for her brain to reset itself and start functioning again. It doesn't. She tells herself to stop staring at them. She can't. It's Finn and Mary Lassiter in the cattle show tent all over again—except it isn't. This is gentler, and easier, and *sweeter*, somehow, and that makes it so much worse, so much more mortifying, as something stirs awake in Remy's chest.

She tears herself away at last, face burning. She shouldn't look at Finn, but she does. It's clear Finn saw the two women kiss, too. Of course she did. But she isn't watching Kit and Striker now. She's staring back at Remy with that same challenge in her eyes, the one she's given before, the one she gave just days ago after their encounter with Imogen Walters.

For the second time tonight, Remy feels like she's been taking a test without realizing it. She has no idea if she's passed this time. Her chest feels strange and warm, like her heart is unclenching for the first time in years.

"I can't believe you brought a greenhand aloft in this wind," Kit is saying now, her arm still wrapped around Striker. "You're going to get someone killed."

"Nah," Striker says, and she catches Remy's eye and grins. "I was pretty sure she could handle it."

XIII

CAS

Years ago, the Sterling family's cook, Mrs. Smothers, had tried to teach Cas to bake bread. She'd guided him carefully for the first few loaves, but when left unsupervised, Cas had set a loaf to rise in a too-small bowl and then forgotten all about it. When he finally remembered to check on it the next morning, the bread dough had risen so much that it had overflowed the bowl. Dough oozed out over the sides and clung in a sticky mess to the towel he'd draped over the top. Mrs. Smothers had to scrap the whole thing.

As Cas settles in aboard the *Memento Mori*, as he tries to settle in to himself, that's what the pressure in his chest feels like—that unchecked bread dough, rising a little larger every time he thinks about what comes after this. It's not as if this is a new sensation; he's been grappling with this sort of dread for years, kneading it down during supper parties and dances, holding out until he's safely back at home and can let himself fall apart. But he shouldn't be feeling this way *now*. Not when everything else feels so right. He wants to revel in these next few days—but the thrill of the adventure is overshadowed by the knowledge that it's *only* for these next few days.

Cas can keep knocking the air out of the worry, can keep pushing it down. But the bowl won't hold it forever.

By dawn, the worst of the storm has passed, and the crew is at work setting the sails and getting the ship back on course. Cas and the others help where they can, but none of them are sailors. Only Remy manages to do much, and only because Striker has taken her under her wing, showing her the ropes in a very literal sense. Cas, meanwhile, keeps getting in the way. He doesn't understand how everyone else isn't constantly bumping into one another.

Eventually, Kit tells him that his efforts are appreciated but unnecessary, and she kindly but firmly sends all three of them belowdecks.

This turns out to suit Remy just fine. The central area of the lower deck seems mostly used for storage; weathertight wooden compartments line the inside of the hull. With the crew still occupied above, with the storage compartments practically begging to be searched, Remy declares it the perfect time to get started on their investigation.

"How much rigging can one ship even need?" Cas asks. He's just opened one of the storage compartments to find that it, like the last two he checked, is stuffed with coils of rope.

"Quite a lot, clearly," Remy says from the compartment beside him. After giving up her disguise in the captain's office yesterday, she's changed back into her old skirts, though Finn has kept the trousers. "I can't even remember half the names of the lines Striker taught me an hour ago."

"She turned around quick, didn't she? Or at least she turned around on *you*. You made quite the impression on her last night."

Remy has been rummaging through a pile carpenter's tools as if expecting some secret to be buried underneath them. Now the clanking of metal on metal pauses. "I suppose," she says. "But I figure we should make the most of our time here, right?"

"By learning to sail?" Cas asks.

"By getting information. It'll be much easier to ask the crew questions if they trust us. Once we've won them over, maybe we can get some answers about that symbol."

"Right," Finn mutters. "You and that damned symbol."

She sounds a little irked about this; Cas doesn't ask why. "Well, *I* think it's a good plan," he says as he shuts the rope coils back in their place. "I'm great at winning people over."

Remy snorts. "Are you?"

"Of course! I'm very charming!" He moves on to another storage locker, which thankfully doesn't hold rope. Instead it holds bolts of spare sailcloth, which is nearly as boring. "Do we even know what we're looking for?" he asks.

"It's not a specific *something*," Remy tells him.

"Right, but all of this seems fairly normal."

Remy shrugs. "The Order members always *seem* normal, until they don't. Just look at Pastor Dekker."

The pressure in Cas's chest tightens a little. He pokes at the sailcloth, pretending to examine it. The sight of Dekker on the wharf back in Boston had rattled Cas more than he'd like to admit. But Dekker has always unsettled him. There was a day several years back when Cas's mother had invited Pastor Dekker for tea and laid out a puffy gown for Cas for the occasion. Cas had put on the dress and immediately felt sick—this happened quite a lot back then. He was nearly fourteen at the time, and his mother had been trying to drag him from the practical clothes of a girl into the comely fashions of a woman. She'd ordered a whole new wardrobe of lengthened skirts, against his protests—stiff, stifling dresses that made Cas's skin crawl, and that sometimes left him struggling to breathe, no matter how much Penelope let out the waistlines.

On the day of the tea with Dekker, Cas had scrambled out of the terrible gown and shoved it underneath his bed. He'd sat on the floor of his room for a long time. When he finally made himself go downstairs—wearing what he thought was a reasonable compromise, an old, shapeless work shift and his father's hunting jacket—his mother had looked him up and down and then struck him, hard, across the cheek.

It wasn't the first time his mother had hit him—but it was the first time she'd done so in front of company. As Cas had clutched at his stinging face, he'd waited for the pastor's horror. Instead, Pastor Dekker had patted his mother's arm.

"I see now what you were describing," the pastor had told her calmly. "You mustn't blame yourself, of course. Some children grow out of these unruly behaviors, but others require a firm hand. I'll prepare something in my sermon tomorrow. It's clear your daughter needs strict guidance about her role within God's kingdom."

That Sunday, as Cas had sat in his family's box at church, he'd stared down at his own hands, but he could still feel Dekker's gaze burning into him as he lectured. He could feel the whole congregation watching. Cas didn't *want* to care what they thought of him—but he did. Of course he did. There were plenty of other sermons after that, on plenty of other Sundays, until finally, slowly, Cas had stopped fighting. He'd started trying harder to push down that growing dread in his chest. He'd started trying to play the part. It's never been good enough for his mother—but it's good enough for nearly everyone else. After all this time, Pastor Dekker probably thinks he's won.

Cas wonders what sort of sermon the pastor would write if he saw Cas now.

"Look at this," Remy says, and Cas shakes himself and abandons the crate of sailcloth to join her. Remy is holding a smooth white box that's barely the length of her hand. No, not a box—it's a miniature coffin. The lid is painted with a nautical scene of a ship tossing in the waves. When Remy slides the coffin open, a delicately carved skeleton figurine stares up at them from the inside.

"Jesus, Mary, and Joseph," Finn breathes.

Cas pokes at one of the skeleton's tiny hands. It lifts when he touches it—the shoulders must be jointed.

"Is this a toy?" he asks, torn between fascination and horror. "Christ, that's creepy."

"I think the box is made from bone," Remy says. "Not human," she adds at Cas's revolted look. "Probably whale's tooth. Scrimshaw."

There's a sudden movement on the deck just above them, and Remy's eyes go wide. She shoves the scrimshaw coffin into the pocket of her coat. There's no time for further tidy-up, though. A pair of worn boots is already on the ladder, followed by a pair of well-fitting trousers, and then Leo climbs down, blinking in the dim light.

"Oh, hello," Leo says, taking in Cas, Remy, and Finn surrounded by several still-open storage compartments. His dark brows furrow. "Are you . . . looking for something?"

"Just tidying up," Remy lies. "Kit said we could help organize these supplies."

"Oh." Shockingly, Leo's expression clears. "All right."

Cas almost wishes Leo didn't believe them. He wishes it were anyone else who had walked in on them just now. Leo's eyes have found Cas again, and he offers a small smile. His dark hair is curling out around the edge of his cap.

"How's your vestibular system adjusting?" Leo asks him.

"Great," Cas says, which is also a lie; he's been sick three times this morning. "It's adjusting great."

"Good," Leo says. His smile is very warm, and it crinkles the corners of his dark eyes. "I knew it would."

Then he leaves them without another word, heading down the narrow passageway and into the small surgeon's cabin; Cas has heard that Leo is the surgeon in question, though he hardly seems old enough. They all listen for the door to latch behind him. They all exhale as one.

"That could've been much worse," Remy says. Then, to Cas, "You seem very friendly with him."

There's something suggestive about the way she says it. Cas feels himself bristling. "Weren't you just saying that we should try to win them over?"

"Well, *he* seemed very friendly with *you*, too."

Cas doesn't know why his face is burning. He doesn't know why his chest feels so tight. Maybe it's the guilt—or maybe it's these suffocating stays still hidden under his shirt.

"Well," he says, returning to the sailcloth and trying to get the lid back in place. "Well. It'll help for your research, right? And it's not as if he'd even be talking to me if he knew."

"If he knew we were snooping around?" Remy asks.

"No, if he knew I—" Cas cuts himself off before he says what he'd really been thinking: if he knew I wasn't really a boy. "Never mind. Doesn't matter." He tugs at his shirt, trying to adjust these damned stays. They really are uncomfortably tight. Maybe he can ask Remy to help him loosen the laces later. Cas doesn't like lying, though he's done an awful lot of it in his life. *Is* he even lying about this? It doesn't feel that way.

Remy has brought out her research journal, and now she sets up the scrimshaw coffin to sketch a rough imitation of it on one of the journal's pages. Finn has opened another storage locker, but she isn't looking through it. She's looking at Cas. There's a canniness in her gaze that makes Cas wonder if she knows exactly what he's thinking.

"What?" he snaps.

Finn turns back to the contents of the locker. "You don't have to answer this," she says in a low voice. "Only . . . well, we've seen now. Plenty of the crew here are women. Even the first mate is a woman. It seems like it's . . . safe, here, for us to travel as ourselves."

She hasn't actually asked anything—and yet Cas knows what she's getting at. She's wondering why Cas had set himself apart yesterday, after Remy had said that she and Finn weren't boys. She's wondering what's different for him. Cas wonders it too, a little—even as he's felt the relief in having said it. Even as he thinks, at the heart of it, that he *is* traveling as himself.

Cas sits down on one of the crates. "Have you ever just . . . *wanted* something," he says, "for your whole life, even though you never really imagined it was possible?"

Finn's gaze darts to Remy, her cheeks reddening under her freckles, and maybe Cas should leave it here. He and Remy are on tenuous terms already. Cas has spent years agonizing over Remy's look of betrayal after he'd told her about her father—but hadn't she betrayed him, too? Remy had promised she'd believe Cas—and then she'd immediately gone back on that promise, and everything had broken apart.

Remy has stopped her sketching now, watching him. Cas backtracks.

"I mean," he says, "all right. So. All of us have wished sometimes that we were men, right?"

It's hardly a question—just an assumption. They're all too aware of the societal advantages to be had. It's possible that Cas is *less* aware than anyone else aboard this ship—regardless of his gender, being born to the rich, white, powerful Sterling family has probably shown Cas more of those advantages than most people will ever see. Finn nods, thinking.

"I suppose," she says.

"Because it comes with privileges, right?" Cas says. "Because of all the ridiculous rules about what women can and can't do?"

"Yes. I mean, it's not quite that simple"—Finn glances at Remy again, and her cheeks somehow turn even redder—"but essentially, yes."

"Right," Cas says. His leg is bouncing up and down in that restless way Remy always used to laugh at him for. He plants his heel on the deck to stop it. The *need* to bounce doesn't go away, though, so he gives in and lets his leg do what it wants. "But like you said—those rules don't really seem to apply out here. So here, on this ship . . . do you still wish you were a man? Does it still, I don't know, pull at you?"

Finn considers this for only a moment. "No. I suppose not." Then she says, "But it still pulls at you."

Every instinct in Cas warns that this is too earnest, too open, too *true*. He's breaking his own rules. He's showing something that he'd always sworn would never see the light of day. He should crack a joke and change the subject. He should deflect.

He doesn't deflect. He lets the words spill out of him. "Yeah. It does. And I don't know why, and I don't know what it means, except that I feel like myself for the first time in my life. Like I'm grounded and real and . . ." He swallows. "Right."

He feels *right*. It's terrifying to admit it. He's so aware of Remy listening to this conversation. He's so aware of the old scars still between them.

But Finn nods again.

"That makes sense," she says, and Remy hums in agreement. Cas tells himself to trust this, at least, though his chest is still aching and tight.

For several minutes, they work in silence: Finn searching through her open storage compartment, Cas pretending to do the same, and Remy sketching in her journal. Then Remy snaps the book shut.

"I still can't believe you made us fight them yesterday," she says suddenly, frowning at Cas.

Cas is grateful for the change in subject. "At least it was something. I didn't see *you* coming up with any brilliant plans."

"I was working on a plan. You just beat me to it."

"Should've planned faster, then."

Remy lets out a frustrated groan at that. But Finn pats her on the shoulder.

"It's all right," Finn says, too patronizing to be sincere. "You'll beat him to it next time."

"Not if he just keeps charging in!" Remy protests. "How am I supposed to come up with a plan quicker than he can throw a punch?"

The *he* is Cas—the tension in his chest releases a little, even as Remy swats Finn's hand away, even as Finn points out that it was a book, not a punch, that Cas had thrown. Cas returns to poking through the storage locker in front of him. Regardless of anything else, regardless of what happens next or whether Remy believes his visions, she and Finn seem to believe him about this. They believe him that he's *him*.

Cas decides that's enough for now.

XIV

FINN

The last time Finn had been on a ship, she'd gotten into a fight and broken a boy's nose.

The fight was Kieran's fault, mostly. He'd been fourteen and Finn ten when they were orphaned and sent to America. They weren't quite penniless, but nearly; their parents' meager savings had paid for the funerals and for Finn and Kieran's passage across the sea, but not much else. Before they boarded the packet ship, Kieran had secured the last of their coin in a small envelope tucked inside his boot.

They'd been at sea for only a day before an older boy noticed the coins' clinking. He cornered Kieran with an offer: Kieran could give the boy all his money, or the boy could knock his teeth in. For one glorious moment, Finn had thought her brother might punch him. Kieran was tall and stocky for his age, and with the two Robinson siblings together, they could have held their own. They could have put up a good fight.

Kieran didn't put up a fight, of course. He'd simply started untying his bootlaces.

But the boy had barely even glanced at Finn as he was making his threats. Why would he? She was a scrawny ten-year-old slip of a girl. Finn had waited until his guard was down, until he was gloating over his haul, and then she pushed the boy hard enough that he toppled. Once he was on the ground, she kicked him in the face. Then she kicked him again. Then she picked *his* pockets while he lay moaning and swearing on the deck. The boy's nose swelled up like a potato for two days. Finn and her brother were left alone for the rest of their journey.

After a single day aboard the *Memento Mori*, Finn is already longing for a brawl.

She knows how to strong-arm her way through the world. She knows how to scrap and fight and do whatever she needs to protect herself and the people she cares about. But the strategy Remy has proposed here—making nice with the crew, winning their trust... Finn doesn't know how to do *this*.

Cas does, clearly. On their first day abovedeck, he runs headlong at their mission of befriending the sailors. It's no secret that Cas is well liked in Windover; like Remy, Finn has always assumed his high esteem came mostly from his family's money. But the Sterling name means nothing here, and Cas is quickly making friends without it, or in spite of it. There's no way of hiding his pampered background, after all. It must be obvious to everyone aboard that Cas has never in his life scrubbed so much as a spoon.

Still, he's so affable and eager to help that no one much seems to mind. He lets Nessa, Kit's seven-year-old daughter, teach him how to tie a few basic knots, and then he ties them so poorly that Nessa gets to spend a full hour teaching him again. He asks about the cook's recipe at lunch until the cook drafts him into kitchen service—though after Cas nearly cuts off his own finger with a paring knife, he's relegated to washing dishes. Then, when the dishwashing bucket turns up a drowned cockroach, Cas knocks over the whole tub in a panic and swears so loudly that half the crew comes running to see what's the matter. A few of the sailors take to calling him "the Little Prince" after that.

"Just wait till one gets into the molasses tin first thing in the morning," Immortal Gabe says fondly while Cas mops up the mess on the galley floor. "*That'll* give the Little Prince a proper scare." Cas presents him with a rude gesture, though it's undercut by the grin that he can't quite hide over the word *prince*.

In the afternoon, Cas, Remy, and Finn reconvene in a quiet corner of the main deck to share what they've learned. Remy sets up a small chess set she found in storage that morning and persuades Cas to play against her as they talk, though she keeps pausing their game to scribble notes in her research journal.

"That creepy little skeleton toy is Nessa's," Cas reports as he waits for Remy to choose her next move. "She told me the captain's partner made it for her as a gift. He's the one who carved the ship's figurehead, too. Nessa said it's supposed to be some sort of joke—although she couldn't explain the joke to me or tell me why it was funny."

Remy writes all of this down, then studies the board. Even with her attention split, she's very obviously winning. She always wins at chess. "Did you ask her about the symbol?" she asks.

"Yes," Cas says. "She wasn't sure what I was talking about. And then she got distracted telling me a story about a mermaid who eats rocks."

Remy snorts. "Well, *that's* helpful."

"It could be. Are there any mermaids who eat rocks in the Order of Lazarus?"

"Maybe you should try talking to sources who aren't seven years old."

"What have *you* found out, then?" Cas snaps.

Remy doesn't answer right away. She might be busy contemplating their chess game, but it's more likely she doesn't have any answer to give. From what Finn has seen today, Remy hasn't made much progress. She's always tended toward a roundabout manner of investigating—and the roundabout manner can take a while.

The problem here is that Remy doesn't *have* a while, and all of them know it.

"I'm working on it," Remy says at last. "I'm trying to find the right approach." She advances one of her pawns, and Cas immediately brings out his knight to capture it. Remy groans. "You do realize that I'm going to take your knight now, don't you?"

"Well, yes, but I got your pawn," he says. "So it's an even trade."

"A knight for a pawn isn't an *even trade*."

Cas gasps and pinches the pawn in question as if trying to cover its ears. "Well, *that's* very rude."

"This is your problem, you know," Remy tells him as she swipes his knight and sits back. "You always take the most obvious attack, even when it's clearly a trap. You really haven't gotten any better at this since we were ten, have you?"

"I am aware, thank you," Cas says, frowning down at the board.

Immortal Gabe is lingering a few yards away. Finn isn't sure whether Remy or Cas has noticed him watching, but *she* has, and she's prepared to redirect them if their conversation veers back toward anything they don't want overheard. But Gabe's interest, as it turns out, is only on the game. When Remy calls checkmate three moves later, Gabe comes over to clap Cas on the back in a sympathetic sort of way.

"Rough one," he tells him, then turns to Remy. "Can I call next match?"

Finn wishes Remy's surprise weren't quite so apparent. "Do you play?" Remy asks.

Gabe laughs. "Whose board do you think that is? The captain got us all in on it—he's a chess genius. Though I'm not too bad myself. So—are you up for the challenge? Or is there a waiting list?"

That calculating glint has returned to Remy's eye as she tells Gabe that, no, there's no list, and, yes, he can have the next match. She starts resetting the board. Carefully, she asks, "Do you think anyone else would be interested in playing afterward?"

And Remy has, at last, found her approach. She spends the rest of the evening playing match after match with the crew, all while maintaining a steady conversation. Her mastery of the game lets her keep control of the board, and it leaves her opponents distracted, more focused on finding a countermove than on carefully watching their words while they do. That night, when they've retired to the fo'c'sle, Remy writes down every detail that the sailors had let slip: The ship's age and history. The last few stops the *Mori* had made before landing in Boston. The next few stops the *Mori* had planned to make before the captain had changed course for Eden. Finn falls asleep to the sound of Remy's pen still scratching out notes.

By noon the next day, Remy has outplayed nearly the entire crew—with the notable exception of Captain Hobbes himself. At one point midmorning, when the captain had passed by as

Remy and the ship's cook were locked in play, Remy had tried to challenge him to the next match. The captain had ignored her outright and instead turned to the cook.

"I trust that the lunch preparations are finished," Captain Hobbes had said in a cool tone, "if you have time to play games with our passengers."

Based on the cook's nervous blinking, the lunch preparations were *not* finished. He'd muttered a concession and hurried down to the galley. The captain had strolled off without another word.

"I wouldn't take it personally," Mita says later when Finn and the others sit down with her for lunch. "The captain has a lot on his mind. And as good as he is at chess, his partner is the undisputed champion here."

"Only because he's been playing longer," Leo argues. "Captain told me once that his partner used to train with Philipp Stamma back in London."

Remy frowns. "Well, that can't be right. Didn't Stamma die nearly a century ago?"

Leo hums noncommittally and takes a bite of hardtack. Mita stirs her coffee.

"That's a very obvious nonanswer," Remy tells them, and Mita chuckles.

"Hang around this ship long enough, and I think you'll find that we all have to accept a few mysteries," she says, which makes Remy frown more deeply and Cas burst out laughing. He must know as well as Finn that Remy does not do well with accepting mysteries.

Finn stares down into her own coffee mug, watching the loose grounds swirling in the dark. Even as she spends more time with these sailors, she can't quite get over the strangeness of hearing them talk so casually about the captain and his partner. When Finn had seen Kit and Striker share a kiss—when she'd had her suspicions confirmed—her mind had recoiled on instinct: *Sodomy. Unnatural. An abomination.* The words were automatic, a reflex built out of so many years of turning them on herself.

And yet it's different, somehow, to try to point that reproach at another person—particularly when everyone else aboard this ship seems so utterly unfazed by the two women's flirting in front of the entire crew. Or by the references Immortal Gabe has made to his own past lover in Oaxaca. Or by the captain's love life. Even when those awful words flit through Finn's mind, she can't manage the same heat for them that she once might have. She's only going through the motions.

After two days of mingling with the crew, then, these are their standings: Remy is respected. Cas is embraced. And Finn is tolerated, she suspects, mainly because of her proximity to the other two.

Of everyone aboard the *Memento Mori*, the only resident Finn has managed to win over is the cat. The cat now spends her days trailing after Finn and mewling expectantly for Finn to pet her. The cat spends her nights curled up at the foot of Finn's bunk. When Finn, Remy, and Cas gather back in the fo'c'sle that afternoon, the cat follows them and immediately climbs onto Finn's lap, knocking her head against Finn's hand until Finn agrees to scratch her chin.

"Kit says we'll reach Bangor tonight," Remy says. "Which means we'll be at Eden tomorrow. We're nearly out of time, and even with all of this"—she takes her journal from her pocket and shakes the newly filled pages—"we're still no closer to finding out what that symbol means."

"We could ask the captain," Cas suggests, massaging his temples, as if Remy's urgency is giving him a headache. "He's the most likely to know, isn't he?"

"That," Remy tells him, "is a terrible idea."

"Why is it terrible?"

"If he's a member of the Order of Lazarus—"

Cas cuts her off with a scoffing sound. "I don't think he's in the Order. Does he really seem the type?"

"I don't know," Remy says, her irritation clear. "We still hardly know anything about him."

"Right, but does he seem like the *Order's* type? Aren't most of these secret societies neck-deep in their garbage about 'the superiority of the white race'?"

Remy falls quiet for a moment. It's clear she hadn't properly considered this until now, though Finn thinks it's a decent point. The cat pokes Finn's hand. Finn resumes her scratching.

"I suppose," Remy says at last. "But he could be working with the Order even if he's not a full member. There has to be *some* connection here." Remy *needs* there to be some connection here; this is what she really means. Finn can see the desperation clouding her judgment even if Remy won't admit it. Remy turns to her. "Finn, what have you found out?"

Finn has given up on trying to win over the crew. Instead, she keeps her head down. She keeps quiet. She listens. Nothing she's caught has been particularly damning, though she's overheard a few cryptic comments about the ship's cargo. Perhaps the ship *is* carrying some sinister delivery for the Order—or perhaps the captain is simply dodging his import taxes. She relays the comments to Remy either way. Remy makes a note.

Finn *doesn't* tell Remy that she's starting to suspect Cas might be right. The longer they stay aboard this ship, the more difficult it is to believe that any of these sailors would involve themselves with a group like the Order of Lazarus. Finn has been listening for the usual—*anything strange, anything that seems out of place*. But that isn't what she's heard.

Instead, almost by accident, she's been catching pieces of the crew's histories—these sailors who follow their captain with unwavering trust. Mita, who had apprenticed on half a dozen other ships before she found the *Mori*. Kit and her daughter, Nessa, who had been forced from their family home in Mexico after the Texas Revolution, when the new republic's constitution had exiled free Black residents. Striker and Leo, who had bounced around the streets of New York before joining up with the captain when Striker was fourteen and Leo barely ten. It doesn't escape Finn's notice that these are the very same ages she and Kieran had been when they'd come to America. She's not sure that it matters. Her mind notes it anyway.

Finn can feel something shifting inside her, day by day. It's as if some axis in her heart has tilted, and suddenly her compass is askew, the whole map knocked sideways by a few degrees. She keeps losing her heading.

"It just isn't much to go on," Cas is saying as he peers over Remy's shoulder to read her notes. "We have what— A few unanswered questions? A few 'mysteries' that you might have to learn to live with?"

"It's enough to prove that they're keeping secrets," Remy snaps.

"Sure," Cas says. "But so are we."

Finn thinks of the hidden panel in the hold, the smuggling compartment tucked out of sight. How much of this crew's secrecy comes from the simple nature of their business? How much comes from the nature of the community that the sailors have formed here—this floating kingdom with rules all its own? The captain has plenty of reason to be wary of outsiders. Finn keeps replaying the expression on Remy's face the other night when she'd seen Kit and Striker kiss. Remy had looked shocked, certainly. Embarrassed, even. But disgusted? Repulsed? Any of the horrified reactions Finn had half expected from her?

No; not so much. And despite her continued suspicions, Remy certainly hasn't seemed repulsed by either of the women since. Just today, she took Striker up on her offer to teach her to shoot. They spent nearly two hours together practicing on the deck.

It feels too dangerous a thing to dwell on. Finn is playing with fire.

"What I'd really like is to take a look around the captain's office," Remy says now. "It's clear he isn't willing to talk to us, so that's our next best option. But we'll have to be careful about it. We'll need the right opportunity."

XV

REMY

Remy's opportunity arrives only a few hours later.

By evening, land has appeared off both the starboard and larboard sides of the ship. The crew navigates with ease among the shoals of Penobscot Bay; it's clear they've sailed this route many times before. When the bell on the mast starts to clang for all hands, Remy makes her way to the bow, searching the shore for the lights of a town.

There's no town to be found—just the mouth of a river and a deserted stretch of rocky beach lined with trees. The only light comes from a white granite lighthouse perched on a lonely bluff.

"This can't be Bangor," Remy says.

Immortal Gabe flicks her shoulder as he passes. "It's *near* Bangor."

"Why are we stopping, though? There's nothing here. No port, no dock—"

"That's the point, isn't it?" Gabe says. "No port means no customhouse. The captain is mates with one of the lighthouse keepers here, Gilly—he works as a sort of middleman for us. Saves us the trip up the river, *and* helps us avoid prying eyes." Remy's face must give away her surprise, because Gabe laughs. "You did know that this was a smuggling rig, didn't you?"

Remy returns to the rope winch near the quarterdeck, where Kit has tasked her, Finn, and Cas with disassembling pieces of old rigging and twisting it into fresh spun yarn. It's mindless, tedious work, and Remy suspects the true purpose is less about the spun yarn and more about keeping the greenhands out of the way. Cas is absently spinning the winch's handle, though he hasn't attached anything to its hooks.

"I think you've forgotten something," Remy tells him as she settles back into place beside Finn. Cas ignores her. Remy selects a length of frayed rope and angles herself for a good view of the deck while she picks apart the strands. She can easily work out the sailors' various tasks by now: trimming the sails, dropping the anchors, preparing the ship's longboat to launch. Frustration tugs at her, threatening to turn into panic. Somehow she's wasted two days filling her mind with sailing knowledge instead of anything she can actually use.

"Are you all right?" Finn asks.

But the question isn't meant for Remy. It's for Cas, who's still spinning the empty rope winch with an oddly blank expression on his face. Something pinches at the back of Remy's mind, a snippet of a half-remembered song she can't place.

Cas hasn't answered. Finn pokes him in the shoulder. "Cas. Are you all right?"

He blinks as if focusing himself. "Hm? Yes, I'm fine. Why?"

"You're being unsettlingly quiet."

"No, I'm not," he says. Finn arches an eyebrow at him, and he spins the winch with more aggression than necessary. "*You're* being quiet."

"It's much stranger from you," she says, and Cas wrinkles his nose at her.

At the ship's starboard side, Gabe and the others have the longboat ready to lower. Remy had expected them to load it up with the casks from the hold's hidden compartment, but either the smuggled whiskey has a different destination or it's going to shore later. The longboat seems to be empty. The captain straightens his coat and retrieves his hat from Kit as the two exchange a few words.

With a thrill, Remy realizes what's about to happen. "I think the captain is going ashore," she says.

This announcement evokes none of the excitement she'd hoped from her two companions. Finn makes a neutral humming sound; she clearly knows Remy's intention but hasn't decided yet how she feels about it. Cas gives the rope winch another spin for good measure. He's clearly missed Remy's intention altogether.

"That means he won't be in his office," Remy says in a low voice. Cas's face doesn't change. "Which means *we* can spend a little time there without being disrupted."

This finally gets his attention. Of the three of them, Cas would have been the last person Remy thought would balk—but now his eyes widen. "You want us to break into his office? Right now?"

"Unless you're too busy making spun yarn," Remy says. "I don't think we'll have another chance like this. We can slip away while the others are launching the boat. It's not as if we'll be missed."

"You did say that you wanted to be included in any future thieving," Finn reminds him.

"Well, I didn't realize how often it would come up!"

He looks ill at the very thought. Or maybe he just looks ill—his face is too pale, and sweat glazes his brow despite the chilly wind. Another memory plucks at the back of Remy's mind—those evenings playing chess with her father in his study. One evening in particular. She pushes it away.

"You can stand lookout if you don't want to get your hands dirty," she tells Cas. "But if we're going to do this, we need to do it now."

Cas nods, though he doesn't look pleased about it. They wait until the longboat is lowered over the side. When they slip belowdecks, the top of the captain's hat has just disappeared beneath the ship's rail.

The lower deck is quiet. Remy retraces the path that Mita had taken them on on that first afternoon. Within moments, they're standing outside the door of the captain's office.

Finn steps forward to examine the latch. "I might need a knife," she says, peering at the crack. "Or ... wait ..." With a disbelieving air, she tests the knob. It turns.

The door opens.

Remy's heart has started to thrum a little faster. This feels like a good omen. It's almost too easy.

"Does it even count as 'breaking in' if the door isn't locked?" she asks.

"Nothing's technically broken," Finn reasons. "But I do think it's frowned upon all the same."

"Only if we get caught." Remy turns back to Cas, who's rubbing his forehead as if reluctant to even witness the crime taking place here. "You'll keep watch?" she says. "Good. Make a noise if someone comes, and then try to keep them talking so we can get away."

Cas nods again. And with that, Remy and Finn slide into the captain's office.

The space seems much larger now than it had with seven people inside. Remy surveys the room with an odd sense of familiarity. How many times have she and Finn been here before—poking through an office, or digging through some archive they've conned their way inside? She's unspeakably grateful to have Finn by her side for this. Finn has already started in on the books lining the wall.

"Those are proper barrister's bookcases," Remy says as Finn lifts one of the glass doors. "They must've cost a fortune to install. Who needs this many bookcases on a sailing ship?"

"Captain Edward Hobbes, apparently," Finn says.

"There's an awful lot we don't know about this man."

Finn takes out one of the books to study. "We know he's fond of reading. And chess. Sound like anyone else you know?"

Remy ignores this and turns her attention to the desk. The charts are gone now, though a clip on one side holds a stack of letters in place. Remy's eyes snag on the signature of the topmost page: *M. Díaz.*

"Mita mentioned this," she says, tugging the letter free to show Finn. "She said this note was the captain's best lead about something."

"His missing partner?" Finn guesses.

"Probably." Remy skims the note, trying to scrape through the fatty pleasantries to find the meat underneath. Díaz's handwriting is atrocious, and the message is infuriatingly vague; it could be some sort of code. Remy wishes she'd kept her journal with her instead of leaving it in the fo'c'sle earlier. She's desperate to copy down the note's contents. She'll need more time to make sense of this.

Still, a line near the end gives her pause: *It seems the rumors may have merit. Two sources now confirming a reaper's glass recently acquired at Eden.*

"You've never heard of a reaper's glass, have you?" Remy asks, and Finn shakes her head.

There's a sudden shout from outside the door. A scuffling sound. In the bare second afterward, Remy prays to a god that she barely believes in for her panic to be misplaced.

The door wrenches open.

Captain Hobbes stands in the doorway. One hand grips Cas by the collar. The other holds a pistol.

The pistol is trained on Remy.

Remy has found that, in moments of the highest stakes, her terror can reach a threshold where it overflows into nothingness. She knows, rationally, that this is bad. She knows that she and her friends are done for. And yet she feels nothing at all as she stares down the gleaming black barrel of the gun, the captain's letter still in her grasp.

"Put that down," the captain says in a low voice.

Numbly, Remy returns the page to his desk and holds up her hands in surrender.

"And you," the captain tells Finn, jerking the pistol in her direction. "Drop it."

Finn glances at Remy, then sets down the book she'd been flipping through. She raises her hands as well.

"Did you think I'd gone to shore?" the captain asks them. "Couldn't even wait for the boat to hit the water, could you? I wondered what you'd do if you thought you had an opening. I called the boat back up as soon as Kit lost eyes on you. It seems my suspicions were not unfounded."

He says all this in his usual measured tone, but there's a sharpness buried underneath the words. Only now, as she wades through this strange void of emotions, does Remy realize her own foolishness. She's accused Cas of walking straight into traps during their chess games—and now she's done the very same thing. Of course it was too easy to break into the captain's office. He'd *designed* it to be too easy. And yet Remy had rushed in without a second thought. Now she's not only thrown herself into the fire but Finn and Cas alongside her.

The captain's pistol is on Remy again. She's never been held at gunpoint before. She only even touched a gun for the first time earlier today. How strange that one small twitch of the finger can be all that stands between life and death.

The captain releases Cas's collar and steps back from the doorway—a wordless command. Remy and Finn both file out of the office. The captain twitches his head toward the ladder, and all three of them climb abovedeck.

When Remy stands in the cool night air, when her emotions come flooding back at last, it isn't fear she feels—it's shame. The scene on the deck is the worst kind of humiliation. The entire crew is here to bear witness. As the captain tells the other sailors what's happened, Remy stands with her friends at the base of the mainmast, trying and failing to come up with a plan. What explanation can she possibly give for looking through the captain's private papers? What excuse is there after being caught red-handed?

She can't think. She can't bring herself to look at anyone. And yet as she stares down at her own boots, the imagined reactions that her mind supplies might be even worse: Mita's eyes widening in shock at the captain's words. Kit shaking her head. Striker's face shifting from confusion to betrayal. Striker, who'd turned around on her, who'd been teaching Remy about the rigging and how to shoot a rifle.

This is unbearable.

Remy rounds on Cas, who's standing uselessly at her side. "Some lookout *you* are," she hisses. She knows her anger isn't really with him, and yet it feels good to hit something, to find someone else to blame. Cas doesn't even look at her. He's shaking slightly.

The voices from the *Mori*'s crew have sharpened. Striker has started up a long stream of Yiddish, almost to herself; Remy doesn't need to understand the language to hear the anger in its tone. Kit is arguing with her daughter.

"Go down to the cabin," she tells Nessa.

Leo steps forward to lead the girl below. He gives Remy and the others a wide berth as he does. Striker's tirade reaches its peak and reverts to English at the end as she bursts out, "I *knew* they were thieves."

The captain turns back to the three of them now, studying them with his piercing gaze. "Bring up their bags," he tells Striker. "Let's see what else they've taken."

As Striker shoves past her, Remy finds her voice at last. "We haven't taken anything!"

"Forgive me if I don't accept your word on that," the captain says. "We've all seen you poking around. Asking questions. You're not as subtle as you seem to believe. Leo mentioned he found you *organizing the supplies* the other day—he may not have recognized the lie, but I did. You'll find I'm not as quick to trust as some of my crew."

He glances at Mita as he says this. His tone is still perfectly calm—Remy almost wishes that the captain *would* yell at them. This unnerving composure is worse.

Striker returns with their carpetbags a few moments later. When she upends Remy's, spare clothes and books tumble out in a pile. Striker picks up Remy's copy of the *Grimoirium Verum* and thrusts it at the captain as evidence.

"Yours?" she asks.

But the captain's eyes have narrowed. "No."

He reaches past the book in Striker's hand to instead pluck something else from the deck: Remy's journal.

Remy's stomach clenches. She doesn't instruct her body to move—it simply lunges forward, driven by some feral instinct to seize the journal back. To protect it, no matter the cost. Striker is on her in an instant, restraining Remy as easily as she had two days ago.

"That's *mine!*" Remy shouts, struggling to get away.

"And it's on my ship," the captain says. "This is what you've been scribbling in, isn't it?"

He flips back the journal's cover, lets the pages open where they may. In horror, Remy watches the spine settle near the end—her most recent entries. Everything she's written down since she, Cas, and Finn boarded the *Memento Mori*.

"Ah," the captain says. "Notes on my ship ... my crew ... *me* ... And you thought we'd send you on your merry way in Eden? You were going to deliver all of this to your Order of Lazarus."

Remy protests before she even realizes what he's said: "It's not *my* Order!"

"It's not enough that you people have been hunting my partner. Now you're spying on me, too, and putting *my* people in danger, and—"

"Wait," Remy says as the understanding dawns. "That isn't—"

"I—" Cas starts, but the captain pushes onward.

"I should have tossed you overboard after all." He's flipping through the other pages now, eyes darting over years and years of Remy's investigation. "I should have— Wait."

He pauses. Reads. Turns the next page more slowly. Remy shakes herself free of Striker's grip at last, but she doesn't grab for the journal. She watches the captain have the same realization she herself had just moments ago.

At last, Captain Hobbes says, almost in wonder, "You're not with the Order of Lazarus."

"No," Remy says. "And neither are you."

For a long moment, they both stare at each other as if meeting for the very first time.

"I think . . ." Cas says, taking an unsteady step backward. "I think I need to . . ."

Then his eyes flutter back into his head, and he collapses.

XVI

CAS

Cas hadn't been prepared for another vision so soon. The visions usually come months apart; two within a fortnight is unprecedented. And he's missed all the usual warning signs. Yes, the nausea has been worse today, but he's been feeling sick ever since they took to sea. His body is still adjusting, like Leo had said. When the headache started, he'd chalked it up to dehydration—a natural thing given how often he's still running for the railing. He'd blamed the growing soreness in his chest and ribs on the same.

His chest has been aching for days now, anyway. He knows he's kept the bindings on too long. But he's afraid to take them off, even to sleep—what if there's another call for all hands? What if he has to rush above with no time to refasten these goddamned stays? Surely someone would notice, or *everyone* would notice, and all this would be over even sooner than he's braced for. The game would be up. Except it isn't a game, not really, and it probably never was, and the idea of being forced back into who he used to be feels nearly unbearable after this brief golden period of being who he *is*.

So maybe this is the inevitable reckoning. Cas has known all along that it was coming. As the deck around him fills with swirling sparks, he can't help but think that of course, of course, these past few days of feeling *good* and *right* would have to come with a price.

Then he's in the vision.

He's bracing himself to see Henry—to have to watch Henry bleed out on a forest floor, just like Mr. DeWindt. Even as they've been sailing for Eden, time has been ticking away. Maybe Henry's fate is already sealed. Maybe he's going to die either way.

But the vision doesn't show Henry. It's Finn. Again.

That's unprecedented, too—Cas has never ever seen the same person's death twice. She's in a different place this time, though. Not the streets of Windover. Now Finn runs through a darkened pine forest. That same shadowy figure is moving through the trees, pursuing her with a steady vengeance.

It's all so much worse now that he knows her. He'd known *of* Finn that first time he'd seen her die—but he hadn't *known* her. Not her wry sense of humor, or the way she quietly watches everything around her, or the look on her face back in Boston when she'd agreed to help cut his hair. Now he's seeing double: this terrified girl running from her death and then, superimposed, the girl he's been getting to know for the past week or so—with her practiced glower, and the depth of caring she hides underneath.

He has to tell her, doesn't he? Oh god. Cas really, really has to tell her.

The forest around them gives way, and then Finn stands on a stretch of solid rock. The rock ends in a cliff. Below, the ocean churns. It's a drop of at least a hundred feet, a wall of worn granite spiderwebbed with jagged lines. Finn is so small as she stands there on the top of it, a dot in this sprawling landscape.

Finn peers down at the water for only a moment before glancing behind her. The dark shape in the trees draws ever closer. Cas thinks she's going to take off running again, just as she did in the first vision.

She doesn't run this time.

With some newfound resolve, Finn plants her boots on the rock. Turns slowly. Squares her shoulders and faces the shadowy figure that's now twenty feet from her. Ten feet. An arm's length away. It towers over her, and Finn's face screws up in defiance. A snarl. She's yelling now. The words are silent, everything is silent, but even without words, her fury is a blaze. Cas wants her to run, to save herself—and yet maybe this is the next closest thing. Maybe there's no way to outrun this fiendish creature, and so the only thing left to do is scream at the injustice of it.

The shadowy hand plunges at her again, reaching through her chest. Closing on her heart. Finn's eyes go blank as the spark in them snuffs out.

And then sound hits him again all at once, and Cas can't breathe.

"Cas. *Cas!*"

He's lying on his back on the deck of the ship. Hands grip his shoulders. His awareness radiates from there. Pain fizzles from one side of his skull—he must have hit his head when he fell. He tries to inhale, but his lungs feel tight. He blinks.

"Oh, thank god," Remy breathes. It's her hands that are gripping him, her voice calling his name. "Are you all right?"

Cas tries to answer, but he can't catch his breath. Finn is crouched at Remy's side, not running now, not shouting up at a demon. Not dead yet. The relief will come later. Around them, Cas feels eyes: Kit, Striker, Mita, the captain. He can't make out any of their expressions. But Remy looks like she's seen a ghost.

Pass it off as a normal fainting spell. Don't let on that anything unusual has happened.

Cas sits up and immediately regrets it—for a long moment he can see only black spots blooming in front of his eyes. He hugs his knees and tries to breathe. He needs to wave them all off, assure them that he's fine, everything's fine. But his chest is so tight, and his lungs aren't working, and surely by now the world should be sliding back into focus. Instead it's still fuzzy and far away.

The thought finally bobs to the surface of his mind: this isn't right.

People are speaking, though Cas can't make sense of the words. A soft British voice asks something. Remy shakes her head.

"I don't know," Remy is saying. "He's told us that he's had these ... fits ... before, but I don't know if ..."

Her voice fades out. Did she stop talking, or did Cas just stop hearing her? His ears are buzzing. Maybe Remy has put together what's happened. Maybe *now* she'll believe him about these goddamned visions.

He blinks again, and then Mita is kneeling on the deck in front of him.

"Can you stand?" she asks. "Can you make it to the surgeon's cabin? I can help you, if you'd like."

Cas likes Mita well enough—he likes laughing with her at mealtimes and playing cards with her and Leo and Immortal Gabe when the night watch is quiet. But joking and cards are one thing. This is something very different.

"I'm all right," he says, or tries to. It comes out a wheeze. "I can—"

But when he starts to his feet, he sways, and there's nothing to do but grab on to the arm Mita's offering him. Remy and Finn are still staring as if waiting for instruction. Cas can't look at them. If Remy *does* believe him now... is she going to ask whose death he's just predicted? Is he going to tell her? He needs time to think.

At least with Mita he can make up some lie for the moment. Mita steers him to the ladder. Cas leaves behind Remy, Finn, and their questioning looks. Then Mita is helping him down and through the passageway to the tiny, stuffy surgeon's cabin, and then Cas is sitting on the wooden bed bolted to its wall. He's tugging at his chest bindings and trying to breathe and wishing the world would right itself at last.

Mita says very quietly, "Do you need help with your bindings?"

Cas has misheard. He must have misheard.

"What?" he hears himself say.

"I don't mean to overstep, but it might help to loosen them, if they're constricting your lungs. Can you manage a deep breath?"

His mind is too fuzzy to process any of this. He does as she asks. The breath hitches in his chest, pinched too small under the tightly laced stays. Mita nods once.

"May I help you loosen them?" she asks. "Or can you manage it yourself?"

Cas can't manage it himself.

He feels the moment when the laces come free. He pulls away the stiff fabric, and his lungs expand properly again, and the fresh air floods in. Slowly, his vision clears. Cas wads the discarded stays into a ball and clutches it against his chest. The fabric of his loose shirt feels strange on his back.

"I'll bring you a cup of water," Mita says, and he has the distinct impression that she's giving him privacy to gather himself. As she ducks out through the cabin's door, she adds, "Just breathe, lad."

Cas breathes.

He breathes, and he tries to sort through everything from the past five minutes. The vision of Finn. Finn's empty, dead eyes. Remy's terrified face when he came to. His bindings. Mita's question about his bindings. She'd said it so calmly, as if it were a perfectly normal thing to ask about.

She'd known he was binding his chest, then. She'd seen right through him. She'd known—

Slowly, though, he's registering her words. Specifically, he's registering that last *word*.

Just breathe, lad.

She'd known what sort of boy he was, or wasn't. And she'd called him *lad* anyway.

There's a knock on the door, and Mita appears with a tin cup of water. She hands it to Cas. He drinks.

"You knew," he says at last.

Mita doesn't ask what he's talking about. "I... surmised," she says.

"But you didn't say anything. You didn't tell everyone that I wasn't a boy. You didn't... you didn't *challenge* me on it."

Mita nods, careful and slow, like Cas is a wild deer that she's trying not to startle. "I didn't think there was anything to challenge," she says simply.

The anxiety in his chest has started to deflate again. He feels strange, like all his skin has been scrubbed raw. It's probably the fever; his temperature always runs high for a few days after a vision. Even so.

"You were right about the . . . ," he says, just to be saying something, and he holds up the wad of bindings. "So. Thank you for that. Shouldn't have left them on for so long, I suppose. Or had them so tight."

Mita eyes the bundle of stays. "May I?" Cas passes it over, and Mita smooths the fabric and studies it for a moment. "Not very breathable. And difficult for you to adjust by yourself, I imagine. True?"

This might be the strangest conversation Cas has ever had. "True enough."

"We can likely design you something better, if you'd like. I'm not much of a seamstress, but I'm sure someone has a vest near enough to your size that we could tailor. If we add the right lining, we could shape it in a way that suits you without being so formfitting." She hands the stays back. "Entirely up to you, of course. I just figured I'd make the offer."

Definitely the strangest conversation Cas has had. And yet he's been trying not to think about what he'll do next—whether to try to readjust those damned stays or just give up any effort at hiding his chest. It's a choice between discomfort in two different ways, for two different reasons.

"That . . . would be amazing, actually," he admits.

"Are you feeling steadier?" Mita asks. "You're welcome to rest in here. The captain and your friends can sort out their issues. You had us all worried for a minute there, though."

"I'll be all right."

It isn't an empty brush-off this time. Cas actually means it. Mita nods again, reminds him to ask if he needs anything, and reaches for the door.

Before she can open it, Cas asks, "Does everyone . . . ? I mean, do the others . . . ?"

She can fill in the rest of the question, surely. She turns back, her face contemplative. The neckerchief that's tying her hair away from her face today is a vivid gold color—the glow of a newly risen sun.

"Some might have an inkling," Mita says. "I honestly can't say. But I *can* say that, whether you choose to tell them or don't, no one aboard this ship will give you any trouble. You have my word on that. They're a good crew. They believe people about who they are."

Cas's mind is cycling through every interaction he's had since he came abovedeck on the *Memento Mori*. Every jab and nickname from Immortal Gabe. Every knot-tying lesson with Nessa. Every card game and meal with the crew. Mita is smiling now, though Cas isn't sure if it's at him or if she's just smiling to herself.

"They've always believed me, anyway," Mita says. "When I told them I was a woman, they believed me like no one else had before."

Cas is staring at her. Stop staring at her. He focuses on his hands folded on his own knees. He lets his mind cycle for just a little longer. It changes nothing, and it also changes everything.

He'd just assumed this was the kind of thing no one else in the world would ever understand.

When he finally lets himself look back up at Mita, she's still smiling, and this time, it's definitely for him. "Yes, lad," she says. "Me, as well."

XVII

REMY

Captain Hobbes instructs Striker to take Remy and Finn belowdecks. For several years at least, the two of them sit locked in the ship's dining room, waiting for the captain to decide their fate. It isn't years, really; it probably hasn't even been a quarter of an hour, but time has become a strange, stretching thing. Remy is here at the table, fiddling with Immortal Gabe's chess set, which had been left out from her afternoon games—and she's also far outside herself, torn between trying to make sense of her racing thoughts and trying not to think about anything at all.

The chess set is a feeble attempt at distraction, especially since Finn refuses to play against her. Finn is infuriatingly quiet as she watches Remy move the pieces around on her own. Remy wishes Cas were here. *He'd* agree to play, or he'd crack a joke, or he'd do something to break this awful silence.

But Cas hadn't been cracking jokes this evening, had he? Even before he collapsed. Maybe it's better that he's still off with Mita somewhere. Even now, as she wonders frantically what the captain and the others are discussing up on deck, her mind won't stop playing through that moment when Cas had slumped unconscious, his body going perfectly still except for his eyes darting beneath their closed lids.

Remy pokes at one of the chess pieces. He was having one of his visions, wasn't he? This has to be what happened. Remy wants to deny it, but the denial feels hollow. She's fairly certain that they've all just witnessed Cas falling into a dream of a death that hasn't happened yet.

She's also fairly certain that she's seen this before—though not from Cas.

Don't think about it. Do everything you can to avoid thinking about it. Remy plays through a sequence of chess moves with herself, and then she plays through it again. She tries to focus on memories of her father's chess table back home, and the countless evenings she spent there with him, playing in front of the fire.

This is her mistake, though; one specific memory from those days keeps poking through. Her father had been a little quiet on that particular night. He'd complained of a headache. He'd called their game short. Still, the evening could have blended into the hundreds of other evenings just like it—

Until Remy had watched her father collapse on the floor of his study. Until she'd watched him lie there, motionless, except for his closed, darting eyes.

A key rattles in the door, and Captain Hobbes steps inside, alone. He's carrying Remy's research journal. How much of the journal did he read? The idea of it makes Remy feel sick—all her private notes laid bare. All her scheming about the Order of Lazarus might have swayed the captain's opinion of her, yes—but the journal holds plenty of scheming about the captain's own crew, too. He might very well have decided by now that Remy, Finn, and Cas are more trouble than they're worth.

"May I sit?" Captain Hobbes asks.

Remy knows she ought to be groveling for forgiveness—but she can't tear her eyes from the journal still in his hand. *Her* journal. "It's your ship, isn't it?" she hears herself say bitterly.

The captain winces at his own words echoed back to him. "I'm sorry about that. Here."

He holds out the journal for her—an olive branch. Remy accepts it. The book's familiar weight in her hands helps settle her, just a little.

The captain does sit; he takes the chair across the table from Remy and Finn. Remy holds her breath as she waits to hear the verdict of his deliberations.

She has to breathe eventually, though.

"So?" she says at last in the silent room.

"I've sent the longboat to shore with our cargo," the captain says. "We'll be keeping the ship moored here overnight. A fog is rolling in, and we'll have better visibility in the morning for navigating back through the shoals."

None of this answers any of the questions that are currently tying Remy's stomach into knots. She's terrified to ask, but she asks anyway: "And?"

"And what?"

"What are you planning to do about . . . us?"

The captain eyes the chessboard. "Should we play?"

The lack of an answer has Remy good and rattled. She's clutching her journal so tightly that one of her knuckles pops. Maybe he hasn't decided on an answer just yet; maybe his deliberations are still happening. Remy has spent the past two days distracting Captain Hobbes's sailors with chess games while secretly prodding them for information. Or not so secretly—what had he said? *You're not as subtle as you seem to believe.* Maybe the captain is trying to turn her own strategy around on her now.

But he hasn't thrown her off the ship yet. He could've easily put Remy, Finn, and Cas on the longboat with the cargo and banished them to shore—and he hasn't done that, either. If Remy can keep her wits about her, maybe she can play her way out of this.

She starts lining up the pieces on the board.

Remy has no memory of learning *how* to play chess; she only remembers playing it. Her father had started putting the game's pieces into Remy's chubby hands before she was even old enough to talk. On those evenings when they'd play in his study, he was always narrating his strategies, pointing out different patterns and lines of attack. Sometimes he would mark down all the pieces' positions and then let Remy try out various sequences: if this bishop moves here, and then the pawn moves there . . . She'd play one line through to its conclusion, then reset the board and try it a different way, again and again, until she'd finally uncovered the best possible move.

Her father never cared about which of them won or lost; he was too busy teaching. Sometimes, when Remy would reach for a piece, he'd clear his throat. When she peeked up at him, he'd be arching one eyebrow at her: *Look closer.* There would always be something she'd missed, some trap she'd overlooked. She would draw back her hand and rechart her options.

There will be no helpfully arched eyebrow tonight, though, as she and the captain choose their colors. Finn has shifted to sit at Remy's side, watching the two of them with silent intensity. Remy moves first, and she opens their game with a simple but reliable gambit. The captain counters it easily with a gambit of his own. Remy has to force herself to breathe, to take her time planning her moves. She braces herself for whatever questions Captain Hobbes plans to ask of her.

For several turns, though, he doesn't ask anything at all.

"What is this?" Remy says finally. "What are we doing?"

The captain blinks at her. "We're playing chess."

"But aren't you going to . . . I don't know, interrogate us?" She's been debating whether to bring her knight into the center or to keep her focus on the wings, but—center it is. "Or did you find out everything you wanted to know when you stole my journal?"

The captain's head cocks slightly as he studies the board's new arrangement. "I read your journal; you broke into my office and read my private papers. I think we're even." He pauses, then brings his own knight to meet hers. "I'm not much in the mood for interrogating tonight, to be honest. And I suspect we *both* have questions for each other."

Which is fair enough. "What's the meaning of that symbol carved into your ship's figurehead?" Remy asks him.

She can feel Finn's gaze burning into her—it's possible Finn hadn't expected Remy to jump straight in like this. But the captain seems unfazed as ever.

"The one sketched in that book of yours?" he says, nodding at her journal. "I assumed you knew."

"I wouldn't be asking if I did." Remy considers her next move carefully—but she might need to cede some of her own territory to better set up an attack. "You wanted to know, before, why we stowed away on your ship in Boston. That symbol is why.

I've been trying to identify it for years, and your ship is the only other place I've seen it. I thought it was a symbol of the Order of Lazarus."

"It's not a symbol *of* the Order; it's much older than their group. If anything, I expect they've been trying to research it, same as you."

Remy waits for him to go on, but he doesn't. He moves his pawn, and then, for several long moments, he gives Remy the quiet she needs to think through her next strategy. Immortal Gabe had called the captain a chess genius, and Remy already sees why; against the other sailors, she could quickly take control of the board, but Captain Hobbes keeps countering in ways she doesn't expect. When she finally takes her turn, the captain makes his own move a second or two later, and Remy is back to working through every possible sequence, scrambling just to keep up.

"Who was it who taught you to play?" the captain asks after several more turns.

Remy's mind offers up a series of images: the chessboard in her father's study. The glow of the fireplace. Her father's body slumped on the floor, closed eyes flicking as she'd waited, panicked, for him to come to. She can't think about it. "Who taught *you*?" she counters.

"My partner."

"The one who's missing. Who you were looking for in Boston. Mita told us he was your—" She breaks off, though, suddenly embarrassed. How on earth had she intended to finish that sentence? His lover? His sweetheart? His ... oh god ... *paramour*?

But the captain simply says, "I am in love with him, yes, and he with me. We've been together for nearly twenty years."

Remy's face is burning. Why is her face burning? None of this is new information. Yet she feels strangely unfooted—not by Hobbes's easy admission that he's in love with a man, but by his easy admission that he's *in love*. With anyone. He'd said it with such confidence, with total certainty in both his partner's feelings and his own.

What would it feel like to be so sure? Remy can't even imagine it.

"Why did you think he was in Boston?" she asks, redirecting.

"It's not that I thought he was *in* Boston, necessarily—more that I hoped someone in Boston might know where he'd gone, or why he's been out of contact."

"And did you find an answer?"

"I'm not sure yet. This sort of investigation always seems to take multiple paths at once, doesn't it? Judging by your journal, I'm guessing you understand that better than most."

Remy has made another claim on the center of the board, and Captain Hobbes studies the pieces, then continues studying them. It's the longest yet that he's had to spend contemplating a move. Remy allows herself to feel the slightest pinch of pride at that.

"I noticed that there were two handwritings," the captain says. "In your journal. Most of the notes were written in one hand—yours, I imagine—but the pages at the front were written by someone else."

The pinch of pride vanishes. Remy's thoughts have gone rogue again: Cas lying unconscious on the ship's deck. Her father lying unconscious on the rug in his study. It doesn't make any sense; Cas and her father are nothing alike. And yet Remy can see the threads between them now: The way her father had been so distracted, just as Cas had been distracted earlier tonight. All the other times her father had shut himself away for days with no good explanation. And there were rumors, even before her father disappeared. Mrs. Sanderson had latched on to a few strange coincidences—clients of Mr. DeWindt's law firm who, with his help and at his suggestion, had put together their last wills and testaments only a week or two before they'd happened to die. The rumors never really took off; after all, the deaths were accidents. There was no way Mr. DeWindt could have had a hand in causing them.

But he might have known they were coming. He might have known when some unfortunate person in town had an urgent need to get their affairs in order.

All his books about prophecies and omens. Remy has been assuming that he'd found out about the Order of Lazarus first—that all his research on the supernatural had stemmed from the strange interests of this group he was investigating. But what if she's had it backward? What if he'd started researching the supernatural in an attempt to understand the things he was seeing? From there, he certainly could have learned about the Order and its workings.

Or the Order learned about *him*.

She's not sure how long she's been keeping the captain waiting; it's clearly her turn, though she can't recall which piece the captain just moved. In her mind, she can practically feel her father's arched eyebrow: *Look closer*. But she *can't* look closer at this. Everything about this night has shaken her. Over and over, she tries to shove the thoughts back into the window seat bench in her mind, and over and over, they break free.

She moves her rook forward without really thinking about it, just to be doing something—it's sloppy, but for possibly the first time in all her years of playing chess, she doesn't really care.

"The other handwriting is my father's," she tells the captain. "That journal is his. He was taken by the Order of Lazarus for a time, but he was able to spy on them, and to send his notes back to us for safekeeping."

"And you've been continuing his research," the captain guesses. "I'm sorry to hear that he was taken. My partner has had encounters with the Order as well. The encounters were not pleasant."

He captures the rook—Remy saw that coming—and then levels her again with that piercing gaze.

"You mentioned, the other day, that you and your friends are going to Eden because you're looking for someone."

"I don't think my father is *in* Eden," Remy admits. "But I'm hoping someone in Eden might know where he's gone, or how I can find him."

The captain actually chuckles at that. "It seems you and I have similar missions."

"And there's someone else—Cas's friend. He *is* at Eden, we think. He was taken, or sent away, by the same Order member who confronted my father just before he disappeared."

"I see."

"Do you think that the Order might have taken your partner as well?" Remy asks.

"I very much hope not. And even if they had, I don't think they'd be able to hold him for long. No, I think it's more likely that he's been driven into hiding—either for his own safety or for ours."

Something aches in Remy's chest—an ache that started there years ago, when she first received the journal from her father explaining why he couldn't come home. *I plan to run, though not to you; I won't endanger you or our daughters.* Similar missions, indeed.

"Your partner wouldn't tell you if he was going into hiding?" she asks.

The captain's smile is a private one. "He can be a bit... impulsive, to be honest."

"But if you don't think your partner's at Eden, why did you tell us you had business there?"

"You've read my letters. I assume you saw the note about a recent acquisition at Eden."

Remy glances at Finn, who shrugs. "A reaper's glass, right?" Remy says.

The captain nods. "It's something my partner has mentioned, though never in much detail. He's also called it a reaper's mirror, or Death's looking glass. My understanding is that it's akin to a scrying device."

"What does the Order want with it, then?"

"Nothing good. I have theories, but they're *only* theories. The Order has been searching for a reaper's glass for a long time. If it's true they've finally found one... the situation might well be dire enough to force my partner to go underground."

Remy studies the board for long enough to realize she's been cornered; the captain will have her in checkmate in two more moves. There's nothing she can do to escape it. She can't even remember the last time she *didn't* win at chess, and yet the loss doesn't sting as she'd expected. The night has held too many revelations already.

"So your business in Eden is to get this reaper's glass from the Order?" she asks.

The captain nods slowly. "We'll all be safer with it out of their hands. And I have a more selfish motivation as well. If the reaper's glass really is some sort of scrying tool, I might be able to use it to contact my partner, even while he's in hiding."

Remy feels as if she's staring at a sky of constellations, but she can't quite untangle yet where one shape ends and another begins. "Wait," she says. "How would it help you contact your partner?"

Again, he doesn't answer this question, but a different one. "You asked about that symbol on our figurehead," he says. "It's called the Mark of Death. It's a reaper's sigil—a loose transliteration of what appears on a person's soul just before that person is to die."

Remy stares at him. "Pardon?"

"Forgive me—*soul* may be overly simplistic." He waves a hand, as if the word choice is the unbelievable thing here, rather than the entirety of what he's saying. "Essence, anima, what have you ... Alas, the language falls short. As it so often does. Roughly put, when a person is Marked for death, they're placed on a sort of ... list. A record of those who a particular reaper has been tasked with collecting. The Mark is what helps Death find that person when their time comes."

A hundred questions are storming through Remy's mind. A thousand. The only one she manages to pull from the squall is this: "You carved a Mark of Death into your own ship?"

"A version of one, yes. If you study it more closely, you'll notice a few minor adjustments I made. The Mark acts as a sort of summoning spell—a beacon for Death. Marking the *Mori* is what usually allows my partner to find me, even when I'm far out to sea."

The pieces are coming into focus now, all the mysteries she's jotted down in her journal over the past few days: The skeleton toy the captain's partner had supposedly carved for Nessa. The grim reaper figurehead that's meant to be a joke. The alleged training with a chess master who died nearly a hundred years ago. A special scrying device that could offer the captain a means of contacting his partner. *A reaper's mirror. Death's looking glass.*

Captain Hobbes has made the final move; Remy's king is in checkmate. He doesn't bother to gloat. Instead, he says, "I sent Gabe to shore with the longboat earlier. I believe he intends to build a bonfire on the beach, since we'll be staying here overnight. I also believe he's appropriated one of the casks of spirits we were meant to sell in New Brunswick. It seems he's planning quite the blowout."

He stands, hands clasped neatly behind his back.

"Once your friend is feeling well enough, come meet me on deck," he says. "We'll row over to join the celebrations. We have a lot to discuss, now that we've established that we're on the same side. And I think we could all use a drink."

"Your partner," Remy says, while her mind breaks down everything she'd thought she knew about the world and starts trying to relearn it anew. "He's . . . ?"

"Death," the captain says. "Yes. My partner is Death."

XVIII

FINN

It's past ten when Cas finally emerges from the surgeon's cabin, and nearly eleven by the time Finn and Remy have caught him up on the evening's revelations. His color has improved, and he seems more like himself than he did earlier this evening; if anything, he's even louder and cheerier than usual. Finn wonders if he's overcompensating.

All three of them join Captain Hobbes on the last boat that's rowing over to the festivities. Thick fog has settled over the bay, just as the captain had said it would, and the patch of shore where they land the boat seems to exist in its own world. There's the beach, the lighthouse, and Immortal Gabe's bonfire, blazing now as the crew throngs around it. Everything else is erased into mist.

While the other sailors stay by the fire, drinking and talking and playing music on a pair of violins that are slightly out of tune, Finn, Remy, and Cas trail along behind the captain as he paces the shoreline, talking. They climb the bluff to the base of the stone lighthouse, with its lantern shining out through the fog, and they retrace their steps to the water's edge, where the waves foam across the rocks at their feet. And as they walk, the captain tells them about Death.

Apparently the captain's partner—lover—whatever—isn't the *only* Death. Apparently he's one of many Deaths spread across the globe. Apparently he's a reaper, a sort of shepherd of souls. Captain Hobbes relays all this as if it's perfectly straightforward: Death, or some human personification of it. A whole legion of Deaths, each with their own list of souls to take. Finn has known for years the impossibilities this world can contain, and even she feels herself standing in awe. She can only guess at what Remy makes of all this.

Remy listens politely, nods, asks the right questions—but she always does. It's her usual approach to the research: she's curious, seemingly receptive in the moment, betraying nothing about how much she actually believes.

"So you're in love with . . . Death," Cas says for what must be the dozenth time.

"Yes," Captain Hobbes says.

"And you think he's gone into hiding because of something the Order is planning."

"I think it's a possibility, yes."

"How on earth did you and Death meet?" Remy asks.

"I was Marked. I appeared on his list."

"You . . . died?" Cas says.

Hobbes offers a wry smile. "Not exactly."

He tells the story in the same measured tone as always, but Finn senses a remove in his expression: this is a story he's practiced enough times that he can tell it without having to *feel* it. He tells them about the merchant crew he'd sailed with in those days, running shipments up and down the New England coast. About the storm that overtook their ship off Cape Cod one night. The ship breaking apart on the rocks. The sailors trying to swim to shore through an icy sea. Their voices going quiet in the waves around him.

"Death took us one by one," the captain says. "Until it was nearly my turn. I was just clinging to life when he asked my name, and I told him. And I asked his. And we talked. It wasn't love, not yet—but it was a connection, I suppose. He'd been alone for a very long time before that."

"And that was it?" Remy says. "He just . . . let you live?"

The captain smiles. "As I said—he can be a bit impulsive. Reapers aren't meant to intervene when a person is dying. But on that day, he did. He pulled me from the sea and brought me to safety, and he wiped the Mark of Death from my soul, and so I lived."

"So you're immaterial," Cas says. "No, that's not it. Immediate. No—immense. No—"

"Immortal," Remy says. She peers into Cas's cup, empty of whiskey once again, though Finn swears he ran back to refill it just a few minutes ago. "Christ, you're three sheets to the wind, aren't you?"

"No," Cas says. "But getting there. It's medicinal."

"It absolutely is not," Finn tells him.

"I'm not immortal," Hobbes says. "Death saved me once, but I'll appear on his list again in due time. And grateful though I am for this life I've been able to live, I've made my partner promise that when my time comes up again, he won't interfere."

For years, Finn has watched Remy read every book she can get her hands on about these kinds of supernatural forces, and for years, she's watched Remy dismiss it all as nonsense. Something is different about her now, though: she isn't dismissing this. Perhaps it's the captain's straightforward manner. Perhaps it's the fact of the captain himself telling it. Perhaps it's everything about this night, charged and daring and so far removed from their old lives that anything feels possible.

They've circled back to the bonfire now. The captain pauses for a moment just beyond the fire's glow, watching his crew as they make merry.

"I'm choosing to trust you with all of this," he says slowly, "in the hopes that you'll trust me in return. If we set sail again at first light, we'll be at Mount Desert Island by late afternoon. We each have our own aims at Eden. If the Order truly has acquired a reaper's glass, I'd like to retrieve it from them. You"—he nods at Remy—"are looking for information about your father, and you"—at Cas now—"need to rescue your friend. I think all of us can help one another in achieving those aims."

"Yes, please," Remy says at once. "We'd like that very much."

"Good." The captain extends a hand, and Remy shakes it. "Once we're back at sea tomorrow, we'll begin forming our plan. For now..." He gestures at the bonfire. "Gabe has prepared quite the event, and it would be a shame to waste the evening on business. Go, please. Enjoy your night."

He drifts away to speak with a newcomer on the edge of the group—this must be the lighthouse keeper, Gilly, who's briefly entrusted his post to his partner so he can come down to see the revelry. The dancing bonfire light has turned the beach into a sort of devil's carnival, though there's a surprising warmth about the whole scene. Two of the other sailors, Mita and Leo, call Cas over, and he tips his once-again-empty cup at Finn and Remy in a kind of toast.

"Enjoy your night," he echoes, grinning. He looks dead tired under the smile; Finn suspects that his episode earlier tonight took more of a toll than Cas wants to let on. Perhaps she should suggest the three of them return to the ship early. Perhaps she should try to force him to get some rest.

It's too late; he's already gone. Finn and Remy are left standing there, looking at each other.

Something is definitely different about Remy. When she catches Finn's eye, the corner of her mouth tips into a smile, and then it keeps going, wild and a little daring, lighting up her whole face. It's as if some rope in her has cut loose, like she's a sail opening to the wind for the very first time.

There is no way in hell Finn is going back to the ship right now.

From there, the night starts to smear together, like a watercolor painting soaked with too much water. All the colors and details blur until only the general shapes remain: Whiskey. The dueting violins. A few hands of a card game that Finn can't name, though she swears Immortal Gabe is changing the rules every time he explains it to her. More whiskey. Dancing. Remy letting herself be dragged into the circle, pink cheeked and clumsy and shockingly unembarrassed at not knowing the steps. Yet more whiskey. Remy taking Finn by the hand and pulling her into the dance, too. The warmth of their intertwined fingers. The sound of Remy's real laugh as Finn tramples her toes.

When they take a break from dancing and go to refill their cups at the whiskey cask, Kit and Striker are there. They're clearly several rounds in as well; they're leaning on each other, arms tangled together, bodies interwoven so comfortably. Kit detaches herself and gently pushes Striker forward.

"She's got something to say to you," Kit tells Finn and Remy.

Striker looks like she's in physical pain. "Is this really necessary?"

"I think so, yes."

Striker groans, then groans again. "I'm sorry," she says at last, "that I accused you of thievery, although in my defense, you were acting very much like thieves, and so I do think I had good reason to be suspicious."

Now Kit groans instead, burying her face in Striker's shoulder.

"I'm sorry that we were acting like thieves," Remy says. "Although in *our* defense, we'd only just met you and didn't know who we could trust."

Striker nudges Kit's face with her arm. "I think my apology was better."

"I'm not sure either of those *were* apologies," Kit says.

"So we're good?" Remy asks, and Striker gives a curt nod.

"We're good."

They're evidently good enough that Striker pours Remy another drink and beckons her back toward the fire, grinning. Some of the other sailors have gathered there, hearing the local news from Gilly and sharing their own news in return. Finn trails a little behind Remy and settles outside the circle herself, not quite joining the conversation. To her surprise, Kit sits down beside her.

"You two have known each other for quite a long time, haven't you?" Kit asks, nodding from Finn to Remy.

Finn wonders what she might lose by answering this question. "Long enough," she says.

Kit smiles. "I've found that some people form their bonds instinctively—through some intuition, some natural compatibility. And then some bond over time, through shared history. But the two of you strike me as a pair bonded by both."

"You and your . . . Striker seem like that, too."

As soon as the words are out, Finn regrets them. She's a dunderhead and a fool. She can't even decide which part is the most embarrassing: her fumbling phrasing in trying to describe what Striker is to the mate, or her implicit comparison of the relationship between these two women—who are clearly involved in a romantic, *physical* way—with the relationship between herself and Remy. Who clearly aren't.

You and your . . . Striker. Finn wants to die.

But Kit only closes her eyes and angles her face toward the bonfire, basking in its warmth. "I suppose we are. We've been through a lot together—and I was a mess when I first came aboard. I was sure I'd never love again after my husband died. But even back then, from the beginning, she and I just . . . matched."

Finn is still wearing her old scapular under her shirt, and the wool feels hot on her skin. *Sodomy. Abomination.* And yet the awful words won't stick. How can they? Their power comes from shame, and Kit has none to grab on to.

Finn has only ever known the shame. She's not sure what this life is without it. Years of secret trysts, of sneaking in and out through back doors, of guarded conversations that can happen only in whispers and so usually don't happen at all. Of bodies pressed together, but only in the dark.

And here Kit lounges with the firelight bright on her face, talking so freely about the woman she loves.

"I think the whole ship is a bit like that, really," Kit is saying, her eyes still closed. "It takes work, obviously. And time. But I think we all felt that same spark at the beginning—like this is where we're supposed to be. Nessa and I never planned to stay, you know; the captain was only meant to help us relocate. But before we'd even made it out of the gulf, I knew the *Mori* was where I wanted to raise my daughter."

Her eyes are open now, reflecting the dancing flames.

"She's seen enough ugly parts of the world already," Kit says quietly. "So now we're building a better world for her, out here. Out on the water."

"Damn right we are," Striker says as she flops down on Kit's other side. Finn ought to look away before they kiss, but she doesn't. There's no need. Finn has been watching this crew for days, but it's only now, here, at the base of a lighthouse surrounded by fog, that she's starting to appreciate what they've created together. That she's starting to believe it.

"When you and Leo came aboard," Kit says, her head resting on Striker's chest, "how long did it take you to decide you wanted to stay?"

Striker considers this. "About five minutes?" she says, and Kit laughs. "It was like mishpachah, but different. You recognize family, though. Whether or not they're by blood."

There's another story written on her face; Finn doesn't know the details, and yet she recognizes the fierce protectiveness in Striker's gaze as she looks down the beach toward her brother, who's sitting with Cas and Mita. Finn's chest aches as she thinks of her own brother. Of Kieran's boyish smile. Of his boots drumming against the side of the stone bridge over Cedar Brook.

"To *real* family," Kit says, raising her cup in a toast.

Striker taps the cup with her own. "To the people who feel like home."

XIX

CAS

"I think this is the best party I've ever been to," Cas says.

He, Mita, and Leo have settled in one of the beached longboats away from the fire. Leo is perched by the lantern at the boat's prow, a sewing kit spread out on the bench beside him.

"Do you spend most parties sitting off in the corner sewing?" Mita asks, and Cas grins.

"No, but maybe I should. Do you?"

"Yes," Leo says without looking up. "Or reading. Can you hand me those scissors?"

Cas hands him the scissors. Back in the surgeon's cabin earlier that evening, Mita had asked Cas's permission to recruit Leo for their tailoring project; she'd declared Leo to have the best sewing skills of anyone aboard the *Mori*. Cas had agreed to this, though he'd cringed as Mita filled him in on the particulars of their task, as Leo processed the *why* of it in real time. But Leo had only blinked, then blinked again, then said, "All right. So where do we start?" He'd approached it like a puzzle, focused and businesslike as he and Mita worked out the design.

Someone did, in fact, have a vest near enough to Cas's size. Over the last several hours, while Cas and his friends were speaking with the captain, Mita and Leo have been hard at work repurposing the vest into an alternative to Cas's stays. Now, their creation is nearly finished: a waistcoat of sorts that Cas can wear over his shirt, reinforced with stiff sailcloth to flatten the front without having to pull his chest so tightly.

Leo ties the end of his thread in a tidy knot and clips the tail. "I'm not really one for parties, usually," Leo admits. "This is nice, though. Here, see how this fits."

Cas accepts the waistcoat and tries it on. As he fastens the buttons and tugs down the hem, he can feel himself settling back into that warm quiet he'd felt when he'd seen his own reflection in Boston. For days, it's all been bumping together inside him—the joy, but also the apprehension, waiting for the reckoning to come. The reckoning apparently isn't coming. He can still hardly believe he gets to just . . . *be*.

"Better?" Mita asks when he's been quiet for too long.

"Yes! Yes, this is . . ." All of Cas's instincts tell him to say something blithe and insincere, but he pushes those instincts away to instead say the truth: "This is perfect. Thank you."

Mita beams at him. "Glad we could help."

"Hand it back for a moment," Leo says. "I just saw a spot I missed on the side."

As Leo patches up an area where the stitching came loose, as Cas sprawls back on one of the longboat's benches to wait, he can feel Mita studying him. For once, he lets himself be studied. He hadn't wanted to pry, earlier. He'd hesitated to ask. But as they've been sitting here some distance from the bonfire, as they've been working, Mita has slowly offered up pieces of her life before. She's talked about growing up along the coast of England, already an outsider because of her race, but knowing there was something else, too. She's talked about the slow-dawning realization that the word *woman* could hold her better and more fully than anything else. She's talked about the pockets of community she'd found in London and Liverpool, and the nagging sense that something was still missing for her among the pale-skinned Brits living in the shadows back on land.

Her father had been a sailor; he'd left his home in Gujarat to crew a merchant ship with the British East India Company. And so Mita had followed in his footsteps and taken to sea, bouncing from ship to ship, honing her carpentry skills. Then she'd found the *Memento Mori*.

"The captain has a habit of picking up strays," Mita had said, smiling out at her fellow sailors spread across the beach. "Particularly strays who struggle with certain... *rules* of Western society. Most of our crew could be tried as sodomites or mollies under one definition or another. Captain Hobbes seems to pull in all manner of degenerates like us."

"I don't think it's degenerate," Cas had said without thinking, and Mita had laughed.

"Aye, *we* know that. Until everybody else catches on, though, we have to stick together."

Cas had liked the way she'd said *we*—an invitation. Like Cas could be included in that *we*, if he wants to be.

Now someone calls Mita's name from across the beach, and she goes to join the others at the fire, leaving Cas and Leo alone. Leo is quiet as he makes the final adjustments. Cas had offered to help a few times, but he's never had much patience for sewing, and after Leo had seen his staggering, lopsided stitches, he'd politely taken the fabric back.

"I'm sorry about my sister," Leo says. "I heard her yelling at you and your friends earlier."

Cas is glad that Leo had gone belowdecks with Nessa before Cas had *truly* caused a scene. "Can't really blame her, can I? We shouldn't have lied to you all." Cas watches Leo tilt the waistcoat back and forth in the lantern light, checking his work. "*I* shouldn't have lied."

Leo pauses. "When did you lie?"

Cas raises an eyebrow at him. Leo waits. Cas gestures at the waistcoat in his hands, then at his own chest, then back at the waistcoat. Leo makes a skeptical humming sound.

"What?" Cas asks, frowning.

"That's not really a *lie*, though, is it?" Leo says as he trims the final few threads. "It's just . . . something that hadn't come up. Here."

He watches Cas refasten the waistcoat like an artist watching his painting find its place on the gallery wall. Cas takes a deep breath. The vest is a hell of a lot more comfortable than his old stays.

"Striker's just protective," Leo says. "Of me. Of all of us. Do you have any siblings?"

"No. Remy and I sort of grew up together, but . . ." Cas isn't sure why he's even brought up Remy; Leo doesn't need to know the ugly details of their history. Something about the party, the crew laughing and dancing around the bonfire, Mita's openness earlier about her own journey, seems to have cast a spell over the night. "It's complicated," he says.

Leo doesn't press for more. "I think that's normal, probably. Anyway, my sister and I have been sailing with the captain for a long time now—but before that, for years, it was just the two of us on our own."

"Why did you leave home?" Cas asks, then immediately regrets it. "Sorry, I shouldn't— Never mind. You don't need to answer that."

"If I don't want to answer, I won't answer. It's fine." Leo starts tidying up the sewing kit, fitting the needle and thread into their small leather case. "Our parents thought there was something wrong with me, back then; I was too quiet, too . . . odd. Too easily overwhelmed. Not what they'd hoped for in a son, I guess." He gives a wry smile, as if he knows, somehow, that Cas might relate. "And when things got bad, my sister took me and ran."

Cas doesn't know what to say to any of this. "I'm sorry."

"I'm not," Leo says, so emphatically that Cas is certain he means it. "Everything is a thousand times better here—for me *and* for her. And the funny thing is that I'm *not* so quiet anymore, and I *don't* get overwhelmed so easily. Because everyone here just lets me be."

He folds up the sewing kit and tucks it into his pocket.

"And look, you didn't know any of that about me until just now. So was I lying before?"

"Of course not," Cas says—and only when he sees Leo's smirk does he realize how he's been set up. He snorts. "All right, fine, you've made your point. Are you coming over by the fire?"

"For a while, maybe." Leo thinks for a moment. "And when it gets overwhelming, I'll come back here and read."

There's something calming about Leo's straightforwardness; Cas keeps expecting to misstep, and then keeps being surprised that he hasn't. Maybe Cas should feel guilty for enjoying himself while Henry's still in danger—but it's not as if he can do anything about the delay. Besides, the guilt can't get a good foothold tonight. They'll reach Eden tomorrow; in the meantime, Cas follows Leo across the beach. He joins the crew, and he listens to Gabe tell an outrageous story about the time he nearly got into a duel with a whaling captain, and he laughs harder than he has in years.

It really is the best party Cas has ever been to.

XX

FINN

Eventually, the bonfire burns low. The whiskey runs out. The music tapers off until it's only Immortal Gabe singing a long, heartbreaking ballad in Spanish while tears course gently down his cheeks.

In the end, the night is this: Remy and Finn lying side by side on the rocks by the water's edge, Remy's coat spread beneath them like a blanket, both of them gazing at the stars. It's just like a dozen other nights the two of them have had before at Dungeon Rock—but it's also completely different. *Remy* is different. Finn can't stop staring at her.

"How are you managing all of this?" Finn hears herself ask.

Remy rolls onto her side to look at her. Her hair has come loose from its braid and now tumbles out around her, salt-sprayed and curlier than it ever is back home.

"What do you mean?" Remy asks. "The whiskey? It's very likely that I'm *not* managing it." She laughs, that same easy, unabashed laugh that's been coming so readily tonight. "Ask me again in the morning."

"No, I mean . . . Death. The captain. Everything he's told us tonight. It's a lot to take in, even for me. So I suppose I'm just wondering . . . ?"

Remy studies Finn's face. "You want to know if I believe it."

This is precisely what Finn wants to know. She waits.

Remy flops onto her back again. The button of her collar has come undone, showing several more inches of skin around her neckline than Finn is used to seeing there.

"Do you know, I've always envied you," Remy says. "The way you're so . . . *certain* about everything. You always have been."

Finn tears her gaze away from Remy's skin. She lies on her back, too, facing the stars. "I don't think certainty is something to envy."

"Why wouldn't it be? You know what you believe in, and you've always seemed so sure of yourself. You're so sure about what's true."

Her voice holds the same earnest longing that Cas's had the other day: *Have you ever just . . . wanted something, for your whole life, even though you never really imagined it was possible?* Finn wants so many impossible things. But Remy is wrong about certainty; in Finn's experience, it's more curse than blessing. There are too many certainties that Finn can't unknow, truths she wishes had stayed buried.

What use is it to know what you want when you also know that you can't have it?

"I've spent all these years reading my father's books," Remy is saying. "All about spells and sigils and demons and prophecies, and I kept thinking that if I could just learn everything, and put the pieces in the right order, I'd find some kind of answer. About *any* of it. And instead it only feels like I've got more questions. And now, with these past few days on the ship, and with everything the captain's told us tonight . . ."

The stars are sprawling out above them—somehow both closer and farther away than they seem to be back in Windover.

"I have no idea what to believe anymore," Remy says. "I have no idea what's real. I just wish I had some sort of . . . *proof*, you know? Something irrefutable. So that I could stop wondering and just *know*."

And that's something Finn does understand.

When she was very young—back when she was much less certain, when she still went to Mass every Sunday and still believed the Virgin Mary might bother with someone like her—Finn used to pray for a sign. She used to ask the Blessed Mother to show her a miracle, however small, however insignificant. Something real and undeniable that could put to rest forever the doubts that always plagued Finn's heart. Kieran seemed to believe so easily. Their mother did, too. Finn *wanted* to believe like that, *wanted* to have that same unshakeable faith.

There's an irony to it now. The thing that solidified her belief in a higher power was the very same thing that damned her.

When Finn sits up, her head doesn't spin as she'd expected. The whiskey is losing its grip on her. Later, perhaps she'll try to convince herself that the liquor had a hand in this foolhardy decision she's about to make, but it won't be true. Her mind now is clear.

"Can I show you something?" Finn says.

"Of course."

Remy sits up now, too, and the coat on the ground bunches under her. They face each other, cross-legged, Finn's trouser-clad knees pressed against Remy's skirt-covered ones. When Finn holds out her hands, Remy doesn't hesitate. She lays her own hands on top, pressing their palms together.

"Here's the rule," Finn says.

Remy laughs again. "Oh, there are *rules* now?"

"Only the one, but you have to agree to it, or else I won't show you anything at all. Here's the rule: you're going to have about a billion questions after this, but you aren't allowed to ask any of them."

"What?" Remy says. "No questions at all?"

Finn waits.

"Not even one?"

Finn continues waiting.

Remy's mouth opens again, then closes. She nods, clamping her lips together in a theatrical show of shutting up.

Finn closes her eyes.

She finds the flames more easily this time—when she searches that pit inside her, the fire there is flickering more brightly than it had been when she'd needed it back on the Boston docks. Perhaps bringing it out that day had stoked it, given it oxygen after years shut away. Perhaps *everything* about these past few days has stoked it.

She reaches for that spark of energy. That inner will. *Vitalis vis.* They'd only ever told her the Latin, but Finn had looked up the translation later, when everything was over and done. *Vitalis*, meaning "life-giving." *Vis*, meaning "strength." Also, "force." Also, "essence." What was it the captain had said? *Alas, the language falls short.*

But the fire doesn't—it's burning strong as ever, like it's begging Finn to bring it to the surface again. She needs only the smallest flicker, though. Not enough to hurt. Just enough to *show*. She imagines catching a single spark of it in her cupped palms.

And then she pushes it out of her.

She knows the moment it works. Even if she hadn't opened her eyes to see the spray of sparks—the striking of invisible metal to invisible flint—Finn *feels* the heat on her fingertips. She feels it release. She hears Remy's sharp intake of breath. When Finn meets her eye, Remy is staring at her open-mouthed.

"What was . . . ?"

She catches herself, though, and cuts off her own question before it can form. Her hands are trembling slightly. Finn had expected Remy to pull away when she felt the sparks there, but she didn't; if anything, she's grabbed on to Finn's hands ever more tightly. Her fingers are warm, just as they'd been when she'd clenched Finn's hand in the hidden smuggling compartment in the hold the other day. Finn can't tell if the pulse she's feeling there is Remy's or her own.

"Show me again," Remy breathes. There's an eager wonder in her voice. Something in Finn's heart is reshaping itself, letting go of a weight she hadn't known she was carrying. This fire inside her has always been inextricably tied up with the worst day of Finn's life. The worst thing she's ever done. She's spent so long trying to bury it. And now, as she shows it to Remy and sees not fear, not horror, but *awe* on this beautiful girl's face—this is a miracle in itself. Years of self-disgust washing clean. A baptism. A confession. Something bigger than any sacrament.

Finn turns both of their hands over so that Remy's are underneath, supporting her own, as she faces her palms toward the velvet sky.

This time, when Finn reaches for the fire, she doesn't push it out of her all at once. Instead, she draws the energy to the surface and holds it there—warm, humming, alive. She lets it crackle through her hands and knuckles and the tips of her fingers until the sparks all merge and form the smallest of flames in the center of her palm, like the nub of an invisible candle. The flame dances, then steadies, dances, then steadies. They've both leaned close enough that their breaths make it flicker, though the light between them doesn't go out.

"Lord," Remy whispers.

Finn watches the glow of the tiny flame paint Remy's cheeks. Their faces are much closer together than she'd realized. Close enough that she can see the individual shadows of each of Remy's eyelashes. Close enough that they're breathing the same air. Close enough that they could kiss.

Finn releases a long breath, and the fire flickers out. But they stay there for a long moment, staring at each other. Finn's heart is a fluttering thing. For one wild, delirious moment, she thinks Remy is going to lean in and close the gap between them.

Remy doesn't lean in.

The questions she'd promised not to ask are written on her face in the moonlight. The answers are there, too. Finn can see them. Remy knows now, whether or not she's willing or ready to believe it.

"Some kind of optical illusion," Remy says. "From the bonfire."

It's a sham of a guess—a pretense of denial. The bonfire has nearly burned to ashes by now, anyway.

"Or static electricity," Remy says. "It didn't feel like electricity, though. It felt . . . warm. And *gentle*. It wasn't like anything I've ever felt before."

Magic, Finn thinks, offering it like a gift. Magic, magic, magic.

"Lord," Remy says again. Then a third time, the word feathered by a laugh: "*Lord*. Did it hurt, when you . . . ? I'm sorry, I know that's technically a question."

Finn shakes her head, though. "No, it didn't hurt. Did it hurt you?"

"No," Remy says, marveling.

And Finn ought to leave the matter here. She ought to keep to these safer waters, just as she always has—let Remy think it over. Trust that she'll come to the truth of it in her own time.

But she thinks of the *vitalis vis*, and Kieran, and the way Cas had looked at her earlier tonight—the dread in his eyes when he'd come to on the deck.

Time is a luxury Finn might not have.

"I understand, you know," Finn says. "Why you've held off on believing what's in your father's books. I know why you've kept it at such a remove. Because it's all tangled up, isn't it, and if it's true, if you actually believe it's true, then you know what it means for . . ."

Her courage falters, though, before she can say, *your father*. Remy drops her hands.

"What are you talking about?" Remy says.

The safer waters are well behind her now. Finn kicks out into the surf. "I believe Cas, about his visions. And I believe everything the captain told us tonight. And all of your father's books. Well, most of the books—some of them are garbage, of course." She waits for Remy to laugh. Remy doesn't laugh. "And I've let you believe what you need to up till now, but it's all getting so much bigger than us, and—"

"*Let* me?" Remy cuts in. "You've *let* me believe it?"

Finn is quiet.

"I don't need you to protect me," Remy snaps. "Is that what you think you're doing? Like when you ran off on your own to make a distraction back on the wharf? Why are you always so goddamn secretive? Lord—I feel like I don't even know you sometimes. And now you show me this"—she gestures wildly at Finn's hands, the sparks well and truly extinguished now—"but you say I can't even *ask* you about it?"

All at once, Finn is tired, exhausted, dragging with fatigue. She's swum out too far, and now she can't swim back, and she doesn't have anything at all to say as Remy waits, and then stops waiting, and then stands, grabbing for her coat, which Finn is still sitting on.

I am a fool, Finn thinks as she shifts awkwardly to the side so Remy can snatch the coat away and storm off. I am a fool, I am a fool, I am a goddamn fool. The cold of the rocks creeps through her trousers and freezes her skin, and still she sits there. I am a fool, and Remy is not, and Remy deserves so much better.

To think that, just moments ago, Finn had wondered if Remy might kiss her.

The sun is rising as they all row back to the *Mori* at last. The high of the night is wearing off, and the hangovers are setting in, and the crew is far surlier than usual as they work to get the ship underway. Finn nominally helps for a while, though really she's just grabbing any excuse to avoid going down to her bunk, where Remy will doubtless be. Finn isn't ready to face her again just yet—or possibly ever.

But exhaustion tugs at her, and there's only so long Finn can stall. When she finally retires to the fo'c'sle, Remy isn't even there. It's only Cas, sitting in the middle of the floor, struggling to remove his boots. He grins up at Finn when she pushes through the curtain door.

"What a night, yeah?"

"Sure," Finn says.

"Did you know that you can just go off and read somewhere, during a party? Like if it's too noisy, you can just . . . take a break?"

Finn squints at him in the dim light. "Were you off reading somewhere?"

"No, but Leo was! Isn't that grand?"

Finn rubs a hand over her face. "Sure."

He's clearly still in his altitudes; Finn would guess it even if he *weren't* tugging at his left boot as if baffled by how to get his foot out of it. But as Finn tries to squeeze past him, he grabs her arm.

"Wait," he says. "Finn, wait."

In an instant, his demeanor shifts, and the two of them are right back on Windover Common.

"I have to tell you something," he says, with the same frantic energy he'd had that night when he called out to her across the darkened square.

Finn's throat suddenly feels very tight. "You're drunk," she says.

"No. Well, yes. It doesn't matter. I—"

"You should sleep. You can tell me in the morning."

Cas scowls at that. "I *hate* sleep." He still hasn't let go of her sleeve. "Look, Finn, I have to tell you. I have to do this. You know about the visions. You know how I—"

"*Cas.*"

The sharpness in her tone seems to cut through his resolve, and his grip on her loosens. Finn unhooks her arm.

"Go to bed," she tells him. "Don't say something you're going to regret."

He falls silent at last and lets her pass.

Finn doesn't even bother taking off her own boots. She climbs into her bunk fully clothed and rolls over, her back to Cas, facing instead the sloping wall where the hull folds in around them. This shouldn't be a surprise. It *isn't* a surprise. She's known her own fate for years. And yet the seriousness on Cas's face just now was too close to a confirmation—Finn can't unsee it. The curse of certainty.

Ever since Cas told them about his visions back at Dungeon Rock—ever since he told them what he sees each time—Finn has had only one guess about what he'd wanted to tell her that night when he'd called out to her on Windover Common.

Finn is going to die—and Cas has seen how it will happen.

Perhaps when they wake, when the alcohol has worn off, Cas will have forgotten all about this conversation. But he won't have forgotten his glimpse into Finn's future. And Remy won't have forgotten what Finn showed her beneath the lighthouse's glow. I brought this on myself, Finn thinks for the thousandth time, as she clenches and unclenches the fingers that she'd used to burn her own name onto that terrible page years ago. She runs her hand over the brown strands of her scapular. She thinks about praying. She doesn't pray.

I brought this on myself.

XXI

CAS

"What exactly is this reaper's glass you've been searching for?" Remy asks the captain. "What is it meant to look like?"

They've gathered belowdecks around the ship's dining table, though it's been repurposed now for a kind of war council with a handful of sailors and Cas, Remy, and Finn. Captain Hobbes sits at the table's head, his elbows resting on the arms of his chair. It's nearly noon, but everyone here looks haggard and bleary; even the always-unruffled captain seems distinctly ruffled by last night's revelry.

The captain rubs a hand over his beard as if trying to wipe away his own exhaustion. "To be honest, I don't know. The official texts aren't much use here. Most of our knowledge about reapers comes from either sailors' lore—a dubious source—or from my partner directly. And he isn't here to ask. A reaper's glass could mean a literal spyglass or mirror—or it could be more metaphorical."

"Do you know what the Order wants with it?" Remy asks.

"From what I understand, this glass has the means to create a spiritual connection with Death. Just as I would use it to contact my partner, I suspect the Order would use it to find him. They've been trying to draw out Death for years."

Cas, for his part, has a pounding headache, either from his vision yesterday or his drinking last night. Probably it's from both. Every time someone says *Death* to refer to the person, his head throbs a little harder.

"The list in your book," Captain Hobbes says to Remy. "The disappearances."

"Oh, right," Cas says. "The ritual murders."

"They're not—" Remy starts, but then she pauses to consider. "You think they *are* ritual murders."

"I think they may have been the Order's attempts to lure my partner to their seminary—at least in part. A few years ago, he went to retrieve a soul there only to find a trap laid for him. The Order didn't manage to hold him, obviously—but it was a narrow escape. Ultimately he had to stop visiting Eden even when a soul there was Marked."

A hopeful thought occurs to Cas. "Wait. Does that mean no one at the seminary can die?"

"My partner doesn't take their lives," Captain Hobbes says. "Only their souls, once their bodies can no longer hold them. A person can still die there—but they won't have a shepherd to guide them to whatever comes next."

Hopes, dashed. Cas tries to hide his disappointment. He turns back to the table, to the spare bit of paper he's commandeered so he can sketch aimlessly as they talk. His concentration is a wayward thing even *without* the headache, and he can focus better with a pencil in his hand.

"That's a rotten hand to be dealt," Remy is saying.

"The souls at Eden may have found their own way to whatever lies beyond," the captain says. "Or they may still be wandering. It *is* a rotten hand. My partner did not make the decision lightly to abandon them."

Finn is jammed so close beside Cas at the table that their elbows keep bumping. She hasn't yet mentioned their conversation from the wee hours of this morning, which is a relief and an agony all at once.

"Back to the reaper's glass, though," Cas says. "How are you supposed to steal it back when we don't even know what it looks like?"

The captain turns to Remy again. "What do you know about the Order's leader?"

"The Reverend John Smith? Not as much as I'd like. I know that his followers in the Order call him the Shepherd. I know he has influence with powerful people. I know he did his schooling in England and founded the Eden seminary a few years after he moved to America."

"And you know he's something of a collector," Captain Hobbes says.

Remy opens her journal and starts flipping through the pages, looking for something. "I suppose. I have letters from a former student there. He mentioned Smith's library and archive a few times."

"To answer your question," Captain Hobbes tells Cas, "if Smith does have a reaper's glass, I think he'll be keeping it with the other artifacts in his collection." He must see the blankness in Cas's stare, because he adds, "It should be labeled."

"So you need access to the archive," Remy says. "That's good. Any records of my father's time at Eden will be in the archive as well. I've only been able to piece together a bit about the building's layout . . ."

As she shows the captain a diagram she's drawn on a page of her journal, Cas returns to his own sketching. He's not sure how it still manages to hurt every time Remy mentions her father. Objectively, Cas knows that this isn't truly about him; objectively, he knows that Remy's dismissal of his visions has more to do with grief and denial and a much deeper sort of hurt than he'll ever be able to understand. Knowing this doesn't lessen the sting.

The table has gone quiet. They're all looking at Cas expectantly. He has no idea what the question was. "Sorry?"

"We're talking about Ashworth," Remy prompts. "Breaking into the archive is one thing, but getting Ashworth out will be another matter altogether."

Her eyes have drifted to the sketch in front of him. Cas is only half-conscious of what he's even been drawing—a face in profile. Only now, as he looks down at it, does he recognize the high forehead, the long, sloping nose. The face is Henry's. And yet it isn't quite Henry now—it's a younger version of him, less polished, less deliberate. The earnest parts of himself that, lately, Henry always seems to want to hide.

"I'll admit that I'm curious," Captain Hobbes says—his eyes have found Cas's drawing, as well. "Do you know why the Order took your friend?"

Cas trusts Captain Hobbes, really—but there's no way to explain why the Order took Henry without explaining everything else and telling him about the visions. How would the captain react to *that*? How would *any* of them react? Cas has been breaking all his old rules lately—but this feels like too much. And he's sitting here squeezed between Remy, who doesn't believe him, and Finn, who's going to die. Cas still doesn't know how to tell Finn about the monster that's coming for her—but he can't do it like this.

Slowly, Cas says, "I think they believe Henry is someone he isn't. Or that he can do something he can't. Once they realize they've made a mistake..." He thinks of the blood on the forest floor, the pair of severed eyes. "I don't want to find out what they'll do to him."

It's a half answer, and the captain must know it. He doesn't push. Remy is still staring down at Cas's drawing. Cas crumples it, suddenly self-conscious.

It's Kit who finally breaks the silence.

"None of this is going to be a straightforward break-in, is it?" she says. "It's going to take time to search through the archive. We'll need a distraction. And that's not even starting on how we're going to get inside, or find your friend, or *find* the archive in the first place."

"Can't we just ask?" Cas says.

Remy laughs, as if she thinks Cas has made a joke. But he isn't joking. The beginnings of a plan have been shaping in his mind ever since the captain described the Reverend John Smith as a collector.

"No, really," he says. "I can write ahead and request a meeting with the Reverend Smith—I'll ask him to give me and Henry a private tour, including the archive."

"He doesn't even allow his own students inside the archive," Remy says. "Why on earth would he let *you* in?"

"Because my father wants to make a donation."

Every eye in the room is staring at him. Cas forces himself to keep talking.

"He's one of these collector types, too," he explains to the captain. "And he's been looking for the right institution to include in his will, to send all his books and papers where he knows they'll be well cared for. Now that Henry has enrolled at Eden, he's thinking of donating all of it to the seminary."

"Is he really?" Remy asks.

"No, but it's a good pretense, isn't it? And Henry can vouch for my father's collection. Smith seems like the type to get excited about original Jonathan Edwards manuscripts, doesn't he?"

The captain's raised eyebrows indicate that there's truth to this.

"Dekker can vouch, too," Remy says suddenly. Her eyes are wide as she tells the others about Pastor Dekker, his involvement with the Order, and their sighting of him at the Boston docks. "He was boarding a ship that was heading for Eden. He might very well have arrived there already."

"That could complicate things," Kit says.

"Or it could help." Remy turns back to Cas. "It's not as if Dekker will have time to write your father and confirm the story—but he can confirm to Smith that your father's collection is real."

"Right," Cas says, trying very hard not to think about the possibility of having to face Dekker in all this. "I'll say that my father sent me in his stead to see the archive specifically. Once Smith has shown it to us, I can signal you somehow, and then Henry and I will keep him occupied elsewhere while you do your searching. When everything's done, Henry will come with me back into town, claiming he's just escorting me to the hotel—and then we run."

It sounds so simple as he says it aloud—surely too simple. Cas waits for someone to tell him that this is a terrible idea.

But Captain Hobbes only says, "Your father has an original manuscript by Jonathan Edwards?"

"Oh, he has several. Never shuts up about them, either. He's much prouder of all his old books than he'll ever be of me."

It's meant to be a joke, but no one laughs. Captain Hobbes is studying Cas in that same intense, bookish way he'd studied them all on their first afternoon aboard—though now it's as if he's reached a new chapter, one that's making him reexamine everything he's read so far.

"So?" Cas says when the silence has stretched for so long that he thinks he might actually scream just to break it.

The captain looks to Kit, and his shoulder twitches—the closest he's ever come to a shrug. "This could actually work."

As the captain starts scribbling notes, as he and Kit start talking through the details in a verbal shorthand that's nearly impossible for anyone else to follow, Remy leans in close to Cas, dropping her voice low.

"You're forgetting something, though," she says. "If you're leveraging your family connections, if you're meeting with Dekker . . ."

She breaks off when she seems to realize the others can still hear her; there's no room for private conversation here. But Cas knows where she was heading. He's been bracing for it—as if he could forget this particular consideration.

"I know," he tells her, keeping his tone light. "It's fine. I'll sign the letter with my full name, make all the proper introductions. Dress the part and everything. It's not as if I've forgotten how to curtsy in the past week."

He can feel the eyes on him again. He tugs at the hem of his newly tailored vest. And yet the eyes here are not hostile; Mita had been right yesterday, when she'd said the crew would accept him.

Mita is watching him carefully now, a question in her gaze. Cas gives her a short nod. Mita nods back.

"Great," Cas says. "So it's a plan."

Cas's leg is jittering again, rattling the table. He plants his heel on the floor—firm. He turns back to Finn.

"Do you still have my old clothes from Boston?" he asks.

They stay in the dining room for hours, until Cas's mind has turned to porridge, until he's paced the perimeter so many times that he swears the floorboards are starting to wear thin. He writes out a letter explaining the pretense and requesting his meeting with the Reverend John Smith. Then he writes the letter out three more times, twice because Remy and Captain Hobbes can't stop picking at the wording, once because his handwriting is becoming illegible. He lets Kit quiz him on his story until she's satisfied with his delivery. He tries to pay attention as Remy and the captain trace routes on the map and discuss the path they'll take through the woods that surround the seminary.

As the afternoon wears on, though, Cas can feel himself slipping. He's never had the patience for the finicky logistics at which both Remy and Captain Hobbes seem to excel. They're both bent over the table, the twin architects of this scheme: Remy, with her obsessive knowledge about Eden and the Order of Lazarus, and Captain Hobbes, with knowledge about nearly everything else.

"I'd like us to drop anchor here," Captain Hobbes is saying, marking his map beside a small outcropping just south of the town. "Out of view of the main docks. The *Mori* is too noticeable—we can't risk the attention. We'll need to send a boat into town tonight, though, to deliver the letter."

Immortal Gabe is balancing his stool on its back two legs. "I'll go. I've got a connection in Eden who can probably take it up to the seminary."

"Somebody you slept with," Striker fills in, and Gabe's stool legs land with a *thud*. "Don't look so shocked—your 'connections' are always men you slept with the last time we were in the area."

"Not always men," Kit points out.

Gabe has recovered enough to return his stool to its precarious stance. He smiles dreamily at the ceiling. "Well, this one is. And he's handsome, too—you ought to see his—"

"Gabe," Kit tells him. "Focus."

"He'll help us out. I can row over tonight with the letter. We'll get the Little Prince's appointment arranged."

"Good." Captain Hobbes notes something on one of the half dozen lists spread before him. "Mita, how many crew will you need to manage on the *Mori* when our party goes ashore?"

The realization hits Cas like a plunge into ice water. "Wait. You aren't coming with us?"

Mita eyes him ruefully. "My skills will be of the most use here, on the ship. I've no talent for sneaking around, and if things go badly inside, I'm not much of a fighter."

"You fought me well enough," Cas says, rubbing at the nearly faded bruise on his forehead from their disastrous brawl in the office.

Gabe snorts. "From what I've heard, that says more about your fighting skills than hers, mate."

Cas forces a laugh at his own expense and resumes his pacing. The pressure in his chest has started to grow again, though, pushing at the sides of its bowl. It shouldn't be a shock. Cas knows the plan. He already knows who's going to be beside him when he steps inside the seminary.

But he thinks of the reassuring smile Mita had offered when Cas explained what he intended to do.

He's only just now considering who *won't* be beside him.

It's fine, though. More than fine. It's better this way. Even with all the captain's scheming, there's no small amount of risk involved, and it's better that Mita will be out of danger—one less person to worry over. Cas definitely isn't spiraling. He's already plenty worried about Henry, who might be injured, or dying, or dead even now, even as they're planning his rescue. What if they're too late? What if all this is for nothing? Cas hasn't seen Henry's death—not like he saw Remy's father's—but that doesn't mean it isn't coming. For every death Cas foresees, there must be hundreds or thousands he doesn't.

Finn has been sitting quietly at the table all afternoon, occasionally murmuring questions but mostly just watching as the plan comes together. Finn, whose death Cas *has* seen. Finn, who *will* be there with him when he meets the Reverend John Smith tomorrow.

All right, yes—Cas is spiraling. He paces, even though there isn't enough space to do it properly. The room is too small, packed with too many people. The ceiling is too low.

Everything feels like it's closing in on him.

It's a relief when the bell rings for all hands a few minutes later. A sailor from abovedeck reports that they'll be dowsing sails soon; the island is in sight. Cas helps gather up the maps and papers from the table, but when the others head up to the main deck, he mutters an excuse about getting his clothes together for tomorrow and stays below. It's not as if he'll be missed. He's not even sure what dowsing the sails means, much less how to do it.

Cas finds the cloak—the velvet-trimmed abomination his mother had forced on him the day they'd run away to Boston—bundled in Finn's carpetbag in the fo'c'sle, just as she'd said it would be. He spreads it over the makeshift table in the crew's quarters to assess the damage. Finn had folded and packed it meticulously—and yet the bulk of the cloak is made from silk, and it's been shoved inside a carpetbag at sea for several days. It's taken on just enough moisture to wrinkle spectacularly.

The little black-and-white cat is sitting in the cabin's open door now, her eyes fixed on the miles of expensive fabric spilling over the table's edge. She mewls.

Cas frowns down at her. "What do you want?"

The cat mewls again. Then she slinks over to the table, leaps up, and settles into the pile of velvet around the cloak's hood, her paws tucked out of sight beneath her.

Cas sighs. He doesn't have the heart to move her—not when she looks far more comfortable nestled in his old clothes than *he's* ever felt in them. Instead he fetches a jar of fresh water and sets to work dampening and smoothing out the worst of the creases. This, at least, is something he can manage. A concrete task. It's easier to focus on tidying up his old cloak than to fret about what's coming in this next day or two. Or, worse—what's coming after that.

"Need a hand?"

Cas startles, but it's only Mita—she's standing in the doorway, tall enough that the kerchief in her hair brushes the top beam.

"Sorry," Cas says, drying his hands on his trousers. "I can come up on deck if they need more people."

"No, no. They're managing well enough. I thought I'd see if you wanted company."

There's an unspoken weight to the offer, and on the heels of the gratitude Cas feels toward Mita comes a rush of annoyance at himself: he must not have hidden his nerves back in the dining room as well as he'd hoped. He must not be hiding *any* of this well.

Mita is eyeing the cloak still spread over the table. "This is it, then?" she says.

"This is it."

He'd forgotten how *long* the cloak is—hardly the fashion these days, but Cas's mother has always favored exorbitance over style. If he keeps the buttons fastened up the front tomorrow, he might be able to get away with trousers under it instead of a dress. The idea brings more comfort than he'd anticipated. He's already been planning to wear the cloak for the full visit, anyway; he needs the hood to cover up his recent haircut. And the cloak's hem nearly reaches the floor. If Cas is wearing his new sailors' duds underneath, if he's wearing his vest, who but he will even be the wiser?

"I think the captain might have a flatiron somewhere," Mita is saying, running a finger over the dampened wrinkles. "What is this, silk? Can it take an iron?"

"Honestly, I have no idea," Cas says.

"Probably better not to risk it, then. This is a bit grand for traveling clothes, isn't it?"

Cas snorts. "You haven't met my mother."

It feels wrong to invoke his mother's name here, though—like he's holding open the back door and inviting a pack of angry wolves to dinner. Mita must see something on his face; her dark eyes are soft as she studies him.

"Cas," Mita starts.

He reaches for the water again just to have something to do, but he misjudges the distance and knocks over the jar. Water slops across the table, splattering both the cloak and the cat, who leaps to her feet and yowls at Cas.

"*Damn.* Sorry." Cas tries to grab the jar before it rolls off the table but misses—Mita catches it just before it hits the floor.

"Cas." Her tone is too serious, too gentle. She sets the jar back in its place, upright but empty. "You know that you don't have to do this," she says very quietly.

She isn't talking about the wrinkled cloak. Cas suddenly feels very wobbly in a way that has nothing to do with the swaying ship or the drinking last night. There's a rock lodged inside his throat. There's a pressure behind his eyes. He hasn't cried in front of another person in years, but somehow the tears are right there now, a moment away from spilling over. It's absurd. It's humiliating. He needs to pull himself together.

"Truly," Mita is saying. "The choice is yours. No one will blame you if you change your mind. There are other ways that they can gain entry. The captain can figure out another way."

Surprisingly, Cas finds that he believes her. When he'd first come up with this plan, it had felt like their one shot—the only possible way to rescue Henry and correct Cas's mistakes. But they have allies here. A crew behind them. Cas has spent the entire afternoon watching the marvels that can happen when Captain Hobbes and Remy DeWindt both set their minds toward the same puzzle.

Of course there are other options. And it would be easier—wouldn't it?—to hand this problem over, to let someone else fix it.

"Cas," Mita says again. "Lad. Talk to me."

He rubs the back of his neck, lets the sheared ends of his hair tickle his fingers. *Lad.* Every time, it makes something settle back into place in his chest. Freeing up space there. He can swallow the rock in his throat at last.

"I can do this," Cas says.

"That's not the same thing."

"I'm *going* to do this." Cas makes himself meet her gaze—it's still soft, still gentle, but steadying, too. He wonders who steadied Mita when she was younger and smaller and less sure of her place in the world. He wonders who steadies her now. "I won't say that I *want* to, because . . . obviously. But at the same time, maybe I . . . do? Because Henry is my friend, and he's my responsibility, and I want to help him. And this is the best way I can do that."

He probably isn't making any sense—but Mita is nodding, easy and trusting, the same way Finn had nodded after his stumbling explanations belowdecks the other day. Back then, Cas might have said all this, but he wouldn't have meant it. Now it doesn't feel like a false reassurance. It feels true.

The cat seems to have forgiven him; she paws at the wet spot on the silk, then sidesteps it to nudge her nose against the back of Cas's hand. He pats her on the head a few times. She purrs like a roll of thunder.

The clothes were never really the problem, anyway, were they? All of Cas's chafing against his old dresses was never really about the dresses themselves. It was everything they signified: the life laid out ahead of him. The person he was expected to be. The person people saw when he wore them—not Cas, but Miss Cassandra Sterling, a role he'd never had a say in playing. Cas spent years of his life waiting for the day when he would wake up and realize that, somehow, the role suddenly fit. Hoping for that day? Dreading it?

It didn't matter. The day never came.

In a way, this thing he's preparing to do is a strange kind of familiar: Cas has been putting himself through this for years. The difference now is that he knows the possibilities, knows that something else can exist afterward. That *he* can exist. That there *is* an afterward. Cas can take up the role again for a little while, can use his old name to introduce himself at Eden—and it won't change a thing about who he is. He can wear a dress or this outrageous velvet-trimmed cloak, and it won't change how Remy and Finn and Mita and the crew of the *Mori* know him.

The clothes are just clothes.

Mita is still quiet, waiting. Giving him space. Cas thinks of that looking glass in the hotel room back in Boston. What a glorious thing, to see himself at last. What a glorious thing, to be surrounded by people who can see him, too.

"It's like a costume," Cas says finally. "Honestly, it's always been a costume. I can wear it for one more day. For this."

And Mita says, "All right. We'll be behind you, then. Anything you need."

"Thanks."

It's insufficient. It's all Cas has. The patch of silk where he spilled the water *is* looking less wrinkled than the spots around it. Cas refills the jar, and slowly, Mita helps him dampen the rest of the wrinkles, moving over the cloak's fabric section by section. When they're finished, they hang it to dry from one of the empty bunks. It really is a ridiculous thing to wear. His mother has awful taste.

The cat is whining from the floor. Mita picks her up and lets her perch on her shoulder like a bird.

"After all of this is over," Mita tells Cas, "I hope you know that you have a place here, if you want it. You're welcome to stay aboard the *Mori* after we rescue your friend. You're welcome for as long as you like."

It's as if she's read his mind—except that he's been afraid to think it, hasn't he? It's more like she's read his heart. She's caught sight of this terrified hope fluttering around inside him, a hope Cas has been trying to ignore all this time as he's worried over what comes next for him. And now she's offering that hope a branch to land on.

He feels wobbly again, but it's somehow less horrifying now. He doesn't trust himself to speak. He manages a nod.

This is who steadies Mita now, Cas realizes as they climb the narrow stairs to join the rest of the sailors. This ship. This crew.

When they emerge abovedeck, the late afternoon sunlight is varnishing the boards of the ship with gold. The sun has dropped low over the island's coastline. Cas squints out over the larboard rail, waiting for his eyes to adjust to the new light.

But when he takes in his first sight of the island, his breath catches.

Cas has seen this place before.

Steely waves churning against a wall of granite. A spidery cliffside a hundred feet tall. A forest of pine trees lining the peaks, their tips stabbing into the sky. Less than a day has passed since Cas watched the scene that's going to play out atop these cliffs.

This is the place where Finn Robinson dies.

XXII

REMY

At last, the *Memento Mori* stands safely at anchor, tucked out of sight behind a smaller islet about a mile off the eastern coast of Mount Desert Island. Gabe takes the ship's jolly boat ashore to handle the business in town, but he's gone for hours, and there's not much any of them can do until he returns. Cas paces the length of the deck for a while before wandering below again; after he's gone, Remy has half a mind to start pacing in his stead. Her anticipation is building with each passing clang of the watch bell.

"Come on," Striker says at last, pushing a spare rifle into Remy's hands. "You need an outlet."

It's as good a distraction as any. Striker ties a line around an empty water cask and tosses it over the side; once the evening's ebbing tide has pulled it out a few dozen yards, it becomes their target. Remy's aim is a little better than it had been during her first shooting lesson with Striker, though she has yet to actually hit the cask. At least the splashes of her bullets in the water have gotten closer to it.

"It's about commitment," Striker tells her as she reloads the rifle. "The aiming is more mental than physical. Once you've got it in your sights, you've just got to pull the trigger. Don't let yourself falter."

She makes it sound so easy, but Remy has spent her entire life faltering. The arduous process of reloading the rifle allows far too much time for worrying. What if Immortal Gabe has run into trouble in town? What if Smith rejects Cas's letter? What if they make it inside tomorrow and Remy still doesn't find out anything about her father?

Or what if she does?

Finn sits quietly by the mainmast, watching the lesson, the cat asleep in her lap. She and Remy haven't spoken about their argument on the beach last night; they probably never will. But Finn's words have worked their way into her mind more than Remy would like to admit.

"Commit to your shot, take a breath, and go," Striker says. "That's all there is to it."

Remy peers through the rifle's sight. "I'm very committed."

Not committed enough, it turns out. She still misses the cask by several feet.

Just past eight bells, the jolly boat returns at last. Immortal Gabe looks very pleased with himself as he presents the captain with a letter. Remy recognizes the handwriting of it immediately—the same spidery penmanship as the note she'd found in the dead Pastor Cole's grimoire.

"My mate said the reverend was practically falling over himself to write back," Gabe tells them as Captain Hobbes studies the letter. "He's even invited the Little Prince to stay for tea after their meeting, see?"

"That's good," Captain Hobbes says. "That gives us a window when we know Smith will be away from the archive."

Remy ought to feel calmer at having this settled, but she doesn't. She leaves the rifle with Striker, and she and Finn go to inform the Little Prince in question.

They find Cas alone in the galley, pouring the last sludgy dregs from the coffeepot into a dented cup. When he sees Remy and Finn in the doorway, he holds out the pot for them, then seems to remember it's empty and tucks it back onto the narrow countertop where he's sitting.

"Sorry," he says. "I can make more. Probably. Maybe."

Remy hands him the letter. Cas's mouth silently forms the Reverend John Smith's words as he reads them.

"Tomorrow at four," he says at last.

"Tomorrow at four," Remy agrees.

It's soon. It's an interminable wait. Remy wonders if any of them will sleep tonight. Finn has hoisted herself up onto the countertop beside Cas, her boots dangling a few inches above the floor. Cas's fingers are drumming against the side of his cup, tapping out a tinny rhythm he seems hardly aware of.

"Are you sure about this plan?" Remy says.

Cas laughs, though there's no real humor to it. "Why does everyone keep asking me that? *Yes*, I'm sure. Yes, I can handle it. Kit made me rehearse my lines a thousand times already. It's going to be fine."

"That's not what I meant. It's not that I don't think you can handle it. It's . . . well . . ."

But Remy's words fail her. There's a hole in their plan—one that Remy is aware of and Captain Hobbes isn't. Because the captain doesn't have all the information. When he'd asked earlier about why the Order had taken an interest in Henry Ashworth . . .

But even now, Remy can't bring herself to raise the question aloud. It's too tangled: Cas collapsing on the deck yesterday, and the memories of her father, and the spark of very real fire burning in Finn's hands. *I believe Cas, about his visions.*

Finn comes to her rescue.

"Are we sure it's a good idea for you, specifically, to go inside?" Finn asks Cas. "They took Ashworth because they think he's the one having visions, right? But if he's told them what really happened . . ."

"He wouldn't," Cas says straightaway. "I don't think Henry really *knows* what happened that day. And even if he has pieced it together, he's not going to tell them that I'm the real cause; he wouldn't throw me to the wolves like that. He does have some sense."

"You trust him, then."

"Of course I do."

Maybe Remy is imagining the cutting way he says it; maybe this *isn't* meant as a stab at her. She deserves the stab regardless. She thinks of Cas's drawing back in the dining room—the unmistakable sketch of Henry Ashworth. After she and Cas had fallen out, she, at least, found Finn. She ought to be glad that Cas has had someone else to trust in these intervening years.

He's still drumming his fingers against the side of that damned coffee cup.

"Lord, aren't you jittery enough without *more* caffeine?" Remy asks him.

The drumming stops. "It's only my second cup tonight," he says, frowning. "Or maybe third. Besides, it helps my brain go . . . you know. Quiet."

"I don't think that's how caffeine works," Remy says.

"Maybe not for *you*."

He takes a noisy, drawn-out slurp from the cup, pulls a face, and then does it again. The second slurp is even longer. It's possible that he's hoping Finn and Remy will have left by the tail end of it, but neither of them moves.

"I've been thinking," Cas says suddenly. He's turned to Finn now. "Our part tomorrow doesn't really need two people. Maybe you should stay here instead of coming to the seminary with me."

Finn's eyes narrow slightly. "Why?"

"There's no *why*—only I can do it just as easily by myself, so—"

"Isn't it better to have backup and not need it than the other way around?" Remy asks.

"Sure, but this plan isn't exactly safe. Anything could happen tomorrow. You and I have our own reasons for doing this, but Finn—"

"I'm part of this now, too," Finn cuts in. "Same as either of you. I'm not going to sit here on my arse waiting to see if you both make it back."

Her tone leaves no room for argument. Cas doesn't argue. He finishes his coffee in one long slurp and wipes his mouth with his sleeve.

"I don't like that Dekker might be there," he says. "He's too close to my parents—he's bound to question whether my father would actually send *me* for something like this. And he already hates me."

"I don't think anyone hates you," Remy tells him. "It's annoying, actually."

"You don't remember all those sermons about *honoring thy father and mother*? Or the time he went on for nearly three hours about women accepting their proper place in the world, *lest they be cast into the fires of hell?*"

Remy blinks at him. "I do remember that, actually. I didn't know he was talking about you."

"Well," Cas says, "everyone else did."

He doesn't look at all like himself as he sits, deflated, staring into his empty cup. Or maybe this *is* himself—only a layer of him that Remy hasn't seen since they were children. A layer she hasn't wanted to see.

When they all crawl into their bunks in the fo'c'sle later, Remy is certain she's not alone in her tossing and turning. She tries to walk her mind through that familiar scene: her father's homecoming, watching herself run into his arms. Something isn't right, though. This isn't Remy as she is now; it's Remy as a child, ten years old. The scene she's imagining isn't the future. Maybe it never has been. It's a pile of memories, all of them long past.

When she looks to the future, it's only fog. And Remy isn't sure anymore if she wants to know what lies beyond it.

In the late afternoon, seven of them board the longboat: Remy, Finn, Cas, Kit, Striker, Leo, and Captain Hobbes himself. The sea is calm as they leave the *Memento Mori* and row toward the wooded shoreline of the cove just south of Eden. Remy is given a set of oars and a seat behind Striker, where she can watch Striker's movements and try to keep pace. Cas and Finn aren't given oars at all.

"You're really not going to let me row?" Cas asks for the third time as the boat glides across the water.

"You'll be headed to tea in an hour," Kit reminds him. "How will it look if you show up red-faced and sweaty in your fine clothes?"

Cas scowls down at the fine clothes, which are currently draped across his lap. "So I'm supposed to just sit here?"

"That's the idea, yes."

"I'd happily trade you if I could," Remy says, grunting a little as she pulls her own oars. "My arms feel like they're on fire."

"Right, but that's the whole point!" Cas says. "That's how you know they're getting good and muscled!"

Beside him, Finn buries her face in her hands. "Jesus, Mary, and Joseph. Are you still on about the muscled arms?"

"I didn't know you wanted muscled arms," Striker says.

"Doesn't everyone?" Cas asks, and Striker laughs.

"You should talk to Gabe," Leo tells him. "When we're back on the ship. He has a whole muscle-building routine that I'm sure he'd love to teach you."

This seems to placate Cas a little; his twitching hands go still as he and Leo chat until the bottom of the boat groans against the rocky shore.

The cove here is only a short walk from town, but it's nicely secluded, with a stretch of piney woods blocking it from view. It's also deserted. Who would bother landing their boat here when the Eden docks are just a mile farther? Only someone looking to avoid attention.

Once the boat is secured, they all settle in for their final preparations. Finn helps Cas pin the front of his hair, arranging it so the hood of his cloak will conceal the cut of it. Captain Hobbes and Striker march off to scout their perimeter. They'll all rendezvous here later tonight, after Cas and Finn have returned to town with Ashworth, after Remy, Kit, and Captain Hobbes have trekked back from the seminary. After they've found whatever there is to find.

Remy can't think about it too closely. She feels nearly as twitchy as Cas. When Leo produces a pack of playing cards from the pocket of his jacket, Remy leaps at the distraction.

"This deck is all spades," she complains as she surveys her hand.

"No, it isn't," Leo tells her. "Besides, you're the one who shuffled it."

"Well, apparently I shuffled all the spades to myself."

"It could be a message," Kit says absently. She fans her cards in Remy's direction. "You know that these decks evolved from tarot cards, right? They have the same suits, just with different names."

Remy feels a little cross at this. She's read about tarot, of course; it's come up in some of her father's books, alongside all the other magical nonsense the Order of Lazarus is studying. Except she can't quite convince herself that it *is* nonsense now, can she? Not after everything the captain has revealed. Not after her conversation—more than a conversation, really—with Finn on the beach the other night.

"What suit would spades correspond with?" Leo is asking. "In tarot?"

"Swords, I think," Kit says. "The suit of intellect. It's all about turning plans into action."

Remy feels even more cross when she draws yet another spade into her hand. "You don't really believe in all that, do you?" she asks Kit.

Kit shrugs. "I'm humble enough to know that I don't know everything."

Striker and the captain circle back from their patrol in time to save Remy from having to reply. Striker leans on Kit's shoulder for balance as she kicks the mud from her boots.

"It's just as the map showed," Striker tells them. "You three will be able to follow the brook for most of your hike up the mountainside. The road into town is just through those trees for when our two little actors are ready. Oh! Speaking of."

Cas and Finn have rejoined the group, fully costumed. Finn is back in the dress she'd been wearing when they'd left Windover, her hair tucked up under a mobcap. Cas has buttoned his cloak all the way to the ground so that the trousers underneath it are hidden. With his hood pulled up, with him in his old cloak, it's almost as if the last few days never happened. This is the version of Cas that Remy might pass on the street in Windover without either of them acknowledging each other.

It's an odd sensation. And yet this is what proves that all of it's been real—because the sight of Cas wearing women's clothes now *is* so odd.

Cas grimaces as he spreads his arms in presentation. "Well?"

"You look very strange," Leo says, frowning. Then he seems to hear himself, and his eyes widen. "I'm so sorry—that was rude, wasn't it?"

But Cas's expression has cleared. "No, it was perfect," he says. "I *feel* strange. Let's get this over with, shall we?"

He starts toward the trees, where Striker had gestured. Leo gathers up the cards. Remy assumes that Finn will follow Cas, but she pauses. She catches Remy's eye. She tips her head away, one eyebrow raised in wordless invitation.

She and Remy step to the side, out of earshot of the others.

"Are you ready for all of this?" Finn asks in a low voice. "You seem..."

There are a thousand ways she might finish that statement. Remy doesn't like any of them. Of course she isn't ready for this. She's been preparing for years, studying the Order from afar—and now she's here, and it's all impossibly real, and none of it feels real at all.

"Tell me it's going to be fine," Remy says.

"It's going to be fine," Finn says. "Truly."

Remy wishes she could believe her. Something inside her is unraveling, like the strands of old rigging for the rope winch. The fear is picking her apart, piece by piece.

Finn is watching her as if she already knows everything Remy is thinking. She always does.

"What if I don't find anything?" Remy asks. "What if, after all of this planning...?"

But she can't say it. Is she more frightened that she won't find answers—or more frightened that she will? She doesn't know anymore. It's all terrifyingly out of her control.

She thinks about the tiny flame Finn had conjured in her hands beneath the lighthouse. About the rifle lesson with Striker that morning. About committing to the shot. She thinks about tarot, and the suit of swords, and turning plans into action at last.

Then Remy stops thinking at all. For once in her goddamn life, she simply acts.

She leans down and kisses Finn on the cheek.

It's quick. A brush of lips. Finn is very still. She smells like lye soap and saltwater. Even after they're separated, Remy can feel the warmth of Finn's skin on her own lips.

Remy has pulled back, but she doesn't pull away.

She's standing too close. She can't move. Thought returns to her all at once: Why did she do that? What was that kiss on the cheek supposed to mean? A goodbye? Good luck? It shouldn't have meant anything at all. How many other people has Remy kissed just like this? Her mother, her sisters.

But not like *this*. The action is the same, and yet the effect is impossibly different. This feels like something entirely new—some bridge Remy hadn't realized she was crossing until she'd crossed it, a thoughtless gesture that's now turned everything fraught and electric.

Finn stares at her, unblinking.

Remy can't stop thinking about what would have happened if Finn had turned her head, just a little.

"I . . ." Remy says, though there's nothing to say.

Finn stays quiet, as if daring Remy to finish that sentence. Remy doesn't. In the end, it's Finn who steps away first.

"See you soon, then," Finn says, as if nothing at all has happened.

Then she's gone—hurrying away after Cas, leaving Remy standing there dazed, reeling. She could follow, could call out to Finn—but she doesn't. She feels torn in too many directions. It's all a tangle in her mind. All the years she's spent helping her mother, cobbling together the family's finances. All the years that she's dedicated to her father's mission of taking down the Order of Lazarus.

And now a third direction that Remy hasn't felt herself pulled before. Something selfish. Something longing.

"It's time to go," the captain says. Remy hadn't even heard him approach. "We need to be in place when your friends give the signal."

Remy puts it all away. She tucks it into the window seat bench in her mind and follows the captain up the beach. Striker and Leo wish them luck; they'll be waiting here with the boat when Remy and the others return.

Remy can't afford to think about anything besides what she's about to do. She walks with Captain Hobbes and Kit into the woods.

XXIII

CAS

Cas had thought that Eden would be something like Windover—the same small, tidy, tight-knit community. In reality, Eden is even smaller. It's also far more run-down. The gray-shingled homes and warehouses seem to lean into one another, all huddling together against the spray of the sea. The mountains loom above them, casting everything in shadow. A few locals give Cas and Finn odd looks as they make their way to the center of town, but no one stops them.

Cas hires what must be the only hack on the island to take them up to the seminary. The town around them gives way to forest again almost immediately. The ride is only two miles, but Cas can feel his nerves building as they climb the mountainside. Finn is stoic as ever. She's barely said a word since they left the cove. Their knees bump together with every jostle of the carriage's wheels.

Cas peers through the coach's grubby window, watching the sea as it dodges in and out of view through the trees. How far are they now from the cliffs in his vision?

"You could still head back from here, you know," Cas says. "Just take the hack back into town, wait with Striker and Leo in the cove—"

"And leave you to manage this alone?" Finn cuts in.

"I won't be alone. I'll have Henry."

"Not to be rude, but I have far less trust than you seem to that Henry Ashworth will be of any help."

"That's still rude, though," Cas tells her. "Just because you say 'not to be rude' doesn't make it less rude."

"The plan is that I'm coming with you. So we're sticking to the plan. Why do you keep pressing this?"

Cas doesn't answer. He tries to keep his face blank, but Finn is studying him, and for the barest moment, he thinks that she *knows*. That she's guessed what he's seen. There's something about her widened eyes or the pallor of her face. Or maybe she's just as nervous as he is.

"I'm coming with you," Finn says again, like that settles the matter. And it does. Cas goes back to staring out the window. They don't speak again.

At last, the carriage rumbles to a stop on the front drive of the Eden Theological Seminary. The college looks out of place here among the trees, and even more out of place after the drabness of the town. It stands three stories high, built of warm, rich stone, more like a fine mansion or manor house than a school. A broad front porch lined with columns towers over them.

Cas pays the driver, and the hack and horses rattle back the way they came. And then Finn and Cas are standing at the front doors. Cas straightens his hood and checks that his cloak is still fully buttoned.

"Ready?" he says.

Finn nods. Cas pulls the bell.

The wait is agony, though it can't last more than half a minute. Then the door opens and a fair-skinned, middle-aged, well-dressed man stands on the threshold. "May I help you?" he says.

Cas puts on his most charming smile. "Miss Cassandra Sterling," he says, bobbing into a curtsy. "Of the Massachusetts Sterlings. I have an appointment with the head of the institution, please, if you could just let him know that we've arrived."

"Of course." The man's eyes land on Finn, and for a moment Cas thinks he's going to bar her from coming in—but he steps back and gestures to them both. Just like that, they're inside.

The entrance hall is all pastel wallpaper and portraits of old white men. The candles in their wall sconces paint the room in a warm, welcoming hue—much brighter and much less murderous than Cas had been imagining this place.

"Tea will be served in a few minutes," the man is saying. "I can take your cloak, and then I'll show you through to the dining room."

Only when Finn kicks the back of his leg does Cas process the man's words. This is not the plan. They're supposed to meet with Reverend Smith straightaway, convince him to show them the archive, and then keep Smith distracted with tea afterward, while Remy and the others do their business. They're not supposed to have tea *first*.

"Oh," Cas says, scrambling to fix this. "I had thought . . . That is, I'd hoped we might begin with a tour, to get our bearings before sitting down to tea. The invitation had said—"

"The tea is ready now," the man says, as if no further explanation is needed. Cas catches Finn's eye, hoping she might offer something. Finn's face is perfectly blank.

He tries again. "My maid..."

"She can help in the kitchen while you dine. She'll rejoin you later."

The man rings a bell mounted on the wall, and a moment later, an elderly white housekeeper with a sour expression joins them. She and the man exchange a few words, and then she gives Finn a slow look up and down. Her expression grows even more sour.

"Come on, then," she says, with no introduction at all. To the man, she adds, "Let's hope this one is properly trained, at least."

It's all happening too quickly, and despite Cas's earlier attempts to send Finn back, he feels a panic seize him at the prospect of being separated. As she's ushered away, Finn pauses for a moment to glance back at him. She meets Cas's gaze. She nods once.

Then she turns and follows the housekeeper away.

A nod. What does a nod mean? Cas has no idea.

"This way," the man says, steering Cas in the opposite direction. Then, again: "I can take your cloak."

"That's all right." Cas clings to it with a ridiculous fear that the man might try to snatch it off him. "I'm a little chilled from the travel. I'll keep it with me." The man's lips purse, but he doesn't argue.

He leads Cas to the dining room, which is enormous and painted in cheerful yellow. A wall of windows on the table's far side shows the pine forest outside, stretching up the mountain into eternity. A familiar figure stands at one of the windows, hands clasped perfectly behind his back as if he's posing for a portrait.

Cas is already running toward him. The world has narrowed to a single point.

"Henry!"

For nearly two weeks, as Cas has been imagining Henry in this place, he's feared the worst: Henry being interrogated, beaten, tortured. Henry's eyes cut out of his head like Mr. DeWindt's. God, ever since they boarded the *Mori*, Cas has been counting down the days to Henry's potential murder.

So as he takes in Henry now—uninjured, unharmed, looking better rested than Cas has seen him in years—the relief nearly knocks him over. Henry turns. His face breaks into a smile. It's poor decorum for Cas to throw his arms around Henry—but it's also poor decorum to call Henry by his Christian name in public, and Cas has already done that. So decorum be damned. Henry grips him back tightly. This doesn't feel like public, anyway. It feels like the two of them are alone in the world, just as they should be.

"I can't believe you're here," Henry murmurs.

"Me neither," Cas says. "I'm so glad you're all right."

"Goodness," says a familiar voice behind them. "How . . . enthusiastic."

And Cas and Henry aren't alone in the world at all, because Pastor Dekker is standing ten feet away, watching them. It's emotional whiplash. Cas can't catch his breath as he and Henry scramble apart. He'd known Dekker would probably be here—he's been steeling himself for it; he's reviewed this plan with Kit and Remy a dozen times over—but it's like trying to mentally prepare for an earthquake. No imagining of the event can stand up to the actual moment when the ground beneath you begins to roll.

Beside him, the real Henry has vanished, replaced by that proper, perfect version of himself.

"I apologize, Pastor," Henry says without looking at Cas. "I'm afraid I forgot myself for a moment."

"It seems both of you did," Dekker says. "You'd think it's been months instead of days since you last saw each other."

"Oh, don't tease them," a woman beside him says. "I think it's very sweet."

The woman is older, her blond hair streaked with gray, and she stands near the table's head in a dress that's clearly expensive. The hostess of this gathering, then. Cas is still trying to get his thoughts straight. His hands are shaking. There are too many people in this room, and he can't think of a single thing to say. He tugs at one of the buttons on his cloak, trying to steady himself.

Thankfully, Dekker interprets his silence as good manners instead of shock. "Waiting for a proper introduction, I see? Good; your mother would be pleased. Mrs. Smith, let me present to you Miss Cassandra Sterling. Miss Sterling, this is Mrs. Smith. And, of course"—now he gestures toward the pale, slight man on Mrs. Smith's other side, who Cas hadn't even noticed until now—"the Reverend John Smith. President and founder of the Eden Theological Seminary."

"A pleasure to meet you, Miss Sterling," the Reverend John Smith says.

His voice is quiet. His graying hair has curled untidily around his ears, and when he bows, his tiny wire-framed spectacles slide down his nose. Cas has been bracing for a more imposing figure. Smith is supposed to be the leader of this place—the alleged mastermind behind the Order of Lazarus and very likely a murderer.

This man doesn't look like any of that. This man looks like he should be keeping the books in the back room of an antiques shop, and probably not a very profitable one.

"Mr. Ashworth has told us so much about you," Mrs. Smith is saying, beaming at Cas. "What a joy that you've come to visit us from so far! I don't get to play hostess nearly as often as I'd like up here, and look, you've given me an excuse to set out the good china. Should we sit?"

Henry pulls out a chair for Cas. Cas accepts it numbly. As Henry takes the seat across the table from him, Cas searches his face for some hint of distress, for some fear directed toward Dekker or the Reverend Smith. But his mask is faultless, perfectly composed.

Henry is studying Cas right back, gaze raking him up and down. Cas thinks he's going to suggest again that someone take Cas's cloak, but instead he says, with a small, polite smile, "You look very nice."

Cas feels a little sick.

From the seat beside Cas, Mrs. Smith has leaned in conspiratorially. "You and I are going to be fast friends—I can tell," she's saying. "I spend far too much time surrounded by all these *men*. How delightful to get to visit with another woman once in a while!"

Cas is sure his face will give him away, but Mrs. Smith's smile doesn't flag. He grits his teeth. He smiles back at her.

"Absolutely," he says.

This is going to be a disaster.

XXIV

FINN

When Finn had first taken up her position as a maid at the DeWindt house, the staff was run by a housekeeper named Mrs. Hewitt. She'd been nearly seventy when Finn arrived, and she had little patience for training the new housemaid entrusted to her—this sullen ten-year-old girl who Mr. DeWindt had only taken on out of pity. For Finn's first few months employed there, the housekeeper patiently guided her whenever Mr. DeWindt was around and then shouted at her when his back was turned. She detested Finn, which was convenient, because Finn detested her right back.

Then, three months after Finn started there, Mr. DeWindt disappeared. The household was in chaos, and Mrs. DeWindt was always in her room, and there was no longer anyone at all to keep the housekeeper in check. Mrs. Hewitt kept a carpet rod that she whacked against Finn's knuckles far more often than she did any of the carpets. She berated Finn at every turn. Once, when Finn had accidentally burned the chicken for a Sunday supper, she made Finn place her own bare hand against the hot coals inside the oven—a reminder against future mistakes. Finn still has the burn scars on the side of her right palm.

When the DeWindts' money was running out, when the family had to start letting their household staff go, Remy convinced her mother to dismiss Mrs. Hewitt first.

Finn hasn't seen Mrs. Hewitt in years. She heard the old woman kicked the bucket last winter. Yet from the moment Finn meets the head housekeeper at the Eden Theological Seminary, she's taken straight back, as if Mrs. Hewitt has been resurrected and placed here specifically to make Finn's life more difficult.

"You'll be working on supper," Mrs. Not-Quite-Hewitt says as she pushes Finn into the seminary's kitchen. "The students will be dining later, so you're to help with preparations for their meal. You can manage that, can't you?"

"Of course, ma'am," Finn says through a taut smile.

Mrs. Not-Quite-Hewitt shoves a paring knife and a sack of potatoes at her.

The kitchen is spacious and bare, free of the fine decor they'd passed in the non-staff portions of the building. Half a dozen other servants hurry to and fro, heads bowed over their work. Mrs. Not-Quite-Hewitt stations Finn and the potatoes at a table in the center of it all. She clearly considers Finn someone who needs an eye kept on her. She isn't wrong.

In the front pocket of the housekeeper's apron, a jagged, jangling lump protrudes—the outline of a heavy ring of keys.

Finn picks up a potato and sets about formulating her next move. If she can slip away for a few minutes, if she can find the library on her own and mark the window there, Remy and the others will still be able to sneak inside. They'll still have time to do their searching while Smith is occupied. It's risky—but their original plan held plenty of risk, too. Better to try it and see what happens than to let the opportunity slide past.

Finn loses her grip on the half-peeled potato, and it shoots from her hand. She dives as if to catch it. She doesn't catch it. The potato bounces away from her, and Finn bounces off

Mrs. Not-Quite-Hewitt's expansive skirts and lands on her arse on the floor.

"Clumsy girl!" Mrs. Not-Quite-Hewitt snarls down at her. "Have you never worked in a kitchen before?"

"I'm sorry," Finn murmurs, head ducked, hands balled up under her. "I'm sorry. I'll be more careful."

"Lord, help me."

The housekeeper has tipped her gaze skyward—an actual prayer, then, instead of blasphemy. Finn takes the moment of distraction to tuck away the stolen keys now clamped in her fist, burying them in her pocket. The housekeeper sighs, then sighs again.

"Give me the peeler," she says at last. "You go over there and see that the ovens are stoked."

Which isn't a job at all—it's a dismissal, a nonsense task to keep Finn busy but not underfoot. Finn couldn't have planned it better herself. The hearth is on the wall nearest to the door, with a stock shelf in the corner that half obscures any view of it. Finn retreats there, offering apologies all the while.

She checks the ovens. They're hot enough already. So long as she's quick, Finn won't be missed.

As soon as Mrs. Not-Quite-Hewitt has moved on to criticizing how one of the other servants has chopped the carrots, Finn turns and simply walks out of the kitchen the same way she'd come in.

The hallway outside is too quiet after the bustling staff area. Finn strains her ears, trying to get her bearings. There are voices from somewhere, though Finn can't place their direction. She has yet to see a single student here. Perhaps they're all still in class. The dining room must be nearby, though—and, yes, from a few doors down, Finn catches the cheerful rise and fall of Cas's voice. He says something she can't make out; it's met with easy laughter.

At least their diversion seems to be going well, then.

Above her, the floorboards creak. Footsteps. The scrape of a chair. Now that she's listening for it, it's clear this is where most of the voices are coming from. The seminary's classrooms must be on the second floor. Is this where the library will be, too? It's as good a guess as any. Finn creeps up the staircase.

The doors on the second floor are all labeled. Each has a tidy metal placard noting the room's use, which feels like a miracle. Finn hurries along the hallway, scanning the names on each side. A classroom. Another classroom. A study room.

And there, on the door beside it: *Special Collection and Archive. For faculty use only.*

Finn takes out her keys.

A door bursts open at the end of the hall—one of the classrooms. Finn freezes. A flood of nearly a dozen boys, most around her age, pours out into the hallway. They jostle and bump their shoulders together, celebrating the end of their lessons, perhaps. A stern voice from within the classroom snaps something about poor form, and the boys' voices drop off momentarily—though as soon as the door swings shut behind them, several of them burst into laughter again.

Finn is still standing at the library door, keys clenched in her hand. The group is coming straight toward her. She racks her mind for some excuse to give. Perhaps she's been sent to fetch something. Perhaps she's been asked to check the fires in the classrooms. One of the students glances her way, and for a painful, stretching second, their eyes meet.

The boy's gaze drifts right over her, though. The group hurries past and starts down the stairs. None of them acknowledge Finn whatsoever. Why would they? She's a servant.

Finn exhales. She has never been so grateful to be invisible.

After the students have disappeared, after their voices have faded, she turns back to the locked door and pretends that she belongs here. She tries the keys one by one. The fourth attempt fits. The lock clicks.

Finn lets herself into the Order of Lazarus's library.

The room is dark, with heavy curtains over the windows to keep sunlight from fading the collection. The shelves along the walls stretch nearly to the ceiling, with glass doors like the bookcases in Captain Hobbes's office. It's all so much bigger than Finn had been imagining it. She's suddenly overwhelmed by the scope of Remy's task. She hears the tremor in Remy's voice: *What if I don't find anything? What if, after all of this planning . . . ?*

It's possible that Remy was right to worry.

Still, there's nothing Finn can do to help now—nothing but the task assigned to her. She can't think about the moment after Remy had said that, about the warmth of Remy's lips on her cheek, about the heat coursing between them when Remy didn't move away. Finn pads across the room. Peeks behind one of the heavy curtains. Unlatches the window. Eases it open, just a crack. She marks the corner of the lowest pane with the bar of soap Kit gave her, leaving a white streak across the glass, just bright enough to be seen from the ground.

Through the glass, the pine forest sprawls out across the mountainside. Somewhere in those trees, Remy is hiding with Kit and the captain. Waiting for their cue.

And now Finn has given it.

Had Finn imagined that yearning in Remy's dark eyes earlier after Remy had kissed her cheek, as the two of them had stared at each other, neither of them stepping back? Finn has spent so long wanting Remy to look at her that way; she doesn't trust her own senses. She won't let herself hope. Besides, Remy has far too much on her mind right now, far too much to carry. She hadn't been thinking clearly.

Finn locks the library door behind her and hurries back the way she came.

One of the doors on the first floor is labeled, too. Finn hadn't noticed when she passed it earlier. Now, though—as she catches the voices in the dining room, still chattering, still distracted; as she thinks about the impossible vastness of the library upstairs— the placard on the door at the end of the hall gives her pause.

President's Office.

Finn shouldn't risk it. She should return to the kitchen before the housekeeper notices. She should stick to the original plan. But doesn't any good plan leave room for improvisation? The president in question, the Reverend John Smith, is still sitting down with Cas for tea. His office will be unoccupied.

And if Remy doesn't find answers in the seminary's library, surely this office will have *something*. Finn can't let her walk away from this empty-handed.

Three tries, Finn decides. Three keys. If the door won't unlock with one of them, she'll take it as a sign that this is a terrible idea and give up. The first key she tries doesn't fit. Neither does the second.

The third opens the door.

It feels like fate. Finn shuts herself inside, then scans the room. It's a typical office for a house like this: dark-paneled, expensively decorated, and exorbitantly large. An ornate carpet covers most of the floor. The desk has been relegated to the far corner of the room; evidently this rug is too fine to even have furniture placed atop it. Finn takes a vicious pleasure in stepping all over it with her working-class boots.

There's a scuff on the floorboards along one edge of the carpet. Not a scuff—a white chalk mark. Someone has drawn something on the flooring underneath.

Finn toes up the corner of the rug, then keeps going. The chalk shape slowly emerges as she rolls the carpet clear. She recognizes it in pieces:

The pentagrams drawn in each of the corners.

The circle that takes up most of the room.

The names written on the serpent that's been sketched around the circle's edge.

The triangle at the easternmost point.

The two dark, smoky marks within that triangle—almost like footprints.

The design is far more complex than what Finn had drawn on the floor of a barn six years ago. But the intention is the same.

This is a summoning circle.

For a long moment—longer than she should—Finn stands frozen. Staring at the floor. At the evidence of a ritual not only attempted, but successfully performed. Finn knows what the footprints mean. A demon stood here. It was summoned. It was forced into a human form—the better to make a deal with.

Inside the triangle—inside this careful perimeter where the demon would've been bound—are numbers. Coordinates.

These numbers can't be Smith's work; they aren't written in chalk. They're scrawled straight into the wood of the floor. Scratched by a fiendish hand.

Finn clenches and unclenches her own fists. She feels the spark there. It's been pushing at her more and more, as if showing Remy that glimpse on the beach had awakened something long sleeping.

She needs to get out of here.

She tears a scrap of paper from a book on the Reverend Smith's desk. She copies down the numbers. She shoves the scrap under the collar of her dress. She rolls the rug back out across the room, checks the corners, checks that everything is in place.

The room looks untouched, perfectly reverted. The only thing that's changed between Finn's entering and her leaving is the pounding of her own heart. She relocks the door with trembling fingers. It's not that she hadn't known what Smith and the Order were capable of. It's not that she hadn't understood the threat here.

But she feels shaken to her core. All of this is real in a way it hadn't been before.

Smith summoned something. He summoned a demon. He made a bargain with it, and the demon gave him information. Coordinates leading to . . . something.

And now Finn has those coordinates, too. She can practically feel the scrap of paper burning against her collarbone as she darts back toward the kitchen.

She nearly makes it, too.

She's just rounded the corner into the staff area when one side of her head screams with pain. Someone has seized her by the ear. It's the burn of the coals against her bare hand. It's the carpet rod striking her knuckles.

Finn stares up through watering eyes into the furious face of the housekeeper.

XXV

CAS

Cas has never been a very good judge of character. He knows he struggles to read between the lines. He knows he's too quick to take people at their word. More than once, at parties back in Windover, he's been commended for his ability to brush off a slight as if completely unbothered. The truth is that Cas usually hadn't realized it *was* a slight until someone else pointed this out. Louisa Springer had delivered her rude comment with a perfect smile; how was Cas supposed to know? If she'd wanted to offend him, she should have made it more obvious.

But for all his shortcomings in reading *people*, Cas can read a *situation*. All these years living under his mother's roof have given him a keen sense for when the mood in a room is about to turn.

As Cas sits at the dining table with Henry, Pastor Dekker, and the Reverend and Mrs. Smith, he can feel the storm clouds gathering.

Still, he can't put his finger on what, exactly, is wrong. Pastor Dekker's vaguely judgmental gaze is nothing new. Mrs. Smith's only crime is her misguided attempt at womanly bonding. And her husband has barely said two words since they sat down. Could the Reverend Smith really be the man who killed Remy's father? It seems far-fetched. Twice already, Cas has watched him push his spectacles farther up the bridge of his nose, only for them to immediately slide back down again a moment later.

Henry has him unsettled, though. Cas can't stop staring at him across the table. He looks ... fine. Better than fine. He looks *happy*—perfectly at ease, or as easy as he ever is in company. He smiles as a servant brings out the tea, and he compliments Mrs. Smith on her table settings, and when Pastor Dekker makes some inside comment about one of the waitstaff, Henry laughs, as if he's in on the joke. With *Dekker*. Who he and Cas both hate.

This has to be an act, doesn't it? Henry must be pretending that everything is fine for Cas's sake. Or he's playing along with Smith and Dekker until he can escape. And yet Cas can't quite scratch that itch of doubt that's settled in his mind. This whole time, he's been thinking of their journey to Eden as a rescue mission.

Henry doesn't look like someone who needs rescuing.

"I'm afraid I only have green tea to offer," Mrs. Smith is saying as the servant fills Cas's cup. "It can be such a trial to get supplies up here, and we've run short on black tea of late."

Cas assures her it's no issue, though truthfully, he'd prefer coffee over any type of tea. Even better, he'd prefer a glass of strong brandy. He thinks of the bottle Remy had stashed in the faerie king's tree. He wishes Remy or Finn were here now. Henry won't meet his eyes.

This *has* to be an act. Cas knows better than anyone how Henry can plaster a smile over whatever he's really feeling; it's a skill both of them have honed. If Cas can sit here making pleasant conversation even as his instincts scream out warnings, Henry is more than capable of doing the same.

"It's my fault, anyway," Cas tells Mrs. Smith, with a demureness that would probably appease even his unappeasable mother. "I'm the one who gave such short notice before encroaching on your hospitality."

"Nonsense!" Mrs. Smith says. "You've no idea how delighted we were to receive your note. Darling, weren't we delighted to receive Miss Sterling's note?"

"Delighted," the Reverend Smith murmurs.

"In any case, thank you," Cas says. "I'm grateful for your warm welcome. You've all been so kind."

Mrs. Smith is positively beaming as she calls for a tray of cakes. Even Dekker seems impressed. Christ, Cas feels dirty.

Despite what his mother might believe, Cas *does* know proper manners. He spent too many hours being forced to copy out lines from his mother's etiquette manuals; now the social rules of the modern young lady will be seared in his mind forever, whether he wants them there or not. The etiquette books are ridiculous—full of arbitrary and increasingly specific behaviors a lady must never engage in, such as rocking in a rocking chair, or tapping her foot to music, or using the word *stomach*. Or *beat out*. Or *stoop*. His mother's favorite of the books is called *The Ladies' Guide to True Politeness and Perfect Manners; or, Miss Leslie's Behavior Book*.

Cas *hates* Miss Leslie.

There was a time when Henry hated Miss Leslie, too. Whenever Cas was nursing his aching hand from an afternoon writing lines, Henry would take the book and read out excerpts in a ridiculous, pompous voice that left them both rolling with laughter. They made a game out of it for a while—testing how many ways they could covertly spite Miss Leslie at a single dinner party before one of their mothers caught on.

Now Cas watches Henry take a perfectly measured sip of tea. He needs to scrape through this facade. He's desperate to poke the real Henry out of hiding, if only for a moment.

Henry must feel him staring, because he gives in at last and looks up. Cas lifts his knife. Miss Leslie has several strong opinions about serving oneself at a table, including this: *There is always a butter knife. To take butter from the dish with your own knife is an abomination.*

Without breaking eye contact, Cas uses his own knife to scrape a generous portion from the table's butter dish.

Henry's expression doesn't change. Damn his inscrutable face.

"I must admit, I was surprised when the Reverend received your letter," Pastor Dekker says as Cas spreads butter on his cake. "I didn't realize you'd be traveling this way."

"Nor I you," Cas says. "But isn't it nice to see a familiar face so far from home?"

"Of course. Still, had I known, I would have delayed my own journey so that I could accompany you. But your parents never mentioned you'd be traveling."

Cas can't dwell on the absolute nightmare that would've been sailing here with Dekker instead of the crew of the *Memento Mori*. "The trip was a bit . . . spontaneous," Cas admits.

"And the donation that your father is considering? Was that a *spontaneous* decision as well?"

"Not exactly," Cas tells him. "Although it *was* recent. He took an interest in this place after Hen—Mr. Ashworth enrolled here. That is, I brought the idea of the donation to my father, and he was quite enamored with the prospect. Though if I'm honest, I did have an ulterior motive."

This is all part of the story Cas practiced with Kit yesterday, and it lands better than he could have hoped. Mrs. Smith actually claps in delight.

"Oh yes!" she says. "You were looking for an excuse to visit our young Mr. Ashworth, weren't you?"

Cas bites his lip as if embarrassed. He can't quite blush on cue, but with the right dip of his chin, the right coy smile, he can give the *impression* of a blush. It works on Mrs. Smith, at least. Henry's gaze is still on Cas, though a question seems to be forming on his face.

Immediately after her condemnations about butter knives, Miss Leslie writes: *It is nearly as bad to take a lump of sugar with your fingers.* Cas takes a lump of sugar with his fingers. He plops it into his tea. Henry raises one eyebrow at him.

But any further reaction is stifled when the Reverend John Smith breaks his silence at last.

"Does your father often send you as his emissary on matters such as this?" Smith asks. His voice is mild as ever, and yet the sound of it makes everyone else at the table straighten slightly, as if their general has called them to attention. Smith doesn't seem to notice. "I am, of course, thrilled that he would consider our humble institution to house his collection. But I must say, his sending you in his place is a bit . . . unconventional."

Cas tries not to grimace at that. "Well, as I said. The donation was my idea."

"Even so. Your father allowed you to travel all this way alone?"

"I had my maid."

Henry must sense Cas prickling, because he intervenes before the thorns can do any damage. "I think you'll find that Miss Sterling can be very determined once she's set her mind to something," Henry tells Smith. "Wouldn't you agree, Pastor?"

"That's one way to put it," Pastor Dekker says. Cas suspects he would've preferred to put it in ruder terms.

"Well, I think it's good for a young lady to travel!" Mrs. Smith says. "And to have some independence. It makes a person resilient." She turns to her husband. "Imagine if I'd never left my hometown before you decided to move us off into this wilderness! I wouldn't have lasted a month."

Smith surveys her over his cup. "What a relief that you've learned to survive with only green tea."

The awkward silence gives Cas a moment to plan his next words. "This does seem a surprising place to build a school," he says. He looks at Henry, then adds, "I don't know that I could stomach it—even the ride up from town had me almost beat out by the time we reached your front stoop."

Henry chokes on his tea. It's victory at last—so Henry *does* know what Cas is doing. He knows exactly the ways Cas has scandalized Miss Leslie. The old Henry is still inside somewhere.

"I don't mean to offend, of course," Cas tells the Reverend Smith while Henry coughs into a napkin. "I'm sure you had a very good reason to choose such a remote spot."

"Of course," Smith says. "There are features of the natural landscape on this island that are unmatched anywhere else on the globe. And I believe our isolation here is an asset, not an obstacle. It keeps our students from distraction. Allows for quiet contemplation."

Henry seems to have recovered; he tips his head at Cas. "Your father has a similar philosophy, doesn't he?"

"Ah," Smith says. "Is that what caught his interest in our work here?"

"Oh yes," Cas says. "My father is a firm believer in quiet contemplation." Even with Henry's mask back in place, that brief glimpse underneath it has Cas feeling less alone. He decides to push his luck. "And he was intrigued by some of the other ... *projects* ... that he'd heard you might be pursuing here."

Cas expects Smith to redirect the conversation—to leap into a monologue about some pointless missionary work or the charitable causes Remy had mentioned.

He does *not* expect Smith to say, "You must mean our Order of Lazarus."

Cas stares at him. For a long moment, the table is perfectly silent.

"Or do I misunderstand?" Smith asks.

Cas forces himself to breathe. He forces a smile, though he feels suddenly off-balance, as if he's missed a step while climbing the stairs. "No, not at all," he says. "I had just thought that your secret society would be kept more ... secret."

Mrs. Smith laughs and nudges Cas with her elbow. "Oh, now you've done it!"

"Have I said something wrong?"

Smith pushes up his spectacles yet again. "Not intentionally," he says. "But I'd hardly call our Order a *secret society*. That term has such a connotation, doesn't it?"

Cas isn't entirely sure what *connotation* means, but he's entirely sure it's deserved. "Does it?"

"Consider this," Smith says. "The Freemasons have a temple with their name out in the open in every major city in America. The members of the student society at Yale are working to build their own hall in the middle of New Haven. Even the Order has to advertise itself with the right people so that we might find funding for our work. None of us are keeping our existence a secret. Why would we? We've done nothing wrong."

The way Cas sees it, there are plenty of other reasons to keep secrets: Safety. Protection. Freedom. He doesn't say this. Maybe Smith doesn't have to worry about these things. Under the table, Cas smooths his cloak over his trousers.

"The Order of Lazarus isn't a *secret society*," Smith says. "It's a fraternal organization working toward a better world."

"Fraternal?" Cas asks before he can stop himself. He's looking at Mrs. Smith, but it's her husband who answers.

"We all have our roles to play," Smith says. "My wife doesn't need to be a member herself to contribute to our Order. Though God created the sexes equal, each has their own responsibilities, do they not? We value our women for their work in the home, their nurturing of children—"

"Oh, do you have children?" Cas cuts in.

His only thought is to make Smith stop talking. Pastor Dekker is sitting at Smith's right hand, nodding along with all of this, and Cas feels like he's right back in the Windover church, listening to another sermon about keeping women in their proper place. His skin is crawling.

But as soon as the question is out, Cas knows it was a mistake. Mrs. Smith had been reaching for the butter dish, but now she drops the knife. It clatters off her plate and leaves a smear of butter on the tablecloth. Her mouth has opened in a soundless *oh*.

"I'm sorry," Cas backtracks. "I hadn't meant to pry, I just—I misconstrued. I'm sorry."

"It's quite all right," Mrs. Smith says. She's smiling again, though it's gone watery. She dabs at the tablecloth with her napkin, but the stain has already set in. "Ah, Mrs. Hughes—do you need something?"

The housekeeper has appeared in the doorway.

"May I speak to you, ma'am?" the housekeeper asks, her face sour as ever.

Mrs. Smith leaps to her feet, clearly grateful for the excuse to step away. "I'll just be a moment," she says, and then she and the housekeeper are gone.

No one speaks after the door has shut behind them. Cas stares into his teacup, feeling like an ass. Any triumph from the Miss Leslie game is long vanished. Henry has gone back to not looking at him. At the head of the table, Smith finishes his cake, then wipes his mouth with a napkin.

"I think we should talk about why you're really here, Miss Sterling," Smith says.

Cas blinks at him. "About the donation?"

"We both know that's not the whole of it, don't we?"

And here it is: the storm Cas has been waiting for since he sat down. That first rumble of thunder. Cas's thoughts race, trying to process what Smith means, and yet his body seems to catch on before his mind can. His heart is hammering. He can't quite breathe. The dread is seeping through him like an icy rain.

"You can speak openly here," Smith says. "I think that will make everything easier. I know about what happened on the beach that morning, when you brought Mr. Ashworth into all of this. That wasn't the first death you'd seen, was it?"

Something is rattling against the table. It takes Cas several seconds to realize that it's *him*, his own fingers drumming out a panicky rhythm. "I don't know what you're talking about," Cas hears himself say.

Smith's smile is thin. "But you do, of course. Don't worry—you're not the first person I've met to have visions. I understand why you've kept them a secret. It's a difficult thing to believe, isn't it? But I want you to know: *I* believe you."

Miss Leslie would call Cas's tapping fingers *beating the devil's tattoo*. It's forbidden, of course. Cas clamps his hands into fists. He doesn't give a damn what Miss Leslie thinks, but he knows he's betraying his own nerves. Smith will see right through him. Cas tugs at one of the buttons on his cloak, trying to steady himself.

Henry has leaned across the table toward him. "It's all right," he says quietly. "He can help."

"Let me tell you a story," Smith says. "And then you can tell *me* whether that story resonates. It's a story about a child who caught glimpses of the future. Who could see in advance how a person would die."

The rules Cas made for himself years ago are crumbling apart in his hands. It's all been for nothing. Because Smith *knows*. How does Smith know? How much did Henry accidentally reveal? How much did Smith put together on his own?

"A terrible thing, really," Smith goes on. "Such a heavy burden for one so young to bear. The child was probably frightened. Confused. Who could blame her for trying to hide?"

Cas isn't watching Smith now; he's watching *Henry* watch Smith, captivated. In the space of a minute, Smith has transformed—the turtle of a man is gone, replaced by this quiet commander who seems to cast a spell over the room. There's a strange gravity to him, pulling them all in. It's like the sway Pastor Dekker holds over his congregation, only amplified a dozen times over, compelling and horrifying all at once. Dekker has nothing on *this*.

"But eventually, the child saw a death that was different from the others. A terrible monster. A demon. A vision so frightening that it pushed her from her silence at last." Smith pauses, then says, "Or at least that's how it was supposed to happen."

One thought makes its way through the clamor in Cas's mind: *Finn.* Smith knows about Finn. He knows about the demon, about the death that's coming for her. And that strange last line—*how it was supposed to happen*—lands heavy in his gut. What has Smith done? What is he going to do? If he knows that Finn is here, under his own roof . . . Finn never should have come here. Cas saw the demon chasing her on this very island, saw the light leave her eyes—and then he brought her here anyway.

If Finn dies tonight, it's going to be Cas's fault.

"I'll admit that Mr. Ashworth's involvement was a surprise," Smith is saying. "You know what they say about the best laid plans. But we realized quickly the mistake that had happened. Our good Pastor Dekker was prepared to return home to collect you, Miss Sterling—and then you arrived here all on your own. It feels a little like fate, doesn't it?"

Dekker nods at him. "As God wills it."

And Cas makes himself move at last. He stands abruptly. His chair scrapes on the floorboards.

"It's not fate," he says, relieved to find that his voice sounds a thousand times steadier than he feels. He's still clinging to the button of his cloak. "And it's not God's will. I'd like to leave now. Please call a carriage for me and my maid."

"You understand why I can't do that," Smith says.

"A horse, then. Or I'll walk."

Cas starts for the door, but Pastor Dekker is on his feet and blocking it before Cas can round the table. Smith hasn't even risen from his seat. His voice is infuriatingly calm.

"You're not well," Smith tells Cas.

"I'm perfectly well!"

"But I can help you. We can help each other. These visions are a burden for you—but they would be a blessing for our Order. The keystone for our most important work." He studies Cas over the rim of those damned spectacles. "We've been waiting for you for a long time."

Cas knows then that he isn't going to be allowed to leave this place. Not without a fight. Whatever Smith wants from him—whatever he wants with Cas's visions—he finally has it nearly in his grasp.

He's not going to let it go willingly.

The door of the dining room flies open to reveal Mrs. Smith. Behind her stands the housekeeper, and behind *her*—barely visible over the housekeeper's shoulder—stands Finn, her eyes wide.

"I need to speak with Miss Sterling for a moment," Mrs. Smith says, unaware of the scene she's interrupted. "Mrs. Hughes has just told me the most distressing thing."

Only now, as Cas stares at Finn in the hallway outside, does it occur to him that none of the men know she's here. None of them know that the girl Cas has brought as his maid is the same girl who's meant to die by a demon's hand. Henry might have recognized her, but she was sent off to the kitchen only moments after arriving; he never even saw her.

Cas may be trapped here. But Finn doesn't have to be.

Cas has tugged too hard on the button of his cloak; the thread has come free at last. He clutches the loose button in his hand, lets the edge of it bite into his palm. The Reverend Smith, shockingly, waves at his wife in bored agreement, as if he's uninterested in these womanly affairs.

"Very well," he tells Mrs. Smith. "Bring our guest to the parlor when you're finished. I think we're through with tea. But don't take long." His gaze burns into Cas as he adds, "Miss Sterling and I have a lot to discuss."

XXVI

REMY

These are the steps by which Remy, Kit, and Captain Hobbes are meant to sneak into the seminary:

Step one—Approach from the woods, following not the main road but instead a streambed that cuts up the mountainside from the cove to the edge of the school's grounds.

Step two—Watch the building from the trees until Cas and Finn mark and unlatch the window of the seminary's archive.

Step three—Enter through the window.

It's a straightforward plan, but that's its advantage. The ideal plan is concrete, specific—flexible enough to allow for contingencies, but stable enough to provide the solid ground from which those contingencies might flow. Remy has spent years thinking about this place but only a short time envisioning herself actually entering it.

Now, with their task finally at hand, this is how the steps play out:

As planned, Remy and the others approach from the woods.

As planned, they watch from the trees until Kit sees the signal.

As planned, they enter through the window.

The archive, as it turns out, is on the second floor, but they've accounted for this possibility; Kit scales the brick wall easily enough and then lowers a rope for Remy and the captain to climb. Remy burns her palms a little in the effort, but she manages. She clambers over the windowsill. And then they're inside.

As planned.

There are few things as satisfying, in Remy's opinion, as a scheme coming to pass exactly as it's supposed to. Plan and execution in perfect alignment. Even as she stands in the archive of the Eden Theological Seminary, even as the importance of this moment hammers in her chest, she pauses for a beat to appreciate the accomplishment. She wipes her hands on her skirt.

Heavy curtains block any outside light from entering the archive. When Kit pulls the window shut and draws the curtain back into place, the room is almost pitch-black. She flicks the curtain open again until the captain gets a lantern going. Kit stuffs her jacket along the crack under the door so the lantern light won't be visible from the hallway. Then she stays stationed there, listening for any approaching footsteps.

Which leaves Remy and Captain Hobbes to their investigations. The bookcases tower over them. The highest shelves are barely visible in the eerie, flickering lamplight. But the collection holds more than books, just as the captain had predicted. Through the shelves' glass doors, Remy can make out other shapes interfiled with the tomes: crates, jars, artifacts. Maybe the captain *will* find his reaper's glass here. And Remy will find . . . something.

This is where the concreteness of the plan falls apart for her. She takes in the infinity of paper in this room with a mix of awe and alarm. The research journal in her pocket is nothing. It's a joke. She's spent years starving, hoarding every crumb of information she could find—and now she's staring at a feast.

However much time Cas can give them with his distraction, it's not going to be enough.

No time to waste, then. Remy shakes herself. She can do this. How many other libraries and archives has she searched before today? How is this any different, really?

It's completely different, of course, and her pounding heart knows it. She chooses to ignore it.

The captain has already found the shelf listings—a set of bound catalogs laid out on a table in the center of the room. Remy joins him there. She gets to work.

She starts with the index of historical records. Anything she can learn about the time her father spent here might offer some guidance for where to look next. But the shelf listings, infuriatingly, don't have their materials filed by date. They're filed by subject. Names, mostly. They're alphabetical, more or less, though a little disorganized from years of late additions. Remy holds one of the ledgers close to the lamp and skims the list of names under *D*, searching for *DeWindt*. Searching for her father.

He isn't there.

Of course he isn't; it would be too easy. Maybe Smith keeps his more private records somewhere else—or maybe he's destroyed the records of her father. Remy thinks of Finn. It's comforting to know that Finn was in this room only a short while before her. Even now, Finn is still inside this very building.

Remy reads the list of names again, more slowly now, just in case—until she spies a name she hadn't noticed the first time: *Joseph Dekker.*

The shelf listing points Remy to a cabinet on one wall. Pastor Dekker's file there holds a large sheaf of papers. Remy brings them back to the lantern to read. Nearly all of them are letters written by Dekker and addressed to Reverend Smith. But these, at least, are arranged chronologically. The most recent is dated barely a month ago. Remy flips through the stack, searching for anything Dekker might have sent around the time Remy's father was taken.

She finds something. More than one something. And her eyes land on the name she'd been looking for in the first place:

The man is Charles DeWindt, Dekker had written eight years ago. *I plan to sound out what he knows and, if he's amenable, to recruit him to our cause.*

Remy reads.

Her years of investigation have prepared her for this—reading in bursts, taking in as much information as quickly as possible and boxing it up in her mind to sort through later. And she can do it all with her attention torn: anytime she shut herself in her father's study, she was always listening for her mother to call or for her sisters to come knocking at the door.

Across the table from her, the captain suddenly sets down the catalog he's been looking through. He darts to one of the shelves with surprising swiftness.

"Did you find something?" Kit whispers from beside the door.

"Possibly." The captain rolls over one of the shelves' ladders. The wheels are well oiled, thankfully; the ladder glides along its tracks without a sound. "*Materials for a reaper's glass,*" he says. "That's what the listing calls it. Maybe Smith didn't *find* the glass. Maybe he's been trying to make one."

"Is that even possible?" Kit asks.

She abandons her post to help the captain with the ladder, and Remy returns her focus to the letters. To the story that's unfolding before her. But now, even as half of her rushes to read the letters from Dekker, the other half is watching the captain and Kit. The captain has brought something down from the shelf.

"This can't be it," he says in a low voice. He's holding a large, opaque jar in both hands, and Kit takes it. "Díaz's sources said the glass was a recent acquisition. This is too old. Look at the dust. And..."

He checks the card tied neatly around the jar's mouth.

"Smith has been storing this for over eight years."

Remy is outside her own body. She watches herself fold up the letters and tuck them in the pocket of her coat. She can see, suddenly, the sequence of moves ahead of her, the chess pieces as they come into focus. She does not want Kit to open that jar.

Kit opens the jar. She tips it toward the light, peering inside. She draws in a breath.

"Ashes," Kit says. A pause. "I think it's remains."

A freezing terror has started up Remy's spine.

"Human?" the captain asks.

"Can't say for sure. But I think... Oh god. I think that's a molar."

The front walk outside the DeWindt family home is set on a slope toward the street. The gradient is so slight that Remy might not even notice, except that every spring, when the snow starts to melt, it pools on the pathway and then refreezes into a perfectly smooth sheet of ice. Every spring, at least once, Remy steps out onto the path and finds herself sliding, slowly and steadily, toward the road, with nothing to grab for purchase and no means of stopping herself. All she can do is scramble for balance and hope that the street stays clear.

Remy doesn't remember crossing the room, but she's standing beside Kit now, staring at the jar. She can see the writing on the card for herself. The date, eight years ago: *18th of June.*

A single day after the postmark from her father's journal.

Remy waits for a crash. She keeps waiting. It doesn't come. There's no violent impact, no fall off a cliff. There's only that slow slide down the end of an icy path, inevitable and surprising and not surprising at all. Maybe she's known, on some level, that this was coming. It hadn't felt real. It's not real now. And yet the gravity has her, pulling her away, pulling everything out of her control.

The captain is up the ladder once more. There's another jar on the shelf there: smaller, transparent, with something suspended in the clear liquid inside.

"Is that . . . ?" Kit asks, then gags.

"Eyes." The captain's voice is barely a whisper. "Why would he preserve the eyes?"

And Remy's emotions have officially hit their capacity. She doesn't have room for any more of them. The terror is gone, leaving only a strange, empty calmness as she stares at the jar in the captain's hands.

Kit has straightened suddenly, listening. She darts to the door, then back again, dousing the lantern as she does.

"Someone's coming," she hisses, gesturing toward the window. "We need to go."

But Remy can't move. She can't stop looking at the jar. The things inside are hardly eyes anymore. They're swollen from the preservation liquid, and their irises and pupils are clouded blue gray. But Remy knows that, underneath, the irises were once a deep brown. The same brown that she sees in the mirror every day. The brown of her own eyes. The brown of her father's.

Because the truth of it is staring her in the face now: Cas's vision was true.

Her father is dead.

Afterward, Remy will wonder why she didn't stay. She should have stayed. She could have ignored Kit's warning that someone was coming, could have brushed off the captain's insistence that they flee. If she were Finn, she might've hidden in the stacks of the library, waited for the perfect moment to enact her revenge against the Order of Lazarus. If she were Cas, she probably would've run fist-first at the Reverend Smith himself.

Remy had thought these days aboard the *Memento Mori* had changed her. But she's still the same frozen, flat, obedient girl she's always been, too caught up in planning and thinking to ever take action. And all the plans she's made have crumbled to nothing by now.

So she follows. She does what's expected of her, just as she always has. She's already hiking back through the woods, trailing along behind Captain Hobbes and Kit, before it even occurs to her that she'd had any other option.

The woods have grown dark around them. Kit and the captain are talking in low voices, but Remy can't hear what they're saying. Kit tries to ask her something. Remy can only shake her head. The letters from Dekker are still in her pocket, and the jar of her father's ashes is tucked under the captain's arm, cradled.

The captain had wrapped the second jar inside a piece of cloth and brought that with them, as well.

Over and over, Remy hears the captain's voice whispering, *Eyes.*

Her emotions have yet to return to her. She's numb. Deadened. Still, instinctively, her mind is reaching for the puzzle of it, trying to work through the knots. Trying to untangle them. Inside the archive, she'd read the letters quickly, gathering as much information as possible but processing none of it.

Now, as they walk, her mind starts to process, whether she wants it to or not. She feels herself putting the story together.

It was Dekker who first grew suspicious of Remy's father. He saw the pattern in the pro bono clients of Charles DeWindt's law firm who died only a week or two after DeWindt had met with them. It was as if DeWindt could predict in advance where his services would be needed. Dekker started watching the lawyer. Following him. He tracked him once when DeWindt visited a bookshop in Boston that was known for selling arcane texts. He tracked him again to a similar shop in Andover. He reported all this in his letters to the Reverend John Smith—the Shepherd.

The Shepherd had been looking for something, Dekker knew: an artifact. A scrying device. Something that would give him access to the list of people who were fated to die.

It seemed that Charles DeWindt had come into possession of that artifact. It seemed that DeWindt had a reaper's glass.

Dekker wrote that he would try the friendly approach with DeWindt first—he'd tried to recruit him to Smith's cause. But DeWindt wouldn't be recruited. He wanted nothing to do with the Order of Lazarus. By the next letter, the pastor had moved to the less-friendly approach. He would send men to DeWindt's house one night. He'd have DeWindt seized and put aboard a ship. The ship would take DeWindt to Eden so the Shepherd could speak to him directly.

The Shepherd would convince him. DeWindt would see reason.

Pastor Dekker would stay in Windover, waiting. Once the Shepherd had learned where DeWindt was keeping his reaper's glass, Pastor Dekker would retrieve it and bring it to Eden. If DeWindt wouldn't tell him the location willingly, the Shepherd would force the information out of him.

Remy hadn't finished reading the letters before everything had happened in the archive; she hadn't reached the point in the story when the Shepherd, Smith, must have realized the flaw in his plan.

But Remy has realized the flaw already as her mind works through everything she's read.

The reaper's glass isn't an object. It never was.

It's a person.

Remy's father had spent years trying to research the power that coursed through his own veins. When the Order dragged him to Eden, he'd kept researching. He'd walked their halls, learned their secrets, dug for information. He'd feigned compliance for long enough to gather sixteen pages of notes, and then escaped for long enough to put those notes in the mail. But Smith must have caught him in the end, before he could run. He must have realized that DeWindt was never going to help the Order's cause willingly.

And so Smith had killed him. And Smith had gathered the remains, thinking that he could use them to harness the connection that the reaper's glass had with Death. Thinking that the body itself still held this power.

But someone else had started having visions by then. The power had already moved on to someone new.

And now, that new reaper's glass has walked through the Order of Lazarus's front doors.

XXVII

FINN

"Mrs. Smith tells me you were caught wandering around," Cas says. "Do you care to explain yourself?"

Finn and Cas are back in the entrance hall. Outside the windows, the sunlight is quickly fading; it's going to be dark soon. Finn had hoped the housekeeper and the older blond woman—Mrs. Smith, apparently—would leave her and Cas alone, at least for a moment, to let them discuss this in private. Of course they don't. The housekeeper is out for Finn's blood, and she's not going to miss a moment of this dressing-down.

But Cas doesn't look ready to dress anyone down. His eyes keep darting back and forth, as if he's scanning the hall for exits. His hands are twitching, fidgeting with something too small for Finn to see. He seems to notice her watching. The fidgeting stops.

"Well?" he says.

Finn considers her words. If Remy were here, she and Cas could probably have a whole unspoken conversation without Mrs. Smith or the housekeeper even realizing it. Their history seems to let them communicate sometimes without either of them saying a word. But Finn and Cas have none of that history. Two weeks ago, Finn barely knew him.

At last, Finn says, "I was trying to help."

The housekeeper makes a scoffing sound. But Cas's darting eyes seem to focus at last. They squint a little as he studies Finn.

"And did you?" he asks. "Help?"

"Yes."

The housekeeper scoffs again, clearly seething. "She did nothing of the sort!" she says. "She made a mess of my kitchen, went sneaking off to who knows where, and then tried to tell me she'd gotten lost!" She rounds on Finn, who tries not to flinch. Her ear is still burning where the housekeeper had grabbed it earlier. "Are you so impudent? Or just a fool?"

Probably both, Finn thinks. But Cas has caught her true meaning. It's fortunate that both the housekeeper and Mrs. Smith are focused on Finn now, because Cas is doing nothing to hide the relief that's written plainly on his face: He knows that Finn managed their task. She marked the window. She let the others inside. Their work here is finished.

"Right," Cas says as he tries to gather himself. "Right. Well, your ... impudence ... must be addressed. Don't you agree?"

He looks to Mrs. Smith for approval. Mrs. Smith gives a curt nod.

"You should go back to town," he tells Finn. "Wait for me at ... the hotel. I'll deal with you later."

Finn replays his words in her head, trying to work out some double meaning. "Are you not returning to town with me?" she asks.

"I'm not finished here yet," Cas says. "And I think we've disrespected our hosts enough for one evening, don't you?"

Surely this isn't just to placate Mrs. Smith. Is Cas staying behind because of Ashworth? Perhaps he needs more time to bring Ashworth into their plan.

But Finn isn't going to leave here without Cas—not when he's acting so clearly unsettled.

"I'm supposed to accompany you," Finn says.

"Mr. Ashworth can accompany me. I'll be fine."

"But—"

"*Finn.*"

Something in his tone stops her. Cas isn't just unsettled. He's *afraid*. The darting eyes, the trembling hands—Finn can see it now. He's badly shaken.

She thinks of that restless energy he'd had when he first called out to her on Windover Common. She thinks of him drunk in the fo'c'sle the other night, trying to tell her something. Something Finn already knows. Ever since they reached the island, he's been cagey, casting Finn odd glances. Trying to convince her to stay behind.

"I'll be fine," Cas says in a low voice. "Just go. Please."

And Finn doesn't need years of shared history to be able to read his face now. She knows.

Cas has seen what will happen to Finn if she stays here.

When Finn's mother taught her and Kieran to read, using a dog-eared book of Catholic saints, Finn was always drawn to the martyrs. She used to spend hours studying their stories. There was Saint Ignatius, who was fed to wild beasts in a Roman amphitheater. Saint Dymphna, who was beheaded by her own father. Saint Bartholomew, who was flayed alive—a term Finn had unwisely asked her mother to explain and now can never unknow.

Even back then, Finn didn't feel much of an urge to die in the name of Christ; it seemed to her that Christ had that covered.

But she envied the martyrs all the same. There was a beautiful kind of simplicity to martyrdom. A promise of salvation, like the one Finn had spent so long chasing after in the Knockadine confessional booth. The saints in those stories always faced their deaths with a total sense of peace. They were calm. Accepting. Secure in the choice they'd made.

And Finn *does* stand by her own choice. She'd make the same one every time, even now, as the death she signed for herself in fire closes in around her at last. She's spent so long convincing herself that she accepts her fate—that when death comes for her, she'll face it with that same sense of peace.

But perhaps those saints didn't face their deaths as peacefully as the stories claimed.

Or perhaps Finn just isn't a saint.

Because even as she wants to stand firm—even as she wants to tell Cas no, that she won't leave without him, that if he's staying here, she's staying, too . . .

Finn isn't ready to die.

"All right," she says at last. It's barely a whisper. It's pathetic.

Cas nods.

"Good," he says. He turns to Mrs. Smith again, smoothing the folds of his cloak. "Do you have a carriage you could send for? Thank you. You can have the driver drop her in town. I'm happy to compensate him. I apologize for the trouble. You and I will talk about this later."

This last statement is for Finn. Cas holds out a hand to her as if to shake. It's a strangely formal gesture, but Finn mirrors him anyway. As she takes his hand, she feels something small and round press into her palm.

"Good," Cas says again, and he lets go.

Mrs. Smith sweeps him off to the parlor after that. Finn waits in tense silence with the housekeeper until a buckboard wagon and a pair of horses appear on the darkening drive. She keeps her hands clenched into fists at her sides. She doesn't open them as the housekeeper and driver mutter about her for a few minutes. She doesn't open them as she climbs into the back of the cart.

Only after the bumpy ride back to town—where the driver deposits her outside a ramshackle hotel and then sets off toward the seminary again without a word—does Finn open her hand to see what Cas had pressed there.

It's a button. Blue. The same color as Cas's cloak.

This is what he's been fiddling with all afternoon. Finn stares at it in her own palm. It's a message, isn't it? It must be; he'd handed it over with clear deliberation. Finn has no idea what it means.

Because she isn't the person it's meant for.

Finn takes off running toward the cove.

XXVIII

CAS

Mrs. Smith locks him inside the parlor. Cas doesn't see her do it, but he hears the click of a key outside, and when he rattles the knob, it doesn't turn. He rattles it several more times for good measure. The parlor is just as grand as every other room Cas has seen here; his mother would probably approve of the decorations. The curtains over the darkening windows are embroidered with flowers. A fire dances in the hearth, cheery and stiflingly hot.

Cas tugs at his cloak—does it even matter anymore that he keeps up this disguise? He eyes the fire, then the perfectly flammable curtains. If they're going to lock him in here, maybe he should just set the whole building ablaze.

He won't, of course. Finn is barely clear of this place, and Remy and the others might still be in the archive, and besides, he has to get Henry out. Henry is the only reason Cas hasn't already broken a window and fled into the night. If he can just get Henry alone for long enough to explain the danger here, then he and Henry can . . . what? Their original plan is shattered; Smith isn't going to let Cas go back to town, with or without Henry.

We've been waiting for you for a long time.

Cas has started pacing without even realizing it. Two well-stuffed sofas stand before the fire, and he circles them again and again. At least Finn managed to get the others inside. At least she'll take his message back to Remy. Cas feels useless. He's done it again, hasn't he? Just like in their chess game, he's taken the obvious attack, even congratulated himself on convincing Smith of his story—and in the process, he's walked himself straight into Smith's trap. Now there's nothing he can do except wait, and pace, and hope that someone stronger or smarter will come back for him.

They *will* come back for him, won't they? Even if Remy gets his message, will she know what it means? Will she believe him? These last few days of amnesty between them can't quite outweigh the years of doubt and distrust.

When the parlor door finally opens, Cas squares his shoulders, trying very hard to look like someone who *hasn't* been nervously pacing a hole in the floor.

But it's only Henry. Cas relaxes. As Henry steps into the room, as he shuts the door behind him, Cas listens for the click of the lock again. It doesn't come. Unlocked, then. Maybe he should just grab Henry now and run.

Henry is already settling on one of the sofas beside the fire, hands folded on his knees.

"What's going on?" Cas asks. "Are you all right?"

Henry looks at him oddly. "I'm fine. I'm more worried about *you*."

He waves at the empty seat across from him, trying to get Cas to sit. Cas would much rather keep pacing. He compromises by standing behind the sofa and worrying his fingers into the upholstery.

"The Shepherd said it's all right if I talk to you first," Henry says. "He knows you have a lot of questions."

Something prickles in Cas's mind. "The Shepherd?"

"The Reverend Smith. He says that you've probably been having these ... visions ... for years. Is that true?"

Cas had known this would be coming, and yet he doesn't have an answer. Which apparently is an answer in itself.

"Why didn't you tell me?" Henry asks.

"Would you have believed me if I did?"

Henry flinches at the bitterness in Cas's voice—but this isn't Henry's fault. Cas takes a long breath. He's the reason Henry was dragged to this place, and in a moment, Cas is going to be the one to get him out of this place, too.

"I'm sorry that I lied to you back at Long Beach," Cas says. "And I'm sorry that I got you wrapped up in all of this."

"I know," Henry says. "And I know, rationally, why you kept the visions to yourself. It's just strange—to realize that you've been carrying this enormous secret, and I had no idea."

Cas's fingers twitch toward his cloak. The parlor really is unbearably hot. And it's only Henry here, isn't it? And he's going to find out soon enough, anyway.

"While we're on that subject ..." Cas says, and he flicks back his hood.

The air on his neck is instant relief. He tugs the pins from his hair and shakes himself loose for the first time in hours.

But Henry's eyes have widened. "What happened to your hair?"

"Nothing *happened* to it." Cas fights the sudden urge to yank the hood back up. He tries to focus on unbuttoning the cloak instead of watching Henry's reaction, and yet he can *feel* the reaction happening anyway, like a trickle of something cold landing on his scalp.

"Oh." The realization flattens Henry's voice. "So you *chose* to cut it. How many years have we known each other? And somehow, you still manage to surprise me."

Cas lets the cloak drop to the floor, a puddle of blue silk. He feels strangely calmer despite everything, and he sits on the sofa across from Henry at last. He's afraid to look Henry in the eyes, afraid that his face will hold some emotion that Cas won't be able to unsee—but Henry has composed himself, inscrutable once again.

"Well," Cas says, "a lot has happened in these last few days."

Henry nods slowly. "It's been the same for me. I have so much to tell you. I'm not sure how much of it I'm really meant to share, but—"

"Because I'm not in the fraternity?"

Cas had hoped that might get a snort out of him—Smith is just the sort of old-fashioned boot he and Henry used to laugh at. But Henry sighs.

"This is why I wanted to talk to you first," he says. "I *knew* that you were going to be like this—that you'd dig in your heels on principle alone. But the Shepherd isn't like what you're thinking. Not really. Please don't judge him based on one conversation."

The prickle in Cas's mind has grown into an entire cactus. "You keep calling him that—'the Shepherd.' Like you're one of them. In the Order."

Henry doesn't reply.

"Oh god," Cas says. "You didn't *join*, did you?"

"No, I didn't join!" Then, as if he's well aware that Cas won't like it, he adds, "Yet."

"*Yet?*"

"It's a long process to become a full member. But Pastor Dekker thinks I'm a good candidate. And the Shepherd—that is, Smith—he—"

"You can't trust him, Hen," Cas cuts in. "You can't trust any of them. They're dangerous—that's the whole reason I came here. I'm getting you out."

"I didn't ask you to do that, though. I don't want *out*."

Somehow, in all their days of planning, Cas had never truly considered this particular turn of events. "You can't stay here!"

"I've *been* here," Henry says. "For over a week now. The Shepherd has been nothing but welcoming."

"You don't know him, though. You don't know what he's done."

"Whatever wild story you've gotten in your head—"

"Do you know about the disappearances? About all the people who've gone missing here over the years?"

Henry falters, and Cas would wager whatever's left of his father's gambling fund that Henry *hadn't* known about this. But Henry only says, "I'm sure there's some explanation."

"Yeah! I can think of a pretty good one!"

"You're being ridiculous. The work that the Shepherd is doing here... It's revolutionary. It's bigger than I could have imagined. So few people can actually change the world—and he's well on his way to doing just that."

"What work is it, then?" Cas asks. He doesn't really expect Henry to answer, though, and Henry doesn't. "Right. So the secret society does have *some* secrets."

"It's not a secret, exactly, it's just... difficult to explain." Henry shakes his head. When he runs a hand through his perfect hair, it's left sticking up on one side. "He's going to tell you most of this, anyway," he says, almost to himself. "So that you can understand why it's so important. He can help you stop having these visions, but it's like he said—you'll be helping each other."

"I'm not helping *him* with anything."

"Will you just listen, please? This is hard enough without . . ." Henry glances at the door—still closed. He leans toward Cas, dropping his voice low. "Here's what I know. The Shepherd told me about these . . . entities . . . called reapers. Supposedly each reaper keeps a list of the people who are meant to die. I know it sounds like something out of a fairy tale, but—"

"It doesn't sound like a fairy tale. I know about all of this."

Henry stares at him.

"Like I said," Cas tells him. "A lot has happened."

"All right." Henry smooths down his hair. "So the Order is working on a way to capture one of these reapers. To control it."

Now it's Cas's turn to stare. "Why the hell would they want to do that?"

"Well, if they control the reaper . . . they control the list."

When Cas wrangles his darting thoughts—the captain, Death, the story the captain had told them in the glow of the bonfire—enough to put together Henry's meaning, the realization feels like a kick to the chest.

"Smith wants to be in charge of who lives and who dies?"

Henry must hear the horror in his voice. "It's not about being *in charge*. It's about putting things right. The deaths the reapers are causing—"

"Who says they're *causing* deaths?" Cas scrapes his mind for how the captain had explained it, though the finer points of that night are fuzzy. "Don't reapers just collect the souls of people who've already died?"

"That's not what the Shepherd says."

"And what does *he* know about it?"

"More than either of us, clearly!"

"He's not going to find him, anyway," Cas says.

"Find who?"

"Death. This reaper he's trying to capture. Death's gone missing. Probably hiding from *him*."

Henry's mouth is actually hanging open now. "How do you . . . ?" he starts, then shakes his head. "Look, the Shepherd has been studying all this for years. I'm sure he has a plan. He says the reapers are interfering with God's will. But if he captures the reaper, if he controls the reaper's list, he can keep the right people off it. He can trade out the names."

"Trade?"

Henry seems to realize his mistake at once. "He can keep people safe," he amends.

"No, you said *trade*. He wants to *trade out* the people who appear on Death's list. So that means someone else has to take their place, right? Who's supposed to die instead—the 'wrong' people?"

"The Shepherd can explain it better than I can—"

"And how does he choose who to save?" Cas hears his own voice rising, but he can't stop it. "Is it the people who can pay? The ones in his fraternity?"

"It's not like that. It's not about the money. I know it sounds bad when you say it that way, but—"

"It sounds bad because it's bad! You're talking about trading one life for another!"

"Calm down, please."

Cas has never in his life felt *calmer* after someone has told him to calm down. He's pacing again. He doesn't even remember standing up. "What happened to your big ideals? Your dream senator in Boston? You spend one week with some fanatical preacher who thinks *he* should decide who deserves to live or die—"

"You're getting it twisted," Henry cuts in. "Or maybe you just can't understand."

"I understand plenty!"

"You haven't lost someone, though!"

The words burst out of Henry like an accusation, and Cas freezes. The whole room feels as if time has stopped, the same second playing over and over. Henry closes his eyes.

"The Shepherd and his wife *did* have a child," he says. The past tense of it drops like a rock in the ocean. "She died. In a shipwreck. Some of the sailors on the crew survived, but their daughter ... She didn't make it."

Cas thinks of Mrs. Smith's watery smile. "That's awful. I'm not saying it isn't."

"You saw what my family went through, too. After Cecilia. The Shepherd is just trying to save other families from having to feel that pain."

There's a longing in his voice that Cas hasn't heard there for years. Henry has found purpose here. Meaning. Cas recognizes the fluttering hope of it, like the feeling he'd gotten when Mita invited him to keep sailing with the *Memento Mori*.

"I know it's a lot to take in," Henry says. "But your visions are a part of it. The Shepherd thinks you're connected to one of these reapers—that's where the visions come from. There's a ritual he can use to transfer the connection. He's got it all worked out. When I first arrived, when he first started asking me questions, I was overwhelmed, too. But then I realized it wasn't me he needed."

Cas feels suddenly cold. "Wait. How did Smith know what happened at Long Beach?"

A questioning crease forms between Henry's eyebrows.

"How did he figure out it was me having the visions?"

And Henry answers as if it's the most obvious thing in the world, as if he'd assumed that Cas already knew: "Because I told him. I told him everything I could."

Maybe Cas *should* have known. Everyone else did. Only yesterday, Cas was sitting in the galley with Remy and Finn, insisting that Henry would protect him. And instead, Henry had already sided with Smith. Even if Henry didn't realize the weight of the secret he was handing over, he had to know it was meant to stay secret. He knows Cas better than anyone.

But that's not really true anymore, is it? If it ever was. And maybe Cas doesn't know Henry as well as he thinks. Henry has been burying more and more parts of himself for years, and Cas has watched the dirt piling up and watched that old version of Henry disappearing into the ground and all the while tried to deny it.

Cas should have seen this coming.

After that awful lunch with his mother and Dekker years ago, Cas had gone to Henry's house. He'd tapped on Henry's bedroom window, and Henry had let him in, though he'd grumbled a bit about the risk to their reputations if someone saw. When Cas had told Henry the story—about the flouncy dress he couldn't make himself wear, about his mother's slap, about

Dekker's response—he'd expected a sympathetic ear, at least. He'd hoped Henry might join him in his righteous anger.

But Henry had sighed.

"Why didn't you just wear the dress, though?" he'd asked. "I don't understand why you always have to make things more difficult for yourself."

"I don't make things difficult," Cas said. "They're just difficult."

"Right." And then Henry had rolled his eyes. "Obviously your mother shouldn't have struck you. But honestly, Cassandra—what did you think was going to happen?"

It had been such a slow change that Cas hadn't noticed it until that moment: The way Henry had stopped playing along with his jokes. The way he'd started worrying about how people might talk. The two of them had been twin rebels for years, until the day Cas looked up and found himself alone.

And *that*, really, was when Cas had given up fighting. Dekker's sermons played a part, of course, but the heart of it was always Henry, and the realization that Henry had changed. That Henry had left him behind. With no discussion, Henry had started making concessions about the life they'd planned together. If Cas still wanted that life, Cas would have to concede some things, too.

It's unfathomable now, that he'd wanted that life. It's unfathomable that he'd almost believed that a life with Henry was the best he could hope for.

Henry rubs his forehead. "Don't be like that. You know I'm only trying to help you. And if you'd stop being so stubborn, maybe you'd see that the Shepherd is trying to help you, too."

"I don't want his help!" Cas says. "He's dangerous!"

"That's rich, considering *your* choice of travel companion."

The sharpness in his voice stops Cas first—and then Cas realizes what he's said. "What's that supposed to mean?"

"Don't think I didn't notice. I recognized her in the hallway. During tea, when you mentioned your maid, I just assumed you meant Penelope—but no. Instead you brought *her*, of all people. Even though we've both seen what's coming for her."

Cas's palms are slick with sweat. "You didn't tell Smith, did you?"

"Is that really what you're worried about right now?" Henry huffs an exasperated laugh. "No, I didn't tell him. I probably should have. What were you thinking? You heard the Shepherd. Who knows what sort of dark business she's gotten herself into, to have a demon on her tail?"

"Finn isn't involved in any *dark business*."

"And that's not even mentioning what will happen to your reputation if anyone finds out you were traveling with her. You have to know what people will say."

Cas shouldn't ask—but he asks anyway. "What will they say?"

"Don't be naive. Surely you've heard the rumors." Henry's voice drops low again, though there's a new edge to it. "She's old Mrs. Darner's maid, isn't she? The one who ... corrupts young ladies, or ... *seduces* them, or ... Christ, don't make me keep going."

Cas has *not* heard the rumors. The only rumors he hears these days are the ones Penelope tells him—and she's certainly never brought *this* up. Cas considers this new piece alongside everything else he's learned about Finn. It's new information, and yet not really a surprise.

"Finn is my friend," Cas says. "And she hasn't *corrupted* me."

Henry's gaze rakes over Cas again, lingering on the hair, the vest, the trousers. He raises an eyebrow.

"Oh, go to hell," Cas snaps at him.

"Such crass language," a mild voice says from the doorway.

Smith has traded his dinner jacket for a wool greatcoat. Cas hadn't even noticed the door opening. How much has Smith overheard? But if he's shocked by any revelations about Cas's maid, he doesn't show it.

"I trust you've had enough time to catch up. Did Mr. Ashworth tell you about the ritual? Good." Smith studies Cas for a long moment with that same burning gaze. Cas waits for him to make some comment on his appearance, but Smith only says, "You may want that cloak again. We'll be going outside."

"Is the ritual ready, then?" Henry asks.

Smith nods, then straightens his spectacles. "Two of our members are finishing the preparations as we speak."

Henry steps forward and reaches to take Cas's hands. Cas jerks away. Henry's brow furrows again, stung, but he doesn't retreat.

"Just hear him out," Henry says quietly. "Please. For me. You said you wanted to leave here—well, this is the way you can do that. Once he's helped rid you of the visions, you can go home." He swallows, considering. "*Both* of us can go home, if you'd like. I'd do that for you. We can deal with the gossip in town. And you'll be free from the visions. We can have a normal life together."

Just moments ago, Cas had been ready to beg Henry to leave with him. But something has shifted.

"Normal," Cas echoes. The word tastes strangely bitter on his tongue. "I don't think normal was ever going to work for me, actually."

"Is this about . . . ?" Henry gestures at Cas. With one up-and-down motion, he captures the whole of who Cas has grown into and dismisses it with a flick of his hand. "You know how I feel about you. This doesn't change anything. You want to cut your hair short? Wear trousers when we're at home? Fine. The hair is nothing a good bonnet can't cover. But having *visions* is something else. It's not as if you asked for this power. You don't even want it."

"Why do you think you know what I want?" Cas says.

"Because I know *you*."

He doesn't, though. Henry *doesn't* know him. Whatever has happened in this last week, whatever has awakened inside Cas that he'd been holding back for so long—this is Cas now. And it always *was* Cas, even before he'd realized it for himself.

Henry cannot possibly know Cas, because until a week ago, neither did Cas.

Cas squares his shoulders again as he faces Reverend Smith.

"I don't want your help," he says. "I want to leave."

"And you will—after. As long as you cooperate, this will all be over soon."

Another man has stepped into the room now, and the sight of him shatters any hope Cas may have clung to about fighting his way out of here: the man is enormous. He murmurs something to Smith, who nods again before turning to Henry.

"I'd recommend that you wait here," Smith says. "Pastor Dekker can stay with you. The ritual is necessary, you understand—but it may be difficult to watch."

The panic is catching up with Cas, an icy tangle in his chest that's making it hard to breathe. "Hen," he says.

Henry blinks for a moment. Is that hesitation? Cas is terrified to hope.

"It's safe, though?" Henry asks Smith.

"Perfectly."

"Henry!" Cas pleads.

Henry won't look him in the eyes anymore. "I'll be here when it's done," he says.

A final abandonment. When he disappears into the hallway, Cas is left utterly alone.

"Are you sure you don't want your cloak?" Smith asks Cas, as if he's inviting him on an evening stroll. "The nights here can be cold."

Cas considers the pile of fabric on the ground. Finn might have some choice words for him if he throws it away once again, but she'll probably understand, too. The thought warms him a little. "I'm good."

"Have it your way, then. Let's walk."

Cas stays where he is.

It's part petulance and part fear, a cold knot of terror still working its way up his chest and into his throat. How long can he possibly stall? How long will it take the others to come back here? *If* they come back here. He can't quite ignore the thought as it lodges itself deeper.

Smith sighs. "I had hoped it wouldn't come to this. But frankly, I don't have the patience."

He gestures to the other man, who crosses to a decorative cabinet near the door and lifts down an ornate wooden box. The dueling pistols inside are polished and expensive looking, probably antique—but still functional.

The man trains one of the pistols on Cas. He flicks back the hammer.

"Walk," Smith says again.

Cas walks.

Dusk has settled into night by the time Smith leads them out through the back door. The path they follow quickly shifts from tidy paving stones to dirt as they leave the small garden and enter the woods. The darkness among the trees feels like a living thing. Cas thinks of the shadowy monster—the demon—gliding through this forest in his vision of Finn.

But that wasn't the first vision to have shown him this place, was it? He recognizes it now, as the pine needles underfoot soften his steps, as he watches Smith's silhouette ahead of him. This is the forest where Mr. DeWindt was murdered. Cas never saw the face of the man who killed him, but as they walk, his mind fills in the scene with details it's never had before: The set of Smith's jaw as he carved out the eyes with grim precision. The blood splattering his spectacles after he'd slit the throat. The calmness with which he'd stepped back and wiped the lenses clean so he could watch Remy's father dying at his feet.

Cas feels dizzy. He should try to run, shouldn't he? But the man with the dueling pistols is still at his back, and besides, where is there to go? He can't make it back to the cove on his own, not in the dark. Not without Smith or one of his Order members catching him.

"How much did Ashworth tell you about the details of our ritual?" Smith asks over his shoulder as they walk.

Cas's memory is a blur. "Some."

"It's a straightforward process, at least for what you need to know of it. Of course, if you were a candidate for membership in our Order, I could teach you how to *use* your power, and this transferring wouldn't even be necessary. Inconvenient, isn't it? I've never understood the reasoning for *who* forms this sort of connection with a reaper. But you understand why, with you, we have to move to a different option."

Cas bites his tongue. He doesn't want anything to do with the damned Order, obviously—so why does this exclusion from it make him want to scream?

"Then again," Smith goes on, "we'd likely have ended up here either way. You seem determined to see me as an enemy. Pastor Dekker did warn me that you were stubborn. *Deliberately contrary*, I believe he said."

"That's flattering," Cas says. "So you might as well give up now, right?"

"I can be very persuasive. This ritual is something like a cleansing process—a means of drawing out this power from you and transferring it into an outside vessel."

Cas struggles to keep his footing on the dark path. "The visions aren't a *power*. They're just something that happens."

"Because you haven't even begun to harness the potential of them. Again—why, then, would this power fall to *you*, someone who's clearly not worthy of it? I have a decade of research trying to answer this question. But the Lord keeps many mysteries, doesn't he?"

"Or maybe you're not very good at researching."

Smith ignores him. "Once your power has been drawn out, you'll be free of the visions. And our Order will be able to access the vessel into which the power has transferred. We'll be able to keep using it long after you've returned safely home."

Cas forces a laugh. "Right. Sure."

"I wasn't lying when I told Mr. Ashworth that this ritual is safe."

"Is it going to be *safe* when you cut out my eyes?"

Smith stops walking. When he turns to Cas, it's with the eager gaze of a scientist preparing to dissect a new specimen. "Fascinating," he says. "You saw him, didn't you? Was DeWindt's death the first vision you had?"

Cas shouldn't be giving him any information. This isn't just about him anymore—it's about Death, and the captain, and Remy, and all of them. The weight of it is closing in on him.

"That ritual was a failure, yes," Smith says as he starts along the path again. Something nudges Cas in the back—the cold end of the pistol. He follows, clenching his hands into fists to stop them shaking. "It was also eight years ago, and much earlier in my research. I hadn't yet come to understand back then that the reaper's glass, this power, wasn't something that DeWindt *had*—it's something he *was*. And when he ceased to be, that power manifested in someone else."

Me, Cas thinks with an awful sort of thrill. All this time, as the captain has been looking for a reaper's glass . . . It manifested in me.

"Fortunately for you, we've learned a lot since then. We've refined our process. To be honest, your predecessor *ought* to have been safe, even without the transfer ritual we have now. He could have joined our Order and kept his power, after all. He refused. We caught him one night, trying to board a ship out of town. We couldn't allow that, of course; he knew too much. What you saw, DeWindt's death, was a desperate attempt, a last resort. But if he hadn't attempted to flee—"

"Then you wouldn't have murdered him?" Cas asks.

"There's no textbook for this. We're piecing together a magic that's older than any of us. There are bound to be snags along the way."

"You're calling Mr. DeWindt's death a *snag*?"

"A necessary sacrifice, then."

Which is easy to say when you're not the one being sacrificed.

They've reached a clearing in the trees now. Another man—he must be in the Order, too—is lighting the candles that are positioned around a ring of stones a few feet high. Pinprick lights are glowing from within the ring—no, reflecting. It's mirroring the starry sky above. The stones encircle a pool of water, perfectly still and perfectly clear.

Smith stops at the edge of the pool. He's drawn a silver knife from inside his coat, and the sight of it sets Cas's pulse stuttering. It's the same knife Smith used to kill Remy's father.

But Smith doesn't turn to attack him with it. Instead, he rolls up one sleeve and slices a clean line across his own forearm. He winces, but barely. He tucks the knife away again. Slowly, deliberately, Smith wipes a finger through the blood and begins marking each stone around the water's edge with a symbol Cas doesn't recognize.

"I mentioned, earlier, the unusual natural features of this island," Smith says. "This spring is a special place. The Jesuits used it for baptisms when they formed their mission here two centuries ago—though that only lasted a few years. Now this water takes on a new purpose. It's going to become our vessel—a scrying glass that's bound to a reaper."

Smith had called the ritual a cleansing process, and through the panic in Cas's mind, a memory surfaces: something Remy had said about a freshwater spring here. *It's supposed to have some kind of spiritual cleansing properties. If you believe in that sort of thing.*

Smith seems like the type who believes in that sort of thing.

"The waters that rise from the ground here have a unique ability to draw out toxins," Smith says. "Both physical and spiritual."

He's finished his circle of blood on the stones now. One of the other men helps him tie a handkerchief to the cut on his arm, and he straightens, hands clasped behind his back. Cas's own hands won't stop shaking now. Smith turns to him.

"And these reapers . . . They're a toxin. The connection you have will poison you. So let yourself be cleansed."

"I'm clean enough, thanks."

But Cas can't hide the crack in his voice. It's like the lead-up to a vision, except that instead of silver lights dancing in his eyes, it's only fear—fear pounding in his head, and fear clouding his eyes, and fear threatening to pull him under. Cas keeps waiting for it to crest, for the panic to finally reach its peak, but it doesn't. It just keeps building.

Someone clamps onto Cas's arm. The bigger of the two men has him in his grasp. It's too late to run.

"Now," Smith says. "Let's begin."

As the man drags him toward the circle of stones, Cas tries to fight. He tries to yell. But the world goes silent as the water closes over his head.

XXIX

REMY

When Remy and the others reach their rendezvous spot in the cove, Finn is already waiting for them.

This isn't right—Finn shouldn't be back yet. And where's Cas? Where's Ashworth, for that matter? Remy feels a hum of panic starting in her chest, a lonely emotion in the void of her overwhelmed heart.

Finn leaps to her feet the moment she sees Remy. Her eyes are wide as she runs to her and, bafflingly, presents her with a small blue button.

Remy stares at it. "What is this?"

"I don't know. *You're* supposed to know."

"Where's Cas?"

"He stayed behind. He made me leave without him."

"Why?"

"I don't know!"

Finn usually holds herself so tightly in check; this frenzy in her voice sets Remy's heart racing. The others have all circled them now, watching with concern. The rifle in Striker's hands is gleaming, as if she's been compulsively polishing it for the last hour just to have something to do. Leo's expression is perfectly blank, though a muscle in his jaw has clenched tight.

"This is his," Finn says, waving the button. "*Was* his. He gave it to me, like it was a message. Except I have no idea what he's trying to say."

But Remy does. The memory sneaks up on her. It's their old game—the petitions they used to leave in the faerie king's tree. A ribbon to ask for good weather. A button to ask for...

Cas is in trouble.

With the captain and his crew gathered around her, Remy imagines a chessboard. Time seems to slow as she plays through the possible moves and countermoves in her mind.

One line of moves: Remy tells them what the button means. Will the captain agree to take his crew back to the seminary to rescue Cas? Remy has seen Captain Hobbes's protectiveness, has seen how he values the safety of his sailors—and bringing them to storm the Order's gates would be far from safe. It's a huge risk for them all to take to save someone who boarded their ship only a few days ago.

Backtrack, then. Try it a different way. Remy tells them what the button means, and then tells the captain what she's learned about Cas. She tells him Cas is a reaper's glass. This guarantees that the captain will go back for him—but it also gives the captain control of the board. She thinks of the jar of her father's ashes, of the catalog label: *Materials for a reaper's glass*. Captain Hobbes won't *kill* Cas, surely; Remy trusts that much. But she can't shake the fear that she'd be trading one of Cas's captors for another.

And besides—this isn't her secret to tell.

Backtrack again. Backtrack further. Remy can lie about the button. She'll tell them it's Cas's signal to wait, to keep their distance. When the sailors aren't looking, she and Finn can slip away. They'll return to the school on their own. Maybe it's better to keep the captain here, anyway; he's too clever. Anything he sees or hears about Cas at the seminary might be enough for him to put together the truth.

But this line of moves leaves Remy and Finn to rescue Cas by themselves, and the strategy falls apart there. Remy isn't sure they can manage it alone. She isn't sure that she wants to.

What would Cas do if he were here?

The answer to *that* is obvious. It isn't tactical, and it hinges on a naive assumption of other people's good intentions. Maybe not entirely naive, though. Cas had known the captain was a friend so much earlier than Remy could see it.

Remy takes a long, steadying breath.

"He's in trouble," she tells them. "That's what the button means. Cas is asking for our help."

Remy should never have doubted that the captain would agree, even without his own motive, even without knowing what Cas is—because he springs into action at once.

"All right," Captain Hobbes says. "Everyone arm up. There are weapons in the longboat. We'll approach the seminary from the woods again. I'll signal Mita to bring the ship into the cove—we might need to make a quick escape once we've gotten him back."

The next few minutes are a flurry of preparations: Striker presenting Remy with a spare rifle from the boat. Kit giving Finn one of her knives. Captain Hobbes coaxing a small fire from the greenest branches they can find, calling the *Mori* with the thin plume of smoke. Leo and Striker arguing in Yiddish until Leo plants his feet and shouts, in the loudest voice Remy has heard from him, "I am not waiting with the boat!"

Leo is given a knife as well.

As they all set off again up the mountainside, following the stream, Finn falls into step beside Remy. They haven't spoken yet about what Remy found in the seminary's archive. Remy's not sure she *can* speak about it. In a way, she's grateful to have another task before her, something with clear, concrete steps. Something that will require all her focus. The earlier revelation is neatly boxed up in her mind for now, shoved back inside the window seat.

She can feel Finn watching her, wondering—but when Remy doesn't offer any details about what happened inside, Finn doesn't ask. Instead, she says quietly, "Are you all right?"

Remy shouldn't feel this calm, after everything. Maybe there's something wrong with her. "To be honest, I don't know," she says.

Finn doesn't ask anything else. They walk in silence for a moment. Then Finn brushes her hand against Remy's, laces their fingers together, and squeezes. Grounding her. Holding her.

Remy squeezes back.

The high stone walls of the seminary have just loomed into view when a voice calls out from the darkness ahead of them.

"Stop! You're surrounded!"

Captain Hobbes has been leading their group, and he stops as ordered. Several young men step forward from all sides. These are seminary students, not soldiers, and their makeshift weapons—kitchen knives, gardening tools—look clumsy in their hands. But they *are* armed. And if these young men are part of the Order, they'll have Reverend John Smith's zeal in their veins, driving them to fight.

"Drop your weapons!" the man in front of them shouts.

Remy does a quick count of heads. She can sense Captain Hobbes doing the same calculation. Five students. Six of them. They may be surrounded, but they're not outnumbered.

None of them has dropped their weapons. The captain glances back at his crew, one eyebrow raised, and Remy knows what he intends. She intends to follow him.

She lifts her rifle.

XXX

CAS

Cas's visions showed him a drowning only once.

She was a girl from Saugus of around nineteen. She'd been out in a skiff with a young man, a suitor, probably, when a sudden squall had caught them and capsized their boat. The young man had managed to grab on to it, clinging to the slick underside as he searched for the girl. But she'd been swept too far from him to save. Cas saw her. Cas had watched her frantically paddling in the waves, her head surfacing and then sinking again, her mouth gaping open and closed. There was no sound, just as there's never any sound in the visions, but somehow Cas knew that even if there had been, the girl wasn't crying out in her brief seconds above the water. She gasped noiselessly. Not enough air left in her to yell for help.

They'd dragged her body up from the harbor two days after the accident. She was bloated and blue, and her family held her funeral with the casket closed. Cas read it all in the newspaper.

In the week that passed between the vision and the girl's death, Cas had considered finding her and warning her against going out on the water that day. He'd considered warning the suitor. But he already knew by then that there was no changing the outcome. He'd kept his head down and followed his rule: *Don't tell anyone what you saw.*

Now, as he struggles under the water of the spring, he wonders at the circularity. He's going to feel what the drowning girl felt— one of so many deaths he didn't bother to try to prevent. Maybe it's right. Maybe Cas *should* know the panic and the helplessness and the moment when that girl had sunk beneath the surface and stayed there, her limbs suspended, nothing left in her eyes.

Then the man drags him up by the collar, and Cas gasps in the clear, cold, breathable air. He blinks and blinks again, trying to clear the water from his eyes. Smith stands at the edge of the spring, hands clasped behind his back. Watching.

Cas needs to keep Smith talking. If Smith is talking, he can't order his lackey to put Cas under the water again.

"Henry says you think the reapers are interfering with God's will," Cas says once he's caught his breath. "How do you know they're not *doing* God's will?"

Something flashes on Smith's face—a fury completely at odds with the calm, stoic leader he's presented until now. He covers it again so quickly that Cas can almost believe he imagined it. Almost.

"You've seen who the reapers take," Smith says. "How many deaths have you seen that have come about by natural causes? Has a vision ever showed you someone dying peacefully in their sleep?"

Cas isn't sure why he's never thought about it before. He's tried for years *not* to think about the visions at all. But Smith is right: every death Cas has witnessed has been violent, painful, shocking. The kinds of tragedies that make people shake their heads and say, *What a shame. It just isn't right. Taken before their time.*

Smith can read him so easily. "That's what I thought. DeWindt's were the same, you know. He kept records of every vision he had, and none of the deaths were peaceful. None of them felt like the will of God."

"Maybe it's another of those mysteries God's keeping from you."

That fury crosses Smith's face again, a crack of lightning, undeniable this time.

Cas has made a mistake. Smith nods at the man, and then Cas is under again. The water is bitterly cold. The man's hand on his neck is too strong; Cas can't get away. He needs air. There's no air. This numb, watery world is all there's ever been and all there ever will be. Nothing else is real except this moment.

By the time the man pulls him up again, Cas's lungs are burning. He must have inhaled water. He coughs. Even as his eyes can focus again, his brain feels sluggish and dull.

"I had a daughter, once," Smith says.

Cas coughs again. "Henry told me."

"Did he tell you how she died? It was on the crossing back from England. My wife and I returned as soon as my post there had ended, but our daughter wanted to stay until the end of the summer. Her governess stayed with her. They sailed a month after us. But the crew took them straight into a storm."

The candles encircling the spring are still lit; their flickering glow sharpens the lines on Smith's face. His still-wet blood on the rocks catches in the light.

"None of the passengers survived—but some of the crew did. The very same sailors whose negligence had caused the wreck. You asked why I don't believe that these reapers are doing God's will. Is there any justice to the deaths they've caused? No. And if nothing else, I believe in a just God."

Smith considers Cas.

"She would have been about your age, I think. If she were still alive. Her name was Viola."

Cas knows better, but he says it anyway: "And I'm sure Viola would be thrilled about what you're doing now."

He hears Smith's hand striking his face before he feels it, and Cas is fourteen years old again, clutching his cheek in his mother's parlor as Pastor Dekker tells her that Cas is an unruly child who requires a firm hand.

When Smith speaks again, his voice holds only disdain. "You cannot fathom what was taken from me."

Cas can't stop shivering now—the cold water and the cold night air are too much. Or maybe it's the fear still wrapping its tentacles around him.

"This is only as difficult as you make it," Smith says. "Once you stop fighting, once you cooperate, it will all be over quickly."

I don't understand why you always have to make things more difficult for yourself.

Cas has only a second to grab for a breath before the hand pushes him beneath the water again. The cold is bone-deep and absolute. The edges of his consciousness start to fray. Maybe Henry hadn't been wrong. It's hard to remember why Cas is fighting now. *It's not as if you asked for this power*, Henry had said. *You don't even want it.* And it's true, isn't it? How many times has Cas wished the visions away? How many times has he cursed them, contemplated how much easier his life would be without them? What have the visions ever brought him besides headaches, and heartache, and secrecy?

Remy, he realizes, as he fights to resurface. And Finn. Yes, that first vision had splintered him and Remy apart—but a vision is what brought them back together now. It's what brought him on this journey, what brought all three of them aboard the *Memento Mori*. And if he really does have this bond with a reaper ... Cas thinks of that night at the lighthouse, when Captain Hobbes had told them his story. He thinks of the bonfire, and sitting in the longboat with Mita and Leo, and something flickers to life in his chest—a tiny spot of warmth, pushing through the cold and the fear.

That spot of warmth is still there when the man hauls him up again, and Cas gasps, and coughs, and breathes.

On the rocks around him, the blood markings have begun to change color. The slick red shifts to pale gray, then a white so bright that it seems to glow. Smith kneels for a moment, pressing his palm to one of the rocks. The whole circle seems to pulse slightly at his touch.

But a thought has caught in Cas's mind. If Smith was telling the truth, if this will only be as difficult as Cas makes it ...

"You can't just take it by force, can you?" Cas says. "This connection, or whatever it is ... You can't just steal it, or draw it out with your ritual. Not if I don't let it go."

Smith stands slowly. He doesn't reply, and Cas knows he's guessed right.

"Well, I'm not going to," Cas tells him. "It isn't yours to have."

He flinches as Smith flies at him, leaning in too close, but Smith doesn't raise his hand this time. His face is ghoulish in the candlelight.

"You think it's *yours*?" Smith snarls. "You have no idea the scope of this thing you've stumbled into. You're a child, spoiled and selfish and clinging to your toys just because you can. Stubborn, foolhardy, degenerate—"

"Sure," Cas cuts in. He thinks of Mita's wry smile when she'd said, *degenerates like us.* "Fine. I'm all of that. And this power still isn't yours."

When the man forces him under the water again, Cas struggles—until he doesn't. Until his body stops answering him. Until he's too tired. He loses track of how many times it's been. He's fairly sure he's going to die here.

But that light is still glowing in his chest—and he pours all his remaining energy into keeping it there. Clinging to it. Protecting it.

As the world grows darker and farther away, he imagines this thing he's protecting is a much smaller, much younger Cas. He sees himself at age ten, when the visions were new, when he'd broken the only real friendship he'd had by revealing too much of himself. He sees that child who had learned to keep silent, who'd learned which parts of himself could never ever be shared.

Now Cas imagines wrapping that child in his arms. He imagines holding him by the shoulders, helping him stand and stay standing, the way Mita had on the deck of the *Mori*. He thinks of the crew there, laughing and talking and weaving a whole shared tapestry of their lives, not a secret among them.

And maybe that ten-year-old child was wrong. Maybe there is no part of him that's too wrong or too broken to be seen, if only by the right people. He tries to hold on to the truth of that. He curls around the warmth.

On the fringes, though, just beyond that fragile glow, Cas can't stop seeing the drowning girl from his vision out in the harbor. Over and over, he watches the girl's eyes go dim. He watches her body as it sinks into the sea.

XXXI

FINN

Here, at last, is the brawl Finn has been waiting for. As she and the crew fly at the students in the woods, she feels the same surge of defensive anger she'd felt on the packet ship from Ireland—just before she'd kicked Kieran's bully in the face. Finn has been fighting for years, hasn't she? She's always known that her brother, with his soft edges, wasn't capable of protecting her, so she's learned to protect the both of them. When the uncle who was meant to care for them in America turned out to have died just weeks after their parents, Finn found herself and Kieran work at the DeWindts'. When old Mrs. Hewitt had tried, just once, to turn her displeasure on Kieran, Finn had stepped in front of him and taken the blame. When Kieran had fallen ill, Finn fixed that, too.

But this clash isn't at all like her fight on the packet ship. These sailors aren't Kieran, and they don't need Finn to protect them. If anything, they're far more capable than she is. The captain has neatly knocked one of the students unconscious, and now he's pinned a second, pistol aimed at the man's chest. Kit and Striker each have a man in a headlock, slowly cutting off their air. Even Leo is holding his own in a tussle with a man who'd been wielding a meat cleaver. The meat cleaver is now lying in the dirt.

Finn's knife is still out, and yet she looks around and finds herself superfluous in this fight.

Remy seems to be having the same realization. For a second, they stare at each other. The sailors have this well in hand.

"Cas," Finn says simply, and both of them take off for the building.

They burst through the seminary's front doors with weapons raised—but the entrance hall is empty. Finn heads in the direction that Mrs. Smith had taken Cas earlier. This is the same hallway Finn had crept through on her way to the library, and then on her way to Smith's office. She and Remy aren't sneaking now, though. The Order already knows they're here, and Finn dares anyone to try to stop them.

There's a faint glow from behind a door just past the dining room. Finn kicks the door open, Remy on her heels. The room is a parlor, probably, though it's too dim to make out much among the shadowy sofas and cabinets. The candles are unlit; the only light comes from the fading fire in the hearth. Finn's eyes land on a dark, crumpled shape in the middle of the floor—something silken and blue.

Cas's cloak.

A thrill runs through her. But Cas isn't here now. Without its owner, the cloak looks like something dead.

"Ah, Miss DeWindt."

Remy's rifle is on the voice in the space of a breath: it's Pastor Dekker. Even as he steps out of the parlor's shadowy corner, his dark suit nearly blends into his surroundings. His expression is perfectly calm as he crosses to meet them in the fire's glow.

"What a surprise," Dekker says—just as he'd said nearly two weeks ago on the road outside the tidy clapboard church.

"It shouldn't be," Remy tells him. "Where's Cas?"

"Your friend is fine. Or will be, once the Shepherd is finished."

Finn's pulse is rushing in her ears. If Cas is hurt... If he's dead... She feels something fierce stirring inside her; she feels more alive than she has in years. That inner fire is pushing to be free, and for a moment, the fire in the hearth seems to flicker a little brighter.

"Where is he?" Remy says again. She's somehow matched Dekker's eerie calm, and she holds the rifle steadily.

Dekker's mouth twists. "Do you know," he says, "I always thought it would be you. That's why I stayed in Windover all this time. I had assumed that *you* would be the one to inherit your father's gift. I've been watching your family for years—"

"I know you have," Remy cuts in.

"I've seen you digging." There's a slickness to his tone; it seems to give Remy pause. "You've been researching our group for a long while, haven't you? Reading about all sorts of topics that would set the gossipers' teeth on you if they knew."

Remy adjusts her grip on the gun. "I don't have time for this. *Where's Cas?*"

Finn still has the knife from Kit clenched in her hand. Dekker has barely even glanced her way. She could catch him unawares, could probably take him down. But Remy could shoot him just as easily—and she hasn't yet. She's letting him talk.

What the hell did Remy find in the seminary's library?

"That's how I found your father, before," Dekker is saying. "It was the rumors. I'd heard what people said about him, and when I started watching him, it became obvious he was the one we were looking for. But I watched you, later, thinking that his power would have manifested in you—and it never did."

If Remy is surprised by any of this, she doesn't show it. A sudden, sick thought occurs to Finn—the note Remy had found in the dead pastor's grimoire. The line she'd shown Finn with such hope in her eyes: *We're watching DeWindt.*

But it wasn't Remy's father they'd been watching. It was Remy. And their watching came up empty.

"How does it feel," Dekker asks, "to realize it was never about you at all? All that research, and you've just been dabbling in someone else's story."

"I *knew* it wasn't about me." Remy keeps the rifle aimed at him, her voice still terribly calm. "I never wanted it to be. I only wanted my father back. And you comforted my mother and offered her charity—and all the while you knew exactly what you'd done to him." For the first time, her voice breaks as she says, "You sent him here to his death."

It's the answer Finn had already guessed. It's the answer she's been dreading. Remy is staring down the man who'd taken her father from her—and she doesn't even look angry. She looks empty, overcome, used up.

Well, Finn is angry *for* her.

All at once, the fire in the hearth explodes. Flames erupt, flooding the room. Heat. Light. Finn is burning, but not from the outside—this is the fire *inside* her, the will that's been crackling just beneath the surface. It escapes her now in one wild, furious burst. Dekker swears and throws up an arm to shield himself. Remy ducks behind one of the sofas. But she'd had no need—the fire doesn't touch her. It channels around both her and Finn, leaving them unharmed.

How many years has Finn held herself back from feeling anything too deeply, just waiting for the end? How many years has she spent biting her own tongue, pushing down her rage? Remy does it, too; Finn knows she does. It's how they survive.

But they deserve more. They deserve to cut loose the restraints they've put on themselves—and Dekker deserves to burn.

That first wild burst of fire has passed, but it hasn't gone out—the room has already caught. The curtains over the darkened windows are alight, flames quickly devouring the fabric. The upholstery on the sofas is smoldering. Dekker stamps frantically at his own burning jacket, putting out the flames. His eyes are wide as he takes in the singed fabric, and then Remy.

But Remy looks just as confused as he is. She studies her own hands, her clothes, and finds herself unscathed. She turns to Finn. Finn sees the realization dawning on her face.

When Dekker tracks her gaze, when his eyes land on Finn, too, they hold none of the awe that Remy's do. For the first time, his face betrays his fear.

Good, Finn thinks. You should be afraid.

Remy raises the rifle once more. She fires.

Dekker flinches badly.

But it was only a warning shot; a bullet hole now mars the extravagant wallpaper five feet behind Dekker's head.

"*Where is Cas?*" Remy demands.

Finn can see the calculation in Dekker's mind as he weighs the value of his own life. One of the room's sofas has begun to burn in earnest. The rug will catch next, and then the other sofa, and the curtains will set the cabinets alight, too. The flames don't need Finn's coaxing anymore. They're here, and they're hungry.

At last, Dekker says, "In the woods. The path at the back of the garden. It leads to the spring."

Remy turns to Finn, fire dancing in her dark eyes. Finn can only guess at what she's thinking. This might be Remy's only chance to confront Dekker—to punish the man who took her father from her. The two of them can kill Dekker right here. Shoot him, or stab him, or simply lock him in this room and let the fire have him. Finn will happily shoulder any burden of guilt. Her soul is stained already; what's a little more blood?

But this is Remy's vengeance to take. And she doesn't take it.

"You said you've been watching me for years, right?" Remy asks Dekker, and she shoulders her rifle. "Now you can watch while I take down your Order."

When Remy dashes for the hallway, Finn follows. They both burst through the seminary's back door and into the night. The woods spread out before them, and there, among the trees, is the path, just as Dekker had described it. Their way to Cas.

But Finn feels eyes on her.

She turns.

The windows of the room where they'd just been are ablaze. Flickering orange light spills out into the darkened garden, and for a bare second, Finn swears someone is there, outside the window, as if they'd been watching the entire confrontation with Dekker through the glass. As if they're watching Finn now. The shadows against the wall seem to curl, like something alive. A hand. A tentacle.

But if there *is* a figure there, it doesn't approach. It doesn't move. Finn blinks, and when her eyes reopen, any shape in the shadows has dissolved.

Finn and Remy run into the woods.

XXXII

CAS

Cas is going to crumble.

He doesn't *want* to give in—but he feels himself faltering. The surface of the spring has begun to shimmer. Cas thought it was moonlight at first, or the reflections of the markings Smith had made on the rocks. But this is no reflection. This comes from within. When Cas is under the water, with streaks of silver lacing around him, it's too much like the sparks that always flood his eyes just before he has a vision. He's seen them so many times before, but never like this. Never on the outside.

So Smith's ritual is working. The spring is drawing this power out of Cas, drawing it into the water itself. Cas wants to fight it, but he has none of Remy's dogged persistence, none of Finn's fierce resolve. He's tired, and silly, and useless, and the silver in the water keeps growing brighter. Maybe Smith was right when he'd said Cas was unworthy. Maybe his mother has been right all along. He's just Cas—trying, and failing, and never enough.

Smith's man drags him to the surface again. Cas coughs, and breathes, and tries to hold on a little longer, even though he knows he can't. He tries anyway. He braces himself for the water once more.

It doesn't come.

He doesn't know why it doesn't come. The seconds pass, and the hand is still gripping him by the collar, but it doesn't push him back below. It just holds him there. Slowly, as Cas's lungs and head clear, he can make out his surroundings again. There are voices, though his ears are ringing too badly for him to catch much. Smith still stands at the edge of the spring. He's talking with the other two men—no, three men now. Another has joined them, a student, maybe, red-faced and out of breath. He must have run from the seminary.

". . . appeared out of nowhere," the student is saying. "Griffin and Hill brought a group to hold them off, but—"

"Then they'll hold them off." Smith's voice is matter-of-fact. Whatever the student says in response, Cas can't hear it. His ears won't stop ringing.

But no—the ringing isn't inside his head. It's coming from the *spring*, from the silvery water around him. The surface seems to vibrate as if caught in the moment of a ripple, reverberating like the high, haunted tones he and Henry used to coax from the rims of the Sterlings' good crystal glasses. Henry, who's abandoned him. Henry, who's thrown his lot in with Smith. Cas can't think about it now.

"Griffin and the others know what's at stake," Smith is saying. "They'll manage. We're not stopping now. We're too close."

He turns to the man still holding Cas, and Cas knows what's coming—

A gunshot cuts the night.

Smith pauses. All three of the men look down the path, back toward the seminary hidden through the trees.

"One of ours, do you think?" the student asks.

"No."

And the understanding hits Cas all at once: they've come back for him.

That glowing light in his chest flares to life again, fierce and persistent and defiant. Remy knew what the button meant. She's brought the others to rescue him. Of course Cas isn't going to crumble. He has people on his side now, people who are coming for him. He's not going to let Smith win.

The moment he thinks it, the water around him stills. The shimmering silver goes dark. The humming drops off into heavy silence.

Smith stares down at the water, which a bare second ago had been alight with this power he's been chasing for a decade. Now it's only water again. The power is gone—or rather, it's back where it's always been. Smith's eyes fall on Cas.

"You," he says.

He seizes Cas with both hands, and Cas is too surprised to put up a good fight as Smith drags him from the spring. But there's solid, dry ground under his feet at last. Even as Smith's hands dig into his shoulders, even as he stares into Smith's furious, too-close face, he can see the path behind him. The dueling pistols have only two shots between them, and it's dark; the man's aim won't be good.

"Do you think this is over?" Smith's spectacles are crooked again, but he doesn't straighten them. A stripe of blood has seeped through the handkerchief tied around his forearm.

"Yeah. I do," Cas says.

He jabs at Smith's arm, digging his fingernails into the fresh wound under the bandage—which is disgusting, really, but it's also enough to make Smith cry out. His grip loosens, and Cas breaks free.

He takes off running.

By the time Smith's men realize what's happening, Cas is on the edge of the clearing. Then the trees envelope him. There's just enough moonlight to keep him on the path. Behind him, he hears shouts, the scuffling of boots—Smith and the Order members are giving chase. Cas has to trust that his head start will be enough. He barrels ahead on sheer adrenaline; he'll outrun them as long as he can.

A pistol fires. Then the second. One of the bullets pounds into the pine needles inches away from his foot.

And yet Cas isn't shot. He isn't hurt. Through the trees ahead of him, a voice is calling his name.

Remy's voice.

"I'm here!" Cas yells, heart soaring. "I'm here! I'm—"

Then Smith is upon him.

It all happens very fast: the weight slamming into him. The grunt as they both hit the ground. Smith's silver knife glinting as he draws it from his coat. Cas throws up a hand to knock the knife away, and the blade bites into his palm—he hisses. He tries to wriggle away. He can't. He's trapped under Smith's weight.

"You chose this," Smith snarls. "You could have played your role and walked away, and you refused. So we'll find the next reaper's glass. We'll start again."

Cas scrabbles in the dirt, claws up a handful of pine needles. He throws them at Smith's face. They bounce off his goddamned spectacles. As Smith forces Cas's hand to the ground, as he pins both of his arms, Cas knows this is the end. *The next reaper's glass.*

Smith is going to kill him. He's going to murder Cas just like he murdered Remy's father, and when Cas ceases to be, the reaper's glass power will move on. Someone else will become the pawn Smith needs.

When the knife flies at his eye, this time, Cas can't block it.

The wrongness comes first—the sensation of skin splitting, of exposed muscle and bone that shouldn't be exposed to the air. Then the pain, white-hot and sharp on the side of his face. There's blood. There's a lot of blood. Cas can't see the wound, but he's certain it's bone-deep. Smith raises the knife again, and again Cas twists, but he can't escape. He's never been much for praying, and even now, as he thinks the words, he isn't really praying to a god. He's just asking for his friends.

Please, he thinks. Please help me.

Another gunshot—the dueling pistols? Has Smith's man reloaded and come to finish the job?

But the weight on him lifts, and Cas is free. Smith lurches backward, clutching his shoulder, where blood blooms between his fingers and across his dark coat. He shouts into the woods, at the figure sprinting through the trees.

It isn't the man with the dueling pistols.

Remy dashes toward them with the rifle still in her hands, the tails of her coat billowing out behind her like the wings of some avenging bird of prey. There's something unmoored in her expression, something cut loose, or cut free—or maybe just cut, cleaved into pieces, a girl dissected, all her insides laid bare. Because Remy knows the truth now. Cas can see it on her face. She knows that her father is dead. She knows this is the man who killed him.

Smith's eyes are wide, as if he recognizes her. As if he can see Remy's father there in his daughter's features. For one hanging second, Smith and Remy stare at each other.

Then Smith turns and flees.

Remy's face twists. Her jaw sets. For one terrible moment, Cas thinks she'll go after Smith and leave Cas here alone.

She doesn't, though. She skids to a stop and drops to her knees at his side.

"Christ," Remy says. "Jesus Christ. You're bleeding."

Cas is vividly aware of this. He tries to answer, but all that comes out is a breathy humming sound. Remy helps him sit up. He's clutching the side of his face, trying to hold everything in, but it isn't working. His palms feel slick.

"Christ," Remy is still saying. "Let me..." She peels back his hands to check the damage, and Cas waits for her to balk. Instead, she says, "Oh. That's not so bad, actually. It's not nearly as bad as I was expecting."

Cas's laugh is a frail thread. "It doesn't feel *good*."

"Well, it missed your eye, at least. Here." Already she's produced a kerchief from somewhere and pressed it to the wound. She clamps Cas's hands over the top of it. "Just keep pressure on it. Leo can get you cleaned up. Come on, can you stand?"

Cas nods, though he's shaking badly enough that it might be a lie. Remy hauls him to his feet. He thinks she'll let go once they're both upright, but she doesn't—she keeps an arm wrapped tight around him, warm and solid, and he's seized with an overwhelming gratitude for her. For all of them.

"You understood my message."

"Of course I did," Remy tells him.

The woods around them are quiet now. Too quiet. There's no sign of Smith or the other men—only trees and moonlight and the darkened path, with its creeping shadows.

"Finn," Cas says suddenly. "Where's Finn?"

"I'm here." And she is, running back toward them from the direction of the clearing, a knife in her hand.

"Smith?" Remy asks, and Finn shakes her head.

"I lost him in the trees. The others took off like a bunch of cowards when he ran. Oh Jesus." She must've caught sight of Cas now. Her face is shadowy as she takes in the state of him. Quietly, almost to herself, she says, "I never should've left you here."

"You didn't, though," Cas says. "You came back."

They start toward the seminary as quickly as they can manage, the three of them jogging side by side. The rifle on Remy's back rattles with each step. The path turns, and then the outline of the building emerges through the woods, though there's something wrong about it, too bright for the moonlit night.

Because the seminary is on fire.

"Holy hell—did *you* do that?" Cas gapes at the flames licking from the lowest windows. Smoke plumes into the night sky.

"It was an accident," Finn says. "Mostly."

Remy's arm is still around him, forcing him to keep moving. "We need to find the others. And where's Ashworth?"

The last time Cas saw Henry, he was in one of the rooms that's currently ablaze. Even now, after everything Henry's done, Cas feels a spike of panic—is Henry still inside? But no; he'll make it out. He probably already has. Maybe he's among the students dashing around the outside of the building, trying to douse the flames.

"Henry isn't coming with us," Cas says.

Remy and Finn exchange a look, but neither of them asks. Cas will feel the anger later, the full sting of Henry's betrayal. For now, he only feels tired.

They skirt along the edge of the woods, keeping out of sight, though the figures around the seminary are too preoccupied to give them trouble. A fire, as it turns out, is a very good distraction. There's movement in the trees up ahead—but the faces that emerge are familiar ones, and everything blurs together as Striker, Leo, and Captain Hobbes rush at them. Their whispered voices wash over Cas. Striker tousles his hair, still wet from the spring and probably his own blood. Someone's coat is draped over his shoulders. Cas doesn't know where it came from, but the wool is warm and blessedly dry as they all hurry back toward the road.

"Come on," Striker says. "Kit's getting us a ride."

The ride is an old buckboard wagon with just enough space in the back for them all to pile in. The pair of horses seems perfectly content to have Kit at the reins instead of their usual driver. She's only just flicked the horses into motion, though, when a figure stumbles out into the road ahead of them.

Kit swears and swerves. At least three guns are drawn and cocked in the space of a second. But Cas is already leaping down from the wagon before it's even stopped moving.

"Wait!"

None of the guns fire.

Henry has raised his hands in surrender. He looks terrible in the moonlight, his face waxen, his brow slick with sweat. "It's just me," he says as he and Cas stare at each other in the road. His eyes linger on the bloody kerchief Cas is still holding to his face. The cut underneath it has started to throb. "Are you all right?" he asks.

Which is a ridiculous question. "As if you care."

"Of course I care! I—" Henry shakes his head, then shakes it again, like the denial might brush away everything that's happened tonight. "It wasn't supposed to be like this. He said it would be safe."

"And *I* said you couldn't trust him! And who did you believe?"

"You don't understand. If you'd only listened—if you had just let him help—"

Cas can't stop himself: he laughs at that, hollow and done. "God, you sound just like him. He was never going to *help*. And I told you he was dangerous, and you still left me there. Honestly, Henry—what did you think was going to happen?"

Cas has no idea if Henry even remembers that conversation—until he sees Henry flinch. So he *does* remember asking Cas the very same question years ago, exasperation leaking from his voice. Maybe this schism between the two of them played out already, and Cas just didn't realize it until now.

He knows an apology isn't coming. He waits for one anyway. Striker, Remy, and Captain Hobbes keep their weapons trained on Henry, but they hold, letting Cas have this. Henry's gaze darts to the audience in the wagon. He stiffens slightly, gathering himself. Picking up that mask of cool indifference instead of admitting that he could've been wrong.

When Henry speaks, the disdain in his voice almost manages to hide the hurt. "Are you going to tell me to *go to hell*?"

"No."

Cas looks up at the wagon, where they're all still waiting for him: Kit. Striker. Leo. Remy. Finn. The captain, with his tendency for picking up strays. Down in the harbor, beyond the trees, Cas can almost make out the *Mori*'s sails fluttering in the wind.

"Because maybe you're right," he tells Henry. "Maybe Dekker's right. And if that's where I'm headed—where *we're* headed—I don't think I want you there."

Cas climbs back into the wagon to join his friends.

"Don't go to hell, Henry. We're laying claim."

XXXIII

REMY

They're all quiet as Kit races their stolen wagon down the mountainside. Leo has snapped into business, inspecting the wound on Cas's face and muttering about what he'll need from his medical kit when they're back on the *Mori*. The captain watches the forest behind them, but there's no sign of anyone following. Remy and Finn sit wedged beside each other against the wagon's side, their shoulders bumping together.

Remy thinks of the fire that had swept through the parlor back at the seminary—*Finn's* fire. The glimpse Finn had shown her at the base of the lighthouse was nothing in comparison. Remy can't stop stealing glances at her, trying to relearn each piece: The sharp line of her nose. Her impossibly dark eyes. The gleam of her hair as it whips around her face. She's exactly the same person Remy has always known, and yet something is different. The heat of that fire is still glowing in her now.

On the outskirts of town, Kit leaves the wagon and horses on the edge of the road, and they all set off on foot toward the cove. Even here, the air hangs heavy with the smell of smoke. A plume of it rises above the trees from where the seminary must still be burning. Remy wonders how much the Order of Lazarus will be able to save, and how much will be taken by the flames.

Nothing about this night has turned out as planned.

Cas walks at Remy's side, his shoulders hunched under the captain's elegant coat. "You can say it, you know," he says. "About Henry."

Remy watches the shadows play across his face. "What's there to say?"

"That you were right about him! That I was a fool for ever trusting him. I know you're thinking it."

"I wasn't thinking that." It's the truth. This is what she's thinking now: That Cas's trust is a precious thing. That the way he offers it so freely makes it more precious, not less. That Ashworth is the fool for betraying that trust.

But Remy had betrayed Cas's trust first, hadn't she? She's been the fool far longer than Ashworth. She'd turned on Cas years ago and never looked back; she's the reason he'd befriended Henry Ashworth in the first place. All this is her fault.

"*You* were right," Remy says now. "About my father, about . . ." She can't quite bring herself to say it aloud, but Cas has gone very still, and she knows he understands. "You were right."

Cas lets out a shaky breath. He adjusts the bloody kerchief against his face. "I didn't want to be right," he says quietly.

"I know."

"I'm sorry."

"I am, too."

The *Mori* is waiting for them in the cove, just as the captain had requested. They row out the longboat and help the crew hoist it up, and then bodies are racing fore and aft across the deck, preparing to set sail again. Leo steers Cas down to the surgeon's cabin; Mita follows just behind them. Kit takes up her station near the helm and starts calling orders.

To Remy's surprise, Captain Hobbes doesn't join his first mate there on the quarterdeck. Instead, he takes out a bag that had been nestled in the bottom of the longboat and brings it to Remy, who's standing uselessly by one of the masts.

"I think these should go to you," the captain says. "Yes?"

Remy doesn't have to look inside the bag. She can see the shapes of its contents: two jars. *Materials for a reaper's glass.* She doesn't ask how he knows, how he'd figured it out. Probably her own reaction back in the archive had told him enough to work out the story. She accepts the bag of her father's remains.

"Thank you," she whispers.

"My sympathy for your loss," the captain says. It's such a commonplace phrase, and yet it doesn't sound common coming from him. The captain understands loss, Remy knows. He understands that, sometimes, the language falls short.

"Well," Remy says. She is not going to cry. "It happened a long time ago, I suppose."

"Even so."

Remy brings the jars to the fo'c'sle and puts them inside her carpetbag. She lies down on her bunk. She dozes. She wakes. She dozes again. She doesn't dream. Later, Finn is in the fo'c'sle, too, lying on her own bunk, though her eyes are open. She's watching Remy in the dark. Even later, Remy wakes to find that Finn has fallen asleep. The small black cat is curled in her arms.

At last, Remy returns to the deck, though it's still dark out. The night watch is quiet, and no one tries to speak to her. The *Mori* is well out to sea again; Mount Desert Island has fallen far behind them. All around, there's only ocean.

For so long, Remy has been pouring all her energy into a single purpose: Take down the Order of Lazarus. Make it possible for her father to come home. But that was never a possibility in the first place, it turns out, and without that clear task from her father's letter laid out ahead of her, Remy is lost. She has no idea what she's supposed to do next.

Finn has followed her abovedeck. Not asleep after all, then. For a long moment, Finn stands quietly beside her at the rail.

"Do you want to talk?" Finn asks.

Remy does not want to talk.

She will, later. She'll tell Finn everything, and Finn will tell her how on earth she's supposed to feel about it, and together they'll form a plan. For now, for hours, she and Finn sit side by side, watching the waves, not saying anything at all.

XXXIV

FINN

Cas joins them on the deck just before dawn. Light has started to seep back into the sky, faint and slow, like the edges of dark fabric fading over the course of a summer. Cas's whole head is wrapped in bandages; Leo had to tie them at an odd angle to cover the gash on the side of his face. There's something lopsided and off-balance about him as he settles between Remy and Finn at the larboard rail.

"You look like a proper pirate now, you know," Finn tells him, nodding at his bandaged eye.

Cas laughs, though he sounds tired. "If I do, I'm the only one here. None of *this* crowd is pirates."

There's a bandage around one of his hands, too. He picks at it absently, tugging the tail loose, until he realizes Finn is watching him and lets it go.

"How are you feeling?" Finn asks.

"Oh, you know." He waves the hand in a dismissive gesture. "I'll live, at least according to the resident doctor. Who's a menace, by the way. I know Leo *seems* all friendly and handsome, but then you show up with a knife wound and suddenly he's sticking a needle in your face. Did you know that *stitches* means he *literally* sews your skin back together?"

Remy blinks at him, shaken from her own thoughts for the first time in ages. "I mean," she says, "yes."

"It's in the name," Finn points out.

"Well, I'd never really thought about it before! And it's horrifying! And he acted like it was completely normal, and kept telling me to *relax*, like *that's* possible when there's a needle coming this close to your eye. I feel like I'm seeing a whole new side of him now."

"Not the first of those you've seen, is it?" Finn says, and then, because she knows it will make Remy laugh, she adds, "We both noticed you staring at his arse the other day."

Remy does laugh, a burst so bright and sudden that it seems to surprise even her.

"I have no idea what you're talking about," Cas says, though the half of his face that isn't hidden under bandages has turned very red.

"Oh, come on," Remy says. "You're the one who just called him handsome."

"I never said that!"

"You absolutely did," Finn says, which prompts Cas to call *her* a rude name and Remy to laugh even harder. It's not quite the open, unburdened laugh that Remy has brought out so easily these past few days, but it isn't the polite, practiced kind she used to use, either. Her laughter now is something in between, or something else altogether—a boat weighed down by grief and heartache, yet somehow still afloat. Joy and sadness learning to coexist. Finn imagines folding up the sound of that laugh into a locket and stringing it onto a chain around her neck. Hanging it against her heart.

It's not that the grief is gone; it's just that there's room enough inside Remy for more than grief alone. Room enough inside all of them.

"It's just a factual observation!" Cas is saying. "Objectively, he *is* handsome!"

Remy snorts. "Objectively, does he also have a nice backside?"

"You," Cas tells her, "can go eat nails." He yawns then, too wide to properly hide it behind his hand, though he tries.

"Have you slept at all?" Finn asks.

Cas scowls. "I *hate* sleep."

He'd said the same thing in the fo'c'sle the other night—and as his guilty gaze darts to Finn now, she wonders if Cas remembers more of that conversation than she'd assumed. He looks distinctly caught out.

"We should talk, I suppose," Cas says. "About . . . Well, you know the reaper's glass the captain has been looking for? As it turns out . . . Christ, I don't know how to say this, but . . ."

"It's you," Remy fills in. "Right? The reaper's glass is you."

Cas stares at her for a long moment. "All right, so that's how you say it."

"And it was my father, before you."

When Remy produces the letters from her coat pocket, Finn doesn't know what they are. She doesn't know where they came from. And yet she knows, somehow, what they'll say. This is the missing piece, the final stone on the lever. This is how Remy had known the story before Dekker had told it to her. Cas mouths some of the words as he reads the first letter, then the next, eyes widening in wonder.

"Did you show these to the captain?" he asks as he flips through the pages, faster and faster.

"Not yet," Remy says. "He may have worked out some of it—about my father. I didn't tell him about you, though."

Cas returns the letters to her, then looks out over the water, hands tight around the railing. His knuckles are white.

"I'd like to, I think," he says. "I'd like to tell him. Maybe not today, but . . . He's going to be our best source about all of this, isn't he? About Death, and the reapers, and the Order. Henry told me some of what the Order's planning. What Smith's planning." He swallows. "I think we're going to need the captain's help with whatever comes next."

As Cas lays out the pieces he's learned of Smith's scheme—to capture a reaper, to take control of Death's list—Finn feels that angry fire stirring in her gut. "Jesus," she murmurs.

Remy is shaking her head. "If he pulls that off, if he's able to put anyone he dislikes on Death's list . . . Well, we're done for, aren't we? We're all in Smith's sights now."

"It's not just us, either." Cas eyes Mita and a few other sailors working on the other side of the deck, his expression grim. "I'd wager that every single person aboard this ship is the sort that Smith would happily sacrifice to save one of his own."

"So we'll stop him," Remy says. Simple as that. "We'll take down the Order before they make it that far. Whenever you're ready, we'll bring all of this to the captain."

"And there's something else."

He's turned to Finn now, jaw set, and Finn knows what's coming. She's known it's been coming for a long time. Longer than Cas did, anyway. There's something terrible on his face, and it's better, somehow, for Finn to take back control. Better to tell this story herself. *So that's how you say it.*

"Right," Finn says. "I'm going to die soon."

It's nothing like the confessions Finn made as a child in the Knockadine church. As she tells Remy and Cas about the choice she made years ago, there's no weight removed, no relief in having said the truth aloud. If anything, the weight feels heavier than it ever has before. This burden was never meant to be shared.

But it's all tangled now. She has to share it anyway.

It was the winter when Kieran had fallen ill. Finn was barely twelve, and her brother was sixteen, and he'd tried to brush off the cough until he couldn't brush it off any longer. Finn had sat with him in his little apartment for weeks as he worsened. She'd watched her brother wither away. Eventually, the doctor told her Kieran was going to die; there was nothing left to be done. Finn shouted at the doctor until she was hoarse. Then she begged. Then she cried. Then she shouted at him some more.

After the doctor had left, Finn returned to the DeWindts' house and went straight to Mr. DeWindt's study. He'd been gone for well over a year by then, but his strange old books were still in the window seat bench. Finn had looked through them a few times in secret. She knew they held rituals, spells, magic.

There was *one* thing left to be done.

The demon that Finn summoned was called Marbas. The demon agreed to save Kieran's life; in exchange, Finn would trade the demon her soul. It was an easy decision to make.

She can't look Remy or Cas in the eyes as she says all this—as she tells the story for the first time in her life. But when she explains how she'd signed the demon's contract—how Marbas had unlocked that fire inside her, the *vitalis vis*, so she could burn her own name onto the page—she hears Remy's sharp inhale. Back at the seminary, back on the beach, Remy had looked on Finn's fire with wonder. Now she'll see it for the sin that it is.

"Why would you do that?" Remy asks. "Why would you make that deal?" Finn has spent years studying the subtle shades of Remy's emotions, and yet she can't place what it is that pitches her voice now—hurt, or anger, or disbelief, or something else. Finn's heart is aching.

"Kieran was going to die," she says simply.

"And now *you* are instead! Kieran doesn't know, does he?"

"Of course not." Finn will never ever tell him. "I thought it would happen right then, when I signed—but the demon said they would come back later to collect. And then Kieran was cured, and I've just been . . . biding my time, I suppose."

"Christ," Remy says.

"That thing I've been seeing, in my visions," Cas says, shaking his head. "It really *is* a demon, then, isn't it? Smith was right."

Remy's head snaps toward him. "Smith knew?"

"Not about Finn, specifically, but he knew I'd seen a demon. He said something odd—like he'd had a hand in it, somehow. Like he'd done something to bring the demons out."

"This isn't Smith's fault," Finn says, unsure of why she's agitated by this. "I'm the one who signed the contract."

"But could he have done something that made the demon decide to collect now, finally?"

This gives Finn pause. She'd almost forgotten it in the midst of everything else—but the scrap of paper where she'd written the coordinates is still tucked beneath her collar. She takes it out.

"Actually," Finn says, "you might be onto something. I think he summoned one, too."

As she tells them about the circle she'd found in Reverend Smith's office, about the numbers scratched into the floorboards there, she can see Remy warring with herself—torn between whatever wild emotions she's feeling and the impulse to work at this new puzzle.

"So you think he what?" Cas says. "Bargained for some magic numbers and convinced the demons to come for you at the same time? Where do the coordinates lead?"

"North Atlantic, I think," Remy murmurs, almost to herself. "A few degrees farther south than we are now. I'd have to look at a map."

"But what's *there*? Why would Smith sell his soul for a set of coordinates?"

Finn folds the scrap of paper again and tucks it away. "He might've had something else to bargain with. I doubt he actually sold his own soul."

"Right," Remy says. "Because who would do *that*?"

The anger in her voice makes Finn flinch—because this is definitely anger now. Remy rounds on Cas.

"How long does she have?" she demands.

Cas shakes his head. "I don't know. Usually a week or two at most after the vision, but it's been two weeks since Long Beach, and you're still . . ." He lets that hang: *Here. Alive. Not damned to hell just yet.* "And I've never seen the same person's death twice before. Not until the other night."

Remy's eyes are wide. "Your vision on the deck. That was Finn?"

Cas nods without looking at them, tugging at the bandage on his hand again. Very quietly, he says, "The demon was supposed to take you on Mount Desert Island."

Finn feels very cold—a cold that's completely separate from the early spring chill and the ocean wind. She thinks of that shadow she thought she saw outside the back window of the seminary. The feeling of something watching her in the dark.

"It doesn't matter," Finn says, trying to hold back her shudder.

"Of course it matters," Remy snaps.

"I didn't tell you all this so you could try to fix it. I just thought you ought to know, before it happens. What's done is done, and there's no undoing it."

"No," Remy says.

"What d'you mean, *no*?"

"No. We'll figure something out. There has to be a way around this."

"There isn't," Finn tells her. "Believe me. I've looked."

"Well, we'll look again! We've got all three of us now, we can—"

"I don't want to look again! I understand this is new for you, and I'm sorry. But I've known for years that it's coming. It's fine. I knew what I was doing when I made that deal. Honestly, I'd do it again. Kieran deserves to live."

"And you don't?"

Finn has had every argument with herself a thousand times; she has a thousand rebuttals. "If anything, I was making the demon pay for something it would've gotten anyway," she says.

"I was always going to be damned. Whether or not I made that deal. Might as well leverage the inevitable."

But she hadn't expected, somehow, the deep hurt in Remy's voice as she says, "Do you really believe that?"

Does she? A week or two ago, Finn certainly had. *Unnatural. Abomination.* But her world has tipped off its axis too many times these past few days for her old moral compass to have any use. She realizes, suddenly, that she hasn't been adding to the mental list of sins in her mind anymore. When had she stopped? It's as if she's reached into her pocket and found it empty. The paper is gone; the memory of the list feels like it belongs to someone else.

"I know what I told Henry," Cas is saying, "but I don't actually believe we're all going to hell. Is hell even real?"

"I don't know." So much for certainty. Finn doesn't know anything anymore. "Maybe not the fire-and-brimstone version of it from your Sunday sermons," she says. "But demons are real enough."

She thinks about her scapular. About her old nightmares of hell. About the stories of the martyred saints. About her own realization, as she'd stood with Cas in the entrance hall, that she's not ready to die. That she wants to live.

Finn wants too many impossible things.

"Hell or not," Finn says, "regardless of what comes after—if there *is* an after—I'm going to die. I've accepted it."

It's a lie, and Finn tells it anyway. She tells it without remorse.

"I need you to accept it as well," she says.

XXXV

CAS

When he was nearly eighteen years old, Cas Sterling saw Finn Robinson die. He watched the scene play out two separate times, two separate predictions, the same and yet not the same—and ever since the vision changed, he's been scrambling to understand *why*. He keeps lining up the two forms of it side by side, studying every detail, like a child's game of trying to spot the differences between two pictures.

The setting had shifted, of course. That's the most obvious thing. Apparently, Finn leaving town had altered her path so dramatically that it had relocated the death laid out for her from a Windover street to a cliffside in Maine, a distance of nearly two hundred miles. And now those cliffs are behind them again as the *Mori* sails away, and yet Finn is still here. Finn is still alive. Cas has spent years resigned to the inevitability of the things he sees.

But her death has been changed once. Maybe it can change again.

And then there's the other difference—one less measurable, yet just as significant. Possibly *more* significant. Cas can't stop thinking about how the scenes had each ended. Not the deaths themselves, but the moment before. In the first vision, Finn had kept running until the demon caught her—but in the second, she'd stopped. She'd rounded on the monster. She'd shouted up at it, furious, fighting.

I've accepted it, Finn tells them now.

But Cas has seen the fire that will blaze in her eyes as Finn Robinson turns to meet her own death. Knowing it's coming is not the same as accepting it.

That wasn't the face of someone who accepts it.

Cas and Remy stay standing at the rail long after Finn has gone below. She'd claimed she was tired, which may have been true—more specifically, though, Cas suspects she was tired of *them*. Tired of Remy's stubborn protests and attempts to form a plan. Tired of Cas's empty reassurances. Tired of arguing about it.

Now he and Remy don't talk as they watch the sun creep over the horizon. The ocean before them turns from dark steel to gold. Remy's gaze is fixed on the waves, but there's something distant and hollowed-out in her eyes, like her mind has journeyed to a faraway place and abandoned its body behind. Cas bounces his leg and scratches at his bandages and turns the pieces over and over in his head.

The first time he'd seen Finn's death, Finn was afraid. The second time, she was angry. What had changed in the weeks between the two visions?

He props his elbows on the rail and scans the deck around them. Kit is at the *Mori*'s helm now, chart in hand, her dark eyes flitting from map to compass and back again as she confirms the ship's heading. Nessa is playing with the cat, tossing around a cord she's tied with a monkey's-fist knot while the cat goes wild. Mita is patching a gap in the longboat's planking, wedging old rope fibers between the boards. Her caulking mallet drums against its hull in a steady rhythm—the muffled *thump, thump, thump* of a heartbeat.

Cas turns back to the rail, to the sea ahead of them. What had changed? Everything.

"So... we're coming up with a plan to save her," Cas says finally. "Right?"

Remy doesn't move. "She says she doesn't want us to."

"I know, but we're doing it anyway, right?"

Remy laughs, a short huff of air, like she's just been waiting for Cas to say it. "Of course we are."

When Cas looks over at her, she's still staring into the middle distance, but her fingers have started to fidget—they press silently against her thumb one by one, as if the cogs of her brain are moving so determinedly that they have to make something on the outside of her move, too. It's a mannerism Cas suddenly remembers from when they were ten years old. The workings of a plan about to hatch.

"I keep thinking about what the captain told us the other night," Remy says slowly. "About the Mark of Death. Because the captain had been Marked, too, hadn't he? He'd appeared on Death's list, same as Finn. And then Death decided to spare him, and—"

"And Death scrubbed the Mark from his soul," Cas says as the hope inside him starts to ruffle awake. "So we know it's possible, then. Death has done it before."

Remy is nodding, her fingers still moving. Smith's words drift back to Cas unbidden: *You have no idea the scope of this thing you've stumbled into.* A daunting prospect, yes. But a thrilling one, too.

The sunrise is painting the sky before them a creamy white, the color of a blank canvas. Sea and sky and nothing else, all the way to the horizon. It's like his childhood visits to Long Beach, when Cas used to stand in the shallows and imagine floating off into that vast expanse of ocean, the biggest thing he'd ever seen.

They're well into it now. Somehow, it's bigger than he'd ever imagined.

"We need to find Death," Cas says.

ACKNOWLEDGMENTS

When I first started dreaming of this book years ago, I knew I didn't yet have the skills I would need to write it the way I wanted. I learned how to write *Devils Like Us* by writing it, and the process pushed me in ways I couldn't imagine and leveled up my craft several times over. I'm incredibly grateful to everyone who's supported me and helped this book find its way out into the world.

To my fantastic agent, Beth Phelan, thank you for being a calm, kind, and ever-steady compass in navigating this tumultuous sea that is publishing. Thank you to the entire team at Gallt & Zacker for the wonderful work you do in championing so many important stories.

Thank you to my editor, Camille Kellogg. You saw my vision for this story so clearly and helped me hone it into the truest version of itself. I can't tell you how many times I read one of your notes or questions and marveled at my luck in getting to work with the absolute perfect editor for this book.

Thank you to the outstanding team at Bloomsbury, especially: Hannah Bowe, Laura Philips, Sarah Shumway, Mary Kate Castellani, Briana Williams, Faye Bi, Erica Barmash, Beth Eller, Jennifer Choi, Andrew Nguyen, Phoebe Dyer, Daniel O'Connor,

Valentina Rice, Nicholas Church, and Alona Fryman. Thank you to Marisa Aragón Ware for the gorgeous cover art, and to Jeanette Levy for the design.

In many ways, this book is my love letter to queer community. Thank you to Lambda Literary, and especially the 2018 fellows and faculty of the Writers Retreat for Emerging LGBTQ Voices. I will probably never have the experience of running off to sea aboard a sailing ship with an all-queer crew—but I did get to spend a week with you all in Los Angeles having revelations about gender and queer art and community, and I think that's pretty close.

An extra shoutout to Jen St. Jude, Kirt Ethridge, Jas Hammonds, Sacha Lamb, Avery Mead, Octavia Saenz, and JD Scott. Thank you for seven years (!!!) of your wisdom, humor, and friendship, and for never kicking me out of the group chat, even when I tell you the same nautical fun fact for the eighteenth time or won't stop talking about *Les Mis*.

Thank you to Katherine Ouellette for talking things through when I get stuck and for helping keep me on track with our writing sessions. Thank you to Lakshya for offering your brilliant insight and encouragement on my early draft. Thank you to Natalie Morgan for the countless hours of brainstorming, for cheering me on at every stage, and for coming to the maritime museums with me.

As it would happen, I only started research for this book in earnest a few months *after* I left New England. Thank you to the Leventhal Map & Education Center at the Boston Public Library, the Phillips Library at the Peabody Essex Museum, and Historic New England for your excellent digital resources that allow even those of us in faraway Iowa to access your collections. Thanks also to Richard Henry Dana Jr., who's long dead, but

who wrote two primary sources that were invaluable for learning about life aboard an American merchant vessel circa 1840.

Thank you to my parents, Molly and Al, and to Megan, Kate, Kevin, and Tricia. The seeds for this story were probably planted long ago with that Fisher-Price pirate ship. I love you all.

Finally, thank you to Cara. There are all the obvious ways you've helped shape this book—brainstorming with me, pointing out plot holes, helping me stay grounded when everything feels like a disaster—and then there's this: You see me, and when I'm with you, I *want* to be seen. What a glorious thing.